We That Are Left

We That Are Left

Clare Clark

W F HOWES LTD

This large print edition published in 2015 by
W F Howes Ltd
Unit 4, Rearsby Business Park, Gaddesby Lane,
Rearsby, Leicester LE7 4YH

1 3 5 7 9 10 8 6 4 2

First published in the United Kingdom in 2015
by Harvill Secker

A CIP catalogue record for this book is available
from the British Library

ISBN 978 1 51001 243 1

Extract from *The Time Machine* by H. G. Wells,
reprinted with permission of A. P. Watt at United
Agents on behalf of The Literary Executors of the
Estate of H. G. Wells

Typeset by Palimpsest Book Production Limited,
Falkirk, Stirlingshire

Printed and bound in Great Britain
by TJ International Ltd, Padstow, Cornwall

For Luke, Alice and Frances,
a third each,
because That's Fair

They shall grow not old, as we that are left
    grow old:
Age shall not weary them, nor the years
    condemn.
At the going down of the sun and in the
    morning
We will remember them.

LAURENCE BINYON, SEPTEMBER 1914.

PROLOGUE

1920

It was raining as they followed the coffin from the church. A gusty wind snatched at people's hats. At the head of the procession the rector clamped his arms against his billowing robes and sang, 'We brought nothing into this world, and it is certain we can carry nothing out. The Lord gave, and the Lord hath taken away,' and the wind caught the words and scattered them like leaves.

They stood together at the graveside, Phyllis and Jessica and Oscar, their heads bowed. Behind them Cousin Evelyn held an umbrella over Lettice, its apex into the wind to keep it from blowing inside out. She was expecting again. A girl this time, she was sure of it, she had confided happily to Jessica. She had never felt sicker in her life.

Afterwards they went back to the house for tea and sandwiches. Marjorie helped Jessica with the cups while Oscar shook hands with some of the tenants, red-faced and awkward in their Sunday suits. From his frame above the fireplace Jeremiah Melville observed the proceedings grimly,

1

his hands clasping his stick. Oscar tried not to look at him.

On the other side of the Great Hall Mr Rawlinson murmured something to Phyllis who nodded and stared out of the window. Her black suit emphasised her pale skin, the red gleam of her hair. Rawlinson turned, catching Oscar's eye. Oscar pretended not to see. The lawyer wished only to pay his respects, he supposed, but he would not speak to him. A more tactful man would have chosen not to come.

It was not much of a party. When the last of the guests was gone Oscar left the women in front of the fire and went for a walk. The wind had dropped and the air was damp and chill. It smelled of wet earth and rotting leaves and, very faintly, of the sea.

He walked down through the darkening garden and across the croquet lawn towards the tower in the woods. It still drew him, after so long. At the bottom of the spiral staircase he paused, one hand on the stone arch that led through to the Tiled Room. The floor was thick with leaves and the windows were overgrown with ivy and brambles, tendrils snaking through broken glass to entwine themselves around the rotting benches. The tiles on the walls were grey, sticky with dirt and cobwebs. He rubbed one with the side of his fist. It gleamed in the dusk like the white of an eye.

By the time he reached the top of the tower he was out of breath. The light was paler here. The low mass of the Isle of Wight smudged the horizon, and the breeze sang in the glassless windows. Sir Aubrey had brought him up here once when he was a little boy. Sir Aubrey had not appeared to know that this room was Theo's private fiefdom, that access was permitted only by invitation. He just made Oscar promise he would not tell Godmother Eleanor. Godmother Eleanor thought that the tower was dangerous. Sir Aubrey told Oscar that the tower had thirteen storeys and 385 steps, that it was 218 feet tall and eighteen feet square, not counting the external staircase, and rested on a foundation nine feet deep, that the concrete was two feet thick at the base of the tower and one at the top, that it had taken a team of forty workmen five years to build. Oscar had been so interested he almost forgot to be afraid about Theo finding out. Everything had been numbers in those days, for Oscar.

The window on the west side of the tower looked down over the house. From so high a vantage point the castellated bastions and turrets of Ellinghurst looked like a child's sandcastle, the vast ivied walls that enclosed it to the west hardly more than a curved line of pebbles in the sand. Beyond the sloping lawns the grassy moat was flooded with shadow and the house on its mound was an island, the wide vistas of the park spreading to the south, to the north the dark-clotted woods and hills of the New Forest. Beyond the barbican of the gatehouse Oscar could just make out the river, a blue-black scrawl amidst ink-blot trees.

The farms were to go. It was a good time to sell, Rawlinson said. The agricultural subsidies introduced by the government during the War had increased the productivity of the land and the profits of farmers. There were mutterings in Westminster about repeal but, while the legislation stood, tenants were keen to buy and, with the hikes in schedule tax, it made sense to convert a reduced income into a tax-free capital gain. Oscar had stared at the ledgers that held the estate accounts, the columns of numbers jumbling in his head. If Rawlinson was right about land values the sales would raise sufficient funds to meet death duties and keep their heads above water, at least for the present.

They had not talked about the future. It was too soon. In time, though, Oscar knew, the park would have to go. Rawlinson did not say so but Oscar knew he had already begun to put out feelers. The estate was mortgaged to the hilt and, without the income from the farms, they would struggle to meet the payments. Little by little Ellinghurst would retreat up onto its mound, its drawbridge pulled up against the marauders whose advances paid its debts and kept the roof from falling in.

Oscar did not know if he would stay on at the University. He had insisted to Rawlinson that he be permitted to graduate but he was no longer sure why it mattered. There was no possibility of a graduate research post, not any more, so why not throw it in now and devote his energies to

4

Ellinghurst? The loss, if there was one, was small, selfish. Science would not mourn him. Nearly five years ago Sir Aubrey's brother Henry had been killed by a sniper at Gallipoli. Though only in his early thirties when he died, Henry Melville had already left an indelible impression on the text-books. It was widely agreed among the scientists of Oscar's acquaintance that, had he lived, his work would have won him the Nobel Prize.

No one doubted that he would have gone on to do work of the utmost importance, work that in time would have marked him out as one of the very great scientists of his generation, and yet since his death that work had not been left undone. It had been done by others. The fissure opened by his loss had been stopped, the plaster smoothed over. Experimental physics was a collective enter-prise, like the construction of an anthill. The particular character or contribution of each indi-vidual ant was not of consequence. What counted was the cumulative edifice. Great scientists were rare but not so rare that their work died with them. If a scientist failed to make a discovery one year, then another would make it the next. One way or another, the anthill would inexorably rise.

Ellinghurst was not like that. After three hundred years they were the only ants left. It was chance that had saved Oscar, chance and Mr Rawlinson. He knew to be grateful. In the last six months of the War the British Army had suffered nearly half a million casualties, almost a fifth of the War's grim reckoning. Whatever the truth, he had made his choice. There was a debt to be honoured, a duty to be discharged. The papers were signed and Sir Aubrey laid to rest. He would do what he could, as Sir Aubrey had wanted. He would not be the one to break the chain. Perhaps, in time, the house, the name, would come to feel like his own. By now he of all people should know that names meant nothing.

It was done. Ellinghurst was theirs. Their future was set. There was no purpose in wondering what might have been, or if it was what he wanted after all.

CHAPTER 1

1910

Terence held the chair steady as Theo tied the scarf over Jessica's eyes. He tied it very tight, so tight it pulled her hair and pushed her eyeballs down into their sockets, but Jessica did not protest. She gripped the chair's wicker arms as Terence wheeled her out to the middle of the lane.

'Cheese,' Theo said and she forced a grin. His camera clicked. She could feel the wind tugging at the loose ends of the scarf, the tumble of apprehension in her stomach. The lane was steep here, steep enough that the red-faced lady bicyclists who panted doggedly all the way up the gentle slope through the village had to get off their machines and push. It made their mother laugh to see them. Sometimes when they were motoring, Eleanor would tell Pritchard to drive right up behind them and sound the horn. Phyllis hated it when she did that but the sight of the bicycles wobbling into the verge only made Eleanor laugh harder. She told Phyllis and Jessica that she was performing a

7

Public Service, that the red-faced ladies should be glad of the excitement.

The red-faced ladies pushed their bicycles downhill too. Father said it was because otherwise their bicycles might run away with them and Eleanor laughed and said it was the only thing that ever would, which made Father's lips go thin. Jessica could see the hill in her mind's eye: the bumpy grey lane dropping away like a laundry chute between the high banks of the hedgerows until at the bottom by the gate to Stream Farm it curved sharply right over the river. Theo said that the bath chair would go in a straight line when the road turned so that the worst that could happen was that the chair would tip over when it went into the thick grass beside the Stream Farm field and that was fine because grass was a soft landing. Jessica knew that was not the worst thing that could happen but there was no point in thinking about that. Nanny said it was thinking too much about bad things that made them happen in the first place.

'Ready?' Theo said and Jessica nodded and pushed the ends of her fingers hard into the basket-work of the chair to make herself feel braver. It was stupid to be afraid. Theo said that fear was the reason so many people lived small unhappy lives. Jessica was small for her age, Eleanor was always saying so, but she had no intention of ever being unhappy.

'You know what, Theo?' Terence Connolly said

in his stretched-out American drawl. 'You've made your point.'

'Rules is rules. We said whoever drew the red match, right, Jess?'

Jessica nodded, biting hard on the inside of her lip. She wished Terence Connolly would just shut up so she could get the whole thing over with.

'So the kid's got guts,' Terence said. 'You don't have to make her spill them all over the roadside.'

'You're not being a pansy, are you, Connolly?' Theo said and he jerked the chair, letting it go and catching it again just as it began to roll. Jessica's stomach turned over. Behind her Marjorie giggled. It was all Jessica could do not to climb out and sock her. Marjorie Maxwell Brooks was always at Ellinghurst, because her mother wanted more than anything to be friends with Eleanor and traipsed around after her saying how much she had enjoyed the So-and-sos and where did she get her marvellous eye for colour. Marjorie had adenoids, which meant she breathed through her mouth and her words came out full of 'd's as though she had a permanent cold in the head.

She also had the biggest stupidest pash on Theo that Jessica had ever seen. She could not say a word to him without tittering or going red. Last Christmas, Theo dropped his handkerchief and Jessica saw Marjorie pick it up and press it to her face even though Theo had just blown his nose on it. Jessica had never seen anything more disgusting in her whole life. Marjorie was supposed

9

to be Phyllis's friend because they were the same age but Marjorie just trailed behind Theo like Mary's little lamb and all Phyllis ever wanted to do was read books. When Phyllis died, Jessica thought, she would not want to be buried or even burned up to ashes like Grandfather Melville but squashed flat like a pressed flower inside a huge fat book and afterwards, when someone tried to read it, they would have to peer through the mush of her brain and scrape her dried brown guts from the gaps between the lines.

'You wouldn't have done it, would you, Marjorie?' Terence asked.

'Not for all the tea in China,' Marjorie said, still giggling.

'But I don't like tea,' Jessica said loftily and Theo laughed.

'That's my girl,' he said, squeezing her shoulder, and the rush of pride burned her throat almost like crying.

'Go,' she commanded, and with an almighty push she was flying, hurtling downhill with the wind whipping at the scarf and the bumps in the rough surface of the lane clattering her bones like she was a skeleton, and as her eyes filled with tears her chest tore open with a great white scream that was terror or triumph, she did not know which, and the darkness turned bright with flashing silver stars and she thought that this was what it must be like to be a bird, a bird or a motor racing car, and then quite suddenly there was an almighty jolt and the chair stopped dead and she was thrown, like a bird, through the air and for a moment time stopped and she wondered what came next and how badly it would hurt, before she landed with a thump that knocked the breath out of her in a thick patch of nettles.

Nanny tutted as she rubbed calamine lotion on the nettle stings. She said that idle hands were the devil's playthings and that the stream was no place for a girl who should have been drawing or practising the piano. Then she tied up Jessica's hair again, smoothing the strands with her gnarled red hands. Jessica did not mention the bath chair. She had no intention of getting Theo into trouble. Not that he ever was in trouble, not properly. When Nanny told him off he only pulled silly faces and tickled her in the place on her side that made her go squirmy and said that he knew she was only pretending to be cross.

As for their parents, Theo could have burned the house down and Eleanor would have laughed and told him how pretty the flames were. It made Father furious when Eleanor stuck up for Theo but when Father shouted at him it only ended up in an argument and Theo always won. He had a way of smiling at Father when he was angry that made Father squeeze his hands into fists and walk out of the room.

When finally Nanny stopped fussing over her and let her leave the nursery Jessica ran downstairs and out into the garden but she could not see the others anywhere. Her skin was sore and horribly itchy, and the palms of her hands burned. She licked the hard white bumps, trying to soothe them. They tasted of calamine. She grimaced, wiping her tongue on her sleeve.

It had grown cool, fat clouds clotting the sky. Around the terrace, the roses shivered, their pale heads pressed close together, and the horse chestnuts waved their flat green hands up and down. Someone, Terence maybe, had left a cricket sweater on the wrought-iron bench by the oak tree. Jessica hoped it would rain and the sweater would get spoiled. She did not like Terence Connolly one bit. His mouth was too red and when he talked his voice was loud and American. He was the most awful boaster too. When Father had asked him if he played tennis he had gone on and on about the stupid tournaments he had won until she had wanted to scream. It baffled her that Theo had insisted on inviting him to stay for another whole week by himself instead of leaving the next day for London with his parents. She supposed it must be the Brownie camera that had turned his head. Before they had arrived with their piles of stupid American presents no one had wanted any of the Connollys at Ellinghurst. No one but Eleanor.

Picking up a stick Jessica ran across the croquet lawn, whipping at her thigh as she leaped the hoops. She could go to the stables and see Max, she supposed, but it was no fun riding by yourself.

It was no fun doing anything by yourself. She pulled up at the stand of beeches near the turn in the drive and peered through the gate in the rhododendrons but the tennis court was deserted, its net sagging on its posts. She slashed with her stick at a rhododendron flower, scattering pink petals, then trailed back along the edge of the wood, the stick clattering the iron railings. Above the wood Grandfather's Tower rose up into the sky like Jack's beanstalk in the story. From here she could see the bulge of the spiral staircase on its far side, a fat snake darker than the pale concrete of the tower itself.

Grandfather was Father's grandfather, not Jessica's, but they called the tower Grandfather's Tower because that was what Father had always called it. Jessica's real grandfather had died when Father was young, which was a long time ago because Father was old, much older than other people's fathers. Jessica kept her eyes on the top of the tower as she walked. She liked the way that the closer you got to it the more it looked like it was falling over. It was because it was so tall. Father said the style was Italianate, which meant that it belonged in Venice and not in the New Forest. Eleanor detested it, she called it an eyesore, but it was still one of her favourite stories, how Grandfather Melville had come back from India concrete-mad and been introduced to a lady called Mrs Gleeson who was a Spiritualist, which meant she could talk to dead people. Grandfather Melville and Mrs Gleeson had become very, very good friends, Eleanor said, making her mouth and her eyes go round so that everyone laughed. It was because of Mrs Gleeson that Grandfather Melville had been able to speak to Sir Christopher Wren who had been dead a long time and get his help with the tower's design. Sir Christopher Wren, it turned out, was quite as excited about unreinforced concrete as Grandfather Melville.

'A wiser man might have worried that Wren was a good two hundred years too early for concrete,' Eleanor liked to say, 'but what's a detail or two when you're holding hands in a darkened room?'

Jessica's father hated it when she told that story. Sometimes when she was in the middle of telling it he just got up and went out of the room. Then Eleanor would laugh and tell the other story he did not like, about Grandfather Melville pushing footmen off the top of the tower to test his flying machines. She had always forbidden the children to go up there, she said it might fall down any minute, but they still went. There was a room on every one of the thirteen floors but the top one was Theo's. He said that thirteen was his lucky number. No one was allowed up there but him. Jessica wondered if he would live up there when Father was dead and the whole castle belonged to him.

Slowly she walked up the steps towards the house. Usually she liked to walk along the ramparts because it was fun to jump the gaps in the battlements but she did not feel like it today. The stings smarted on her arms and legs and her bruised shoulder throbbed. She could not believe that the others had deserted her. Somehow in her mind she had imagined them all gathered in triumph on the terrace, Theo raising a glass of lemonade to toast her pluck. Instead, as usual, he had vanished into thin air and she was left all alone, wriggling like a fish inside her sore raw skin. She looked back at the tower. Phyllis was probably there right now, curled up in the Tiled Room, hunched over some book or other. The Tiled Room was octagonal and had painted tiles not just all over the floor but on the walls too. Father said that in India they used tiles because they kept rooms cool. Grandfather Melville must have forgotten about English weather because the Tiled Room was cold as an icehouse but Phyllis did not seem to mind. Jessica wondered if she even noticed. Of all the infuriating things about Phyllis perhaps the most infuriating was the way she always behaved as though books were real and real life just a story somebody had made up without thinking.

The Great Hall was deserted, the doors to the drawing room and the long gallery both closed. Jessica kissed the carved eagle that topped the newel post on the beak and looked up at Jeremiah Melville who glared down at her from his frame above the chimneypiece. All around him on the walls were clubs and shields and crossed pikes and bits of old armour. Jeremiah Melville's ancestors had been farmers, not medieval knights, but he had made pots of money from Indian cotton and decided he did not want to live in a boring manor house but in a castle with a minstrels' gallery and towers with arrow slits, even though by then there were no minstrels any more and everyone just shot one other with guns. Jeremiah Melville had been Grandfather Melville's grandfather.

'Where is everybody, Rexy boy?' Jessica asked, stroking the stone lion that sprawled over the huge fireplace. One day, she hoped, she might persuade Eleanor to let her have a dog. Behind her a sudden shaft of sunlight flooded the stained-glass windows, splashing pools of colour across the stone flags. Jessica put her toe into a lozenge of yellow. She supposed Mrs Maxwell Brooke and Mrs Connolly were still traipsing round Salworth House with Mrs Grunewald, unless they had already died of boredom. As for Eleanor and Mr Connolly, who knew how far away they were by now? Mr Connolly's new motor car was white with red leather seats and shiny silver wheels with the spokes all criss-crossed like a game of pick-up sticks. It only had room in it for two people. When Mr Connolly had taken them all out to look at it Eleanor had stroked its glossy flank and told Mr Connolly that a girl could die happy in an automobile like that, and Mr Connolly had smiled at her like the witch smiled at Hansel and Gretel when she was getting ready to eat them up.

Jessica despised Mr Connolly even more than she

despised Terence. Partly it was because he opened his mouth too wide when he laughed and wore oil in his hair and ugly coats with patterns and too many pockets. Mostly she did not like him because he was too stupid to realise that Eleanor did not care for him any more than she cared for any of the others. He was always staring at her when he thought no one was looking. The day before, when Jessica was lying beside the gallery banisters pretending to be a tiger in a cage, she had heard the door to the drawing room open underneath her and Mr Connolly say 'My God, look at you,' in his American voice that was shouty even when he was whispering, and she had wanted to drop something heavy on his head. She thought that Mr Connolly would be a terrible driver with Eleanor in the car, that he would spend the whole time looking at her and not at the road he was driving on.

A girl could die happy in an automobile like that.

'But of course I'll die, you silly,' Eleanor had said with a gay laugh when Jessica was little. 'We'll all die. But you mustn't worry. I shall be sure to do it very beautifully,' and Jessica had a sudden violent picture of Mr Connolly's white automobile crumpled like a paper bag and Eleanor sprawled with her head thrown back, a shiny line of blood like scarlet nail polish running from her mouth.

She shook her head like a kaleidoscope to make the picture change and scrubbed at her nose. She thought about going up to the nursery but Oskar was probably in the nursery and Oskar was worse than nobody at all. Oskar was Mrs Grunewald's son and the same age as Jessica, which meant that everyone expected Jessica to play with him. She tried to tell Nanny it was impossible but Nanny only put on her stern face and said it was Jessica's job to make sure her visitors had a nice time.

Jessica could not see why Oskar had to be her visitor when it was not her who had invited him, and she did not have the foggiest idea how anyone could tell if he was having a nice time. Oskar could go through a whole day saying nothing at all, just staring into space or reading a maths book, and, when you finally lost your temper with him and demanded to know if he was actually still alive, he only blinked at you in that startled way of his, his eyes like sucked aniseed balls, as though it was perfectly normal for a boy who was not ill to sit quietly all day long and never once yawn or complain or want to run somewhere and break something. He was always writing down numbers, rows and rows of them so tightly packed together there was hardly any white left on the page, and when he talked it was just the same, strings of facts so unspeakably boring you could not imagine ever wanting to know them, let alone learn them by heart. Theo said Oskar was like the Engine in *Gulliver's Travels*, that if you could only work out where to crank him up, he would spool out point- less information for the rest of his life in seventeen languages at once.

In the middle of the hall table there was a big

silver bowl full of pale pink roses. Jessica took one out and, holding it up in front of her, glided across the hall towards one of the suits of armour that guarded the bottom of the stairs. The armour held a pike in one hinged metal hand. The other hand was empty, the arm slightly outstretched. Clasping the cold fingers, she bowed her head.

Will you, Jessica Margaret Crompton Melville, take this man to be your awfully wedded husband? He loves you to the ends of the earth and he wants more than anything else in the world to buy you an Alfonso motor car.

Why, in that case, I will.

Tearing the petals from the rose and throwing them above her head, she processed triumphantly back towards the front door. She had only ever been to one wedding, last year when Uncle Henry married Aunt Violet. It had not been in the least romantic. Uncle Henry was twenty-five years younger than Father but he was still ancient. When he made his speech he did not kiss Aunt Violet or say they would live happily ever after or anything. When Jessica asked Eleanor why not, her mother had made a funny face and said surely she knew by now that the Melvilles were the coldest fishes in the sea?

Jessica caught sight of Theo and Terence through the window as they crossed the gravel drive. They were laughing. They had changed into white flannels and Terence was wearing a panama hat. The

19

hat made Terence's face look redder than ever. Jessica stood four-square in the entrance of the Great Hall, her fists on her hips, so that when they pushed open the door, still laughing, they almost knocked her over.

'Where the bloody hell have you been?' she demanded. The swearing made her feel better. She eyed the tennis racquets in Theo's arms. 'You're not going to play bloody tennis, are you?'

'Bloody tennis?' Theo said. 'Where on earth did you get that idea?'

'The racquets.'

'Racquets?' Theo looked down at the racquets and gaped. 'Good Lord. Where the devil did those spring from?' Terence laughed as Theo pushed the racquets into his arms and, whisking Terence's panama from his head, sent it skimming towards the eagle on the newel post. The brim clipped the eagle's beak and skittered upside down along the floor.

'You missed,' Jessica said.

'That depends on what I was aiming for,' Theo said and Terence laughed again, his red mouth wide open. Jessica glared at him.

'You shouldn't leave people out,' she said to Theo. 'It's rude.'

'What's rude?' Marjorie skipped down the stairs. She was wearing a tightly belted tennis dress and shoes so white they made Jessica blink. Behind her, dressed in her ordinary blouse and skirt, Phyllis scuffed her feet, a book dangling from one hand. She kept her thumb tucked between the pages, marking her place.

'Miss Messy here, that's who,' Theo said and, reclaiming a racquet from Terence, he bounced the strings on Jessica's head. 'You should hear the swear words Nanny's been teaching her. The two of them would put a navvy to shame.'

Marjorie sniggered. Jessica glowered at her. She hated it when Theo called her Mess and Messy. Miss Messica Jelville, he would say, as though his tongue had got it muddled up, and Eleanor would laugh and laugh. But at the same time she could not help being glad just a little that he had a special name for her he had made up all by himself. He never called Phyllis anything but Phyll.

'Ready?' Theo said as Terence retrieved his hat. Then he frowned. 'Come on, Phyll. You haven't even changed your shoes.'

'What difference does that make?' Phyllis said. 'I won't be any less hopeless with different shoes.'

'There's no point in playing if you refuse to try.'

'Well, in that case . . .' Baring her teeth in a smile, she turned to go back upstairs, her eyes already on her book. Marjorie caught her arm.

'Please, Phyllis,' she wheedled, glancing at Theo. 'We need you. Don't we need her, Theo? It's much more fun with four.'

'Or you could let them play singles,' Phyllis said. 'You know they'd rather.'

'Would you?' Marjorie asked Theo. 'Would you

really?' And she bit her lip and made her eyes go round at him in a way that made Jessica want to be sick on her snowy white shoes.

'For God's sake, Phyll,' Theo snapped. 'Just play, won't you?'

'I can play,' Jessica offered quickly. 'I've been taking lessons.'

'I don't even know why you want me,' Phyllis said. 'You'll only growl at me every time I hit it into the net.'

'Miss Whitfield says I have a natural eye for the ball,' Jessica added.

'He won't,' Marjorie said. 'You won't, will you, Theo?'

Theo's mouth twitched, his eyes sliding sideways towards Terence. 'Well, I suppose if she were on the other side I mightn't. Then I might even enjoy it.'

'Is that what we on the East Coast call a challenge, Melville?' Terence said.

'For you, most certainly. Have you seen Phyllis on a tennis court?'

'That's it,' Phyllis said. 'I'm not playing.'

'Come on now,' Terence said. The way he looked at Theo suggested some kind of private joke. 'Wouldn't it be a little bit fun to knock that self-satisfied smirk off your brother's face?'

'It'd be a joy and a pleasure. Unfortunately, though, he has a point. My tennis is execrable.'

'Nonsense,' Terence said, still looking at Theo. 'Trust me. It will be a cinch. A snap. A picnic.

A breeze. A piece of cake. A walk, my friend, in the park.'

'Extraordinary,' Theo said. 'In the old country only a matter of weeks and already so fluent in hubris.'

'Just wait till you see me serve.'

'I've heard Terence is fearfully good,' Marjorie confided to Phyllis. 'You'll hardly have to hit a stroke. You can just stand there looking pretty.'

Phyllis rolled her eyes. 'If only Miss Pankhurst could hear you, Marjorie. She'd be so proud.'

'What about me?' Jessica demanded. 'Why can't I play?'

'Are you still here?' Theo asked. Then, putting one hand on the top of her head and another around her chin, he tipped back her face, twisting it from side to side. 'Welcome, ladies and gentlemen, to the Royal Society. Today we will be studying the sadly not-so-rare species, the Spoiled Child.'

'Let go of me,' Jessica protested, trying to wriggle free, but Theo only tightened his grip, his fingers digging uncomfortably into her jaw.

'Mark,' he said, 'the distinctive pout, the ill-tempered frown between the eyebrows. Not uncommonly this will be accompanied by the protruding tongue—'

'Let her go, Theo,' Phyllis said as Marjorie giggled, her hand over her mouth. 'We can let her pick up the balls or something, can't we?'

'And be your slave?' Jessica said. 'No fear.'

'Fine.' Phyllis shrugged. 'We'll see you later, then.'

'You can't just leave me all alone.'

'Oskar's around, isn't he? And anyway, I thought you were putting on a concert?'

'It's not a concert, it's an Extravaganza. And I can't do anything with you gone because you're all in it.'

Theo looked at Terence and snorted. 'When hell freezes over.'

'It isn't for you, actually, Theodore Melville. It's for Eleanor.' She rolled the name on her tongue like an elocution teacher. Her mother was always telling her to pronounce it properly and not like a maid who dropped her 'h's.

'For Eleanor?' Theo said, copying her enunciation. 'Would that be the Eleanor who prizes children's shows above all other entertainments?'

'She'd like it if you were in it,' Jessica said sulkily. Theo did not try to deny it. However short-tempered Eleanor was, however restless or peevish or bored half to death buried in the back of beyond, she was never impatient with Theo. Sometimes she even kissed him for no reason or smoothed the hair away from his forehead. When Jessica's hair escaped her ribbons, Eleanor just winced and sent her up to Nanny.

'Do it with Oskar,' Theo suggested. 'I mean, the boy's pure music hall.' He strummed his tennis racquet like a Spanish guitar. 'Zey call me Oskar Grunewald, ja, zey do. Some days I zay one word, some days even two.'

'Don't, Theo,' Phyllis said. 'That's unkind.'

'It's not unkind if it's true,' Jessica said.

'Actually, it's more unkind if it's true,' Phyllis said. 'And why are you backing him up? I'm the one on your side.'

'No you're not. You're ruining my Extravaganza just as much as Theo, only you won't come straight out and say so. Which makes you worse.'

Terence grinned, showing white teeth. 'Well, ain't you a pistol, little sister?'

Jessica considered the American boy, her eyes narrow. Then slowly she raised her hands, the first two fingers pointing at his head.

'Bang, bang, you're dead,' she said. Blowing the smoke from her fingertips, she stuck out her chin and stalked through the servants' door towards the kitchen.

CHAPTER 2

Oskar had not seen the Children's Encyclopaedia in the library before. It came in eight thick volumes, a two-foot stretch of blue leather that took up almost a whole shelf of the bookcase. He stood on tiptoes to inspect it. At school the encyclopaedias had letters on their spines to mark out which part of the alphabet they were for, but these ones just had numbers, one to eight. Under the number, there was another, much bigger number showing the page numbers for that book, surrounded by a pattern of gold leaves and a scabbard. Oskar knew what a scabbard was because of the Roman exhibition at the British Museum but it was the numbers that caught his attention.

Oskar could not explain how he felt about numbers except to say that they were his friends. His mother smiled when he said that and said she knew what he meant but that it might be better not to tell the other boys at school. She said that, unlike numbers, schoolboys were unpredictable, that they did not always behave the way you expected them to. She did not seem to understand that numbers did not either, or not all the time. Sometimes, when you were ill in bed, they got all agitated in your head, and it was like the day they went together to see the men riding their bicycles in the Olympic Games and he thought he had lost her, primes and squares and cubes pushing and shoving and squashing out the light; except that numbers matted themselves into thick ropes that kept getting bigger and more twisty until you thought your head would burst. But most of the time numbers were smooth and cool and fitted together so you could make buildings out of them. The number buildings were beautiful.

Oskar's mother liked words more than numbers, which meant that she knew lots of stories about them. She told Oskar about the shepherds in Lincolnshire in the Middle Ages who had their own numbers that started *yan, tan, tethera, pethera,* but only went up to *figgit,* which was twenty, because if a shepherd had more than twenty sheep he would scrape a line in his crook and start at *yan* all over again. She said that the word calculate came from the Roman word for pebble because the Romans counted with stones, and that digit, which was a grown-up word for finger, was also a grown-up word for number and that was why numbers were counted in groups of ten, because people counted on their fingers and ten was how many fingers you had for counting on.

'Unless you were Anne Boleyn, of course,' she said. Anne Boleyn was the Queen who married

King Henry VIII when his other wife was still alive so that he could not be a Catholic any more. Oskar did not care for Anne Boleyn any more than he cared for the broken bits of pot at the British Museum, but he quite liked the shudder that came from eleven fingers, and he really, really liked the idea of a number system that went up to eleven before starting again. For a while when he was littler, he had invented his own number system that went up to *dat*, which was eleven, and then afterwards, when he saw that it would work better to have a base that divided by lots of other numbers, to *tog*, which was twelve. His mother said that there had been several clever men in the nineteenth century who had tried to change the number system so that everyone counted in twelves, especially in Britain where there were already twelve pennies in a shilling, but that no one had wanted to listen. She said that it was one of the things that she would never understand, that even when it was quite plain that things would be better if they changed, most people still wanted them to stay exactly the same.

Volume 6, pages 3727–4463. Both 3727 and 4463 were prime numbers. Oscar liked odd numbers better than even ones and primes most of all because each one had its own special shape. He slid the book from the shelf. It was new, the spine stiff and the gold very gold. At home the books were all battered and when you opened them the pages fell out or letters or scraps of paper covered in his mother's handwriting. She was always putting letters and lists in books to mark her place and forgetting all about them. Once Oskar had found a telegram announcing the birth of JESSICA MARGARET CROMPTON MELVILLE STOP; another time a French train ticket from before he was born. The books in the Melvilles' huge library did not look like anyone had ever read them at all.

Carefully he opened the book. When he was small he had asked his mother if Sir Aubrey had read all the books in his library and his mother had laughed and said that not even Sir Aubrey could love Ellinghurst as much as that. She said that according to the estate records most of the books had been purchased by the yard, like silk for curtains, boxes and boxes just to cover the shelves, but that some had been chosen specially by Sir Jeremiah who was Sir Aubrey's great-great-grandfather.

'What else explains so much Scott?' she said and she smiled so that Oskar knew it was a joke even though he did not understand it. He often did not understand the things his mother said but he knew better than to ask her to explain because mostly the explanations were not very interesting. He was interested in Sir Jeremiah, though. It was Sir Jeremiah who had turned Ellinghurst from an ordinary manor house into a medieval castle and built castellations and turrets and a moat with a bridge and a huge arched gatehouse with machicolations and a portcullis and a lookout tower with a hole for boiling oil. Oskar's mother had told Oskar that Sir Jeremiah had been an admirer of Richard the Lionheart and, like the great Crusader king, believed in gallantry and chivalry and the unrelenting plunder of the people for profit. She said that if your concern for the tenants on your land extended only as far as their potential capital yield, it was probably prudent to have a portcullis, just in case.

'No little lily-handed Baronet he,' Oskar's mother said, and Oskar knew from the way that she said it that the words came from a poem. Oskar's mother loved poems. She said that poems could be just as beautiful as mathematical equations but Oskar knew that she only thought that because she did not really understand mathematics.

The first thing in *Volume 6* was a shiny colour plate of the Solar System, the planets suspended in their orbits like swirly glass marbles. Oskar knew about the Solar System. He knew that the rings of Saturn were made up of small particles of ice and rock and that Jupiter was two and a half times the mass of all the other planets put together, with its largest satellite, Ganymede, bigger even than Mercury. He knew that, from where he was on Earth, the Sun was ninety-three million miles away. It puzzled him when other people remarked to his mother on how clever he was to remember so many things. Facts were like books or socks. If you put them back in the same place you always knew where they were when you needed them.

Opposite the picture of the Solar System was a

list of all the things in *Volume 6*. Oskar ran his finger down the list until it came to *THE BOOK OF WONDER*. Oskar wondered what *THE BOOK OF WONDER* was and if that was why it was called that, because it made you wonder. His mother said that words were like chemistry because each one reacted with the one next to it to make something new, but Oskar just found them confusing. He nearly put the book back on the shelf. Then he saw that beneath *THE BOOK OF WONDER* was written in smaller letters, *BY THE WISE MAN*. Then he wanted to know who the Wise Man was too.

He took the book to his window seat. There were eight windows all the same down the length of the library, or actually twenty-four because each one was made up of three arranged in a bay, but Oskar's was the one furthest from the door. It was guarded by a marble bust on a pillar, a man with a curly beard and blank blind eyes. Oskar supposed he was a Roman because he wore a sheet tied on one shoulder so he called him Mr Albus because he was white and *albus* was white in Latin. He always said hello to Mr Albus as he climbed into the window seat, just to let him know he was there. The window had a seat underneath it with a long silk cushion and panelled shutters that, when you closed them, made a little room inside just big enough to sit in or even to lie down in if you were ten and not very tall for your age.

It was peaceful in the window. Oskar wanted to

live in a castle more than anything but, though he looked forward to going to Ellinghurst for weeks, when he was there he often wanted to go home. He liked it in the early mornings when the only other people who were up were the servants busy with their work, and he could walk around and look at things properly without someone asking him what he thought he was doing. But a lot of the time he wished he was sitting with his mother in front of the fire at home, Oskar with a book or a scrap of paper and a pencil, his mother with her spectacles on the end of her nose, writing or reading or folding stacks of letters and putting them into envelopes, not talking but looking up at one another from time to time just to make sure. At Ellinghurst he only saw his mother after tea when Nanny took the children down to the drawing room. The castle was perhaps the most interesting place Oskar knew but it was tiring always being with people who were waiting for you to go away again.

Resting the book on his chest Oskar turned the pages. It turned out that the Wise Man did not just tell people things. He answered their questions, like *WHAT IS THE AETHER?* The Wise Man said that the aether was everywhere, that everything travelled through it, even the planets and their moons. He said it was because of the aether that X-rays could look into people's bodies and tele-graphs could be sent through the air without any wires for the messages to travel along. Oskar knew about telegraphs. Mr Kingsley at his school had told them all about Mr Marconi from Italy, who had invented wireless telegraphy and who was presently inventing a machine that would pick up voice rays from the Next World, which meant dead people. Mr Kingsley said that perhaps in their lifetimes a wireless would be invented that could pick up the voice rays from God.

The Wise Man did not say anything about God. He just said that aether was in everything, even in the electrons in atoms, which were the fundamental building blocks of matter. Oskar had never heard of atoms but the Wise Man said that everything that existed in the world was made of atoms, particles so small that millions of them would fit on the head of a pin. And yet, tiny as they were, they were packed with much, much smaller things called electrons. These electrons were so tiny that the best way to imagine them, the Wise Man suggested, was to picture tennis balls bouncing in violent random motion inside the dome of a cathedral.

At the bottom of the page the Wise Man warned that scientists did not yet know for certain if this was how atoms worked, that it remained a hypothesis, but by then it was already too late. Oskar's head felt hot and bright, lit up from the inside like a lantern. He touched the wall beside him, the stone flowers and the fishbone ridge in the plaster where the hair from a paintbrush had stuck, and the thought of it, that the plaster and the paint and the paintbrush hair and his own hair and the tips of his fingers were all made up of atoms, that everything in the world, whatever it was and however it looked, was made of the same specks of matter, each one a tiny universe with its own wildly ricocheting solar system, the astonishing thrill of it, made the hair stand up on the back of his neck.

The slam of the library door made him jump. Instinctively Oskar slid down inside his window-seat house. He knew that he was allowed to be here, that Sir Aubrey had said he could come whenever he wanted as long as he did not touch the special books in the shelves like cages, but that did not mean that he wanted to be found. Very slowly, to keep himself from breathing, he counted the cubes in his head: 1, 8, 27, 64, 125, 216 . . .

It was only one person. You could tell that from the footsteps. Whoever it was was talking to them-self or maybe singing. He wondered hopefully if it might be his mother. His mother was always singing. Sometimes she and Oskar went to the Clapham Grand, which was a music hall with lots of singing and magic tricks and people telling jokes. His mother sang along with all the songs.

There was a scraping noise as though something was being dragged across the floor, then a crash and another and another. Whoever the someone was they were throwing books on the floor. The crashes made him wince, as though a bit of him

34

was inside the pages. There was another bigger bang, several books at once, and a high shriek of fury.

'Damn you all to bloody hell! I hope all the ghosts of all the dead people ever in the whole world come back in one big cloud and scare you all *to death*.'

The voice was Jessica's. Oskar screwed up his face and prayed on the encyclopaedia for her to turn around and go away. If Jessica discovered his window then she would be sure to tell Theo and Theo would find a way to spoil it. Theo only liked people liking things if he had thought of them first. He closed his eyes and counted faster, 4913, 5832, 6859. Then suddenly there was a loud clatter of boots and the shutters banged open. He turned his head away, keeping his eyes squeezed shut.

'For God's sake,' Jessica said, disgusted. 'I can still see you.'

Unhappily Oskar opened his eyes. He hugged the encyclopaedia to his chest.

'I knew you were here,' she said. 'You think it's such a big secret but we all know. Eleanor thinks you must be soft in the head. She says it's like wanting to sit in a coffin.'

Oskar looked past Jessica at the books sprawled on the library floor. He had once overheard a lady telling his mother that the reason Eleanor Melville refused to let her children call her Mama was because she deplored the institutional inequality of the mother–child relationship, and his mother had laughed so hard he thought she might choke. He wanted to ask her what was so funny but he knew she would only want to know what he was doing hiding behind the sofa in the first place.

'Why did you throw the books?' he asked.

Jessica frowned. Oskar always asked the most idiotic questions. 'Because I felt like it. Why do you hide yourself in here like a corpse?'

'Because I felt like it. I like the books.'

'Only freaks like books more than people. When you're grown up you'll probably marry a book.' Shoving his legs out of the way, she clambered onto the window seat. She could see the garden and, above the woods, the top of Grandfather's Tower like a cut-out bit of paper against the sky. Grandfather Melville had wanted to be buried with his wife in the tower but she had said it was ungodly so instead he had made them burn up his body like they did in India and scatter the ashes from the top. Sometimes, when she saw dust on the skirting boards, Jessica wondered if there were still bits of Grandfather Melville in it, blown inside by the wind. 'Marjorie Maxwell Brooke wants to marry Theo,' she said. 'When she talks to him her voice goes funny.'

Oskar did not know what to say to that. 'Is it tea time?' he asked instead.

'Mama and Mr Connolly aren't back yet. I expect they've had a smash.'

'Don't say that.'

'Why not? Cars smash all the time, especially

when they're driven by someone as stupid as Mr Connolly.'

'I didn't know Mr Connolly was stupid.'

'Of course he's stupid. He thinks Mama likes him because he's charming when really she only likes him because he has a brand-new motor car and he hasn't done anything to annoy her yet.'

Oskar thought of Godmother Eleanor and Mr Connolly laughing together beside the fire after tea the day before, Godmother Eleanor's finger-tips touching her lips as though even the laughing was a secret. Once, when Oskar was little, he had asked his mother why the people who came to stay at Ellinghurst were never the same and his mother had said that Godmother Eleanor changed her friends as often as most people changed their vests.

'She hasn't changed you,' Oskar had pointed out.

'No,' she had said, smiling. 'I think she's stuck with me.'

'Stuck in your vest.'

'Completely jammed.'

It had made them laugh to think of Godmother Eleanor flailing blindly about with her arms over her head, tangled up in her Mother vest. If Jessica had been his friend he could have told her and made her laugh too. It was a funny story.

The suddenness with which Jessica leaned over and snatched the book from his arms startled him. She stared at it, wrinkling up her nose in disgust. 'Truly? The bloody encyclopaedia?'

Oskar blinked. He had never heard a girl swear before.

'What's the matter?' she demanded. 'Never heard a girl swear before?'

He reddened. 'Give that back,' he said, but Jessica twisted away, sliding the book under her bottom.

'Why should I?'

'Because I was reading it.'

'Is it yours?'

'Your father said I could read whatever I wanted.'

'So? It's my book just as much as Father's. If I don't want you to look at it, you can't look at it.'

She tucked her legs underneath her, sitting back on *Volume 6* as if it were a cushion. Oskar bit his lip. He did not understand what she wanted, but he knew enough to know that the more he asked the less likely she would be to give it back. Jessica had always bewildered him. When they were little she had made him play games where he had to pretend he was someone else and when he got it wrong she flew into a temper. Her rages had frightened him. Of course that was long ago, before he went to school and met Sayle and McAvoy and the other boys that trailed after the two of them like the Pied Piper's rats.

'For the love of peace, Grunewald, have some backbone,' his form master chided. 'You bring it on yourself, don't you see? Boys are wolves. They smell weakness.'

38

He told Oskar that when someone hit you you had to hit them back. Oskar could not hit Jessica. She was a girl and good at getting other people into trouble. But he could pretend he did not care. Without saying anything he climbed out of the window seat and started picking up the books that were scattered on the floor. Several of them had landed open, crushing the pages. He smoothed them out as he closed them. Behind him Jessica sighed noisily.

'Fine. Here. Have your stupid book.' She held it out to him. Oskar hesitated. 'Come on.'

Oskar put out his hand. Immediately Jessica snatched the book back, clasping it against her chest. 'Just one thing. What do I get in return?'

'What do you mean?'

'You can't expect to get something for nothing,' she said. 'If you want something you have to pay for it.'

'But I don't have any money.'

'Who said it had to be money?'

'What then?'

Jessica put her head on one side. Then she put the encyclopaedia down on the window seat and crossed her arms. 'Show me your thing,' she said.

Oskar stared at her.

'Go on. Pull down your trousers and show me your thing.'

'No!'

Jessica's mouth twisted. 'Why not? Or don't you have one?'

39

'No. I – I mean, I'm not going to. I won't.'

'Theo was right. You're pathetic. Completely and utterly pathetic.' She stroked the encyclopaedia. 'Well, I'm going to take this upstairs. Not that I want to read it or anything, but the pages might do for paper chains. I'll see what I feel like. After all, it is mine.' She slipped off the window seat, the book cradled in her arms, but she did not leave. She came and stood right in front of him. She smelled of warm hay and calamine lotion. 'You're so stupid. If you'd shown me yours I'd most probably have shown you mine. And I bet you'd like to see what it looks like, wouldn't you? For a girl?'

Oskar could not speak. He could not think. He stared at the floor as the heat rushed through his chest and up into his face.

'Well, wouldn't you?'

'Go away,' he muttered. His ears burned. He thought maybe if he wished hard enough the energy of his wanting her to go away might shrivel her up. Jessica looked at him. Then, putting the encyclopaedia on the floor, she lifted her skirt and pulled down her drawers. Oskar saw smooth pale thighs and between them, a curve of flesh like a white fruit, divided in two. Then, like a theatre curtain, the skirt came down.

'You, Oskar Grunewald,' she said, yanking up her drawers, 'are a lily-livered chicken-hearted whey-faced spineless bloody milksop.' She snatched up the book and hurled it at him as hard as she could. It knocked the breath from his stomach. In a daze he heard her boots on the parquet, the slam of the door. The library tilted and spun around him but, even as the thoughts fell over themselves inside his brain, he knew one thing for certain: nothing in the world was quite the way he had imagined it.

CHAPTER 3

1915

That December was bitterly cold. At Ellinghurst the lake froze thick enough to skate on and the ice on the window panes made curved patterns like the backs of seashells. On the second Sunday of the month, as the grey afternoon sank into dusk, it snowed. Jessica stood in the window of the old day nursery, the lamps unlit behind her, and watched the white flakes as they swirled like feathers in the gathering gloom. Beyond the black humps of the trees the full moon was a smear of silver beneath the thick shroud of the sky. Shivering, she pulled her cardigan more tightly around her shoulders.

Theo was dead. A boy had brought the telegram, riding up the drive on a red bicycle. The bicycle had a silver bell. Jessica had seen it through the window, propped against the stone ledge, the silver bell and the dark cloth tape, beginning to fray, wrapped around the handlebars. As soon as Mrs Johns saw the boy she backed away from the door, calling in a shrill voice for Jessica's mother. Jessica heard Eleanor say something to Phyllis on the gallery landing and then the click of her heels on the stairs, the barely suppressed irritation in her voice.

'Really, Johns, what could possibly be so—' But when she saw the boy the words died in her mouth and her legs buckled and she had to catch the eagle at the bottom of the banisters to stop herself from falling. She did not look up when Sir Aubrey came out of his study, Mrs Johns clutching her apron behind him. Nor did she go to the boy who waited on the doorstep in his too-big uniform, the envelope in his outstretched hand. She clutched at the post like a mast at sea, her face chalky white, her head swaying backwards and forwards.

It was less than three months since the news had come of Uncle Henry, killed at the Battle of Gallipoli.

'No,' she said, her eyes wild. 'No, no, no', over and over again in a bleak howl like the wind in the chimney while Sir Aubrey took a coin from his pocket and gave it to the boy. When the boy handed him the envelope he stared at it as though he had never seen a telegram before.

Jessica clenched her fists, pressing her nails into her palms, and willed him not to open it. For as long as he did not open it whatever was in it had not happened. Not yet. Her father ran the side of his thumb over the typed address. Then, turning it over, he slid a finger under the flap and drew out the slip of paper. Someone gave a strangled cry. Perhaps it was her.

Then, like a jump in the newsreel, Phyllis was standing beside her.

'Father?' Phyllis said, holding out her hand, but Sir Aubrey only shook his head and went on staring at the telegram. His breathing was unsteady and he swayed a little. Phyllis took a step towards him. He blinked and looked up, leaning away from her, shaking his head, his free hand smoothing his tie.

'No reply,' he said to the boy and the boy nodded and straightened his cap and opened his mouth as if he meant to say something. Nothing came out. Instead, he turned around and swung his leg over his red bicycle. When the front door closed the silence was terrible. Jessica stood frozen, mesmerised by the ticking of the grandfather clock, the hiss and sigh of the fire, Eleanor's low keening punctuated by the scrape of her breath.

'Father?' Phyllis said again, uncertainly. Sir Aubrey cleared his throat. Carefully, he folded the telegram and tucked it inside his jacket.

'Take your mother upstairs please,' he said in a voice that was not his. 'She needs to lie down.'

Phyllis shook her head. 'What does it—'

'Killed in action. Fourth of December. I assume we shall know more in due course.' He paused, taking his handkerchief from his pocket. Last Saturday, Jessica thought dumbly as Phyllis put her hands over her face. Theo has been dead since last Saturday. She watched her father unfold his handkerchief and blow his nose. Then he folded it again, one square on top of the other.

'There is no nobler cause than to lay down one's life for one's country,' he said, his voice cracking on the consonants. Eleanor's cries had grown higher and shorter, jabbing the air like tight little stitches. 'We should be proud. Mrs Johns, would you? I . . . there are things I must take care of.' He slid his handkerchief back into his pocket. Then, once again smoothing his tie, he went into his study and closed the door.

After that things continued to happen one after the other in what everyone pretended was the ordinary order. People came and went away again. A white-faced Phyllis poured them tea. Three days later the morning post brought a letter from France. Jessica was in the Great Hall when it arrived. She stared at Theo's familiar spiky hand-writing on the envelope and something inside her burst. Theo was alive. There had been a mistake. It had not been Theo who had been blown to pieces by that shell, not Theo at all but someone else. Did he even know that they had thought . . .? The envelope was addressed to her mother but she tore it open anyway.

The letter was short, covering less than a single page. Theo had always been a poor correspondent. He wrote that they were not to worry about him, that although his battalion had moved forward they considered themselves pretty safe, as they had only the odd stray bullet whistling over and none of the heavy shelling that had dogged their last position. He wrote that all he really wanted was for it to stop raining because the rain turned everything to soupy, sticky mud. But, although the whole world was mud and all the men in it, his boys were in good spirits, buoyed by the rumours that the German trenches were worse. *So at least we're winning something,* he wrote, *even if I would give everything I own for a dry pair of socks.* Below the scrawl of his name he had noted the date.

Jessica sank down onto the stone flags, her arms around her knees, the sobs coming in dry heaves that twisted her ribs. December 2nd 1915. It did not seem possible that the shock could be just as new a second time.

Later, sometime in the lost hours, she rose and went barefooted to the bathroom. There were lights on downstairs and the landing was striped with shadows. The house no longer slept. Time had lost its substance, the old boundaries between day and night broken open. Outside Theo's bedroom door she hesitated. The door was pushed to and a narrow knife of light lit the wooden floor beneath it. Hardly breathing, she nudged the door open.

Her mother stood with her back to Jessica at the chest of drawers. The top drawer was pulled open, its contents spilled out all over the floor. In her hands, Eleanor held a pair of woollen shooting socks, dark green with jaunty yellow diamonds knitted into the turnovers. Slowly, her head balanced as carefully as an egg on her neck, she turned round. She did not say anything. Jessica was not even sure that she saw her. Her face was stretched so tight it looked like a skull with two dark holes where the eyes should have been. Behind her, on top of the chest of drawers, every one of the silver-framed photographs had been turned to the wall.

It had always been the tradition at Ellinghurst to hang the Christmas decorations on Christmas Eve. Boughs of spruce and ivy were cut from the woods and twisted with pine cones and scarlet ribbons and slices of dried orange and sticks of cinnamon, and laid along the sideboards and around the posts of the banisters. The children gathered sprigs of holly to put behind the paintings. There were wreaths on the doors and creamy candles in silver candelabra on the mantelpieces and, in the hall, reaching up so high that you could almost touch it from the gallery, a huge Christmas tree hung with glass baubles and silver stars and lit with hundreds of tiny electrical lights.

The Christmas of 1915 there were no decorations and no friends of Eleanor's with their dancing and their cocktails and their long cigarettes. When Mr Fisher's boy brought the tree up to the house,

Mrs Johns sent him away. The tree jounced as he clattered back down the drive, its hacked-off trunk jutting from the cart like a broken bone. The stars and the baubles and the heavy ropes of silver tinsel that Uncle Henry had brought back from Germany before the War stayed in their boxes in the attic. Eleanor locked the piano. There was no music, no singing. Death filled the house like dirty water, muffling sound.

It was as though time had stopped. The hands of the clocks moved slowly round but the days did not change. For as long as Jessica could remember Father Christmas had come to Ellinghurst at midnight on Christmas Eve, not down the chimney the way he did in books but through the front door because, as Eleanor always said, what kind of lunatic came down a chimney when the fire was lit? Jessica was seven when she saw Father Christmas kissing Eleanor's hand and realised that it was not Father Christmas at all, but M. du Marietta who was Viennese and ate four green apples every morning for breakfast. The next day, after church and before it was time to open the presents, she had sneaked into his room and filled his shoes with a paste of flour and water. Eleanor had been furious. She had had Nanny send Jessica to bed without any supper, even though it was Christmas Day, and said she could stay there until she was sorry, but Jessica was not sorry, not a bit, not just because M. du Marietta deserved it but because of Theo who told her she was a marvel and spun her round and round in the air by her arms. It was one of Jessica's favourite things to balance on her stomach on the gallery balustrade, she liked the dizzy vertigo it gave her, but Theo spinning her was the closest she had ever come to really flying.

The Father Christmases continued to come to Ellinghurst long after they were all too old to pretend. One Christmas it was a financier Eleanor had met in Berlin, another an Italian sculptor. Once it was Mr Connolly with the white motor car. Last year it had been Theo, home from the Front on a week's leave. His hand shook as he gave out the presents. Afterwards he sat by the fire, a glass of whisky in his fist, and Eleanor rested her head against his shoulder, strands of her hair clinging to his scarlet coat.

'Promise me, my darling,' she murmured. 'Promise me you'll always be Father Christmas.'

Theo hadn't promised. He only raised his glass with a slurred 'Ho, ho, ho!' and drained it in a single gulp. He drank a lot of whisky that Christmas. It made him quarrelsome. He tried to argue with Phyllis but she was like their father and would not argue back, so he argued with Jessica instead. She told him he was hateful and that she wished he had not come back. Two full days before his leave was up, he left Ellinghurst and went to London. He did not say why or where he was going. Nanny told Jessica it was not her fault, that there was no fighting the bright lights with a boy Theo's age,

49

but Eleanor was inconsolable. She wept and raged and accused Sir Aubrey of driving him away. It was not fair but he did not say so. He did not say anything at all. He just folded up his face and went into his study and shut the door.

He said it was because of the book he was writing about the history of Ellinghurst, but Jessica knew it was because he was weak. He never stood up to Eleanor, even when she laughed at him with other people's husbands. That was why she did not love him. You could love someone who argued with you, even in the heat of hating them you could love them so hard it hurt to swallow, but how could you love someone without any backbone?

The Christmas Theo died there was no Father Christmas. On Christmas Eve Eleanor did not come down for dinner. The next morning they went to church. Sir Aubrey insisted. They were not the only family in the village, he said, to have lost a son. It was the first time since the telegram that Eleanor had left the house. She leaned on Phyllis as she stepped out of the car, her black dress rustling, her face obscured by a thick veil of black crape. In the graveyard she stopped suddenly, one hand on a lichened headstone. Phyllis murmured something to her and tugged at her arm but she doubled over as though she was being sick, her body wracked with sobs. The extravagance of her grief was like a pillow pressing down on Jessica's face.

By the time they went in the organ was playing

for the first hymn. The church looked as it had done every Christmas since Jessica could remember, the nativity scene with its painted plaster figures in the upended wooden crate that served as a stable, the winter jasmine in tall vases behind the altar, the Advent wreath with its red candles burned down and the white one in the middle, its flame guttering a little in the draught from the door. Jessica breathed in, inhaling the familiar church smell. As they made their way up the aisle, several members of the congregation rose, murmuring their condolences, but Eleanor did not acknowledge them. She clasped her hands together as Phyllis guided her into the family pew, her hunched silhouette impervious to solace.

The parson was fat with several chins and an abundance of curly grey hair. Jessica had never seen him before. She frowned at Phyllis, wondering what had happened to whispering Mr Lidgate and his weak chest.

'Gone to be a chaplain at the Front,' Phyllis muttered.

Jessica had never cared a straw for Mr Lidgate but abruptly his absence was a hole gouged inside her. Once, after one particularly inaudible Collect, Mr Lidgate had stuttered, 'Lord, hear our prayer,' and Theo, matching exactly the parson's hoarse whisper, had murmured in her ear, 'Not a bleeding hope, dearie.' Jessica closed her eyes, her arms tight around her ribs, squeezing herself in. She knew how it worked, from the time she had broken her collarbone. The more you moved, the harder it was to bear it.

The new parson delivered his Christmas sermon, his elbow on the pulpit as if it were the bar in a public house. He said that just because the country was at war it did not mean that God had abandoned them. He told the story of the avenging angel of Mons who had appeared to embattled British troops at the very moment that they had believed themselves vanquished, and led them to victory. Only months ago, he said, a bright white cross had appeared in the sky over Flanders, dazzling the soldiers of both sides who laid down their weapons and prayed. This was, he said, a Christian war. It was Jesus, God's only beloved son, whose birth they were gathered together to celebrate, who had shown them the way, by laying down his life for mankind. Now it was the turn of his people on Earth to make the same sacrifice.

'Sacrifice is traditionally the theme of Easter, not Christmas,' he said, 'but this war has turned our world upside down and us with it. Let us steady ourselves with the certainty that those who have fallen have done so for the salvation of mankind. Let us not grieve. Let us rejoice in their valour and their heroism. Let us give thanks for their willing sacrifice. And on this day of hope let us consider the words of H. A. Vachell: "to die saving others from death or, worse – disgrace – to die scaling heights; to die and carry with you into fuller ampler life beyond, untainted hopes and aspirations, unembittered memories, all the freshness and gladness of May – is not that cause for joy rather than sorrow?"'

Eleanor stood up. Throwing off her husband's restraining hand, she pushed out of the pew. Everyone stared, their heads turning to follow her as she swept up the aisle. For the first time Jessica noticed that they were almost all women. The only men in the church were old or little boys. The porch door banged. There was a silence, then coughs and shushing. The fat parson asked the congregation to rise. As the organ wheezed out the first notes of 'Oh Come All Ye Faithful' Jessica looked at Phyllis.

'Leave her,' Sir Aubrey said.

Jessica hesitated. Phyllis shook her head. Then, closing her hymn book, she followed her mother out of the church.

When the freeze was at its hardest, and the midday sun hardly more than a pallid smear on the lowering sky, Sir Aubrey told Phyllis and Jessica that Mrs Carey was coming to stay. Mrs Carey was Mrs Grunewald, only since the War she had gone back to the name she had had before she was married. She had changed Oskar's name too. Now he spelled Oscar with a 'c' and his surname was Greenwood, like the dentist in America who made a set of teeth for George Washington out of hippopotamus bone. The story of Greenwood the dentist had been one of Theo's favourites.

'What do you mean, they're coming here?' Jessica protested. 'They're German.'

'They're not German in the least. Mrs Carey comes from Sussex.'

'Oskar's father was a Hun.'

'Joachim Grunewald was a composer. An artist. He would have detested this war as much as anyone.'

'So what? He'd still have fought for the other side. Against us.'

Sir Aubrey was silent. He bent his head over his plate, cutting his meat into smaller and smaller squares. The scrape of knife against china set Jessica's teeth on edge. On the other side of the table Phyllis turned a page of her book, her chin propped on her cupped hand. Her dogged deafness enraged Jessica. Did nobody but her read the newspapers? Had they not seen the stories of German soldiers in Belgium, the mutilation and the torture and the bayoneting of babies? Her father looked at the meat on his plate. Then, piercing a piece with his fork, he lifted it to his mouth. The square was small enough to swallow in one go but he chewed it and chewed it, his eyes fixed on the tablecloth. The chewing made Jessica want to break something.

'I won't let them come here,' she said furiously. 'How could you even think of it? The enemy in our house, under our roof?'

Sir Aubrey pressed his lips together and swallowed. 'For the last time, Jessica, Oscar Greenwood is not German. His father was naturalised before he was born. The boy is as English as you are.'

'Except that his father was a Hun. She wears a ring with an inscription in German on the inside. Remember, Phyllis? Mrs Grunewald's ring? She took it off once and showed it to us.'

'Her name is Mrs Carey.'

'She wore a German ring because her husband was a Hun. You can't just change that with a – a piece of paper.'

'The law would say otherwise.'

'So you don't care that Oscar has German uncles, German cousins? You don't care that it might have been one of Oscar's family who killed Theo?'

'For God's sake, Jessica!' her father shouted, banging his glass down on the table so hard that Phyllis jumped. Jessica bit the inside of her cheek to keep her steady and made herself meet her father's glare. She could feel her heart thudding in her chest. His hands were clenched on the table and for a wild moment she wondered if he meant to hit her. There were flecks of spittle in the corner of his mouth and his neck was mottled purple and red. She could see the hairs in his nostrils moving in and out as he breathed.

Then, as if a wire had been cut, he looked away. The side of his hand caught the handle of his fork as he reached into his lap for his napkin, knocking it to the floor. Phyllis leaned down and picked it up, putting it on her own plate.

'I'll ring for a clean one,' she said but Sir Aubrey shook his head.

'I've had enough,' he said and, not looking at Jessica, he wiped his mouth very carefully on his napkin. Then he folded it and put it on the table and pushed back his chair. They listened in silence as the echo of his footsteps receded down the passage.

'Well,' Jessica said. 'He's in a filthy temper.'

Phyllis did not answer. Reaching for the bell she rang it. 'You've finished, haven't you?' she said as an afterthought, eyeing Jessica's barely touched plate.

'What do you care?' Jessica pushed the plate away. The smell of congealing gravy made her feel sick. She supposed it was too much to hope for, that Phyllis would ever take her side. She scowled at her sister but Phyllis pressed her lips together and went back to her book.

'You could talk to me,' Jessica said. 'It would make a nice change.'

'Or you could read,' Phyllis said evenly. 'That would make a nice change too.' When Enid came in to clear the plates she lifted her book from the table to make it easier for her to reach but she did not stop reading. Eleanor detested maids in the dining room, she said it made her feel as though she were eating in a public house, but even she had grown used to it. There were no footmen left at Ellinghurst, not since Harold and Robert had enlisted.

'Coffee in here, miss, or in the drawing room?' Enid asked.

'In here is fine, thank you, Enid,' Phyllis said. Enid put the pot in front of her and set out the cups. Jessica waited for Phyllis to pour. Then, with a noisy sigh, she reached for the pot herself and poured two cups, pushing one in front of her sister.

'Thank you,' Phyllis murmured absently and went on reading. Jessica drank her coffee. She thought about leaving the table but she did not have anywhere else to go. She did not want to be alone. Instead, she pleated the edge of the table-cloth and wondered why it was that Phyllis refused to take any interest in clothes and make-up. Nanny always said that Phyllis's red hair was striking, which was the kind of word people used when they could not find anything nicer to say, but her pale pointed face cried out for a little colour and her chest was as flat as a boy's. She had never shown the least interest in parties even though she was meant to have come out the previous summer. No one had, of course. There had been no Season in 1915, no debutantes or presentations at Court. The War had stopped all that, stopped it dead, just as it had stopped absolutely bloody everything else.

The blackness was rising in her again. Dropping the hem of the tablecloth Jessica kicked at the table leg, swinging her foot backwards and forwards like a pendulum. It hurt her toes, which helped somehow so she went on kicking. The thumps shook the table. Phyllis frowned.

'You shouldn't frown like that,' Jessica said. 'You'll get awful wrinkles.'

'Like this?' Phyllis's frown deepened. Without lifting her eyes from the page she reached for her coffee cup.

'You're not seriously going to drink that?' Jessica said. 'It's got a skin on it.'

Phyllis glanced at the cup, grimaced and put it back down. Jessica leaned over, jabbing at the skin with her spoon. 'For a girl who's supposed to be clever you can be unbelievably dense.'

Phyllis gave a strangled cry and dropped her book on the table. 'Sometimes, Jessica . . .' She held her hands out, palms up. 'What exactly is wrong with you?'

'What's wrong with me? I'm not the one who tried to drink coffee with a skin on it like a . . . like a French letter! Oh, don't look so shocked. If you thought less about French books and more about French letters you'd probably be a lot less miserable.'

'Is that right?'

'You know it is.'

'And there I was thinking I was miserable because Theo is dead. How dense can you get?'

When she slammed the door the pictures shook.

Alone at the table Jessica jammed her spoon into

58

the sugar and twisted it, scattering brown crystals across the starched white cloth. It was usually Jessica, not Phyllis, who was the door slammer at Ellinghurst. Quite out of the blue, the lines of a poem came to her, a poem sent to their mother by Theo, who had never had any time for poetry, after Uncle Henry had been killed at Gallipoli.

War knows no power. Safe shall be my going,
Secretly armed against all death's endeavour;
Safe though all safety's lost; safe where men fall;
And, if these poor limbs die, safest of all.

Dropping the spoon with a clatter Jessica began to cry.

CHAPTER 4

Oscar went to the tower. There were 385 steps in the tower, from the bottom to the top. 385 was not only a prime number and the sum of three other primes but a square pyramidal number, which meant that if you arranged one hundred balls in a 10 x 10 square and then put the other balls on top, 385 balls would be enough to make a pyramid like the ones in Egypt. Sir Aubrey had once told Oscar that the tower had been built without any scaffolding at all, just one piece on top of the other. Like an equation, Oscar had thought. He wanted to count each of the 385 steps as he climbed them and let the numbers drop one by one into his brain, like stones into a pond.

That morning the postman had brought a brown paper parcel tied with string. The parcel contained Theo's uniform from the Front. Godmother Eleanor had laid it out on Theo's bed, on the freshly washed sheets. The waistcoat and breeches were bloodstained, the jacket torn. Everything was stiff with mud. Oscar had not known mud could smell like that, as though mud was not earth at all but made of rotting meat. Its thick reek stopped his throat and crept like a fog under the doors and into the curtains. It was impossible to be upstairs.

Oscar had gone first to the library where everything smelled of wax polish and paper but when he opened the door his mother was in there with one hand on Sir Aubrey's arm and Sir Aubrey was rocking backwards and forwards, just rocking without making any noise, so he had fled outside before they knew he was there.

The buttons on Theo's uniform had tigers on them. The Royal Hampshire regiment. Everyone at school knew all the regiments in the British Army. They talked all the time about how they wished they were not too young to go to war. They said they would give the Hun a pasting and every time they said that someone would look at Oscar. They called Oscar the Boche. It did not matter that he had a picture of Theo in his uniform on the dressing table by his bed. Bash the Boche, one of them would shout, and each one would take turns to kick him or slap him or punch him in the ribs. They said he was a spy and stole the torch his mother had given him for his birthday because they said he would use it to signal to Germans in the night. At the end of term McAvoy had told everyone that Oscar's father had been unmasked as a secret agent, that he had been taken to the Tower of London where he would be executed by firing squad.

He did not tell them that his father was already

dead. They knew anyway, even if they chose not to remember, and if there was any trouble they would have to tell his mother and he did not want that. She said that there was nothing to be afraid of but the truth was that, since the sinking of the *Lusitania*, she had been afraid a good deal. The days of Churchill joking about interning German wine with his dinner were long gone. Now everything remotely German was wicked and disgusting, not just Hock and Moselle but German sausage and Goethe and even Beethoven. In Clapham the greengrocer's shop was smashed up and set on fire for having a German-sounding name, even though the owners were Hungarian and had been there for more than fifty years. His mother took off the poesy ring she always wore on the third finger of her right hand. Oscar's father had given it to her when he proposed marriage. The gold ring was engraved with entwined ivy leaves and, inside the band, the words *du allein* which meant *you alone* in German. Her finger was narrower where the ring had been, as though the gold had rubbed it away.

When his mother told him she was changing their names she said that she understood if it made him sad or even angry. Oscar was only angry that she would not let him be Carey like her, but only a version of his German self. He did not believe her when she said that he was the most English boy you could ask for because his father had chosen to be English rather than just being born that way. Every time he looked at something and the German word for it came into his head first he felt cold inside, as if the boys at school were right and he was the enemy after all. It frightened him that he might do something German in his sleep.

He walked briskly across the lawn towards the woods, gulping the cold air, but all he could see was Godmother Eleanor's face when she opened the parcel. Oscar's father had come to London because his family disapproved of him, but there were plenty of brothers and sisters who had stayed. Before the war Tante Adeline had sent his mother a card every Christmas. She had five sons, all grown up, and dozens of nephews, Oscar's cousins. He knew that statistically the possibility that it was one of them who had killed Theo Melville or the Knox brothers or his mother's friend Mrs Winterson's oldest son was vanishingly small, but that did not stop him from thinking about it all the time. As he pushed open the door to the tower the stink of Theo's uniform clung greasily to his hair and skin, gagging the back of his throat.

It was a moment or two before he saw Phyllis. She was crouched up in a ball on the wooden bench that ran around the Tiled Room, her arms wrapped around her shins like a fledgling fallen out of its nest. A book was open face downwards on the bench beside her. As Oscar backed away she looked up. Her pointed nose was red.

'Oh,' she said. 'It's you.'

63

'I'm sorry. I didn't mean . . .'

'It's all right.'

'I'll go.'

'No. Don't.'

Oscar hesitated. Phyllis sniffed and scrubbed at her red-rimmed eyes with the cuff of her jersey. 'Please don't,' she said. 'We don't have to talk or anything. It might just be nice to . . . be with someone for a bit. You know?'

Oscar nodded. He thought perhaps he did know, a little. He wanted to say he was sorry about Theo but the words stuck in his throat. He thought of something his mother had said to him once, that it was not always easier to say sorry just because you knew for certain that something was your fault.

'You're cold,' he said instead.

She shrugged and pulled her jersey over her hands. 'I'm all right,' she said. She was not wearing a coat. Oscar looked down at his own overcoat, his striped muffler. He had never had a new coat before, not new to him, but his mother had taken one look at him when he came back from school and said that he looked like a scarecrow.

'Look at you,' she had said, pulling him in front of the glass. 'That coat's so tight it looks like your arms are on back to front,' and he had laughed, because that was exactly what it looked like, and he had kissed her on the top of her head, which made her laugh too. The coat was one of Theo's cast-offs and like all of Theo's clothes it was beautifully made, only Oscar had grown three inches since the summer holidays. Three inches was an increase of 4.286 per cent, once you had rounded down the extra decimal points. There was another bigger coat of Theo's in the wardrobe but they had gone to Arding & Hobbs instead and bought a new one. Oscar hesitated. He could hear the rattle of Phyllis's teeth chattering.

'Here.' He pulled off his scarf and thrust it at her. 'You can have it. Not to keep, I mean, I'll want it back later but . . .'

To his surprise Phyllis gave a lopsided smile. 'Thank you,' she said. As she wrapped it round her neck Oscar thought of the matted rag of khaki in Theo's package. In Clapham the streets echoed with marching columns of men. On the Common, next to the bit they had dug up for vegetables, a large square had been commandeered by the War Office for officer training. The soldiers' cap badges glinted in the sun and their polished boots were spotless.

'I'm very sorry,' he said, looking at the floor. 'About Theo, I mean.'

'I know.'

Oscar could think of nothing else to say. He buried his hands in his pockets, only his book was in one of them so he took it out and put it on the table. He thought of the last time he had seen Theo, when he had been home on leave. Godmother Eleanor had never left him alone, sitting on the arm of his chair, running her fingers over his shoulders or through his hair. At meals she sat him beside her and rested her hand on his arm. He thought of Charles II who had grown so tired of his scrofulous subjects coming to him to be healed that he had hired royal strokers to do it for him. That was the way Godmother Eleanor usually touched people too. Not Theo. The way she touched Theo it was as if he was a magnet and her fingers made of iron filings.

Phyllis picked up his book. '*The Time Machine.* Is it any good?'

'I don't know yet. I like the beginning.'

Phyllis opened it. She read the first page, then turned over. Oscar did not like other people touching his things but he did not say anything.

'I like this part,' she said. 'Where the Time Traveller says that there's no such thing as an instantaneous cube. That in order to exist something must have not only Length, Breadth and Thickness but Duration. It has to exist in time. I've never thought of it that way before. That Time could be a dimension.'

'*There's no difference between Time and any of the three dimensions of Space except that our consciousness moves along it.*'

Phyllis's finger found the line. 'Yes.'

'Wells is right,' Oscar said. 'Space and time should be thought of from a four-dimensional point of view. Mathematically, I mean.'

'Is that what they teach you at school?'

'I wish. School stuff isn't nearly that interesting.'

'And I thought it was only girls who weren't allowed to learn anything worth knowing.'

Oscar was silent. Last term his mathematics master had stopped teaching him with the rest of the class. He had given Oscar a list of books and sent him to the library. Most of the books were good. Oscar had particularly liked the one about mathematical rules that turned out not to be rules, like the angles of a triangle always adding up to exactly 180°. The mathematician who proved this was not a rule was called Riemann. Riemann had also invented a new kind of geometry and proposed a hypothesis to explain the distribution of prime numbers which Oscar's master said was one of the most important unresolved problems in pure mathematics, but when he gave Oscar a book about Riemann to read during prep Oscar accidentally left it on his desk. Bernhard Riemann was German.

'Eleanor says you're a Mathematics prodigy,' Phyllis said. 'That you'll win a scholarship to Oxford.'

'Maybe. I'd like to.'

She stared at her knees. 'You're lucky. Eleanor wouldn't let me go. She says that the really clever girls know not to look too clever. Men don't marry clever girls apparently.'

Oscar looked surprised. 'I didn't know that.'

'Uncle Henry tried to change her mind. He said that . . . well, I suppose it doesn't matter now.'

They were both silent. Phyllis tucked her fingers inside the cuffs of her jersey and hugged herself to keep warm. Her pointed face was milky pale and there were purple shadows under her eyes. She looked very tired and sad. Oscar tried to think of something kind to say to her.

'Did you know it's because of your Uncle Henry that they don't let scientists fight any more?' he said at last. 'Not the really good ones, at any rate.'

'Really?'

'My physics master gave me a book about him. Well, more of a journal really. There was an article in it about your uncle.'

'About it being because of him that scientists aren't allowed to fight?'

'No, Mr Hall told me that. The article was about Melville's Law.'

Phyllis smiled faintly. 'Eleanor always says Melville's Law is that the less a Melville has to do, the more time he will spend in his study pretending to do it.'

'Actually that's not Melville's Law.'

'I know. It's a joke.'

'Oh,' Oscar said. He stared at the floor. 'Sorry.'

'The awful thing is I don't actually know what Melville's Law is. The real one, I mean.'

Oscar hesitated. 'Do you want me to tell you?'

'Please.'

'Melville's Law proved a systematic mathematical relationship between the wavelengths of the X-rays produced by chemical elements and their atomic numbers.'

'I don't even know what that means.'

'It means that until your uncle came along, people thought that atomic numbers were semi-arbitrary. I mean, they knew they were based approximately on atomic mass but they didn't think they were fixed or anything. Melville's experiments proved that an element's atomic number correlates directly with the X-ray spectra of its atoms.'

'Is that important?'

'Of course it's important. Before him nobody knew it was true.'

'But does it matter? I mean, does it make a difference, knowing?'

Oscar frowned. 'If you mean what will it change, I'm not exactly sure. There's a lot I don't understand, and we don't exactly do it in school. But knowing always makes a difference, doesn't it? I mean, surely it's the point. Of everything.'

She smiled. Her face was sharp, all points and angles, but her eyes were soft. She did not look as though she was laughing at him on the inside.

'What?' he said.

'Nothing. It's nice to hear you talking, I suppose. You don't talk much.'

'I don't usually have anything important to say.'

'That doesn't seem to stop most people.'

'My mother says it is because I got muddled with German and English when I was small so I decided it was better not to speak at all.' It was an old joke, one he had forgotten he remembered. Then he saw the way Phyllis looked at him and something inside him shrivelled. 'I don't speak it any more,' he blurted. 'I was never any good anyway.'

Phyllis did not answer. The silence made Oscar's throat ache. 'My father used to get so angry with me,' he gabbled. 'He said that German was the language of science and high culture. Even though he hated Germany and never went back. He said that next to the Germans the English would only ever be enthusiastic amateurs.' He hung his head. 'I'm glad he's dead.'

'Don't say that,' Phyllis said fiercely.

'But it's true.'

'I don't care. You're not allowed to be glad anyone's dead, not anyone at all. Not any more.'

The afternoon was darkening. In the grey light Phyllis's face looked very white. Outside the wind was getting up. Oscar could hear the whistle of it in the top of the tower, the sea shush of the rustling trees. Neither of them spoke. Oscar thought of Nanny who did not live in the house any more but in a damp cottage in the village, crowded with feathers and stones and splotchy drawings and samplers with the stitches pulled too tight. The day before his mother had made him visit her and, when it was time to leave, she had cried, the tears clotting in the powdery creases of her cheeks, and said that she hoped Oscar would be a brother to the girls now, with Theo gone.

Phyllis reached out and put her hand on Oscar's arm. The tips of her fingers were yellow with cold. 'Thank you,' she said.

'For what?'

'For telling me about Uncle Henry. For not being like most boys of fifteen.'

Oscar looked at her hand on his sleeve. Then awkwardly, like a game of Pat-a-Cake, he put his on top of it. 'I'm good at that,' he said.

The door banged open.

'Phyllis?' Jessica called out, clattering up the shallow steps into the Tiled Room. Immediately Phyllis slipped her hand out from under Oscar's. 'Oh, I'm sorry,' she said. 'Am I interrupting something?'

'Don't be pathetic,' Phyllis said. 'What are you doing here, anyway?'

'Looking for you, if you must know. You're to go back to the house. The men from Theo's regiment are here.'

'I thought Eleanor—'

'Yes, well, she didn't. Won't. Whichever. Father says you'll have to do.'

The sisters looked at each other. Then Phyllis nodded. She stood up, unwinding Oscar's scarf from around her neck.

'That's all right,' he said. 'You can give it back to me later,' but Phyllis balled it up and held it out to him. Oscar took it. It was warm, like something alive.

'Hold on.' Jessica brushed away the bits of dead leaf that clung to her sister's jersey. 'That's better. You should brush your hair before you go in, though. And put some lipstick on. You look terrible.'

71

'Jesus, Jess, they're here to pay their respects, not go to a bloody dance.'

Jessica watched, her crossed arms hugging her chest, as Phyllis hurried through the gloom towards the Great Gate. At the edge of the lawn a white dog was barking at the grass.

'Are you all right?' Oscar asked.

'Of course I'm bloody all right,' she snapped. 'It would just be nice if for once everyone in this house didn't take their misery out on me.'

Since Theo's death the other Melvilles had grown older, greyer, huddled inside their skins like hand-me-down overcoats, but not Jessica. It was impossible not to look at her. She was so new-looking, so extravagantly, insistently shiny. Even in the murky light of the Tiled Room she glowed as though there was sunshine inside her. Her honey-coloured hair reminded Oscar of the gleam on the smooth underside of his mother's chin when he held up a buttercup to see if she liked butter.

'Eleanor says there's no point to anything any more.' She talked without turning round, as though she were talking to the trees outside the window. 'Not now, not with Theo gone. She told your mother that the darkness was like drowning. That she could not remember how to breathe. Your mother said to remember that she still has Phyllis and me. And Father, of course.' She exhaled a tight little laugh. 'It didn't seem to be much consolation.'

Oscar did not know what to say. He looked at

the floor. Inside his head, like a gramophone record going round and round, he heard the words his mother always used to sing when he went to sleep: *Guten Abend, gute Nacht, mit Rosen bedacht.*

'She can hardly bear to look at us,' Jessica said. 'It's like our being alive makes Theo being dead even worse.'

Morgen früh, wenn Gott will, wirst du wieder geweckt. Oscar bit his lip, squeezing the song out of his brain. *Tomorrow morning, if God wills, you'll wake up again.* He thought of his mother in the library, Sir Aubrey like a broken toy in her arms, the sadness leaking out of him like sawdust.

'It's the shock,' he said helplessly. Jessica shrugged. She kicked at the leg of the bench.

'You and Phyllis looked pretty thick,' she said.

'We were just talking.'

'Just talking.' She looked at Oscar. Then she sat down next to him on the bench. It was dark enough for her face to be fuzzy round the edges, even close up. Sir Crawford had wanted electrical lights all the way up the tower but Trinity House had forbade it. They said that the tower was too close to the sea, that ships might mistake it for a lighthouse. 'You were holding hands. I saw you.'

Oscar made himself think about modular arithmetic, which his teacher called clock arithmetic because it was like telling the time, with one coming after twelve and not thirteen. Like everything, modular arithmetic was better with prime numbers. Jessica reached out and took the scarf

73

from his lap. She did not ask him if she could. She wound it round her neck. Then she cocked her head on one side, considering him. Oscar made himself compute powers going up from one for modulo 5. $2^4 = 1$, $2^5 = 2$. He could feel his ears going red.

'Did you want to kiss her?' she said. 'I bet you did. Boys always want to kiss girls, even the not very pretty ones. But then I shouldn't think you notice if someone's pretty or not. She could look like Mary Pickford and you'd still prefer the encyclopaedia. Unless she was made of sums. Think of that. A girl with long division for arms and hair all curly with quadratic equations. Two times signs for eyes and an equals for a mouth. Look at you, just thinking of her makes you blush.'

She thought it would make her feel better, watching Oscar squirm, but the hole inside her kept opening, wider and wider like a huge black mouth. 'You'd eat pi for every meal,' she said. The important thing was not to stop talking. 'Pi and circumference, with slide rules for knives. You do know it's rude, don't you? To sit there like a codfish saying nothing at all. It's bloody freezing out here. If you were a gentleman you'd offer me your coat.'

'We should go in.'

'Not yet. Those men haven't gone yet.'

'How do you know?'

'Jim Pugh's dog.'

Outside the dog was a smear of white against the grey grass of the mown path. It rolled over, its mouth wide open as though it was laughing. Jim Pugh drove the trap that served, among other things, as the station taxi. His dog rode with him everywhere, sitting up very straight with its eyes bulging and its tongue lolling out of its mouth. No one complained because Jim was not all there. Theo had called them the Village Idiots. He once gave Jim Pugh a bag of bird seed and told him if he planted it it would grow birds.

The hole was not a hole any more but a fat black snake, thickening inside her. Jessica tugged at the ends of Oscar's scarf, wrapping the fringes as tightly as she could around her fingers. 'I suppose you're in love with Phyllis, then?'

'No.'

'You make it sound like there's something wrong with her.'

'No, I don't.'

She thought about arguing with him but the snake was too heavy. It made it difficult to breathe. 'Do you ever think about it?' she asked instead. 'About what it would be like to fight?'

Oscar looked at her. *Guten Abend, guten Nacht.* The tune went round and round, round and round. 'Sometimes.'

'It's the only way to make people believe you're not German, you know. To kill some Germans yourself.'

'I know.'

'Then what are you waiting for?'

'To be eighteen.'

'You could lie. Lots of boys do, it was in the newspaper. Or are you a coward?'

'I don't know. Probably. Are you?' He glared at Jessica. The snake in her chest coiled around her heart, squeezing it tight. Tears burned behind her eyes.

'Why does war have to be so absolutely bloody?' she whispered. Closing her eyes, she slid along the bench and laid her head against his chest. He did not put his arm around her. Beyond the woods the garden with its trees and statues looked grey and grainy, like a picture in the newspaper.

'It's not really Phyllis you like best, is it, Oscar?' she asked softly.

Oscar did not answer. At the end of the path, where the gate led into the park, a man was smoking a cigarette. Though the light was poor and he was some distance off, there was no mistaking him. He leaned against a beech tree, one hand cupping his elbow. He was wearing his uniform, the khaki jacket and breeches that Oscar had seen laid out on the bed, only this time they were clean and pressed. When he exhaled the smoke made a stripe in the air.

On the path Jim Pugh's dog stopped rolling. Scrambling to its feet, its hackles raised, it barked frenziedly at the soldier. Theo Melville did not turn around. Dropping the butt of his cigarette, he ground it out with the heel of his boot. Then slowly, he walked away out of sight. Oscar let his breath go.

Jessica turned her face, looking up at him. 'What is it?'

'I . . . I'm not sure.'

In the twilight her eyes were the colour of new pennies. He blinked at her, dazed. He felt like he had somehow stepped out of his body and did not know how to get back inside. Reaching up, she put her arms around his neck. 'Kiss me,' she said.

Kiss me. Two words, a single fixed point in a swirling sea of flashing dust. Giddily Oscar looked down at her, at the bow of her parted mouth, the smudges of her closed eyes with their thick eyelashes curling up at the ends. She looked just like a film star.

'Well?' she said impatiently, opening one eye.

Squeezing his eyes shut, he pressed his lips to hers.

CHAPTER 5

In the dormitories at Oscar's school, boys were allowed a single photograph on their chests of drawers. In Oscar's first few terms most of the boys had photographs of dogs, except for Brigstocke who had a lady in a silver frame who he insisted to Matron was his aunt but who was actually a dancer called Hilda Lewis. By the second year of the War the photographs were almost all of men in uniform.

Oscar told the other boys that Theo was his cousin. In the picture he was standing on the sloping lawn at the front of Ellinghurst, with the castellated turret and arched windows of the east wing of the castle visible behind him. Oscar had taken it himself with Theo's old Brownie, which he had unearthed in a box of discarded clothes and cricket bats. Theo had a newer grander camera by then but Oscar had still been half-afraid to take it back to Ellinghurst in case he decided he wanted it back. There was a pale circle just visible on one of the windows that might have been a face looking out but which Oscar knew was just the reflection of the sun on the glass. Beneath the stiff peak of his cap Theo was squinting.

He kept the photograph there, even after Theo was killed. The other boys did the same. On clear nights, when the moon silvered the linoleum, the faces of all the dead uncles and brothers gleamed pale as ghosts in the darkness. One evening after supper Oscar came back to the dormitory to find Tuckwell and Jamieson standing by his bed. Jamieson was holding Theo's photograph. Someone had drawn a Prussian spike onto Theo's cap and extended his moustache, curling the ends around his ears. A speech bubble extending from his mouth said *DEUTSCH SCHWEIN* in capital letters. Oscar held his breath and waited to see what the boys would do to him, but Jamieson only spat on his handkerchief and scrubbed furiously at the glass, smearing the ink. Then, without a word, he put the photograph back where he had found it.

After that there was always a black smear on Theo's face and a shadow across the turret wall, as though a Zeppelin was blocking out the sun. Oscar touched the shadow before he went to bed, not for good luck so much as to keep the bad luck from getting any worse. He did not think it worked but he went on doing it anyway, the same way his mother whistled when she saw a magpie and said, 'Good morning, Mr Magpie, where's your brother?' The trouble with luck, she said, was that you never knew if without it things would have been any different.

★   ★   ★

79

It was the term after Theo was killed that Oscar was put into Mr Leach's Mathematics division. By then the only teachers left were either ancient or cripples. Mr Leach had thin hair pasted in careful stripes over his skull and a flat round face with a sharp nose in the centre like the gnomon of a sundial, which was the sharp part that cast the shadow. It was because of Mr Leach that Oscar knew the word gnomon in the first place. According to the dictionary it came from the Ancient Greek for 'that which reveals'.

The only thing Mr Leach revealed was his dislike for Oscar. In one of his first lessons, Oscar made the mistake of pointing out a mistake in the equation Mr Leach had written on the blackboard. Mr Leach rubbed out the equation and wrote *'Insolence, if unpunished, increases'* ARISTOTLE across the top instead. Then he gave Oscar a thrashing in front of the class.

After that he called Oscar the Prince of Mathematics with a sneer that made his long nostrils flare, exposing the hair inside. Everyone knew that the Prince of Mathematics was the nickname for Carl Friedrich Gauss and that Gauss was German. It enraged Mr Leach that Oscar did not follow his prescribed working methods but only wrote down the solutions that rose like bubbles in his head when he looked at the questions. Mr Leach said that answers alone made a mockery of mathematics. Instead, he insisted on strings and strings of gobble-degook he called 'workings'. If Oscar forgot any of it Mr Leach thrashed him. The effort made his eyes bulge and dislodged the pasted strands of his hair.

Oscar could tolerate the thrashings. It was the equations that made him wretched. For one whole term and then another, Mr Leach set Oscar the same pointless problems, over and over again. The workings were like lead weights tied to the numbers' feet. With nowhere to go and nothing to entertain them, they started to jabber and thrash in Oscar's head. At night, in the darkness, he could feel them writhing in the lobes of his brain, as though they were looking for a way out. They did not dance for him any more, or hardly ever. They were dull, their eyes glazed over, their old suppleness fattened with tedium and frustration. Sometimes, when he tried to fit them together they would not go, even though they had gone that way before, and then they grew angry and shouted in his ears. For the first time in his life he was afraid of them.

His mother wrote to him. She sent him a postcard on which she had printed a quotation from Galileo.

The universe cannot be read until we have learned the language and become familiar with the characters in which it is written. It is written in mathematical language, and the letters are triangles, circles and other geometrical figures, without which means it is humanly impossible to comprehend a single word. Without these, one is wandering about in a dark labyrinth.

On the other side of the postcard she drew a picture of a confused-looking Oscar, surrounded by mathematical symbols. Underneath the picture she wrote, *Chin up, my darling, and keep at it. You're all that stands between me and the Minotaur.*

The following term they began Officer Cadet Corps. The Sergeant Major who ran the Corps at Oscar's school said that, if the War kept on dragging on the way it was, they would be the next officers to lead the Allied troops into battle. Once a term, at final assembly, the headmaster read out the names of the school alumni who had been killed. There was a board in the hall with their names on. When it was full they put up another one. Oscar would not be eighteen for two more years but twice a week he learned to crawl through mud and shoot a gun and to plunge a bayonet into a sack of sand. The Sergeant Major told the Corps that there was no difference between a bad soldier and a traitor. At night Oscar dreamed of numbers lining up, soldiers to the power of 10, of 10,000, and his bayonet plunging into them over and over again. The bayonet made a sickening liquid noise as it went in but the numbers did not die. They just kept swarming up at him, more and more of them rising out of the ground as though they were made of muscle and mud.

The only thing that helped was to think about Jessica. Jessica was the only thing in his head that had nothing whatsoever to do with numbers. In his mind he ran one finger over the curve of her forehead, following the arch of her eyebrow, touching very lightly the soft fringe of her eyelashes. Her cheekbone was high and hard beneath the white softness of her skin, and on her neck a strand of her honey-coloured hair lay in a loose curl, like a three.

She was his own personal film, over and over, silent and perfect. He slid his fingers along the curl of her hair, feeling its silkiness, before continuing on down the slope of her cheek. When her lips parted he could see the pink tip of her tongue between her teeth. Very slowly he traced the precise bow of her upper lip, the plumpness of the lower. Their softness made him shudder. Turning onto his front, burying his face in the pillow, he lifted her chin up towards him and leaned down to press his lips against hers. The tip of her nose was cold against his cheek. When the climax came he pressed himself against the mattress to keep it from squeaking on its iron springs and, for a moment, there was nothing, no numbers and no clamour and writhing in his head, only the darkness and the sweet cut-grass smell of her hair.

He played the film so often he almost forgot it was real. But it was real. For a minute at least, perhaps much longer, Jessica Melville had let him kiss her. She had kissed him back. When it stopped she had wiped her mouth with the back of her hand and looked at him, her bottom lip caught between her teeth.

'I'm going in,' she said. And then, 'I'm the first girl you've ever kissed, aren't I?' When he nodded, she smiled to herself. 'Then you'll always love me. For the rest of your life.'

He watched her run back down the path towards the garden. He did not follow her. He did not want to go back to nursery tea and the interrogatory brightness of the electrical lights. He could not imagine how he would be able to talk to Jessica now, or even look at her, not after what had happened. And what about his mother? He could not hope that she would not notice the change in him. The kiss had marked him like a brand. He might as well have purple hair or smudges of lipstick all over his face.

He had kissed Jessica. Jessica Melville who looked like an actress and swore like a sailor, who provoked and infuriated him but whose face, when he thought of it, caused him to jolt as though electrified. Every time he remembered it exploded inside him like a firework: he, Oscar Greenwood, had kissed Jessica Melville. The preposterousness of it made him want to laugh out loud.

He had stayed in the tower a long time. When at last, awkward and half-frozen, he skulked back into the house, there was no sign of anyone. His mother was upstairs with Godmother Eleanor, Sir Aubrey working in his study. The children were served a hurried supper in the breakfast room. Phyllis read her book. He could feel Jessica beside him, the hum of her like an engine running, but

84

he kept his eyes on his plate, pretending to eat. In the back of his throat, he could taste the rotten stink of Theo's uniform.

The next morning, from his bedroom window, Oscar watched his mother and Sir Aubrey walking across the lawn. Behind them the tower rose like an upended pencil from the dark scribble of the woods. Oscar closed his eyes, summoning the press of Jessica's mouth against his, the exquisite shimmer of her in the pit of his stomach, but it was Theo Melville he saw, the smear of his pale face in the twilight. They did not send bodies home from the Front, not any more. There were too many of them. Theo Melville would be buried where he fell, if there was enough of him to bury. It was hard to imagine a man's spirit finding peace amidst the ceaseless thumping of the guns.

People said there was no such thing as ghosts but Oscar knew there were. Not headless spooks with clanking chains like the ones in stories but spirits, traces of the energy that had made them alive in the first place. Human bones and brains and flesh were not alive by themselves. They were made of matter and matter was inert, its atoms completely controlled by the forces acting on it, the nature of the energy in the aether. The atoms themselves could not change their state. They could not start or stop on their own. That was the law of inertia, and all material atoms were obedient to it, whether they formed an engine or a clockwork toy or a human body.

The mistake most people made was that because they could not see energy, only matter, they believed that matter was more real than energy. Oscar did not understand this. A magnetic field existed, whether there were iron filings there to demonstrate it or not. Without a wireless set sound waves passed through the aether unseen and undetected. Why could the same not be true of human life, that the essential energy to animate each individual continued to exist, even when the body was no longer there to prove it? Pierre Curie, the Nobel laureate who with his wife Marie had discovered both radium and polonium, had regularly attended seances. He had hoped that, properly conducted, they might unlock the secret of radioactivity.

And yet. He thought of the yellowing piece of paper Mr Beckers, the new science master, had pinned to the classroom wall, printed in his distinctively Continental script.

A THEORY CAN ONLY BE <u>DISPROVED</u> BY EMPIRICAL EVIDENCE. EVIDENCE CAN NEVER <u>PROVE</u> A THEORY BECAUSE OTHER EVIDENCE, YET TO BE DISCOVERED, MAY EXIST THAT IS INCONSISTENT WITH THE THEORY.

On the train home he asked his mother if the men from Theo's battalion had gone to the woods. 'Why?' she asked. 'Did you see someone?' 'In the distance. Vaguely. I thought maybe . . .'

'That it was Theo.'

Oscar nodded. He wished his mother could not always see inside his head.

'Perhaps it was,' she said.

'Perhaps.'

His mother was silent for a long time. Then she sighed. 'We all saw Theo this weekend,' she said. 'One way or another.'

In June Oscar sat the Matriculation examinations. He scored nearly perfect marks in science and Latin but in mathematics he barely scraped a pass. Mr Leach told the headmaster that he had neither aptitude nor application for the subject and that there was no place for him in his classroom. He meant it as a punishment but it felt to Oscar like a reprieve. He had forgotten almost all his German, except those fragments that slipped in on phrases of music or late at night as he was falling asleep. Languages were like that: untended, the part of the brain that you had cleared for them reverted to wilderness. Oscar wanted the same to be true of numbers too.

They did not go back to Ellinghurst that summer. His mother muttered about Mr Asquith and essential journeys. It was near the end of the holidays, trying to clear a space on the kitchen table amid the mountains of piled-up books and papers, that Oscar came across a letter from Sir Aubrey, folded several times and tucked into a book of poetry.

I wish it were otherwise but I'm sure you can imagine how painful it is for Eleanor to see Oscar. Your boy is grown so tall. Pray God they bring this nightmare to an end before he is old enough to know its horrors.

Oscar would not be eighteen for two more years. It was impossible to imagine that the War could go on that long, just as it was impossible to imagine that it would ever end. The wretchedness was like the black London dust, a thin layer of grime so pervasive you forgot that anything could ever be quite clean. In their street in Clapham almost every house was mourning someone. No one wore mourning like Godmother Eleanor's. They just seemed smaller somehow, shrunk inside their ordinary clothes. The week before he and his mother had seen the local doctor's wife at a supper to raise money for refugee children. She wore a blue dress with a white armband around the sleeve.

'John and I have been highly distinguished,' she told them quietly. 'Charles has died for his country.'

At home afterwards his mother had cried. She said that of all the filthy things about the whole filthy business the filthiest was the idea that death was glorious. She said that it was not right that the dead boys should not be mourned, just so that those who were left behind could go on believing in a sacred war. She and her old friends from the Suffrage movement no longer wrote pamphlets and articles about the Vote. Instead, they campaigned to persuade countries outside the War like America to force a mediated peace. Most of the women were like Oscar's mother and had jobs during the day, so they worked at night. The newspapers damned them as fanatics and hysterics and accused them of being unpatriotic, but his mother only shrugged. She said that if this was where men's brains got us, it was time people listened to women's hearts.

The War swallowed everything. Oscar did not mind so much not going to Ellinghurst, it was easier somehow to keep Jessica safely in his head than to imagine what would happen if he were ever to see her again, but he longed for there to be somewhere left where the War was not. The streets pounded with marching columns of recruits in civilian clothes and, on the Common, beyond the high fence that marked the perimeter of the vegetable fields, face-less soldiers in gas masks threw dummy grenades and squirmed through trenches scored deep into the muddy ground. Even his bedroom had blackout blinds and candles on the bedside table in case of raids and a huge enlistment poster stuck up on the wall right outside the window. On the benches around the pond smashed-up men with crutches or hopeless coughs stared at nothing, while above them the barrage balloons drifted in the sky, nosing the clouds like fat black fish. No one flew kites any more. The flying of kites was forbidden by law. On the High Street grey-faced women queued for meat and tried not to cry.

His mother had a job with an insurance company. There were not enough clerks with all the men at the Front. She worked long hours and fell asleep in her chair after supper. The holidays were long and empty. When he suggested to his mother that they go to the music hall she said that she could not bear it, that the shows were nothing but government propaganda, a blatant recruiting campaign. She said she could not sing along to songs like that. Instead, Oscar went to the flickers. Afternoon tickets were cheap. The projectionist at the Globe on Clapham High Street had lost the right side of his face at Mons and sometimes when a reel spun and sputtered to its end there was a long blank silence, nothing but a flickering white screen and an empty tube of light above the audience in which dust turned in slow circles, and when someone went up to the booth and banged on the door, they found the projectionist rocking backwards and forwards in his chair, his eyes fixed on the film that he could not stop, that ran always and unrelentingly in his head.

The War swallowed everything. It even swallowed physics. Teaching was supposed to be a reserved occupation but at Oscar's school most of the masters who were young enough had joined up all the same. The new science master was a Belgian refugee called Beckers. Mr Beckers had a twisted spine from poliomyelitis so the boys called him Bed Beckers in bad Belgian accents. They liked him, though. He had taught at the University in

Leuven until the German invasion had forced him to leave. Many of his colleagues there had been German themselves. Mr Beckers said that there were no politics in science, that scientists were all on the same side.

Mr Beckers had brought two suitcases with him when he fled to England, both filled with books and papers and scientific journals. The Germans were burning the library and, besides, he said, clothes never fit him properly anyway. He told Oscar that in Europe many scientists had serious doubts about the completeness of Newton's theories and gave him some articles to read. Sometimes, when the other boys were playing rugger or cricket, he asked Oscar to tea in his little room. They sat in front of the electrical fire and talked about physics. Mr Beckers told Oscar about radiation and X-rays and Ernest Rutherford's hypothesis of the atom in which electrons did not bounce randomly around as the Wise Man had thought, but moved in elliptical orbits around a central nucleus. All of Rutherford's experiments supported his theory. There was only one problem. It was impossible. His theory contravened the fundamental laws of physics. Faraday and Maxwell had already proved that an electrically charged particle produces radiation if it is diverted from a straight path. Since Rutherford's electrons were in circular orbits they should have been radiating all the time and therefore losing energy, causing them to spiral down into the nucleus in a fraction of a second.

Rutherford's atom was impossible. It should have collapsed in on itself. And yet it did not.

It was not Rutherford but a Dane called Niels Bohr, Mr Beckers told Oscar, who suggested that an electron orbiting a nucleus does not radiate. This was just as impossible as Rutherford's theory, but yet again the experiments seemed to bear out his hypothesis. Bohr went further. He said that the orbit of electrons around the nucleus was predetermined. An electron could only be stable at definite distances from the nucleus; an electron could jump from one permissible orbit to another and as it did so it either absorbed light or emitted light. It was this emission of light that caused spectral lines, the measurable dark or bright lines emitted by atoms that made up a kind of fingerprint for each element on the Periodic Table and which had mystified scientists since the mid-nineteenth century. Bohr's experiments with hydrogen bore out his assertions, Mr Beckers said, his eyes shining. The Dane had brought order to the exterior of the atom just as Rutherford had brought order to its nucleus.

He had also thrown all of classical physics up into the air. A lot of scientists did not like it. While some hailed his theory as one of the great discoveries of the age many more dismissed it as fantasy. Classical physics depended upon cause and effect: if a happened, then b must follow. Bohr's electron was not only random, it knew in advance at what frequency it was going to vibrate when it passed from one stationary state to the other. Which was impossible. Or was it? Given Bohr's results, what other explanation could there be?

That, Mr Beckers said, was where the story ended, for now. Just as things had started to get properly exciting, the War had come. Laboratories emptied as men like the Melvilles' Uncle Henry signed up to fight and foreign scientists were expelled as enemy aliens. Men who had been colleagues and collaborators were abruptly adversaries, fighting on opposite sides. Their experiments were mothballed. Instead, they were made to work on secret War projects like bombs and poison gas. The books and journals stopped. Letters were censored. The War blacked out physics, just as it blacked out everything else.

Until it ended nothing important would happen ever again.

CHAPTER 6

The summer of 1916 was warm and dry. The War was going badly, the news worse almost every week, but in Hampshire there were still picnics and tea parties and tennis parties and, in the long pink evenings, musical recitals of such mind-numbing dullness that Jessica had to fight the urge to scream obscenities or tear off all her clothes. The other girls had known each other all their lives. The boys were their brothers and cousins and the occasional school friend, shipped in from another provincial backwater to make up numbers. They were pimply, raw-looking creatures, hardly more than starter moustaches with manners. Occasionally someone produced a man who was older, on leave or wounded in the War. Neither stuck around very long. Jessica could not blame them. Anyone with any sense could see that there was nothing to keep them in the country. The only ones that stayed had no legs or could not breathe or they shook so much they could not hold a cup of tea. Everyone was kind to them but it was still a relief when they went home. Their afflictions embarrassed everyone, themselves most of all.

By then Jessica was the only one left at home. In January Phyllis had volunteered as a VAD and gone to London. Eleanor had tried to stop her. She said that Phyllis's first duty was to her family, that there was plenty of war work in Hampshire, that nursing was dull and exhausting and often dangerous, that terrible, unspeakable things happened to unsuspecting nurses at the mercy of wounded men long starved of female company, that surely Phyllis realised that she would be of no earthly use to a hospital, a girl who had never once cared for a doll, let alone a real person, and did she really think Matrons let their nurses wander around all day with the noses in a book, but Phyllis only shrugged and said that she had made up her mind.

'They give the VADs all the worst jobs, you know,' Jessica told her. 'Lavinia Petersham says her sister does nothing but sweep floors and scrub lavatories. She never even gets a day off.'

'So?' Phyllis said.

'So I'm just telling you. You won't be allowed to actually nurse anybody or anything. You'll be a glorified charwoman.'

'What else could I be? I'm barely qualified for that.'

'You don't mind?'

'That my upbringing and education together have failed comprehensively to furnish me with a single valuable practical skill? Yes, actually, I do.'

'You can still change your mind,' Jessica said. 'It's not too late.' But Phyllis only gaped at her as though she had spoken in Japanese. A week later she went to London to start her training. She took Theo's suitcase with her, the one Grandmother Melville had given him when he first went away to school. It was made of brown leather with his initials embossed on the lid. When Eleanor saw it she gasped and pressed her hand against her mouth.

'I liked the idea of him keeping me company,' Phyllis said.

Like a bird, Eleanor's hand lit on the corner of the suitcase. She stroked the scarred leather with the side of her thumb.

'I'd forgotten that old thing,' Jessica said softly.

'I know,' Phyllis said. 'I'm just hoping it won't insist on eating oranges and refuse to open the window.'

'Or retch into its handkerchief when anyone else tries to get into the carriage and mutter about tropical diseases,' Jessica added.

'Or try to catch butterflies out of the window with Eleanor's silk parasol.'

Eleanor gave a sob, pulling the suitcase towards her with both arms. Phyllis glanced at Jessica.

'You can't have it,' Eleanor cried. 'It isn't yours to take. Going into his room, rifling through his things. I shan't let you, do you hear me? I shan't let you.'

Phyllis hesitated. Then she shook her head. 'I'm sorry,' she said. 'He wasn't just yours. He belonged to us too.'

She took the suitcase. When she kissed Eleanor

goodbye at the front door Eleanor turned her face away, her neck stretched taut, and went into the house without looking back.

With Phyllis gone and half the servants, Ellinghurst was silent as a church. Even the horses had been taken for the War. When summer came Jessica went to the parties because there was nothing else to do. She hit tennis balls deliberately into the trees and smoked cigarettes while pretending to look for them. She drew up a list of the boys and asked the girls to score them all out of ten according to how good they thought they would be at doing it. Once she brought a bottle of gin she had stolen from the drawing-room drinks cabinet and suggested to several of the girls that they sneak off and have a proper party on their own. Nobody came. She drank some of the gin and poured the rest into a potted fern. She hoped it died. The girls were drips and goody-goodies, every last one of them.

But then the boys were worse. She thought of Hubert Dugdale, who for months had trailed after her like a spaniel and who out of the blue in August had presented a bouquet of roses to Iris Lloyd Warner. Iris, who was fat and freckled and got out of breath just reaching for another cake. The other girls sighed and squealed and declared the whole thing impossibly romantic, but Jessica thought it was contemptible. It was not that she cared a jot for dreary Hubert Dugdale. It was the principle.

The fire of passion did not burn out just because it was not stoked. It fed on itself, greedily, blazing like a house in flames, terrifying and glorious. That Hubert Dugdale could be declaring undying love to her one week and fondling fat, splotchy Iris Lloyd Warner the next made Jessica despise him even more than she had before. What kind of a sorry apology for love was that which could be dispersed with one sharp puff, like a dandelion clock?

Sometimes she forgot that Theo was dead. Sometimes she went for a whole day without remembering and she was almost happy. She hated herself then, for forgetting. Nanny said that time was the great healer but Jessica did not want to heal. She wanted to hurt, to bleed forever like St Francis of Assisi. The hurt was all she had to offer Theo in return for being alive.

She made an inventory. She went everywhere in the house she could think of, up the spiral staircase of the turret to Grandfather Melville's old smoking room with its curved panelling and the red lamp he had used to signal to the kitchen when he needed something, and along long-closed-off corridors and into dust-sheeted bedrooms no one had slept in since before the War. She went up to the empty attic bedrooms where the servants had slept when there were still enough servants to fill them, and where now there were only iron bedsteads and rows of tin buckets, collecting the leaks from the roof. She went to the gun room with its numbered wooden shelves of boots and gaiters and to Grandfather Melville's racquets court in the tower, its wooden panelling sagging from the walls, its cement floor scorched and stained by years of Uncle Henry's boyish chemistry experiments. She went to the dovecote and the orangery and the gatehouse and the empty stables where a forlorn Max kicked the partition of his loosebox for something to do. She walked around the battlements and through the gardens and between the grassed-over slopes of the old moat and out over the bridge to the orchards and the woods, and for each place, she collected up all the memories of Theo she could remember and put them in her pockets, like leaves.

Some of the memories were part of family lore, stories told so often Jessica did not know if she actually remembered them at all: Theo driving the Rolls-Royce across the croquet lawn with Pritchard running behind like a madman, or flying Mr Floyd the beleaguered tutor's darned woollen drawers from the flagpole. Some were posed, caught forever in black and white: a round-faced Theo on Max at his first Boxing Day hunt or armed with snowballs by an enormous snowman or smiling in the woods with a shotgun broken over his arm and a brace of pigeon hooked on one finger.

The best ones, though, were the ones that were

just hers. She had not thought there were so many. Theo throwing Father's top hat like a quoit over the eagle on the Great Hall newel post. Theo opening a box in the nursery and showing her the stag beetles sprawled inside, intoxicated on the dregs of cocktails abandoned on the terrace before dinner, or swinging out on the knotted rope over the lake and landing in a splash of limbs and silver, or toasting the start of the holidays with stolen champagne poured in tooth mugs, or making her roll again and again down the slope of the moat until her skirt was green and he had singlehand-edly repelled the Mahdi at Khartoum. Lying with her on his stomach on the lawn and plucking the petals of daisies as she strung daisy chains: *worships me, adores me, just wants me for my body*. Opening the door to the old scullery when he was home on leave and finding him crying, curled up in a ball on the floor.

She did not go into the scullery again. That would not be what she remembered.

Eleanor was building a memorial. She had commissioned an architect from London to design it. It was to be a cupola of marble set on Grecian pillars with a statue inside of Apollo and an inscription from Socrates around the lip of the dome: *THE SOULS OF THE RIGHTEOUS ARE IMMORTAL & DIVINE.* When Sir Aubrey said that labour was scarce and that if any work was to be done it should be on keeping the roof over their heads from falling in, Eleanor walked away as though she had not heard him. She told Jessica that when Mrs Waller asked Theo if he liked the sketches for the memorial, the pointer had spun like a dervish and touched *YES* not once but three times. Later, she said, he had spelled out *DON'T CRY DEAREST*, plain as printing. Everyone agreed they had never seen a message from the Other Side come through so clearly.

Eleanor had visited Mrs Waller every Thursday since February. Jessica had presumed she would tire of it, just as she had always tired of everything else, but, five months later and despite petrol supposedly being rationed, Pritchard still drove her to Bournemouth every Thursday after lunch and waited until it was time to bring her back. Perhaps, Jessica thought sourly, her mother claimed the seances as War Work. If so it was the closest she ever got. On Saturday afternoons, when Nanny finally stopped knitting and came up to the house to wrap parcels for Allied prisoners of war, Eleanor always said she had a headache and had to lie down. Other big houses had offered themselves as convalescent homes and hospitals, but Eleanor refused, even when someone from the War Ministry wrote specially to ask. She said it was unthinkable. It was one of the few things she and Sir Aubrey agreed on.

Eleanor never asked Jessica to go with her to Mrs Waller. Jessica was glad. She hated it when Eleanor talked of the Temple, as though it was somewhere holy rather than a room above a chemist's shop. She did not want to look at the scribbled-on scraps of paper that Eleanor flourished at her, flush-cheeked and agitated as though they were something magical and not incomprehensible gobbledegook, or to hear how Mrs Waller moved her hands over the sealed envelopes containing the sitters' questions, so that the words came up through her skin. Mrs Waller could not hear the voices of the spirits. Instead, after each question, she would begin to recite the alphabet until the table tilted, whereupon she would begin again. The letters gained in this way would then be put together into words and sentences. When the spirits were excited, Eleanor said, the table danced on its wooden legs or even rotated like a carousel. On those days the psychical energy of the spirits was so powerful that you could see it, tiny flashes of light in the dim red darkness. On one miraculous afternoon, the table had risen clean into the air, lifted from the pull of gravity by the clamour of voices from the Other Side.

On other days Mrs Waller used the planchette, a heart-shaped piece of wood fitted with a downward-facing pencil that moved at the behest of the spirits, spelling out messages on the piece of paper underneath, or practised the art of automatic writing where her right hand seemed to be owned by someone other than she, the pen in her fingers scribbling madly on whatever paper came to hand. Eleanor said that, once the process

102

had begun, Mrs Waller's trance was shallow enough to allow her to ask questions so that it was almost like having a conversation.

Eleanor kept the scraps of paper in a silk box on her dressing table, even the ones where the pencil marks hardly formed letters at all. She read them over and over, like love letters, until the paper was as thin as muslin. Sometimes, on Thursday afternoons, when the car was out of sight, Jessica crept into her mother's bedroom and took out the pieces of paper. She looked at them for a long time but, though she tried, she could not see what Eleanor could see. It felt like another kind of betrayal.

CHAPTER 7

It was not until the Easter holidays of 1917 that the Yorkshire Melvilles finally came to stay at Ellinghurst. It was a momentous occasion. Sir Aubrey insisted on Phyllis coming back from London for the weekend, even though she said that the hospital could not spare her. He said that there were still some things that were more important than the War.

Evelyn Melville was Father's third cousin once removed or perhaps it was twice. Sir Aubrey had explained it but Jessica had not paid attention. No one but Sir Aubrey had ever met him before and then only once a million years before at a family wedding when Cousin Evelyn was a boy. Now he was a middle-aged solicitor and heir to the baronetcy. He had a wife, Cousin Lettice, and four young sons, the smallest of which was no more than a grub in a blanket and too little to be left behind. The Melville baronets had always lived at Ellinghurst. When Sir Aubrey died, the house and the title would pass to Cousin Evelyn and one of the grub-children would get Jessica's bedroom.

The Yorkshire Melvilles arrived on the afternoon train from London. Sir Aubrey sent the car to meet them at the station. For more than a year Jessica had pictured Cousin Evelyn as a devilish but seductive villain, a black-moustached, black-hearted crook who would stake the whole estate on a single hand of cards, or sometimes as a snivelling Mr Collins, gawping at the portraits and leaving greasy fingerprints on the silver. But the man who climbed out of the car was a perfectly ordinary-looking man with thinning hair and wire-rimmed spectacles. The lenses of his spectacles were the only notable thing about him, so thick that from the side they made it look as though he had four eyes in a row, two of them huge and swimmy. He told Jessica it was his poor eyesight that had kept him out of the War.

The next day, as he and Sir Aubrey walked the estate and looked at ledgers and went to meetings with land agents and accountants, Jessica went with Pritchard to meet Phyllis's train. Anything was better than having to stay with fat Cousin Lettice. Lettice did not leave her baby with the nursemaid like normal people. She liked to hold it and bounce it up and down on her knee. Worse, she kept offering it to Jessica like a present, as though there was no greater pleasure in the world than clutching a sour-smelling sausage that, when you squeezed it, opened its mouth and leaked a disgusting stream of white sick all down its front.

'All babies are heavenly,' Lettice said to Jessica, making cooing fish mouths at the squalling bundle in her arms. 'But just you wait till you have one of your own. You'll love it so much you'll want to eat it up.'

Jessica resisted the temptation to ask whether babies went better with mustard or mint jelly. The Lettices of the world were no fun to tease. They only looked at you in a wounded, bewildered kind of way and said something apologetic about not really liking that sort of joke that made you feel foolish and furious at the same time.

'She's only been here a day,' she told Phyllis in the car as they drove back to Ellinghurst. 'Already she's told me that she knows in her bones that I've already met the man I'm going to marry, which if it's true is frankly the most dispiriting thing anyone's ever said to me.'

Phyllis laughed. She was very thin, almost gaunt, her pale eyes purple-lidded and smudged with exhaustion, but it was the way that she stared out of the window as they crossed the humpbacked bridge that struck Jessica most. She knew how it felt to come back from a term away at school, that fierce mix of yearning and reprieve at every indelible twist in the lane, each achingly familiar field and fencepost lining up with their pair inside her, returning her to herself piece by piece. It made her feel closer to Phyllis, to think that she felt the same way too.

'It's hard to believe anyone that fat has bones,

let alone feels things in them, but there you are, apparently they're infallible,' she said. 'The very moment she set eyes on Cousin Evelyn off they went, marrow positively writhing with certainty. I wonder if they also happened to mention that one day, if she sat very tight, she'd wake up to find herself Lady Melville.'

A flicker of something crossed Phyllis's face. Jessica wondered if she would ask first about Eleanor or Cousin Evelyn. She had rehearsed her answers to both. Instead, Phyllis leaned forward. 'Would you stop the car please, Pritchard? Just here would be fine.'

'Oh God, you're not going to be sick, are you?' Jessica asked but Phyllis did not answer. She did not wait for Pritchard to come round. As soon as he fixed the brake she opened the door and climbed out. Jessica followed her. They were nearly home. Ahead of them the lane cut a channel through sloping green fields dotted with sheep, and the sky stretched milky-blue towards the sea. In the woods the trees were coming into leaf, latticed branches hazed with green. Phyllis held her face up towards the pale spring sun, listening to the birds, the faint throaty call of the ewes to their young.

'If you say anything about how lovely and quiet it is after London I swear I'll scream,' Jessica said.

Phyllis smiled. Then, fumbling in the pockets of her coat, she took out a packet of cigarettes and a box of matches. 'Want one?'

Jessica shook her head, staring as Phyllis put a cigarette between her lips and lit it. She did not know which part provoked her more, the smoking or the fact that Phyllis was not wearing gloves. It was just the kind of thing Phyllis would do to annoy Eleanor, unless of course she had just lost them. Phyllis had always lost things, all her life. It had driven Eleanor to distraction.

'When did you start smoking?' Jessica asked.

Phyllis did not answer. 'We could always have Pritchard take us back to the station,' she said instead, blowing out smoke. Her hands were red and rough-looking. 'There's a fast train to London at half past.'

'You looked up the return trains already?'

'It's one of the things they drum into you during VAD training.' She smiled wryly. 'Always know the exits in case of emergency.'

'Tempting though it is, I'm not sure Cousin Lettice's bones could manage the disappointment.'

'And Eleanor?'

Jessica hesitated. Then she shrugged. 'You know,' she said. The sisters exchanged a look. 'But Mrs Moore has made plum cake.'

'She hasn't?'

'This morning. Especially for you.'

Phyllis groaned. 'Damn that woman. All right, then, it'll have to be the six o'clock. It's a stopping train but what choice do we have? Mrs Moore's plum cake.' She shook her head. 'I dream about it, you know. All the time.'

'You're twenty years old and living in one of the great cities of the world, and you dream about plum cake? Tell me it's not true.'

'I'm twenty years old and living in a hostel in Roehampton with eighty other girls and I don't dream about any old plum cake. I dream about Mrs Moore's plum cake with its soft moist middle warm from the oven and bursting with fat sultanas and walnuts and bits of dried fig like perfect little pieces of heaven . . .'

Jessica put her head in her hands. 'You break my heart, Phyllis Melville, do you know that? You break my bloody heart.'

At tea Phyllis ate two slices of plum cake and held Cousin Lettice's grub baby. It was quiet for her, gazing up at her solemnly as she drank her tea and stared into the fire. When Lettice asked her about her work she replied as though her answers were cables, paid for by the word. The new post was in Roehampton. A convalescent hospital. Yes, Queen Mary was the patron and had visited several times. A private house, requisitioned by the War Office. Yes, specifically for officers and men who had lost limbs. Prosthetics, thousands of them. Legs, arms, sometimes both. Yes, wonderful what the doctors could do these days. One hundred new cases a week and a long waiting list. Longer all the time, yes. Of course, very brave. An inspiration, all of them.

'You too,' Lettice said. 'I do admire you. It must be a terrible strain.' She leaned forward, her face

109

creased with sympathy, her hands lifting and flut- tering in her lap like fat birds, but Phyllis only sat more upright in her chair, her jaw set and her eyes fixed on the fire. 'There is a Home for men like that in Harrogate. You see them sometimes being led along the front, blind, half of them, their faces all smashed up. I tell the boys not to look but of course they do. They can't help it. I mean, one feels for the poor creatures, of course one does, it's too dreadful, but I'm not sure they should let them out like that. You know, in public. Teddy's had nightmares.'

'They should lock them up,' Phyllis said. 'Or drown them. In a sack like kittens.'

'No, well, obviously I'm not suggesting . . . like kittens, goodness!' Lettice said, flustered. 'I suppose that's the famous hospital humour everyone talks about. Nothing so ghastly it can't be joked about, isn't that right?'

Phyllis opened her mouth. Then she closed it again. 'I don't know,' she said wearily. 'You'd have to ask the boys on my ward.' Reaching out she took a cigarette from the box on the table and lit it. Lettice looked distressed.

'Gosh, I don't think . . . I mean, if you don't mind?' she said, scooping the grub from Phyllis's lap. 'I'm sure you understand, the risk of a burn . . .'

The baby started to cry. Phyllis looked at Lettice, her cigarette quivering between her lips. For a moment Jessica thought she might hit her. Instead she gave a strange strangled gulp of laughter. Then,

110

sucking so hard at the cigarette that the tip crackled red, she threw it into the fire and stood up. Behind her on the table their mother had spread the plans for the memorial.

'I wanted you to see these,' Eleanor said to Phyllis, smoothing the paper, but Phyllis turned her head away and said she was going for a walk.

'I'll come with you,' Jessica offered. Phyllis shook her head.

'Do you mind if you don't?' she said. 'I'd like to be on my own.'

There was a silence after she left. A little later Cousin Evelyn came back with Sir Aubrey. He admired the plans for the memorial. Then he sat down next to Jessica. He told her that he found Ellinghurst delightful but when she said it was just as well, given that he would soon be living there, he smiled and said that he was sure that Sir Aubrey would outlive them all.

'Hampshire has its charms, of course,' he said, 'but it can't hold a candle to Yorkshire.' He said that Harrogate was lovelier than Buxton, lovelier even than Bath, and that, if Jessica wanted a complexion like Letty, who had had four children and was still the prettiest woman in Yorkshire, then she should visit them and take the sulphur baths at Harlow Carr.

'Sulphur?' Jessica said, making a face. 'Don't they absolutely reek?' But Cousin Evelyn only went on smiling and said that Harrogate was the most advanced centre for hydropathy in the world.

As for the Kursaal, the concerts there surpassed anything in London or Vienna, even before the War.

'The Royal Hall, Evie dearest,' Lettice corrected him, leaning over to brush an imaginary speck from his sleeve. 'We call it the Royal Hall now.'

She was always touching him, and he her. The next day, in the morning room after church, Cousin Evelyn rubbed his nose against Lettice's and behind their backs Phyllis made a sick face at Jessica, two fingers pointing down her throat, and walked out of the room. Jessica started to go after her but her father put a hand on her arm. He said quietly that nursing was a wretched business, that Phyllis had seen things no girl of her age should ever have to see.

'Did she tell you?' Jessica asked, surprised.

'She didn't have to. Just leave her be.'

Jessica did as he asked, though it did not seem fair. What was the point of making Phyllis come home if she just went off all the time on her own? She trailed resentfully after Lettice as she pushed the grub in its perambulator out for its morning walk. The lawn was too soft for the wheels so they went up the drive and along the path to the old Dutch garden where labourers had begun to sink the foundations for Theo's memorial. Where the path sheared into mud Lettice stopped, one hand on Jessica's arm.

'I hope you don't think it presumptuous,' she said, 'but I get a very strong sense of Theo's presence

112

here. Like being in a baby's room when he's sleeping. That feeling of peace, the hush after the hurly-burly of the day.'

Jessica shrugged. 'Wait till the workmen come back on Monday. There won't be a lot of hush then.'

'Well, no. But that isn't quite what I meant.'

'Besides, I'm not sure hush is what Eleanor's after. She prefers the dead jabbering nineteen to the dozen.'

'Heavens, dear, what a thing to say.'

'Why? It's true. I suppose you believe in all that stuff too? In crossing over and table tilting and voices from the Other Side?'

'If you're asking if I believe that the dead reach out to us, then most certainly I do. Don't you?'

'Of course I don't. It's mumbo-jumbo.'

'Oh, no, dear,' Lettice said firmly. 'There's scientific proof.'

'What proof?'

'You should ask Evie really, he understands it all much better than I do, but a cousin of my mother's is a very renowned scientist, Sir Oliver Lodge, perhaps you've heard of him? He's quite brilliant. He invented the wireless before Mr Marconi, though Mr Marconi being an Italian was very quick to take the credit.'

'What has that to do with the Other Side?'

'Raymond Lodge, Sir Oliver's youngest, was killed in Flanders two years ago. Since then, Sir Oliver has proved scientifically that, even though

113

Raymond is gone, his spirit remains with us. He wrote a book about it, *Raymond*. You don't know it? It sold in mountains.'

Jessica shook her head. She heard the clatter of hoofs on the drive behind the rhododendrons, saw, as the trap rounded the bend, the crown of Jim Pugh's familiar weather-beaten hat. She frowned. She did not think they were expecting anyone.

'We ought to go back,' she said.

The visitor was in uniform. Jessica felt the old sick rush of terror as she saw him disembarking in the carriage porch, even though she knew there was no one else left to lose. On the box of the trap Jim Pugh's white dog leaned stiffly against Jim Pugh, its brown eyes milky with age.

'Shall I stay?' Lettice murmured but Jessica shook her head. She waited until Lettice had jounced the perambulator into the Great Hall. Then, smiling politely, she held out her hand.

The officer's name was Cockayne. He said that he had written to Lady Melville, that she was expecting him. Jessica pretended that she already knew. She told Jim to take the trap round to the stables and showed the captain into the morning room. She rang for tea. Enid brought it. She told Jessica that Lady Melville sent her apologies, she would be there directly.

'It's my fault,' Cockayne said. 'I caught the earlier train.'

Jessica poured tea. 'Milk, Captain Cockayne?'

'Guy. Lemon, thank you.'

He was in the Royal Hampshires, Theo's regiment. Jessica recognised the tigers on his buttons. He told her that the two of them had enlisted in the same week, that they had served together ever since. After Theo was killed Guy had gone on for another half year before he too was wounded. A sniper bullet, he said. Not a good enough shot to kill him. After several months of convalescence, the doctors had declared him fit. In a week he would return to his battalion. He told her all this in a flat voice, like a railway announcement, and all the time he was talking he stared around him, as though he was trying to remember something. It occurred to Jessica that he might not be a soldier at all but a confidence trickster, looking for things to steal. She fiddled with the spoons on the tea tray and wondered how much longer her mother would be.

Then he took some photographs from his pockets. The photographs were of Theo, sometimes alone, sometimes with some of the other men. Jessica took one and stared at it. Theo was sitting in a trench, his back against a wall of sandbags. There was a gun propped up beside him. He looked tired and dirty, his puttees caked with mud, but he leaned towards the camera, a smile creasing his eyes, as though he was confiding a secret. Jessica's heart turned over.

'Who took this?' she asked.

'I did.'

'I thought you weren't allowed cameras at the Front.'

'We weren't. It was Theo's. Theo never cared much for the rules.' He smiled faintly. Jessica looked at the photograph of Theo and then again at Guy Cockayne. His hair was brown, falling forward slightly over his high forehead, but his eyes were a clean clear blue, darker at the outside than in the middle as though someone had circled the irises with ink. The thinness of his face exaggerated his full mouth, the sharp slope of his cheekbones. He did not look like a soldier. He looked like a poet or a medieval saint. He turned his head, catching her staring. She buried her face in her teacup.

'You look so like him,' he said.

'Do I?' The words were bristly. They stuck in her throat.

'You have the same eyes.'

'Lion eyes. That's what Nanny always called them.'

'Lion eyes.' He nodded. 'Yes.'

'She used to say it was all very well having lion eyes but what counted was a lion heart.' She faltered, not knowing how to ask. 'Was Theo . . . was he very brave?'

Guy leaned forward, straightening the row of photographs on the table. His hands were long and narrow, with narrow pale nails.

'Theo was the bravest man I ever knew,' he said at last. 'It didn't matter how bad it got out there, he just refused to be afraid. He said it wasn't courage, just contrariness, bred in the bone. He said you were just the same.'

'He talked about me?'

'Of course.'

'What . . . what did he say?'

'That you were just like him. Ferocious. Free. Undomesticated. The kind of wild creature that would die rather than live in captivity.' He laughed, a choked cough, and ducked his head. 'Sorry.'

Jessica stared at the floor and tried to imagine Theo saying such things about her. All her life she had loved him and looked up to him, she had wanted to be like him, for him to notice her, and all her life she had grieved because he was not looking. Except that he was. He had. He had thought she was like him. The stab of pride bent her double.

The door opened and Eleanor came in. Phyllis was with her. Guy stood. When they sat down Eleanor sat very close to him on the sofa, her leg almost touching his. She wept when she saw the photographs. She said that Theo had talked about photographs with Mrs Waller, that he had grown quite impatient with her when she had not understood. Stripes behind, he had said, and she pointed to the pattern of sandbags behind Theo. Stripes behind. She said it as though it made sense of everything.

Guy drank his tea. Not long after, he said he had to leave to catch his train and asked if he might wash his hands. Eleanor went upstairs to lie down and Jessica waited for him with Phyllis in the Great Hall. He took a long time. When

Jessica went to find him he was standing in the passageway, his eyes closed and his forehead against the wall.

At the front door she shook his hand, feeling the narrowness of it, the long bones moving under the skin.

'Might I write to you out there?' she blurted. 'For Theo's sake, I mean. Because of Theo.'

Guy hesitated. Then he nodded. 'Please,' he said.

The next day the Yorkshire Melvilles left to return to Harrogate. It was raining, a fine drizzle that caught in the trees like smoke. Jessica waited with Phyllis and her father under the stone arches of the carriage porch as Cousin Evelyn helped Cousin Lettice and the nursemaid and the grub baby into the car. When everyone was settled he came back to the porch. His coat glinted with tiny beads of rain.

'Come and visit,' he urged as he kissed Phyllis and Jessica. 'We'll show you why there's two sort o' folk int' world, them from Yorkshire and them that wished the' were.' His Yorkshire accent was abysmal.

'I expect you'll be glad to be back,' Father said.

'Ah, well, you know, the home fires and all that.' They shook hands. Then Cousin Evelyn patted Father awkwardly on the arm. 'Thank Eleanor for us, won't you? I hope she feels better soon.'

Sir Aubrey nodded. 'Safe journey,' he said.

Cousin Evelyn bent to climb into the car. Then he straightened up again.

'I hope you know how sorry I am, Aubrey,' he said. 'This . . . situation. It's not what any of us would have wanted.'

As the car crunched away Sir Aubrey walked out onto the gravelled sweep. He watched as it made its way slowly down the drive, following the curve of the rhododendrons until it disappeared from sight. It was only when the rain began to fall in earnest that he turned and went back into the house.

CHAPTER 8

According to Mr Beckers, the aether did not exist. Or at least it did not exist in the way that Newton and scientists up until the nineteenth century had thought of it, as the invisible essence of which all bodies were made. The questions that had once been considered among the most urgent in physics – How dense is the aether? Is it fluid like water or solid like steel? Which way do the particles of the aether oscillate when an electromagnetic wave travels across it? – had never been answered, but this was not ignorance, Mr Beckers said. It was knowledge. The questions could not be answered because they were the wrong questions to ask in the first place.

The aether was not a kind of matter. It had none of the characteristics of matter, such as mass or rigidity. There was no more purpose in asking about the material properties of the aether than there was in asking about the material properties of time. Some physicists had even argued that modern theories no longer had any need of the aether, that it had effectively been abolished. Mr Beckers said that was a red herring. He said that those physicists just did not like the word, because for so long the aether had been imagined as a kind of material jelly when in fact it was something else entirely.

The aether, he said, was just another word for space.

Oscar was studying for the Cambridge scholarship to read Natural Sciences. Mr Beckers said that if he could only improve his mathematics Oscar had a good chance of winning it. He offered to give Oscar lessons after supper, when the other boys were ragging in the Common Room. Oscar agreed reluctantly, and mostly because it was a relief to have somewhere else to go.

Mr Beckers was gentle and encouraging and under his tutelage the numbers began once again to move, just a little, like wind through grass. Oscar supposed he was glad, though he was afraid Mr Beckers was wasting his time. The prospect of Cambridge seemed impossibly remote, and not just because of the money. By the end of the Michaelmas Term of 1917 any hope that the Americans would finish things off had been dashed by the failures of the summer offensives. Worse, the triumph of the Bolsheviks meant that the Russians were as good as out of the War. With the prospect of victory on the Eastern Front Germany looked stronger than ever.

All through that term and the short dark days of the Lent term that followed, the boys in Oscar's year were called up. Several applied for temporary exemptions to allow them to sit the Matriculation examinations. None was granted. The demand for men was more urgent than ever. Walker, a quiet boy in Oscar's physics set, was advised to keep up his studies in the Army and obtain leave in June for the duration of the examinations. Four weeks later Walker was killed when a tank exploded at his training camp.

Oscar was the youngest boy in the year. In August he too would be called up. All these years he had waited for the chance to demonstrate his patriotism, to prove that he was British to the bone, but now that it was nearly upon him, the prospect of fighting was a cold knife on the back of his neck. It was not so much the newspapers, though they were bad enough, or even the roll-call of the dead that concluded the end-of-term assembly, the same surnames repeating again and again like a gramophone record with the needle stuck. What haunted Oscar were the rumours that drifted through the school like poisonous gas, the executions for cowardice and desertion, the men shot by their own officers to force the rest of the platoon over the top. It was all right in the daylight but at night, in the darkness, the dread came in waves and the stink of Theo's uniform rose like bile in the back of his throat.

To keep it at bay he thought of Jessica. He could no longer summon her face, not exactly, but her body was more certain than ever. He had grown bold with her over the years. She did not resist as he pulled the cardigan from around her shoulders, slowly unbuttoned her silky blouse. Sometimes she straddled his lap. She never wore underwear. Her full breasts were high, like the breasts of the girls in the postcards the boys passed round after lights out, her thighs were white and willingly parted. When he stroked her she stretched like a cat, her head back and her honey-gold hair spilling over her shoulders. Afterwards, as his heart slowed, he slept. It did not stop the dreams coming in the night, the sandbags that erupted in his face, explosions of scarlet and splintery bone.

At the end of March, with the country reeling from the success of the German offensives on the Western Front, Oscar went to Trinity College, Cambridge to sit his scholarship examinations. Beyond the window of the train the sky above the Fens was white-grey and as lumpy as wallpaper paste. In his pocket he had a letter from his headmaster, delivered to his room the night before.

It is a matter of little argument, Mr Harrington wrote, *that the three greatest physicists in history are Archimedes, Newton and Maxwell. Of those three, only Archimedes had the misfortune not to be a Trinity man. As for the current Master of the College, you would do well to remember that it is none other than the great Sir John Joseph Thomson, Cavendish Professor and Nobel laureate. What better guide as you commence your first explorations of our mysterious universe?*

Oscar fingered the corners of the folded letter and thought of Pierre Curie who had once absent-mindedly left a few milligrams of radium in a vial in his coat pocket. The radium had scorched right through the heavy tweed of his waistcoat and left him with a permanent scar on his chest. It seemed to Oscar that the envelope in his pocket was possessed too of its own radiant energy, rays of ink and possibility that penetrated the flesh of his fingertips and made them fizz with anticipation.

Before Thomson the atom had been indivisible, the most fundamental unit of matter. It was Thomson who made them look deeper, Thomson whose discovery of electrons had inspired the work of Rutherford and Bohr. The idea that Oscar might breathe the same air as J. J. Thomson, that he might walk the same corridors and eat in the same dining hall and venture into the same laboratories, perhaps even see with his own eyes the apparatus used in the very first experiments with cathode ray tubes – the thought made his head spin.

There were cadets drilling in Great Court as he hurried around the perimeter, and a huddle of officers beneath the arch that led to Nevile's Court. The next day, going back on the train to London, there were more soldiers and kitbags sprawled like bodies on the floor. The soldiers were drunk. They passed a tin water flask between them, squinting with the hit as they drank. At Baldock one of them was sick out of the window.

Oscar sat in the corner and watched the grey fields unspooling behind the train like a bolt of fabric. All he could think of was how soon he might be able to go back. The interviews had gone well, he was sure of that. He might not have done well enough for the scholarship but surely they would not turn him down. For the first time it occurred to him that perhaps it would not be so bad if the Germans won and the War was over. Then physics would start again.

Physicists are not politicians, Mr Beckers had said. How can they be? Physics is universal. This is what the theory of special relativity tells us. The laws that govern light and gravity apply as much to the furthest corners of the Universe as they do on Earth. And because of the universality of physics the history of the Earth is provincial. What for us is a million years, or four, may be to someone travelling at speed no longer than the blink of an eye.

Oscar had only the vaguest grasp of Einstein's theories, but he knew his story, that a German scientist had renounced his citizenship to avoid compulsory military service and, as the bloodiest conflict in all of Earth's history raged around him, he had looked not only down a microscope or through a cathode tube but up and out at all of the natural world – space, time, the unity and harmony of the entire universe – and seen in all its unimaginable complexity the most universal of universal laws.

Or so he claimed.

The faster an object moves, the vaster it becomes. Where was it the War was hurtling, as it grew bigger and bigger and blotted out the sun? Oscar no longer cared. He no longer cared whether he was German or English or Mandarin Chinese. In Berlin at this very moment there was a boy just like him, his eyes raw from reading, his stomach tipped upside down by the monstrous prospect of war, and in a matter of months one of them would kill the other, and why? Because he happened to be there.

He closed his eyes, leaning his head against the upholstered seat, and reached out for Jessica. *Kiss me,* he said. *Kiss me and let me live.*

Two days before the school was due to break up for the Easter holidays a water tank burst in the attic of Oscar's boarding house. The torrent of water flooded the building and brought down several ceilings on the upper floors. The boys had to be evacuated. It was not safe for them to stay. Camp beds were hastily put up for the younger boys in other houses but, with lessons all but finished for the term, the Sixth Form boys were asked to go home.

The boys sent telegrams, summoning mothers and chauffeurs. Oscar did not bother. The sight of the telegraph boy with an envelope would only mean agonies for every mother in his street. Besides he always went home by train.

It was a little before seven when he reached Clapham. The unlit sky was bright with stars and, beyond the black ramparts of the chimney pots, the moon was a sliver of phosphorus. The house was dark, the blackout curtains drawn, but when he pushed open the front door he saw that the lamps in the back parlour were lit. After months of daylight raids the Gotha bombers now flew at night. He shut the front door quickly behind him.

'Mother?' Dropping his suitcases he opened the parlour door. His mother rose from her chair by the fire, knocking a book from its arm. Flustered, she bent to pick it up. Her cheeks were pink. On the other side of the fireplace, in Oscar's chair, sat Sir Aubrey Melville.

'Oscar, darling, whatever are you doing home?' she said, embracing him. 'Tell me you haven't been expelled?'

'There was a flood. They sent us home early. Sir Aubrey. Please, don't get up.'

'Oscar, old chap. What a pleasant surprise.'

Sir Aubrey's grip was firm but Oscar still could not quite bring himself to believe that he was real. Sir Aubrey did not belong in their cramped parlour in Clapham. He belonged with all the other Melvilles in their gilt frames at Ellinghurst, with its stone shields and vaulted ceilings and the suit of armour that the Black Prince had worn at Poitiers. It

127

shamed Oscar that Sir Aubrey would know that they did not have servants or a billiard room or stained-glass windows with their family crests, and the realisation that it shamed him shamed him more. On the cabinet behind the door there was a bottle of whisky, another of ginger wine. He supposed Sir Aubrey had brought them. There had never been any sign of rationing at Ellinghurst.

'Look at you,' Sir Aubrey said. 'It's been a long time.'

'Aubrey has very kindly been advising me on some business matters,' Oscar's mother explained. She smiled blandly at Sir Aubrey who nodded and glanced at the clock.

'I should be off,' he said. 'I'm late already.' He shook Oscar's hand once more. 'Good to see you again, old chap.'

'You too, sir.'

They waited as his mother fetched Sir Aubrey's coat and hat. When he had put them on she touched her cheek to his.

'I'll write,' she said. 'Love to Eleanor and the girls.'

The door clicked shut. Oscar's mother leaned against it, closing her eyes. Then she opened them again and looked at Oscar.

'We have to talk,' she said.

She had meant to tell him, she said. She had never intended it to be a secret. But the War had come and then conscription and she had not wanted to frighten him any more than he was frightened already. For all of the last long year she had hoped against hope that something would happen, that somehow there would be an end to it and she would be able to confess it, not easily but without this sickening dread, when it no longer mattered any more. Except that there had been no end. The War went on and on, grimly, bloodily, the lines moving neither forwards nor back but only down, deeper and deeper into the shattered earth. It would not be over in six weeks.

She was so very sorry.

He shook his head. It was too much to take in. She poured him a glass of whisky which he did not drink. She drank some herself. It had been her decision, she told him. She had done it to protect Joachim. Then she shook her head. She had done it to appease her parents. They were already unhappy enough that she meant to marry a penniless composer, and if they had suspected impropriety they would have refused to have anything further to do with them. She would not have minded, only without their help they could not afford to live. They had married quickly and very quietly, against her father's wishes, and gone away to France. When they returned they were a family of three.

She opened a cardboard file and handed him a thin piece of paper. His birth certificate, issued by the British Consul in Paris. Oskar Julius Grunewald, born to Joachim Otto Grunewald and Sylvia Margaret Grunewald née Carey on 23 April 1900. His call-up papers would arrive in four weeks.

She had asked for Sir Aubrey's help because she remembered him talking once about a lawyer friend of his whose work these days was all in tribunals. Sir Aubrey had already been in touch with him. The examinations were close, only a couple of months away, but Sir Aubrey was sure that a deferment might be obtained until they were over. He had promised to write personally to the tribunal to plead Oscar's case.

'Why would he do that?'

'Because he can. Because he's fond of you and you're Eleanor's godson and I asked him and like all of us he's had enough of this bloody awful War. Oh, darling, what does it matter why? He wants to help. He will help.'

Oscar went upstairs. He did not draw the blackout. He lay on his bed in the darkness. Beyond the window the sky was alive with stars, the moon so sharp that the intersecting spars of the window frame threw a shadow like a black cross across his stomach. A marked man, he thought. He did not move. Above the chest of drawers, the glass on the wall gleamed like oil, spilling a shimmering smear of light over the polished wood. Light is not a continuous wave but exists in lumps known as quanta. The aether is just another word for nothing. And Oscar Greenwood? A boy with the wrong name and the wrong age and seventeen sunny August birthdays that were not his to have.

CHAPTER 9

On 23 April Oscar's mother sent him a card. It came in a plain brown envelope. On the last night of the holidays she had told him that she did not expect him to keep it a secret, that it was all right to tell people the truth if he wanted to, and he had lost his temper and asked her if she thought he was stupid. He had said that the only thing that could possibly be worse than being German at his school was being a German's bastard. His mother had folded herself up then and nodded and said that she was sorry, and he had wanted to say that he was sorry too, only he wasn't. He was the angriest he had ever been. The card was a cardboard frame with curly edges into which she had put a picture of the two of them in the garden at Clapham. There was no funny poem, no sketches of Oscar as an old man or setting himself on fire with his birthday candles. It did not even say happy birthday, just, *Thinking of you, my darling, today and always, Mother.* Oscar put it in his drawer, under his socks.

The next day he received his call-up papers and

a letter from Sir Aubrey enclosing the application form for a temporary exemption.

The tribunal took place on a Wednesday in May. Oscar was summoned to attend. By then he had already undergone an Army medical and been declared fit. He told the school there was a family emergency.

Sir Aubrey's lawyer, Mr Rawlinson, had a magnificent stomach and the air of a man with somewhere more important to be. He sailed with implacable calm past the waiting clusters of jittery-legged boys, Oscar trailing in his wake. In court he looked at his watch and read out the letter from Sir Aubrey as if he were reciting a shopping list. When the colonel acting on behalf of the Military Representative asked Oscar to clarify the precise reason for his application Mr Rawlinson's sigh was audible.

The tribunal took less than five minutes to dismiss Oscar's application. The colonel stated firmly that if men of mature age had been required to give up occupations there could be no reason to exempt a man who was yet to earn a living. Glaring at Oscar he instructed him to report for duty without further delay. Mr Rawlinson appeared unperturbed. He told Oscar it was to be expected, that the South London Military Representative took a notoriously hard line, and he told Oscar to go back to school. That afternoon he lodged an appeal.

For nearly three weeks Oscar studied for his examinations, not sure whether he would be at school to sit them. He returned to London to attend his appeal. The case was scheduled for first thing in the morning so he was obliged to travel up the night before. At Charing Cross a train had just arrived from Southampton and the station was crowded with army vehicles and ambulances and wounded servicemen hunched over their kitbags. The Germans had reached the Marne. They were closer to Paris than they had been at any time since the start of the War. On a wall outside the station a tattered poster read: THE WOMEN OF BRITAIN SAY 'GO!'

He arrived at the house in Clapham just as his mother walked up the street. He knew there had been shortages, even with the rationing, but it was still a shock to see how thin she was. There were shadows like bruises under her eyes. He asked her if she was ill, if she had seen a doctor, but she only rolled her eyes at him and told him even doctors could not help people getting older. She did not take off her coat and hat. Instead, she held an envelope up in front of her face. The paper was the same colour as her skin.

'It's here,' she said and she coughed, the pain twitching at her face.

'Are you really all right?'

'Of course I am. It came yesterday so I thought it safer not to send it on. Go on, you goose, open it. I'm dying of suspense.' Awkwardly, her arms stiff, she tried to shrug her coat from her shoulders. As she twisted she gasped, her face suddenly ashen.

'Mother, what is it?'

'What will it take to have you put me out of my misery?' she said with a shaky laugh. 'For the love of peace, Oscar. Are you going to Cambridge or aren't you?'

Oscar tore open the envelope and drew out the letter.

'An exhibition,' he said flatly. So that was that.

'But that's marvellous, dearest. Congratulations.' Smiling, she held her arms out. Oscar shook his head.

'What good is an exhibition?' he said. 'I mean, I probably won't even be able to take Matric.'

'That's not true. Sir Aubrey says you have a good chance. A very good chance.'

'And even if I do? Then what? It's an exhibition, not a scholarship.'

'So it's not their highest award. It's still wonderful.'

'But it's not enough, don't you see? It had to be a scholarship, otherwise how can it be managed? An exhibition, it's nothing but prestige. The money . . . we can't afford it. You know we can't.'

'Except we can.'

'I don't understand.'

'It's taken care of. It won't stretch to a valet and your own private motor car but you'll have enough to manage.'

'But how?'

'I'm a part-time highwayman. Your money or your life. I've saved it, you silly.'

Oscar shook his head. 'Mother, no. I couldn't—'

'You could and you will and that's the end of it. Congratulations, darling. I'm so terribly proud of you.' She put her arms out again.

'And what about you? What will you live on?'

'I shall depend on you in my dotage. That's all right, isn't it? You'll just have to be disgustingly successful.' She smiled at Oscar and this time he embraced her, the brim of her hat pressed against his cheek.

'Thank you,' he said. 'Thank you, thank you, thank you.' He could feel her bones through the wool of her cardigan.

'Careful or you'll crush me Best Straw.'

Oscar smiled. Me Best Straw was an old joke between them from the days when Ruby had charred for them. Ruby had considered Mrs Carey a proper lady and had shown her respect by wearing only her best hats to work, in the winter the brown hat she referred to as her Felt, in summer the navy blue Best Straw. It was the highest compliment Ruby Patch could pay a person, that they were worth me Best Straw.

'Stuff your Best Straw and all who sail in her,' he said and he hugged her tighter, lifting her off her feet. She gasped, stiffening in his arms.

'Goodness, you'll crush me too,' she said. The pain sharpened her voice and made her cheekbones stand out like elbows.

'Mother, what is it?'

She shook her head, lowering herself tentatively into a chair. 'It's nothing, a little backache, that's all. Trinity, Oscar, how wonderful.'

'You need to see a doctor.'

'And I will. Oh, Oscar, you clever, clever boy. Now go and have a rummage in the kitchen cupboard. Behind the flour tin. There's a rather special bottle there I've been saving for just a moment like this.'

The South London Appeals Tribunal sat in Wandsworth Town Hall. Oscar took the trolleybus. The Chair of the Tribunal, a Mr Dunlop, addressed Oscar only once, to ask him to confirm his name and age. Mr Rawlinson asked if Oscar's letter from Cambridge might be submitted to the bench. There was a brief consultation between the members of the Tribunal before Mr Dunlop informed Oscar briskly that the decision of the Local Tribunal was to be overturned. Oscar would be granted a two-month exemption to allow him to sit his examinations, after which time he would join his battalion for training.

Before Oscar could thank him they were once more in the dingy corridor outside the tribunal room. On a wooden bench like a church pew a woman was crying, her head bent over her battered handbag.

'That's it?' Oscar asked, stunned.

'That's it,' Rawlinson said and shook Oscar's

hand. The Military Representative in Clapham would very likely appeal in his turn, he said, but the verdict would stand. Penrose Dunlop was an old friend and a thoroughly decent chap. A Cambridge man. He would not roll over just because the MR made a stink. Besides, they were growing weary of the MR at Appeals. His belligerence clogged the court and generated piles of extra paperwork.

'And they wonder why we've still not won the War,' Rawlinson said drily. 'We lawyers would have wrapped it up years ago.'

Oscar did not tell anyone at school about the exemption. There was no need. His birthday had only ever been in August. He wrote to Sir Aubrey to thank him for his help and received a reply by the next post.

I was glad to be able to help, glad and frankly grateful. So often these days it seems as though there is nothing to be done about any of it. Do you know those words of the great Leonardo da Vinci: 'iron rusts from disuse; stagnant water loses its purity and in cold weather becomes frozen: even so does inaction sap the vigour of the mind'? A man of my age, it seems, must endure a heavy burden of inaction: it was no less a gift to me, then, than to you to be permitted to act and, better, see that action yield some small reward. I only wish I could do more. Your mother tells me you have several days between the conclusion of your examinations and the date you are expected with your unit. Come to Ellinghurst for a day or two, won't you, if you can spare the time? We can feed you up before you are reduced to Army rations.

Oscar wrote back to say thank you and that he would have to talk to his mother. Love to Godmother Eleanor and to Phyllis and Jessica, he wrote at the bottom of the letter. The J curved out like the swell of a breast. After all this time he would see Jessica. He tried to imagine what she looked like now, set her up like a doll in a chair in the library or walking on the lawn, but the picture kept slipping, her arms reaching round his neck, the silky fabric of her blouse slithering over her creamy skin. He did not know how he would be able to meet her eyes, not after what he had done to her, what they had done together. She would take one look at him and she would know. The thought was mortifying. But at the same time he could not stop thinking it. If he was to be blown to smithereens, he would do it having kissed Jessica Melville one more time.

The thought was a consolation, even though he did not believe it for a minute.

Oscar and a boy called Hamilton-Russell took the Matriculation examinations alone, two boys in a hall built for one hundred. The footfalls of the pacing invigilator echoed as they wrote. When they were over and his trunks packed, the headmaster shook Oscar's hand and told him to be sure to come back. Oscar did not even trust himself to nod.

His mother was not yet well. Despite her assurances that she was on the mend it was plain that she was tired, even though she had reduced her hours in the insurance company. Her eyes were very big in her face and she had a persistent cough that made her go quite still, as though she meant to fool the pain into going away. Oscar wanted to stay with her but she insisted.

'Go,' she said. 'And be grateful to Sir Aubrey.'

Oscar took his camera. When he alighted at the station Pugh was waiting for him in his old trap. His white dog squatted by his heels, its tail brushing the dusty ground, its coat worn away in patches to show the pink skin underneath. It was too old and stiff to jump onto the box. Pugh had to lift it. The dog leaned against its master's side, its head resting on his sleeve. Oscar took a photograph. He thought of the white stretch of Jessica's neck, the sudden electrical shock of her tongue against his, and the burst in his stomach was as reliable as a chemical reaction.

Even after so many years the War had not reached Ellinghurst. In the soft pale pink of evening, pigeons cooed and the trees were fat with green. Beyond the humped stone bridge the lane narrowed, the hedgerows foamy with cow parsley. Above the woods he could see the turrets of the castle and the vertiginous mast of Grandfather's Tower. It seemed to twist as they approached, the unglazed windows of the belvedere opening like mouths.

Then abruptly they were there, turning in beneath the Gothic arch of the gatehouse with its arrow slits and round turrets and the stone lions with their flowing angel hair and their faces like the faces of bad-tempered babies. Oscar had Jim Pugh stop so that he could get a picture. He tipped the camera against his belly so that the coat of arms was in the centre of the photograph, the evening sun picking out the letters of the family motto, *DENIQUE COELEM*.

'Heaven at last,' his mother always translated with a twist of her mouth as they passed under the teeth of the portcullis, and he never quite knew if it was meant to be a joke. A trailing snatch of goose grass turned in the wheels of the trap. It sighed gently to itself as they trotted past the rhododendrons and up towards the house: *Jessica, Jessica, Jessica.*

Mrs Johns had grown fatter since Oscar had last seen her, her cheeks slack like uncooked pastry. Sir Aubrey and Lady Melville and Miss Jessica were changing for dinner, she told him. Miss Phyllis was in London. Her hospital worked her much too hard, Mrs Johns confided as she led Oscar upstairs. Twelve hours a day, with only a short break for lunch and a weekly half-day off. They were supposed to have leave but Miss Phyllis

140

never seemed to. Still, that was the War, wasn't it, and no one would have chosen it. On the landing she paused, leaning on the banister to catch her breath.

'Look at you,' she said to Oscar. 'When did you get all grown up?'

When Oscar had changed, he took some photographs out of his bedroom window. Then he lay on his bed, trying to swallow the butterflies in his stomach. He supposed there were things eighteen-year-old girls talked about but he did not know what they were. He thought of Theo, the way girls had always clustered around him, trying to attract his attention. Theo had always known what to say. The first gong sounded. He lay a little longer, then made himself get up. On the landing he hesitated, leaning over the banister to see if he could see anyone in the hall below.

'Hello.'

Oscar turned round. Jessica stood on the stairs behind him. The flesh-and-blood reality of her was startlingly unfamiliar, as though all this time he had been thinking of someone quite different. He stared at her, disoriented, rearranging his imaginings around the facts of her. She was tall, in her evening shoes not much shorter than he was. Her mouth was just the same.

He did not let himself look at her mouth. She wore an evening dress of honey-coloured silk, fastened with a sash around her hips, and a long string of pearls and, in her piled-up honey-coloured hair, a pearl and diamond clip in the shape of a flower. Oscar had never seen her with her hair up before. It showed off the length of her white neck, the delicate whorl of her ear. Between the slope of her shoulder and the slender rim of her collarbone, the pale skin dipped in two perfectly triangular hollows. There was a freckle in one of them, like a fleck of molten chocolate. Oscar touched his tongue to his lips.

'Oh,' he said.

Jessica raised an eyebrow. Then, with her hands on her hips, she turned slowly to and fro in front of him like a fashion model. Her mouth gleamed pink.

'Well?' she said. 'What do you think?'

He gazed at her. The hair at the nape of her neck was dark, still damp from her bath. 'You look . . . nice,' he managed.

'Nice? That's honestly the best you can do?'

Oscar flushed. 'Very nice, then. You look very nice.'

When she smiled at him something inside him turned upside down. She took a step towards him, close enough for him to smell the scent of honey-suckle. She put her hands on his lapels and, on tiptoes, touched her mouth to his. Her tongue flickered between his lips. Then it was gone.

'You still think of me, don't you?' she murmured. 'When you're all alone?'

He stared at her. Smoothing the corners of her mouth with one finger, she smiled and went downstairs.

★ ★ ★

At dinner he sat next to his godmother and tried not to look at Jessica. Except for the absence of footmen, no one would have guessed there was a War on. The food was plentiful, the table bright with glass and polished silver. The string of pearls around Jessica's neck curved inwards between the swell of her breasts like an eight that did not meet in the middle. There was something on her lips, a faint wet shine. He kept his eyes on his plate as she talked to her father, her nearness like a pulse in his throat. Twice, she caught him looking at her and her mouth twitched, as though she knew exactly what he was thinking, and the look was like a match to gas, sending a jet of flame up his neck and burning his ears.

After dinner the ladies withdrew. Sir Aubrey offered Oscar a cigar.

'I wanted to thank you,' Oscar said. 'For all you've done.'

Sir Aubrey shook his head. 'Please. It was nothing.'

'It wasn't nothing. Or it won't be. Not if I . . . you know. As long as I make it.'

Sir Aubrey's face stiffened. Oscar knew he was thinking of Theo. Awkwardly, for something to do, he helped himself to port from the decanter, slopping a little on the gleaming white tablecloth. Sir Aubrey smoked his cigar. Oscar did not know what else to say. He thought of his mother, who had always laughed when he said that grown-up parties were the worst torture in the world.

'Worse even than football?' she had teased.

'Much worse.'

'But it's just talking. Isn't it?'

But it was not. It was like chess, only with words which was much more difficult because there were no rules about how words were allowed to move. You had to keep moving them about and hoping it made sense and all the time you had to think about where to go next without making a mistake, without the other person getting impatient and bored with you and working out how to make you lose. But his mother had said you did not have to play it like that.

'Not all conversations have two talkers,' she had said. 'If you know what someone likes best in the world all you have to do is ask them about it. Most of the time they'll talk and talk and you won't have to say a word. You just have to listen. And nod. It helps if you nod.'

Oscar put down his glass. 'I wondered, sir, if you might like to talk about Ellinghurst.'

Sir Aubrey balanced his cigar on the edge of the ashtray. 'Ellinghurst?'

'Yes, sir. If you wanted to.'

'And what exactly is it you hoped I might say?'

'Nothing,' Oscar said, flustered. The smoke from the cigar curled upwards, smudging the air. 'That is, I mean, I know you're writing a book. Or perhaps you've finished it. I just thought you might like to talk about it.'

'I see. So you are being polite?'

'No. I mean, I suppose so.' Oscar frowned unhappily at the tablecloth. The port stain was blue and purple, like a bruise. 'I'm sorry. I'm afraid I've never been much good at conversations.'

Sir Aubrey considered him. Then he shook his head, exhaling a rueful kind of laugh through his nose. 'I'm afraid that makes two of us.'

'You probably get tired of telling stories about Ellinghurst anyway.'

'Not really. Much to your godmother's vexation.'

'My mother used to tell me some of them on the train,' Oscar said. 'About the heating pipes with the special spurs for drying shoes that blew up, and the sprung stage on wheels for dances. And the fireworks in the fireplace of the Great Hall.'

'My grandfather was a great experimenter.'

'Like your brother.'

'Like Henry.'

There was a silence.

'I didn't know you were interested,' Sir Aubrey said. 'Jessica has always maintained that you hated staying here.'

'That's not true.'

'She claimed you were always hiding out on your own.'

Oscar hesitated. 'That part is a bit true.'

Sir Aubrey smiled.

'I always loved the house, though,' Oscar said. 'When I was little what I wanted most of all was to live in the gatehouse.'

'Really? That was always my favourite too. Like a little castle all of one's own.'

'Only then I decided that the tower would be better still, right at the very top in the room with the arched windows. We weren't supposed to go up there, were we? I thought it would be the best thing in the world to wake up in the sky with the whole world spread out beneath you all the way to the sea. Like being a bird. But when I told my mother she said that I'd have to live there by myself. She said she was too forgetful to live somewhere so tall, that she'd always be leaving a book up there or her hat. She said all those stairs would wear her out.'

'Your mother? I can't imagine that. No one has as much energy as your mother.'

Oscar was silent.

'My grandfather had hoped to install a safety elevator in the tower, did you know that?' Sir Aubrey said in a different voice. 'The very first blueprints show a lift shaft on the western façade.'

'You still have them?'

'Of course. I can show you if you're interested.'

'Would you really? It wouldn't be too much trouble?'

'Of course not. I'll look them out in the morning.'

'That would be wonderful, sir. Thank you.' It struck Oscar that this was the first time he had ever really properly spoken to Sir Aubrey and that, despite the way Godmother Eleanor treated him, he was actually very nice. 'So why did your grandfather change his mind? About the lift, I mean.'

'One has to assume he came to his senses,' Sir Aubrey said. He smiled. 'Even my grandfather wasn't so confident of unreinforced concrete as all that.'

Sir Aubrey finished his cigar and retired to his study. Oscar went to join the others in the drawing room but, as he crossed the Great Hall, the door opened and Jessica came out. He gazed at her, her goldenness, the gleam and shimmer of her breasts and hips beneath her silk dress. The bow of her perfect pink mouth.

'Jessica,' he said. He took a step towards her but she held up a reproving finger, tutting softly under her breath.

'Easy there, boy.' A smile played about her lips as, kissing the tips of her fingers, she blew him a starlet kiss. 'Goodnight, Oscar. It was nice to see you.'

'Nice? I thought nice was, you know, not a good enough word.'

Jessica raised an eyebrow. 'For you, Oscar, nice does very nicely.' He stood in the hall, listening to the tap of her shoes as she climbed the stairs. When she reached the gallery she leaned over the banister, her pearls swinging around her neck. 'I told you, didn't I?' she whispered. She was laughing, her cheeks sucked in as though the laughter was a lemon drop in her mouth. 'You'll never forget me, not as long as you live.'

That night, when the moment came, it was with an explosion of such intensity he had to bury his face in the pillow to keep from crying out. At breakfast Sir Aubrey looked up at him from over his newspaper and told him he was the last man in.

'Jessica already up?' Oscar said casually, poking at scrambled eggs.

'Didn't she say? She left early, won't be back till Monday. Some sort of house party, apparently.' Draining his coffee cup, Sir Aubrey stood and bid Oscar a good morning. He did not say whether Jessica had said to say goodbye.

Later that morning, Oscar walked across the lawn to the beech trees. He took his camera with him, the strap around his neck. Near the trees he turned, looking back at the house. The hazy sky gave off a filtered light and on both sides of the path that ran up to the terrace the magnolia trees were in full and glorious bloom. He weighed his camera in his hand, running his thumb over its leatherette sides, the worn nickel fittings. In a week he would be in uniform. They said front-line officers were supposed to be eighteen and a half but everyone knew that they did not wait that long, not any more, and especially not if you had been through public school and the OTC and knew the drill.

He let go of the camera, pulling the strap so that it bumped against his back as he walked. Under the beeches he stopped, staring up into the dappled green of the canopy. A breeze danced among the leaves and ruffled the feathery seed heads of the long grass. He tried to summon Theo's face, the fall of his hair over his eyes, the way he had of leaning languidly against a wall with his hands in his pockets and one foot up behind him, as though his joints were too loose to stand up straight, but it would not come. Instead, he put his arms around the tree and held it. The bark was rough against his cheek. He closed his eyes, inhaling its smell of wind and pencil shavings.

He stood like that for a long time. Then, feeling rather foolish, he pushed himself away, patting the tree awkwardly as a father might pat a weeping child. Dusting the greenish marks from his coat he turned back towards the house. It was on the last tree, above the crook of a branch where the bark creased like skin, that he saw the initials carved into the trunk. Reaching up he traced the shape of them with one finger. TVCM. Theo Vyvyan Crawford Melville. He could smell cigarette smoke. He looked around but there was no one there, only the beech trees and the soft kiss of the grass against his trousers.

On impulse he took the camera into his hands and took a photograph. Immediately he wished he had not. Once, when he had shown his mother a picture he had taken of her while she was sleeping in her chair, she made a face and told him that there were primitive tribes who believed that the camera stole your soul. He thought of that as he pressed his hand against the carving, feeling the shape of it against his palm. *Forgive me,* he said silently. The breeze sighed. Then, putting his palm against his cheek, he walked away.

CHAPTER 10

Before the War it had never occurred to Jessica to think of Ellinghurst as a prison, except in games. The house's high walls, its moat and portcullis and the battlements that curved like an arm around its shoulders, had been there to keep other people out. She had always loved the moment, coming home for the school holidays, when the car passed beneath the arch of the gatehouse and she was home, every stone and tree hers and familiar. She had wished then that she could close the great oak doors with their heavy iron studs that always stood open, so that Eleanor's friends from London had to go back to their trains and all of Ellinghurst and Eleanor would belong to Jessica alone.

By the end of the summer of 1918 the walls had grown so thick it was all she could do not to scream. The newspapers were full of horrified reports of drunkenness and depravity among the young women of Britain who, freed from the restraint of fathers and husbands, were running wild, neglecting homes and morals and producing a plague of illegitimate children. Jessica knew she was supposed to be shocked. Instead, she envied them. She walked down to the village almost every day, ostensibly to visit Nanny and to help with the parcels for the prisoners of war, but really because she had to get out of the house. The silence between her parents was a kind of tinnitus, ringing in her ears.

Her father no longer joined them for lunch. He had his meals served in the library, which he had taken over for his book. No one was allowed in there, not even the maid to dust. Baize-topped card tables had been set up along the length of the room and still the floor was heaped with books and blueprints and ledgers and notebooks filled out in neat columns detailing shooting bags and the contents of the wine cellar. Sir Aubrey emerged reluctantly at dinner, restless to return, but when Jessica passed the windows and looked in he was never writing, only gazing up at the bookshelves or staring into space. In the morning room her mother stroked her scraps of paper from the seance as though they were bank notes.

She wrote to Guy Cockayne. There was nothing to write about so she wrote about Theo. She wrote about the rope with a knot in its end that the gardeners had put up over the lake as a swing one summer and how Theo had climbed the rope and dived off the branch instead, about the Great Bath Chair Races and the drunken stag beetles and the goat in the nursery in a bonnet in time for tea: 'Another sandwich, Nanny?'

How foolish this must seem to you, she wrote and he wrote back, *Tell me more.* His letters were infrequent and very short. He said he was no good with words. Instead, he sent drawings, mostly sketches of soldiers on scraps of paper torn from a notebook. *These men are who I am,* he wrote. The portraits were raw, unguarded, whole lives laid bare in a few strokes of the pencil. She did not show them to anyone. One of the young men was recognisable from the photographs Guy had brought for Eleanor. He bent forward, leaning on his rifle, his eyes fixed on the ground. Another was of a sleeping man, his body slumped against a wall, his cap tipped down over his face. Though the man himself was conjured in a few lines, the badge on his cap was meticulously detailed, the tiger staring out from his wreath of laurel leaves with undisguised contempt.

It was only later that it occurred to Jessica that the man was not sleeping but dead.

In August Jessica kissed a boy called Mervyn. She did not like him. She did it because he was the boy the other girls liked and because she wanted something to happen. She knew it would provoke the other girls, that they would tell their mothers and whisper about her behind her back, but she did it anyway. She could not bear that she was eighteen and the only boy she had ever kissed was Oscar Greenwood. She closed her eyes and pretended Mervyn was Guy Cockayne but it did not help. It was like kissing a dead wet fish. Much worse than Oscar who at least had turned out to be rather beautiful with his big dark eyes, even if he was mute and could not say boo to a goose.

Mervyn sent her a poem. In the second verse he rhymed Jessica with love-sicker. Jessica knew then that she had to get out. If she stayed in Hampshire she would go as mad as one-armed Godfrey Charrington who had been at Ypres and who jumped six feet into the air if anyone so much as clattered a teaspoon.

Summer cooled to autumn. In France the Allies were pushing the Germans back all along the line but in England there was a new enemy. As the Spanish flu swept the country, what poor parties and entertainments there had been were all cancelled. In Bournemouth they opened the windows in the cinemas every four hours to air out the auditoria; they sprayed the trains and the buses and even streets with chemicals to stop the infection from spreading.

Sir Aubrey said it was worse in London. He worried about Phyllis. The hospitals were overflowing and medical schools had closed their third- and fourth-year classes so that the students could work in the wards. It was not just wounded soldiers and the poor who were dying. A man from his club had lost his wife and all three of his grown-up children one after the other, like skittles.

Everyone was frightened, though they pretended not to be. At the Savoy Hotel, he said, the barman had invented a cocktail made from rum and whisky called a Corpse Reviver.

Jessica knew he only told her the stories to keep her prisoner. She told him she would rather die of influenza in London than of boredom in the New Forest. She did not care if she tempted Fate, not any more. She was eighteen years old, for heaven's sake. When was her life going to be allowed to begin?

And then, abruptly, it was over. In London the crowds flooded the streets of the West End like a roaring sea, surging through Trafalgar Square and sending waves of revellers over the steps of St Martin-in-the-Fields and up against the railings of the National Gallery. The night of the Armistice was wet and foggy but the tops of omnibuses were packed with nurses and office girls and yellow-skinned munitionettes waving and blowing kisses, their hair jewelled with rain, while in the crush below, and half-mad with euphoria, girls wrapped in Union flags kissed drunken soldiers and danced with drunken sailors and sat astride Landseer's damp-streaked lions to watch the German guns that had been dragged in from the Mall set on fire. As the flames caught the throng linked arms and, at the top of their lungs, belted out the words to 'Land of Hope and Glory'.

They sang too in the Strand where, for the first time in four years, the street lamps blazed and restaurants threw up their blackouts, spilling a dazzle of light and laughter out onto the teeming pavements. In the Savoy Hotel officers of the Royal Flying Corps swung from the chandeliers, while across the light-spangled river, whooping groups of girls staggered to catch the last trains at Waterloo Station, so intoxicated that they had to be rolled along the platforms like barrels of beer. Discarded on benches and in gutters, the sodden newspapers proclaimed a single word in letters two inches tall: VICTORY.

Jessica was not in London. She walked with her father into Ellinghurst village where the church bells were tolling and let Mrs Holt from the dairy press her against her upholstered bosom. Outside the shop the women gathered in giddy clusters, unsteady as children off a merry-go-round. Sir Aubrey went into the Red Lion and shook hands with the landlord and bought beer for the men inside. Jessica went to see Nanny who cried and laughed and would not let go of Jessica's hand. Jessica looked at all the childish souvenirs on Nanny's mantelpiece, the potato pictures and the clay pots and the samplers with the too-tight stitches, and she wondered what Nanny would do all day, now there was no longer any call for socks.

When her father came out they went home.

That night Jessica cried. She had not cried much

for Theo, not even after he died. The grief that had encased her was stiff and hard, a plaster cast that held her rigid, and the tears too were solid, packed together like the lumps embedded with rock and pebbles that fell sometimes at Hordle Cliff. She cried for Theo and his friends and for Uncle Henry and Mrs Briggs from the bakery's three red-headed sons and Hubert Dugdale who served less than a month as a subaltern before he was killed by a gas attack. She cried for all the boys Theo had brought home to Ellinghurst who would never come again, their laughter drifting up from the tennis court and later from the terrace as they danced to the gramophone in the lavender dusk. She told herself she should be happy but she was not happy. Peace had broken open the plaster cast and it was not joy that flooded out or even the lightness of relief but only a bleak grey desolation. The old world would not come back. With the guns silenced and the bloodshed finally at an end, Theo was no longer dead for as long as the War dragged on.

He was dead for ever.

And still nothing changed. Phyllis wrote to say that she was staying at her hospital. Her father went back to the library. Three days after the Armistice, Mrs Johns' sister received a telegram from the Front informing her with deep regret that her youngest boy had been killed during action on the Sambre. In the afternoon, while Mrs Johns wept in the kitchen, Eleanor went to Bournemouth.

Jessica watched from the landing window as the car swung down the drive and out of sight. Then she turned and walked along the passage. Outside her mother's bedroom door she hesitated. As a child, on Nanny's afternoons off, when her mother was out or in London and the housemaid thought she was in the nursery or playing in the garden, she had sometimes crept into her mother's bedroom. Such trespass was expressly forbidden, of course, but the prohibition had only added to its allure. She had sat at her mother's dressing table, gazing at her reflection in the three-part glass, scooping her mother's hairpins from their porcelain saucer and letting them run through her fingers, or stroking with the tips of her fingers the shivery softness of her down powder puff. She had opened the wardrobes and buried her face in the clothes hanging up there. Once she had even put on her mother's silk wrap and lain down on the bed, gazing up at the silk rose at the centre of the canopy. The thought of her mother undressed and all alone, her hair loose about her shoulders and her day-time self unhooked like a corset, had given her butterflies.

Jessica opened the door and went in. The room was her favourite in all the house, with large windows looking out over the lawn and, through an arch, a circular sitting room in the tower that abutted it, with long thin windows made to look like arrow slits. The furniture had been built for the room, the curved backs of the writing desk and the silk-covered chaise matching exactly the curve of the wall. Jessica ran a hand over the ink well, the box of writing paper edged in black. As a child she had thought that, if she touched the things that her mother touched, if she slipped her arms into her furs and lay as she lay beneath the canopy of the four-poster bed, if she breathed in the same musky, powder-dusted air, the leftover fragments of her, then she might, little by little, become more her mother and less the other person that she was when she was not paying attention, the person that made her mother press her lips together and stiffen when Jessica hugged her good-night as though she were something dirty that might spoil her dress.

How foolish she had been. This room was no more her mother than the abandoned dresses in her dressing-room wardrobes. How could it be? Theo was dead and most of her mother with him, and the room remained just the same. Apart from a framed photograph of Theo on the bedside table that had once been on the mantelpiece, it looked no different from before. There were still flowers on the tables, a fresh cake of soap in the dish on the washstand. It smelled as it always had, of lavender and beeswax. It was no more the encap-sulation of her mother's true self than Theo's mummified room with its fading team photographs was the bedroom of a living boy. Whatever remained of Theo's spirit, or her mother's, they were not here. All that remained of either of them had long ago been dusted away.

CHAPTER 11

Something was wrong. Eleanor was never home so early. From the morning room Jessica heard Pritchard bang open the door to the kitchen passage, his muffled shout as he called for Mrs Johns. She watched from the gallery as together they helped Eleanor into the house. She was shaking and weeping. She could hardly walk. In the hall she screamed and twisted away from Pritchard, her fist raised as though she meant to strike him.

'Don't touch me,' she sobbed. 'Don't . . . don't touch me.' Her legs gave way beneath her and she sank to the floor, her face pressed against the arm of a chair, clutching at it as though it were the one thing keeping her from drowning. Mrs Johns knelt beside her. Very gently she prised her hands from the chair. Pritchard cleared his throat. Mrs Johns looked up to the gallery. Hurriedly Jessica ducked back into the East passage. She was still there when Mrs Johns brought her mother upstairs.

That night, while it was still quite dark, Jessica woke up. She did not know what time it was or what had woken her. She knew only that she

161

needed the lavatory. Sleepily she slid her feet into her slippers and felt her way out onto the landing. A light was burning. She was almost at the bath-room door when she heard her mother cry out.

'Let me go, you bastard!'

Jessica crept to the banisters. On the landing below she saw her father, dressed only in striped pyjamas, and her mother in her nightgown, her plaited hair dishevelled, thrashing in his arms. For a sleep-fogged moment she thought they were kissing. Then she saw that her father had her mother in a kind of lock, her arms held behind her back with one hand, his other over her mouth. Her mother thrashed her head from side to side, trying to escape his grip. She was still shouting but the words were stifled by his hand, Jessica could not make them out. Like competitors in a frenzied three-legged race he dragged her with him along the landing. Even when the stairs hid them from view Jessica could hear her muffled shouts, the thump of her bare feet on the wooden floor. Suddenly there was a gasp like a scream.

'What do you care?' her mother shrieked. 'When have you ever given a damn?' And then there was the bang of a door closing and Jessica could not hear anything any more. She closed her eyes, waiting for her heart to stop thumping, and when she opened them, the house was its ordinary night-time self once again, the lamp burning peaceably on the landing and the stairs creaking to them-selves as they stretched and settled in their sleep.

162

The next day Dr Wilcox came. Jessica had always disliked Dr Wilcox. He had bad breath and a greasy nose that looked like it had been pricked all over with a pin. Last summer, when she had been ill with a bad cough, he had placed his hand on the right side of her chest as he pressed his stethoscope to her sternum, his curve of his thumb and little finger matching the curve of her breast and the base of his palm pressing gently upwards into the flesh as though he were weighing it. Afterwards, though she was seventeen, he had given her a humbug from a bag in his pocket. The humbug was sticky, the stripes blurred as though it had already been sucked.

Dr Wilcox was in with Jessica's mother for a long time. Jessica waited in the morning room. From time to time she heard her father coming out of his study and crossing the hall to the stairs. Eventually she heard feet coming down the stairs, the murmur of Mrs Johns' voice. She opened the morning-room door.

'But of course,' she heard Dr Wilcox say. 'My complete discretion.'

Jessica banged the door. Her father turned.

'How is she?' Jessica said.

'Quite comfortable now, I hope,' the doctor said smoothly.

'What is it? What's wrong with her?'

Dr Wilcox glanced at her father. 'She's lucky to have you to take care of her. A fine nurse like you.'

'Phyllis is the nurse,' Jessica said. 'Not me.'

★ ★ ★

Her mother did not get up that afternoon. Jessica went to see Nanny. She did not want to be in the house by herself. When she walked back it was getting dark. The thickening dusk collected like cobwebs in the dips and shadows of the garden and threw a sticky veil of dust over the trees. She went upstairs to change for dinner. When she came down Eleanor was standing in the Great Hall.

She was hatless and gloveless and soaked to the skin. Her feet squelched in her shoes and her hair clung to her scalp, whippy strings of it stuck to her neck and pale cheeks. She stood quite still, her face serene as Mrs Johns peeled the sodden coat from her shoulders and barked at Enid to fetch tea and warmed towels from the range. All the time that Mrs Johns was fussing about her, and even as she hustled her upstairs, her face remained calm, a tiny smile playing around the corners of her lips.

The next morning she came downstairs as Jessica was helping Mrs Johns with the flowers. Though her face was pale, she was very composed.

'They shall be here at eleven,' she said to Mrs Johns. 'I shall see them in the morning room.'

A few minutes later Jessica's father asked if Jessica might have a word with him in his study. He told her that the police wished to talk to her mother.

'What has she done?'

Her father frowned. 'Really, Jessica. They wish to take a statement. Your mother's Mrs Waller has been exposed as a fraud and I'm afraid your mother was present when it happened. The shock has been considerable.' He shook his head either in pity or anger, Jessica could not tell. 'It's a wretched end to an utterly wretched business. Let us hope we can finally put it behind us.'

The police were polite and plainly embarrassed. The younger one took notes as, sitting very upright in a hard chair, Jessica's mother answered their questions in a small, clear voice.

It was Mrs Coates who had brought Mr Jessop, a middle-aged gentleman with a mournful face and so unassuming in his manner to be almost meek. Mr Jessop was her brother. He had sat with the others as Mrs Waller received the messages from the spirits, the table listing heavily to one side and then to another to spell out its answers. Mrs Waller had announced that the older of Mrs Coates' two sons was clamouring to come through, that he wanted very badly to say something. Frenziedly, as though it were dancing a jig, the table spelled out

H-A-P-Y-B-I-R-R-H-D-A-Y-D-E-R-S-T-M-A-M-A.

Mrs Coates began quietly to sob. Immediately Mr Jessop jumped to his feet. The dazzle of his torch was blinding. There were screams as he pushed his chair backwards, swinging the beam around the table as he moved towards the door.

'Stop it!' someone cried. 'You'll kill her!'

Mr Jessop switched on the electric light. Mrs

Waller jerked, her eyes bulging from her head, and fell like a stone to the floor.

They had thought she was dead. It was not unknown for spirit mediums roused so violently from trance to die, Eleanor said, their hearts stopped by the shock of sudden awakening. Even the striking of a match across the table could burn a hole in the flesh of a sensitive when she was in a transported state. Miss Harmsworth pleaded with Mr Jessop to let her run to the hotel at the corner where they might call for an ambulance but Mr Jessop refused to allow it. He said that no one was going anywhere and when Miss Harmsworth demanded of him what authority he had to tell them what to do, he said the authority of Her Majesty's Government and took a badge from the inside pocket of his coat.

After that everything happened very quickly. Two policemen who had been waiting outside searched the premises and took the details of the sitters. Several, including Jessica's mother, had been too shaken to speak but they had succumbed at Mr Jessop's insistence to an inspection of their clothing. During this inspection it was discovered that two of the group's most regular sitters, Miss Hillsborough who had lost her brother in East Africa and Mrs Carley whose two sons had been killed at Verdun, were wearing special wristbands concealed beneath the cuffs of their dresses. The wristbands were fitted with metal hooks which, as they placed their hands on the table, slid into special slots cut for the purpose beneath the table's edge. When required the two women lifted their hands, so that the table moved without them so much as lifting their palms from its surface.

As for Mrs Waller she was found to have, concealed inside her left sleeve, a rubber bulb containing a clear liquid. The bulb was filled with alcohol. When Mrs Waller leaned her left arm on the cushion on her lap, the alcohol sprayed onto a sealed envelope was sufficient to make it transparent so that, with the red lamp placed conveniently beside her chair, Mrs Waller could read her sitters' questions quite easily for herself.

When she had finished Eleanor rose from her chair and asked if the policemen would excuse her.

'One moment, Eleanor,' Sir Aubrey said. He turned to the taller of the two policemen. 'You mean to prosecute, I hope?'

'That is currently the intention, sir.'

'Surely it's an open-and-shut case?'

'I'm not sure it's ever quite that simple, sir, but I can assure you that Bournemouth Constabulary is very hot on this kind of thing. Well, it's like the black market, isn't it? Scoundrels profiting from other people's troubles.'

There was a pause. Eleanor turned and looked out of the window. The taller policeman cleared his throat. Then, shaking Sir Aubrey's hand, he said they would see themselves out.

* * *

On Tuesday the men came back and resumed work on Theo's memorial. No one sent them away. At tea time they went home, leaving a spade in the top of the heap of sand, its handle sticking out like a flagpole. Jessica walked around the hole, then sat on a stack of stone flags, her legs dangling. The building was to be a kind of Greek temple with a cupola. It did not sound to Jessica like Theo's kind of thing at all.

She had already clambered to her feet when she saw her mother, picking her way towards her across the lawn. They stood side by side in silence, staring down at the muddy foundations.

'I'm sorry,' Jessica said at last. 'About what happened. I hope they lock that woman up for a long time.'

Her mother shook her head. 'Don't say that.'

'Well, I do. What she did – it's terrible.'

'Not terrible. Just terribly, terribly misguided.'

'But she lied to you! She . . . she made you think it was real.'

'Yes, and it was very wrong of her. At first I could hardly . . . well, it was . . . incomprehensible. Unbearable. That was before Theo came to me, came to me right here, where we are standing now, and explained everything.'

Jessica bit her lip. 'Eleanor—'

'Cynthia Waller is a child, of adult size, yes, but a child all the same with a child's innocence, a child's sensitivity. She should have been protected like a child, not left to struggle on alone. And she

168

was worn out, we all saw it. Sometimes she could barely rouse herself from her trance and had to be half-carried out of the room. We knew it was too much for her and yet we let her sit, because we drew our strength from hers. In our own way we are as much to blame for this as she is.'

'She's a fraud, Eleanor. A phoney. She was caught red-handed.'

'And it was a very foolish and hurtful thing to do. But she's not a fraud.'

'But you saw her. You said so yourself.'

'Jessica, Cynthia Waller is possessed of an extraordinary gift. But a spirit medium should sit at most twice a week, it is too exhausting otherwise, the rigours of trance are too much for her. Cynthia was sitting eight, ten times, week after week. Of course she hadn't the strength for it. Not every time, not over and over and over again. There must have been days when the vibrations were weak, when she couldn't see, couldn't hear, but she always sat. Always. She could never bring herself to disappoint anyone. The temptation then to cheat, don't you see? She was a child.'

'So you're not angry?'

'Sad, yes, and disappointed. But not angry.'

Jessica pressed her foot into the mud, making a shape like a flat iron. 'Father says you're to be called as a witness. When the case goes to trial.'

'If it goes to trial.'

'So you'll take her side?'

'I will tell the truth, just as I've told it to you.'

169

'Which will help her, won't it?'

Eleanor did not answer.

'When Theo first . . . when he died, I saw him everywhere,' she said at last. 'I heard his voice, heard his feet on the stairs or the sound of him whistling. He used to whistle all the time, do you remember? I was sure I was going mad. But I was not mad. All that time he was talking to me and I did not listen, because I was afraid. Cynthia taught me how to listen. To understand that death is not the end but only another world we have not yet learned how to see. It is because of Cynthia that I am no longer afraid.'

Jessica said nothing. She stared at the ground.

'It is so terribly hard for them, the ones who have passed,' Eleanor said. 'They feel alive, you see, just as they always did. They have not changed their form or their character, only their vibrations. And yet they must watch their loved ones weep and weep for them as though they are gone for ever. It breaks their hearts.'

A robin lighted on the handle of the spade. It looked at Jessica, its head on one side. Its black eyes were very bright.

'You asked me if I was angry with Cynthia and I said I was not. It's not true, not quite. On Thursday Theo will wait for me and wait for me and I will not come. He will think I have forgotten him. I cannot forgive her for that.'

Jessica stared at the robin. Then abruptly she turned. The robin flew away.

'I'm cold,' she said. 'I'm going inside.'

They walked together in silence back to the house. Jessica wrapped her arms around herself, rubbing her hands against her sleeves to bring some warmth back into her cold fingers. In the hall Jessica's mother pulled her gloves off, one finger at a time. Jessica watched her lay them on the sideboard, one on top of the other. In a moment, she would be gone and perhaps the longest conversation they had ever had would be over. If I died, she wanted to say, if it had been me, would you have grieved like this for me? Instead she swallowed, forcing her lips and jaw to unclench into indifference.

'Father says Dr Wilcox has recommended Egypt,' she said. 'A change of scene.'

'So I gather.'

'And what about me?' The question came out more shrilly than she had intended. 'What will happen to me? Where shall I go, if you go away? Do you mean to leave me here, shut up inside this place like a dungeon?'

Her mother frowned. 'But I'm not going anywhere.'

'Father said—'

'Your father can go to Timbuktu for all I care. I belong here.'

'And me? Where do I belong?'

Her mother looked at her blankly.

'I'm nearly nineteen, Eleanor. I should be in London, dancing. Going to parties and falling in love. Instead, I'm stuck here, in the middle of nowhere, with no one to talk to but you and your . . . your bloody ghosts.'

Eleanor said nothing. Carefully she placed her hat on the sideboard.

'Life goes on,' Jessica said. 'Whether you like it or not.'

Her mother turned, her eyes burning. 'For you,' she hissed. 'Life goes on for you.'

CHAPTER 12

When the Armistice was announced on a dull grey Monday morning in November Oscar was at a training camp near Rhyl. He locked himself into a lavatory cubicle and cried. All through that autumn, as he had marched and drilled and succumbed to measles and learned about poison gas and machine guns, the Bulgarian, Turkish and Austrian armies had collapsed one by one into surrender but Oscar had wound his puttees and scratched his rash and known he would die. His physics books lay unopened on the shelves. There was no point in contemplating the future or a world of infinite wonder. His own world was proscribed, preordained. He would drill and drill and then he would die. He would die face down in the mud, his mouth pressed like a lover's against the rotting cheeks of those who had gone before. That was the way of it, lives laid down upon lives like sedimentary rock. Their orders came through on the last day of October. They would be in France by Christmas.

Less than two weeks later it was over. The celebrations in the camp were wild, the men shouting

173

and singing as though they meant to drown out all the horrors of history. Later, as the drunkenness soured, there was a good deal of slurred swagger about precisely what they would have done if they had only had their chance at the Hun. The brutality of their imaginings frightened Oscar. For the first time it occurred to him that, if you took away a man's freedom and gave him instead a greatcoat and a pistol and a belly full of hate, there might come a time when he no longer wanted to change back. Oscar drank and drank and waited in vain for the elation to come. After the first desperate weeping purge of relief he felt only shame. Through the static of the alcohol in his blood, he could hear the whisper of it, that he and all these other grotesquely undamaged men who roared and cheered and stamped their boots in triumph had cheated, because the triumph did not belong to them and because young and strong and whole as they were, they would only ever be pale shadows of those who had gone before.

They did not go home. Demobilisation would take time, the Commanding Officer informed them. The British Army was four million strong and the logistics were complex. Last in, last out, that was the way of things. The men would remain at the camp until informed otherwise. Oscar wrote to his mother to tell her he would not be home for Christmas. Her letters back were brief, her handwriting lopsided. He hoped she was not letting herself get too tired.

Nobody knew what was happening. The camp crawled with rumours. Some said that it was to be turned over to the Canadians as a demob centre for Canadian soldiers stationed in the south-east and that they would all be allowed to go home, others that only 'slip men', those with the written guarantee of a job, would be demobbed. Three weeks before Christmas the story went round that they were to be shipped off to Russia to support the White Army against the Bolsheviks. They would fight after all. In Siberia in December the temperature at night reached minus twenty degrees Fahrenheit. Some twenty thousand men were already on their way.

It was snowing in Rhyl when Oscar received the letter from Mrs Doyle who lived next door. Mrs Doyle's youngest son Jimmy had lost both legs at Loos and sometimes late at night you could hear him crying through the wall. Beyond the window Oscar could see the flakes swirling black in the glare of the unshaded outside light. Mrs Doyle said she was sorry to write when it would only alarm him but she did not think she could wait any longer. His mother was very ill. She asked if Oscar might be able to come home.

The CO granted Oscar a week's leave. The two middle-aged women sitting opposite him on the train patted his knee with their gloved hands and told him they were proud of their boys. They wore tweed overcoats buttoned to the neck and gauze masks on elastic over their mouths. When

175

they muttered together about the preventative effects of vinegar and quinine the gauze pulsed in and out of the space between their lips. Oscar thought of the little girls in the village school in Wales who sang as they skipped with their ropes in the playground at dinnertime.

I had a little bird
Its name was Enza
I opened the window
And in flew Enza.

Mrs Doyle was just leaving as he arrived at the house in Clapham. She blinked at Oscar and said it was not right, not when everything was supposed to go back to normal. She said that she would be back again the next day, that a friend of his mother's, a young nurse who had proved a great support to her, had promised to look in that night and check that she was comfortable.

'How long has she been ill?' Oscar made himself ask.

'A while, dear. But worse these last two months.'

'Why didn't she tell me?'

'What good would it have done?' Mrs Doyle said. She patted his hand, her face creased with pity. 'It'll be a shock, dear, I know. Try not to show it.'

It was a shock. His mother turned her head as he opened her bedroom door and smiled. Her face was grey, all cheekbones and protruding jaw. Her hair was grey too. She was so thin she scarcely made a bump in the bed.

'Darling,' she said.

He read her poetry as she drifted in and out of sleep. He did not try to understand the words but there was something calming about the steadiness of the metre. The room grew dark. Oscar did not turn on the lamp. Instead, he held his mother's hand, listening to the faint wheeze of her breath, in and out, his thumb moving gently over the bumps of her knuckles.

The doorbell made him jump. When he opened it Phyllis Melville was standing on the doorstep, a brown paper bag in one hand. She was wearing a vividly striped knitted scarf wound several times around her neck and a red velvet hat like a squashed pancake. He blinked at the brightness of her.

'You came,' she said.

Oscar waited downstairs while she tended to his mother. For something to do he boiled the kettle and laid the fire in the parlour. There was no coal, of course, but somehow his mother had got wood, enough to be stacked on both sides of the fireplace. There was something very comforting in the ordinariness of the ritual, the first tentative lick of the sputtering match, the blue-green shrivel of the newspaper as it caught. Oscar leaned closer and blew, coaxing the flame into life. In Rhyl someone else lit the fires.

When Phyllis came back downstairs he had made a pot of tea. He offered her a cup.

'I ought to get back,' she said, picking up her coat from the arm of the sofa. 'I've a very early start.'

'Just half an hour,' he said. She hesitated. Then she put down her coat.

'All right. But only if we can have a proper drink.'

'I'm not sure there's anything in the house,' he said, but Phyllis was already opening the corner cupboard, taking down glasses and a half-full decanter of whisky. She poured them both two fingers.

'Water?' she said.

'Like that is fine.'

She sat in the chair by the fire, her feet tucked under her and the glass cradled in both hands. She hardly looked any older than she had done three years before except that she had cropped her hair short like a boy's. It suited her. She did not speak. Instead, she took a gulp of her drink. Oscar took a small sip of his. He had never liked the taste of whisky.

'She's dying, isn't she?' he said. 'Tell me.'

'She has cancer.'

It shocked him to hear the word out loud. The tumour had originated in the lung. Now it was in her bones. It made them brittle and easily broken. She had fractured two ribs just from coughing. When Oscar asked about radium treatment Phyllis shook her head. Radium pellets could be inserted into a contained growth, but the seeds of his mother's cancer were no longer contained. They had scattered, germinating and taking root in several places. There was nothing else that could be done. The specialist at the Cancer Hospital had prescribed morphine for the pain and told his mother to come back when she could no longer manage at home.

'How long does she have?' Oscar made himself ask.

'Weeks. A month, maybe.' Her gaze was grave, steady. 'I'm very sorry, Oscar.'

Oscar was silent. He thought of the cancer seedlings, pushing up like cress through the soft marrow of his mother's bones. 'Do you mind if we don't talk about it any more?' he said.

'Of course not.' She did not try to say anything else. The silence stretched and settled between them like a cat but Phyllis did not shift about in her chair or clear her throat or glance at him with the smile-frowns that people used when they wanted other people to say something but did not know how to ask. She gazed into the fire and there was a concentration about her silence, as though whatever it was she was thinking was interesting and important. The flames lit her pale face like a lamp.

In the grate a log collapsed, sending up a flurry of sparks. An ember winked on the rug. Phyllis stretched out a foot and stamped it out. Then she stood up and fetched the whisky decanter from the table. Propped up on the mantelpiece was one of the photographs Oscar had taken at Ellinghurst, a detail of a gargoyle on the gatehouse. Oscar had manoeuvred the camera until the gargoyle's mouth was lined up with one of the chimneys on the main house. The gargoyle looked as though it was smoking a fat cigar. Phyllis smiled.

'I like that,' she said. She held out the decanter to Oscar who shook his head, then sloshed some whisky into her own glass. 'How long before you're demobbed, do you know?'

Oscar shook his head. 'You?'

'Same.' She sipped her drink. 'It's funny, for the last year all I've wanted is for it to be over but now it is I can't imagine it somehow. Going back to doing ordinary things again. Wearing ordinary clothes. Not being afraid to look at one's letters or in the newspaper.'

'Being ordinary and not feeling guilty about it. That's what I can't imagine.'

She blinked at him in surprise. 'Yes. That's it exactly. When I think about the boys on my ward, all I can think is that the War isn't over for them at all. That perhaps it never will be.'

His mother had told him a little about Phyllis's hospital in her letters. The men there had all been blown to bits, one way or another.

'They're terrible pranksters,' Phyllis said. 'One private's arm flies off every time he salutes. He says it's a fault with the prosthetic but we all know he's a bet with the others on whether he can knock an officer's hat off.'

180

Oscar smiled and thought of Jimmy Doyle in his wheelchair.

'It's like a madhouse during the day,' she said. 'Like herding eels. But then at night, when the lights are turned down and it's quiet and they can't sleep and there's time to talk – you'd give anything, then, just to take away some of their pain.' She was silent, staring at the fire. Then she took a big gulp of whisky. 'Sixteen shillings a week, that's what Mr Lloyd George reckons an arm to be worth. Although if you've got a half-decent stump they'll cut that to eleven and six. Anything above the neckline, not a penny. Apparently a smashed-up face isn't worth anything at all.' The sudden savagery in her voice reminded Oscar of his mother. He felt himself closing inside, like an anemone touched with a finger.

'The ones that make it, they're like very old men. All their friends are dead, and now they're just waiting to be dead too, except that they've still got years and years left of being young.' She shook her head. 'I'm sorry. You don't want to hear all this.'

'It's all right.'

'No. No, it isn't. We should be talking about peace and . . . and Charlie Chaplin.'

'*A Dog's Life.*'

Phyllis smiled lopsidedly. 'Something like that.'

'I must have seen that film five times. The part where he eats the cakes, do you remember?'

'I'm afraid I haven't seen it. Though if it has cakes in perhaps I should. I like cake.'

'But not the pictures?'

'The pictures too. It's just . . . well, I haven't been for a while.'

'It's one thing to say for basic training. You see all the flicks.'

'I'd go with the other nurses, except the cinema near us only ever shows those hateful romances. You know, *Hearts of the World*, things like that. I don't suppose you saw *Hearts of the World*.'

'Only the poster.'

The poster had shown a German soldier flogging a screaming girl with a cat-o'-nine-tails and underneath the title, in big white letters, A LOVE STORY OF THE GREAT WAR. By the time Oscar came home after his examinations *Hearts of the World* had been showing at the Clapham Roxy for weeks and weeks and still in the evenings the queue stretched right around the corner.

'My friend Maud went three times,' Phyllis said. 'She said that it made her hate the Germans so much she felt giddy. She knew that it was propaganda but she didn't mind. She wanted it. The giddiness and the hate.'

Oscar thought of the men on Armistice Day, baying for German blood.

'Perhaps hating is better than thinking it's all for nothing,' he said. 'Perhaps hate makes it mean something.'

'But what if we can't stop? What if hating is all that's left of us?'

'But it isn't, is it?' Oscar said. 'It just isn't.'

'No,' she said very quietly and she went on looking at him with her grave pale eyes and he looked back at her and he did not say anything because there was a truthfulness in looking that was plainer and more fluent than anything he could think of to say.

He stayed for a week. His mother had good days and bad days. On the good days she sometimes wanted to talk to him about what might happen after she was gone. He learned to recognise the change in her expression, the careful steadying of the breath in her clogged lungs, the way she picked with a nail at a seam in the counterpane. Usually he contrived to escape the room before she could begin. He heard a knock at the front door or remembered a letter he had to write or the kettle he had left boiling on the stove. He did not always manage it. Once she caught him by the wrist and made him sit.

'Not talking about it doesn't make it any less real,' she said. She told him that the Melvilles were to be his guardians. The arrangements had already been made. When he protested that he was more than capable of managing on his own his mother squeezed his hand.

'I know,' she said. 'But I'm not. Let me look after you a little longer. Please?'

Another time she had him bring her a small silk pouch tucked at the back of her dressing-table drawer. Inside he found her gold poesy ring and another just the same, only larger. Oscar turned it over in his fingers to read the words engraved inside the band. *Du allein. You alone.*

'It was your father's,' she said. It had never occurred to Oscar that his father had worn one too. His mother slid hers onto her left hand. She was so thin that she had to hold it to keep it on. It was the tradition in Germany, she told him, for a betrothed couple to exchange poesy rings. The rings were worn on the left hand until a couple exchanged marriage vows, and afterwards on the right. Oscar wondered why his mother had never told him this before. He had always presumed she wore the ring on her right hand because she did not want to remember.

'We were better at being engaged than being married,' his mother said. 'You might want to try it the other way around.'

On the bad days he brought her tea she did not drink and watched her sleep, the pain moving across her face like clouds. Sometimes, muddled with morphine, she mumbled words he could not hear, her head twisting from side to side as though she were having an argument with herself. To calm her Oscar read poems out loud. He took down books at random from the shelves, Gerard Manley Hopkins, Christina Rossetti, Thomas Gray. In the Gray, on the frontispiece, someone had written *Thoughts that breathe and words that burn, with all my love,* and the date, *August 1899.* A month later his parents had married. Oscar touched the ink with the tips of his fingers. It shamed him, reading those words, how much he had wanted to be someone else's son.

At nights he lay on his bed, his door open in case she cried out, and stared up at the ceiling. As a child, sent to bed before sundown, he had liked to fix his eyes on the crack above his bed until the ceiling began to swarm, making patterns of waves and grids that undulated, grey and silver, in and out of the pale paint as though they were breathing. Sometimes, if he hardly blinked at all, little black figures would appear from between the lines, clambering over and between the curves and angles. Sometimes they were people and sometimes they were numbers with legs. He had liked them. But when he tried it now, he seemed to have forgotten the knack of it. However much he looked, the ceiling of his room remained resolutely flat and white.

The day before he was due to return to Rhyl the country held its first General Election for eight years. The newspapers dubbed it the Coupon Election because Lloyd George and the Conservative Bonar Law had issued a coupon to the 159 Liberal candidates giving an assurance that, if they stood for election, no Conservative candidate would challenge their seats and that the arrangement would be reciprocal. The arrangement meant that the outcome of the election was a foregone conclusion but, as his mother said, surprises weren't everything. She had Oscar help her to a chair in the window so that she could watch as groups of men and women made their way along the street towards the Town Hall.

'Eight and a half million women,' she said. 'Can you imagine?'

They had finally won. For the first time in history women over thirty, if they met a minimum property qualification, were eligible to vote, along with almost all men over twenty-one. On this day across the country, more than twenty-four million men and women, nearly three times as many people as before the War, would take their turn at the ballot box.

'We only went and damn well did it,' she whispered, clasping Oscar's hand in hers, and in Oscar's throat there was an aching lump of pride and fear and sadness that he could not swallow.

She insisted that he left her while she dressed. It took a long time. When at last she called Oscar to help her downstairs it was plain that the effort had exhausted her. In the parlour she sat down shakily, her breath ragged and shallow.

'Hat,' she said, holding out her hand, but when she raised her arm to put it on the shock of the pain made her whimper. The hat fell to the floor.

'Let me,' Oscar said. 'Now. The coat.'

He knelt beside her chair, sliding her arm into the sleeve as gently as he could manage. She looked at him, her face ancient with pain.

'Come on,' he said. 'We can't let that bastard Du Cros win.'

Du Cros was the Conservative candidate for Clapham. Everyone knew he would win, he was a coupon candidate with only an Independent standing against him, but that was hardly the point. Du Cros had always been passionately opposed to votes for women.

'I can't, dearest,' she whispered. 'I just can't.'

She dozed a little after that. He did what he could to make her comfortable on the Chesterfield. She did not have the strength for the stairs. By half past three it was already almost dark. Oscar did not switch on a light. Instead, he left his mother sleeping and went next door to the Doyles' house. When he came back he knelt by his mother's side and very softly told her it was time to wake up. She opened her eyes, staring dazedly at the wheelchair in front of her.

'We'll have to hurry,' he told her. 'I promised Jimmy he'd have it back before opening time.'

The chair was the newest kind, with rubber tyres and a reclining back. Oscar set it to its most recumbent position and placed several cushions around the frame. Then, very carefully, he lifted her into the chair.

'You don't need a coat this way, see,' he said, tucking a blanket around her. 'Or your Best Straw, for that matter.'

His mother managed a smile. 'I bloody well do. If any day deserves me Best Straw it's today.'

It was freezing when they came out of the Town Hall, the air sour with fog. Oscar pulled the blankets more tightly around his mother. Then, removing her hat, he set it in her lap. When he kissed her cheek she caught his wrist with her good hand, pressing his knuckles to her lips.

'Thank you,' she murmured.

He smiled at her. 'Ready?'

'Ready.'

Careful not to jolt her, he lowered the chair down the step of the kerb and into the middle of the road. There was no traffic, only a ghostly grocer's van on the other side of the street with its rear doors open, the horse stamping and rattling in its traces. Oscar bent down and, locking his elbows, pushed the chair out in front of him. Then, with a wild whoop like an Apache Indian, he broke into a run. The grocer's horse shook its blinkered head, blind to the fog-blurred figures flying down the road behind him, their laughter unfurling behind them like streamers.

CHAPTER 13

At the start of the War Jessica had gone with her mother and Phyllis to Southampton to meet the soldiers coming off the crammed troop trains. They had stood among the crowds waving off the ships for France, gaily dispensing paper bags filled with chocolate and cigarettes. The atmosphere had been one of a vast Sunday picnic, the newly enlisted soldiers singing and laughing and blowing kisses with a good deal of 'Ooh, la, la!' and 'See you in time for Christmas!' Part of Jessica had wished she could go with them.

Now they crept back silently, in dribs and drabs. Many were missing limbs or parts of their faces. Tom Dodds whose father had a small farm on the Ellinghurst estate had a hook instead of an arm which he used to drag brambles from ditches and to close gates. The oldest of the Scovell brothers had been blinded by gas. His mother had insisted on having him home, though Mrs Briggs said it would be kinder if he was in a Home. She did not say kinder to whom. The three Scovell brothers had always gone around in a pack like

189

fox cubs and had often come up to the house to play tennis with Theo. Arthur Scovell was the only one left.

Phyllis came home too. On her last leave, a snatched two days before Christmas, she had told her parents she meant to stay on at the hospital for as long as they needed her, perhaps until the autumn. She did not say why she had changed her mind. Her letter was brief, hardly more than the time of her train. Jessica went with Pritchard to meet her. When she saw Phyllis she gaped.

'Your hair,' she said.

'I like it, before you say anything,' Phyllis said.

'Actually, I was going to say that it suits you.' She considered her sister, her head on one side. 'Which was the Tudor king, the sickly one that died? Before Bloody Mary.'

'Edward VI?'

'Exactly. You look like Edward VI, in that picture in the National Portrait Gallery. The one Nanny always insisted was one of the Princes in the Tower.'

'Poor little mite,' Phyllis said and they both laughed. Nanny had never managed to pass that portrait without saying it. Phyllis looked older, Jessica thought, but also more elegant somehow, despite her shabby overcoat and a hat that looked as though someone had sat on it. Perhaps it was the hair. It emphasised her elfin face, the delicate line of her jaw.

'Thank God you're home,' Jessica said. 'I can't tell you how ghastly it's been.'

Later she lay on Phyllis's bed as her sister dressed for dinner.

'Archaeology?' she asked. 'But why?'

'What's wrong with archaeology?'

'You're really interested in bits of broken pot?'

'I'm interested in the people that made them, in the great vanished civilisations of history. Aren't you?'

'Not much. I prefer my civilisations with a bit of life in them.'

'I imagine the Egyptians felt the same way.'

Jessica rolled over, staring up at the ceiling. 'I can't stay here, Phyll. It's killing me.'

'Killing you?'

'Don't give me that look. You know what I mean.'

'Then leave. You're eighteen. You have a choice.'

'Do I? Did you know the house in London is being sold?'

'Father said something about it, yes.'

'No one tells me anything. You have no idea what it's been like here, walled up like one of your bloody Egyptian mummies. I got so desperate before Christmas I even wrote to Mrs Carey begging her to take me as a PG, but she never even answered. Can you believe it? All those years of paying Oscar's school fees and not even a post-card. If there is a Season this year I'm going to miss the whole bloody thing.'

Phyllis was silent, buckling her shoe straps. Suddenly Jessica sat up. 'If you're going to be at university in London perhaps we could persuade Father to take a flat.'

Phyllis shook her head. 'I've already arranged rooms in the college hostel.'

'A hostel? But those places are beastly. Didn't you have enough of inch-deep baths and single gas rings during the War?'

'I told you, it's all arranged.'

'I'm sure you could unarrange it if you wanted to.'

'But I don't want to.'

Jessica stared at her sister. Then with an exasperated sigh she flung herself backwards onto the pillows. 'I can't believe you. You're as bad as Eleanor. It's as if both of you actually want me to die an old maid.'

'I'm afraid you may not have a choice.'

'What are you talking about? You're supposed to be helping me, Phyll, not crushing my last crumbs of hope.'

'All right, then. Here's some advice. Do something.'

Jessica frowned. 'Have you even been listening to me? I've tried everything.'

'Have you? What about getting a job?'

'A job? The War's over, Phyllis.'

'There are still jobs.'

'For men. Come on, things aren't what they used to be but they're not quite that bad yet. Not until Cousin Evelyn throws us out onto the street.'

'Except you said it was killing you.'

'And it is. It is.'

'Then do something. Make your own life, instead of waiting like Rapunzel for the last of the knights-errant to ride up on his white charger and offer you his.'

'Why do you think I haven't cut my hair?'

'Ha ha. I mean it.'

'So do I,' Jessica said. 'It's not as though I'm asking for much. Before the War Eleanor would have dragged us to London whether we wanted it or not. I don't know if there'll even be Court presentations this year but—'

'Is that what you want? To be paraded in front of a crowd of chinless horrors like a prize cow? Have you forgotten that last summer before the War, how Theo loathed every minute of it? How he spent every ball and party plotting his escape?'

'Of course I've not forgotten. And I don't give a fig for all that ghastly polo and Royal Ascot stuff. I want to go to nightclubs and dance all night and drink too much champagne and fall madly in love. I'm eighteen, Phyll. I want to live.'

Phyllis was silent, staring at her reflection in the dressing-table glass.

'Don't you want that?' Jessica said. 'To fall into someone's arms and to know that every minute you've ever lived, every thing you've ever done up until that moment was nothing but the overture. To know that all of a sudden you're not sleep-walking any more, you're wide awake, and nothing will ever be the same because you're not the same you that you were the day before, that something fundamental has happened that has changed you, something chemical, so that together you make something completely new like – like hydrogen and oxygen making water. Do you really not want to know how that feels?'

Phyllis gave her a strange look. Then she stood up. 'Goodness,' she said tightly. 'I never knew you were such a hopeless romantic.'

'You should try it,' Jessica retorted. 'Better a hopeless romantic than just plain hopeless.'

It was not entirely true, that Jessica did not give a fig about the Season. Theo had hated it, it was true. He had done wicked impressions of the awkward girls clutching their dance cards, the braying young men who pushed them around the dance floor like wheelbarrows and boasted of their conquests. The English upper classes, he said, thought it as vulgar to be good at dancing as it was to be clever or to speak French with anything resembling a French accent, and yet they insisted on trampling girls' feet night after night in a round of parties that nobody but the florists and the caterers and the dressmakers profited from in the slightest. He called it the Slave Market. He still received dozens of invitations. Sometimes, when he was bored, he used the heavy cards as projectiles, flying them with a flick of his wrist across his bedroom into the fire in the grate. The

194

cards did not burn well. Just like debutantes, Theo said. Too thick to be any fun at all.

Jessica had vowed then that she would never allow her mother to make her come out. In those days, though, it had been different. It had never occurred to her that her mother would listen to her, that there might be a time when Eleanor did not want to be in London. The promise of parties and theatres and glamorous dresses had been as much a part of her childhood as Ellinghurst. It had been easy to despise it all then, when there was no avoiding it.

At the same time she thought of the girls she had been at school with and the girls at the parties in Hampshire and she knew she could not bear it, if the Season turned out to be exactly the same.

On the last Saturday in February Princess Patricia of Connaught, a first cousin of the King, married Commander the Hon. Alexander Ramsay in Westminster Abbey and the Yorkshire Melvilles returned to stay at Ellinghurst. Cousin Lettice could talk of nothing but the wedding. She told Phyllis and Jessica that the Princess had decided on her marriage to relinquish her royal titles.

'No one asked her to,' she said. 'She had to ask the King's permission especially, but she insisted. She would not outrank her husband. Isn't that lovely? She could have had any royal prince in the world but she followed her heart and chose a commoner. Of course, he absolutely worships her.'

'What is it about you girls?' Cousin Evelyn said, pressing his wife's hand to his lips. 'So silly about weddings.'

This time Cousin Lettice brought the whole brood. The three elder boys ran in circles through the house and across the garden, chasing one another with sticks, while the baby gaped like a landed fish in its perambulator. Cousin Lettice said that boys were like ponies; they needed to be exercised or they grew skittish and prone to bite. She did not mind about mud or torn buttons or dirty hands that marked her skirts. When the boys made wigs of pondweed she only laughed and said she liked their hair better when it was blond.

Phyllis was reading a book about Egyptian hieroglyphics. She explained to the boys that, because hieroglyph meant god's words in Egyptian, the ancient Greeks had believed the system to be allegorical, even magical, the key to secret, mystical knowledge.

'Look how complicated it is,' Lettice said. 'You must be awfully clever.'

'Is there a picture for every word in the world?' Lettice's oldest boy asked Phyllis, peering at the page.

'Not quite, though there are nearly five thousand. What they mean depends on context, do you know what that means? On their place in the sentence. It might be figurative or phonetic or symbolic or all three, all at the same time.'

The boy looked blank. Phyllis smiled at him. 'See this eye? Depending on the sentence it might be the word for eye or something done by an eye, like seeing or understanding. Or it could stand for the sound the word makes when you say it out loud: I as in you and I. And sounds can be used on their own or as part of a longer word like, let's see. Like I-ced buns. I don't suppose anyone wants an I-ced bun, do they?'

The boys shouted for joy and bounded out of the morning room towards the kitchen, Phyllis in their wake. It was easy for Phyllis to manage without love, Jessica thought. She fell in love with things: Greek myths or the French Revolution or hieroglyphs or John Donne. She always had. When they were younger Phyllis had pinned a line from a poem on her bedroom wall, something about treading softly because you tread on my dreams, and Jessica had laughed because the only dreams Phyllis had were of lessons and books and people who were imaginary or centuries dead and what possible harm could things like that come to, even if you trod on them quite hard?

Lettice smiled, listening to the whooping, the clatter of boots across the Great Hall. The baize door banged. Then, frowning sympathetically, she put her hand on Jessica's.

'How is your mother?' she asked. 'Evie told me a little of her troubles.'

Jessica shrugged. 'She's all right.'

'I wondered, has she found someone else? Another

sensitive? It must be hard for her, cut off so cruelly from Theo like that.'

'You can't be cut off from something you were never in touch with in the first place. The woman was a fraud.'

'Evie said. Poor Eleanor, it must have been ghastly. That's why I wondered, not that I would ever wish to interfere, but I wondered perhaps if she might like an introduction to Sir Oliver? You remember, the scientist I told you about, my mother's cousin. He only works with mediums who are prepared to be put through his tests, you see, so they're all absolutely above board. Then again, his sittings are almost always in London so perhaps that would not be convenient.'

Jessica put down her cup of tea. 'Eleanor would have to go to London?'

'I'm afraid so. One of his ladies is in Hampstead, or is it Hampton? Is there even a difference? I'm afraid I'm quite hopeless when it comes to London. All I know is that Sir Oliver comes down from Birmingham quite regularly to sit with two sensitives, both of whom have been scientifically proven to be genuine. But perhaps London would be too much for your mother?'

Jessica looked at Cousin Lettice, her eyes gleaming. 'Oh, no. Not at all. London would be absolutely perfect.'

Later, as Phyllis led the boys in a game of Sardines, Jessica walked across the lawn towards the woods.

198

It was cold and she put her hands in her pockets to warm them. Above her the leafless branches of the trees drew black patterns on the darkening sky. The door to the tower stood open. She peered in. When she was little it had been the job of one of the under-gardeners to clean the Tiled Room but there were not enough under-gardeners for that kind of work, not any more. The tiles were grimy, furred with sagging spiders' webs, the floor thick with dead leaves. The varnish on the wooden benches was starting to peel. She held a piece of it up to her eye, looking through the tiny yellow lens. Scotch-tinted spectacles, she thought, and dropped it. When she scuffed the leaves with the toes of her shoes they rustled like old ladies' skirts.

She had forgotten how many steps there were. She was out of breath when she reached the top. She leaned on the sill of one of the empty window arches, looking out. It was a long way down. In the trees below the rooks were stirring, the harsh cries cutting the air. This had been Theo's den, the place he took boys to do whatever it was boys did when they were out of sight of grown-ups. Everyone else was strictly prohibited. Jessica could still remember the thrill she had felt when, one dark evening, bored and restless, Theo had whispered to her that he was going to the tower and that she could come if she liked, if she promised not to be a nuisance.

'Not Phyllis,' he had said. 'She'll only spoil it.' She had nearly burst with pride and triumph.

The woods had been very dark, the staircase too, the concrete walls ducking and shivering in the tiny light of Theo's matches. When they reached the top Theo had let off the firecrackers that he had in his pockets and, though he aimed them at her feet, she had not screamed, not once, but laughed and almost meant it because she knew he was only teasing. Then he had lit toffee papers and dropped them out of the window and she had watched entranced as the scraps of flame floated down like butterflies and were swallowed by the night.

That night at dinner Cousin Evelyn expressed his surprise that Grandfather's Tower was still standing.

'Structurally it's perfectly sound,' Father said.

'I see,' Cousin Evelyn said, laughing. 'So it's only conceptually that it's on shaky ground. Oh, come on, Aubrey, old chap. The thing's a monstrosity.'

When Father glared at him Cousin Evelyn only laughed more. He said that Aubrey knew as well as anyone that Yorkshiremen could not help speaking their minds, it was the way they were made. There was no point in beating round the bush. The truth might be painful but at least it was clean; it was untruths that festered. Which was why, he said, he wanted to lay some plain facts on the table. He was not normally a man for mixing business with pleasure but this was a family matter. He wanted no whispering behind people's backs.

He had done all the calculations. At current rates

the value of the Ellinghurst estate put likely death duties at close to thirty per cent. As and when the estate passed on, there was no liquid capital available to meet that obligation. Even the sale of the London house, which would raise a fair sum, would provide only temporary relief. The mortgage burden on the estate was crippling, a legacy of poor investments and heavy borrowing by Sir Crawford and the ruinous agricultural depression that had followed. Land might be sold to raise the necessary funds but it would require the divesting of most of the estate. What land remained would almost certainly be insufficient to support the house, particularly one as expensive to run as Ellinghurst, and that was before one attempted to fix the roof and do all the repairs that had been ignored during the War and were now urgently in need of attention.

Alternatively, the house could be sold and the land retained intact. There were other smaller properties on the estate that might serve as well and be a great deal more practicable, and there were investors prepared to pay reasonable sums for properties that might accommodate a school or some other type of residential institution that required only limited grounds. It might even sell as a hotel. There was a market for castles, it seemed, even the Victorian imitations. Or the estate might be sold in its entirety. There were good reasons to argue against continuing as a landowner in an uncertain future when, if he liquidated his holdings, a man might clear a sizeable capital sum that could secure not only his future but those of his children.

'Your children,' Sir Aubrey said. His face was white.

'Or yours. If you chose to sell now the girls could net a sizeable capital sum. Land prices are stronger than they've been for years. Indeed, now might be exactly the right time.'

'And the baronetcy? You'd "liquidate" that too, I suppose, if you could.'

'Aubrey, this is difficult, I know.'

'Difficult? It's intolerable.'

'None of this has to happen in your lifetime, not if you don't wish it. But I wanted you to understand the situation. I wanted to be clear.'

'You've been very clear.'

'Then I—'

'You've been very clear indeed. You intend to destroy the Melville family.'

'The estate is not the family, Aubrey.'

'How can you say that? There have been Melvilles at Ellinghurst for three hundred years!'

'Then we've had a good run.'

Sir Aubrey stared at Evelyn, his mouth working. Then, standing up, he threw his napkin onto his plate and stalked out of the room. Jessica and Phyllis exchanged a look. It was Phyllis who went after him. Cousin Lettice looked at her lap.

'I'm sorry to spring this on you, Eleanor, my dear,' Evelyn said. 'But the facts must be faced.'

'Must they?'

'I'm afraid they must.'

'This is our home,' Eleanor said. 'My son's home.'

'With the greatest respect, Eleanor, Theo would have faced exactly the same problems we do. The world has changed. We must change with it.'

'And so my son's home, his memorial, becomes – what? – a madhouse? A school for delinquents? My son died, Evelyn, while you were busy feathering your nest and fondling your fat little wife, but what does that concern you? You're going to be rich! It was a wretched squalid War but someone has to win. That's the way things are. The world has changed and we must change with it. Pile it high and sell it cheap. Why not? My boy is dead. There's nothing he can do to stop you.'

'Eleanor,' Lettice pleaded.

'Why should I care?' Eleanor declared. 'I've always loathed this house. It was Theo who loved it, Theo whose spirit fills every room.'

'But spirits are free, aren't they?' Lettice said. 'Your son is with you always, Eleanor, wherever you are.' She looked helplessly at Cousin Evelyn.

'You could always ask him,' Jessica said. 'If he minded, I mean.'

'Jessica, dear, I'm not sure . . .'

Jessica ignored Lettice. 'Don't you see?' she said to Eleanor. 'If you could only talk to him the way you used to, perhaps the house wouldn't matter so much. To either of you. Whatever happened, you'd still be together.'

Eleanor stared at her daughter. Then, one hand pressed against her mouth, she stumbled from the room.

CHAPTER 14

Sylvia Carey's funeral took place on a bitter Friday afternoon at the Church of the Holy Trinity on the north side of Clapham Common. Oscar's mother had never been a church-goer but she had liked this one for the grace of its architecture and the picturesqueness of its setting, and because it had been the church of William Wilberforce and the Clapham Sect, who had done so much for the abolition of slavery. It was one of her favourite stories: how Wilberforce, presenting his Abolitionist Bill for the first time in Parliament, had insisted on laying out for the House the full horrors of slavery. He spoke for three hours. When he was finished, he said, 'Having heard all this you may choose to look the other way but you can never again say that you did not know.'

They had walked here often on Sundays, bringing scraps of bread to feed the ducks, then circling the pond towards the stand of copper beeches behind the church. Sometimes, hopeful of more crumbs, the mallards had followed them, the gleam-green drakes in their smart white collars jostling their plump brown wives. It made Oscar and his mother laugh to turn suddenly and see them stop, their heads carefully averted, as though they were playing Grandmother's Footsteps.

A week before he was due to be demobbed, Oscar had received a letter from Mrs Doyle. His mother had been moved to the Hostel of God, a hospice run by the Sisters of Margaret that over-looked Clapham Common. Oscar knew then that she was dying. At Christmas, when Dr Seeley had first proposed the hospice, his mother had turned him down flat. She had no intention of dying, she protested, and anyway she would rather be dead than hidden away in a convent as if cancer was something to be ashamed of. Dr Seeley had given way, startled by the vehemence of her refusal. Oscar went again to his Commanding Officer and asked if he might be released early. This time permission was not granted. It was seven days before he could return to London.

He took her home. She was very weak. Dr Seeley said she had only a few days left and that she would be more comfortable with the nuns but Oscar knew he was wrong. She lay in bed, fragments of consciousness clinging to her like cobwebs, as he sat with her, her wasted hand in his, and read her poetry and told her all the stories he could remember of their lives together and all the things that scientists were going to discover, now that the War was finally over and it no longer mattered where you came from but only what you could see. He thought she smiled. Then, one morning a little after dawn, she began to shiver. Her temperature soared and she fell into a restless twitching sleep from which he could not rouse her. At noon the twitching ceased. When Dr Seeley came he offered Oscar his commiserations and instructed him to disinfect the house to prevent the spread of infection. He said it would be best to burn everything in her bedroom that could not be boiled, just to be sure.

The funeral service was brief. Afterwards the congregation gathered on the steps of the church while the coffin was carried to the hearse. The pond was a sheet of beaten pewter and the leafless trees made cracks in the white ice of the sky. Oscar stared at his feet. His shoes were very shiny. He wondered who had polished them and how it was that he had got here.

It was Phyllis who took his elbow and steered him to the motor car. He sat between her and Sir Aubrey as they drove in silence to the graveyard. Jessica and her mother were in a second car behind them. It had been explained to him that the burial would be attended only by immediate family and his mother's most intimate friends. The rest of the mourners would go back to the house in Clapham where refreshments had been arranged. Later he would have to face them but not now. There were more words at the graveside, a blur of white faces and black hats. People pressed his hand. He climbed back into the motor car.

'Nearly there,' Phyllis said.

They drove back past the church on the Common. There was a lady in a brown hat walking alone along the pavement. She raised a hand to adjust her scarf and for a moment it was her. Oscar's heart lurched. It was only when he looked again that he saw it was not her, nor even like her. His mother was walking with the angels, wasn't that what the vicar had said? Reunited with her husband in Heaven. Oscar had found himself wondering if that might be open to negotiation. His parents' marriage had not been happy. Embittered by his own failures, Joachim Grunewald had resented his wife's independence, her passionate convictions. He had wanted her at home, as thwarted and aggrieved as he was.

'Of course Wilberforce never troubled himself with the bondage of women,' Oscar heard his mother say quite clearly, as though she was sitting next to him in the car. 'It was only men that he believed were born equal.'

The parlour was full and uncomfortably warm. People were smoking and drinking tea and whisky and glasses of wine. Someone had put out plates of sandwiches. Oscar saw Sir Aubrey pick up the gargoyle photograph from the mantelpiece and stare at it. Then, smiling a little, he put it back. Women he vaguely recognised kept coming up to Oscar and pressing his hand. The smell of the whisky and the wine and the pipe smoke and the half-chewed insides of people's mouths as they

talked all mixed up with the faint smell of disin-
fectant made him feel sick. He squeezed through
the crush towards the door, nodding at the faces that
loomed towards him, mumbling at him with their
wet lips.

'Excuse me,' he said, again and again. 'Excuse me.'

The landing at the top of the stairs was empty.
He leaned against the wall, his forehead against the
cold plaster. Then, twisting round, he slid down
the wall into a squat and put his arms over his
head. There was the click of a door.

'Oscar?'

She still came to him, still comforted him as he
was tipping into sleep. Sometimes she was Jessica
in her silk dress with the string of pearls around
her neck and sometimes Jessica from the tower
or a slippage of the two, her clothes melting from
her as he took her in his arms.

'Oscar, are you all right?'

He looked up. Jessica frowned at him, her hands
on her hips, her hair bright as butter against the
black of her suit.

'You should really come downstairs,' she said.
'It's quite rude, you know, hiding away up here.'
When he did not answer she sighed. 'I'm sorry,
you know. About your mother.'

Oscar put the heels of his hands over his eyes.
Lagrange's Four-Square Theorem states that every
positive integer can be written as the sum of at
most four squares. Given this theorem, prove that
any positive multiple of eight can be written as

the sum of eight odd squares. How many times had he played this game, sitting here on the landing before his mother woke and the day was allowed to begin? He tried to arrange the numbers in his head but they only slipped and stuck like defective typewriter keys.

JUST BLOODY KISS ME, they punched out instead.

He did not know what was wrong with him. His mother was dead and all he wanted was to kiss Jessica, to kiss her and kiss her until there was no room left inside him for anything but kissing, no feeling but the feeling of her face against his face, her mouth on his.

GO AWAY, the metal arms banged out against the inside of his skull. *KISS ME. KISS ME. KISS ME.*

Jessica scuffed at a worn patch in the carpet with the toe of her shoe. 'I'm not surprised you couldn't stand it down there. All those ghastly old people trying to look mournful while stuffing their faces with cake.' She considered him. Then she sat down on the stairs, wrapping her arms around her knees. 'You know in India they take their dead to the banks of a holy river and burn them with wreaths of flowers. Then they scatter the ashes on the water. People say it's barbaric but how could it possibly be more civilised to shovel the dead into the earth like a dog burying a bone? At least the Indian way is beautiful. Romantic. You can't do romantic with cups of tea and egg sandwiches.'

Oscar did not answer. He heard the sound of footsteps on the stairs.

'Oscar?' Sir Aubrey called up. Jessica leaned over the banister. 'Jessica? Have you seen— Ah, there you are. What are you two doing hidden away up here?'

'Oscar just needed to be on his own for a bit.'

'Right. Of course. Still, it'd be best if you could come down, old chap. You too, Jessica. People are leaving.'

'We're coming,' Jessica said. When her father was gone she turned to Oscar. 'Are you packed? Father says you're coming home with us tonight.'

Oscar shook his head.

'You should. Eleanor hates to be kept hanging about.'

'I'm not coming with you.'

'But of course you are.'

'I'm not. I want to stay here.'

'Really? On your own in this house, where she actually died?'

'Just go away,' he blurted, the words out before he could stop them.

Jessica shrugged. 'Fine. But don't shout at me. It's Father's stupid idea to take you to Ellinghurst, not mine.'

Downstairs she trailed after Phyllis as her sister gathered up dirty glasses. She hated funerals, she decided. She wished they could leave. She knew Eleanor did too. Her mother had barely talked to

211

anyone, just stared out of the window with her cheeks sucked in. Her father on the other hand had insisted on talking to everyone, even the old Suffragette ladies with their moustaches and their skirts made of horse blankets.

'You could help too if you wanted,' Phyllis said.

Jessica picked up a half-empty teacup and followed Phyllis into the back parlour. The room was crowded with books, stacked in piles on the table in the window and on the mantelpiece and the piano and the fender stool and in the corners on the floor. Phyllis nudged the books on the table to one side and put down her tray of dirty glasses. Jessica added her cup to the pile, then idly picked up a book, glancing at the spine.

'You'd have thought someone might have tidied up,' she said. When Phyllis did not answer she sighed. 'Oscar's refusing to come to Ellinghurst. He says he wants to stay here. Don't you think that's a bit creepy?'

'I think it's exactly what I'd want if I was him.'

'He can't stay here by himself.'

'Then maybe one of us should stay with him.'

'One of us? Do you really think Father would agree to that?'

'For God's sake, Jess, Oscar's as good as family.'

'I wish someone had told him that before he tried to slobber all over me.'

A woman in an apron sidled up to Phyllis, muttering something about more whisky. Phyllis nodded. 'I'll see to it. Tell Father about Oscar, would you, Jess? We should see what can be arranged.'

Jessica nodded absently, peering out of the window into the small square of garden at the back where a few leafless plants straggled in pots. It was impossible to believe that she had begged to come and live here, that she had imagined Clapham to be the answer to her prayers. No wonder Mrs Carey had never invited any of them to visit. Except Phyllis, of course, and then Phyllis was always so busy being good she never noticed anything. It made Jessica think of the houses one saw from the train as one neared Paddington Station, not quite as run-down perhaps, at least here the windows were unbroken and there were no strings of ragged laundry to get dirty again before it was even dry, but it had the same make-shift feeling, the rooms too small and the walls too thin. And so crammed with stuff! Jessica half expected a shopkeeper to sidle up to her, murmuring prices.

'I don't suppose you'd let me hide in here with you?'

Jessica turned around. The gentleman was old, perhaps as old as her mother, tall and broad in an elegantly cut suit. His hair was thick and winged with silver. In one hand he held a glass, in the other a bottle of whisky.

'Emergency measures,' he said. 'I'm not very good at funerals.'

'I don't think anyone is good at funerals.'

213

'I don't know. The Women's Legion out there seem to be having a whale of a time. I suppose if you've been a Suffragette you learn to take your pleasures where you can.'

Jessica smiled.

'Drink?' he asked. When she shook her head the man sloshed three fingers of whisky into his glass and put the bottle on the piano. Then he came to stand next to her in the window. He did not introduce himself. He smelled nice, of leather and cigars and an unobtrusive woody cologne.

'Even Sylvia's most staunch defenders would have to concede that she hadn't the least aptitude for gardening,' he observed.

'Didn't your nanny ever tell you it was wrong to speak ill of the dead?'

'And what about the dead plants? Look at that poor – whatever that brown thing is along the back wall there. Dead as a doornail.'

'It's a clematis. That's what clematis look like in March.'

'How do you know that? Are you a farmer?'

'Yes, I'm a farmer. I farm clematis.'

'Very shrewd. Everyone will always need clematis eggs.'

Jessica laughed.

'I have to admit,' he said, 'I always thought of farmers as an unsightly lot. Not that I ever go to the country, you understand, but one hears things. I appear to have been misled.'

'Are you flirting with me, Mr . . .?'

214

'I'm trying. I'm not sure it's entirely successful but I am trying. Lovely girls expect it, don't they?'

'Do they?'

'You're no help. I shall have to go and find another lovely girl and ask her. The trouble is there are so exasperatingly few of them, particularly at funerals.'

'Perhaps you go to the wrong kind of funeral.'

'Lovely and heartless. Now that's an even rarer breed.'

'Better than ill-mannered and drunk.'

He laughed. 'How about lovely and heartless and ill-mannered and drunk? If you can manage all that and a few exaggerated facial expressions, you can forget the clematis. You're nine tenths of the way to being a bona fide film star.' He lowered his voice confidentially. 'You do know that's why men love film stars, don't you?'

'Because they're ill-mannered and drunk?'

'That helps. But mostly because their expressions are so blessedly unambiguous. We men are simple creatures. Idiots, really. It's unreasonable to expect us to work out for ourselves how a girl is feeling. We need her to make it easy.' He brandished his fists, his face contorted in a grimace. 'Angry.' Then he gasped, a dying swan, the back of his hand pressed tragically against his brow. 'Sad.' He shrugged. 'I'd like to see a law.'

'A law obliging girls to pull faces?'

'Precisely. Title cards too, while we're at it. And an orchestra. Life's significant moments should come with a rousing score. That way one would never miss them.'

'That isn't very reassuring.'

'On the contrary. One would never make a mistake again.'

'And what about the girls who couldn't pull faces? What would happen to them?'

The man sipped his drink thoughtfully. 'They'd have to be disposed of. Humanely, of course, but the law's the law. An example must be set.'

'Help. Then I shall have to practise.'

'You shall. You'll need lessons, of course. If I can be of any assistance . . .'

'I think I can manage.'

'Ah, but can you really? Show me your "I'm wildly, absurdly in love with you" face.'

'My what?'

'Come on,' he said. 'Your life's at stake. Show me.'

Jessica laughed awkwardly, rolling her eyes. 'I shall do no such thing.'

'But it's easy.' Seizing her hands, he sank to his knees. She gaped at him, too startled to laugh, as he gazed up at her, his face slack with adoration. Then, shrugging, he stood, dusting the knees of his trousers. 'I'd strongly advise lessons. I shan't be able to do a thing for you otherwise, come the revolution. Perhaps we should discuss it over lunch.'

'Lunch? I don't even know your name, Mr . . .?'

'Cardoza. Gerald Cardoza.'

She hesitated. He smiled at her, his eyes on hers

216

as though he could read every thought in her head. To her mortification Jessica could feel herself blushing.

'Jessica Melville,' she said.

'Jessica. "And fair she is, if that mine eyes be true."'

'What?'

'Never mind. So, Miss Jessica Melville, do you absolutely loathe the Savoy?'

CHAPTER 15

The teapots were empty, the plates of sand-wiches mostly crumbs, and still people lingered. Oscar ached for them to be gone. All afternoon he had shaken people's hands and repeated the same phrases, over and over: thank you and you're very kind and it was good of you to come, until the words were nothing but blobs of sound without any meaning. He gazed blankly at Godmother Eleanor as she bore down on him, the emerald in her lapel glaring at him with its cold green eye.

'Help me find Jessica, won't you?' she said. 'I told her quite plainly we were to leave by half past at the latest.'

Sighing impatiently she flung open the door to the back parlour. Two figures were outlined in the window. One was a man, the other his mother. She was laughing, her head thrown back, and something inside Oscar turned over and then she turned and it was not his mother at all but Jessica who had never resembled her in the least. Oscar pressed his fingers against his temples. He could not understand why it kept happening, why he kept making the same mistake.

'Eleanor,' Jessica said smoothly. 'Do you know Mr Cardoza?'

'What on earth are you doing, hiding away in here?' her mother demanded.

'I was looking for a book. Ah, here it is.' Jessica snatched a volume from the arm of the sofa. 'Mr Cardoza is an old friend of Mrs Carey's. From her Suffragette days. Mr Cardoza, this is my mother, Lady Melville.'

Mr Cardoza smiled and held out his hand. 'How do you do?'

Eleanor considered him. Then, placing her hand in his as though it was something unpleasant she meant him to dispose of, she turned to Jessica. 'Find your father. Now. Tell him we leave in five minutes.'

'Eleanor, please,' Jessica admonished. 'Mr Cardoza, have you met Oscar Greenwood, Mrs Carey's son?'

'My deepest sympathy,' Mr Cardoza said. 'I was very fond of your mother.'

'Thank you.' Mechanically Oscar shook his hand.

'Your father,' Eleanor said icily.

'It's time I was going,' Mr Cardoza said. 'Lady Melville. Mr Greenwood, thank you. It was a beautiful service.' Then, with a private smile at Jessica, he gestured towards the door. 'Miss Melville?'

Smiling, Jessica swept out of the room, Mr

Cardoza in her wake. Eleanor folded down the corners of her mouth like an envelope. Then, without a word, she followed them.

People stood in the hall in their coats, saying their last farewells.

'You're so kind,' Oscar said, again and again. 'Thank you. Thank you for coming.'

Sir Aubrey shook Oscar's hand. He looked very old and weary, the skin pouched beneath his eyes. 'I only wish I could persuade you to come with us.'

'Don't worry, Father,' Phyllis said. 'Mrs Mulley will take care of everything.'

Mrs Mulley was the local woman that Mrs Doyle from next door had suggested to take care of the funeral tea. A widow, she lived with her sister in a flat in Balham. When Phyllis had asked if she might be able to stay she had agreed on the condition that she could go home and fetch some things.

'If she comes back,' Sir Aubrey said.

'Of course she'll come back.'

'I'd rather we waited to be sure. Then we can give you a run back to Roehampton on our way.'

'Don't be silly, Father. You're late enough as it is.'

'Then at least let me give you the money for a taxi.'

'I don't want a taxi. There's a bus that goes almost all the way.'

'A bus? Phyllis, darling—'

'Aubrey, for the love of God,' Eleanor snapped. 'Can we just go?'

Jessica stood on tiptoes and pressed her cheek to Oscar's, kissing the air by his ear. Her skin was soft and very warm. Then they were gone. Phyllis and Oscar stood alone in the hall, side by side. Someone had left a plate on the hall table. Phyllis picked it up. Then, gently, she put her other hand on Oscar's arm.

'Well done,' she said. 'You did it.'

The tears massed in his throat, behind his nose and eyes, a force like a fist against the back of his face. He turned his head away.

'Come here,' she said and she put her arms around him, holding him like a child. The top of her head barely reached his chin. He put his hands over his face. He was not crying but somehow the tears slid between his fingers and down into his cuffs, and his body shook.

'I know,' Phyllis said softly. 'I know.'

They stood there together for a long time. Then Oscar took a deep breath and pressed the tips of his fingers hard against his eyeballs.

'I'm sorry,' he said.

'Don't be.'

'You don't have to stay, you know. I'll be quite all right.'

'I know. Shall I make some tea?'

Oscar shook his head. 'Where will she sleep?'

'Mrs Mulley? She says there's a bed in the box room, is that right?'

'It's hardly more than a cot. She should have my mother's room.'

'Absolutely not.'

'She won't catch anything, if that's what you're worried about. They even sprayed the mattress.'

'That's not what I meant. I just thought . . .'

'What did you think?'

'That it's too soon. Her room, all her things . . .'

'They burned her clothes. They took them away and burned them.'

'Oh, Oscar.'

'It's not as though she's going to need them.'

Phyllis put a hand to her forehead. 'Let's have some tea,' she said.

He could not look at her. The thought of sitting down, of drinking tea, it made the blackness surge up in him, an uncontrollable force like the force pulling on the edges of the universe. He twisted round, his hand finding the handle of the cupboard under the stairs. He threw it open, ripping coats frenziedly from their pegs and hangers.

'What does any of it matter? Let's just get rid of all of it.' He thrust his mother's mackintosh cape at Phyllis, then her astrakhan coat with the fur collar. The coat had been expensive but she had said it would last her a lifetime. It turned out a lifetime was not so very long after all.

'Here,' he said. 'Take them. I've no use for them. Or these.' He pulled familiar items from shelves and cubbyholes: a travelling rug, a Chinese parasol, a pair of worn leather gardening gloves, stiffened into hands, shoving them at Phyllis. She stared helplessly at the pile in her arms.

'Oscar,' she said.

'And these.' He swept a pile from the upper shelf – a rabbit fur stole, a fringed shawl, a gauzy scarf patterned with peacock feathers – and bundled them into a ball. 'Take them. Take all of them.' Bending down he rummaged wildly in the bottom of the wardrobe, pulling out an umbrella, galoshes, a tennis racquet in a wooden press, a pair of walking boots encrusted with mud. When he dropped them chips of earth skittered across the tiled floor.

'Oscar, stop.'

'Why? She's dead, isn't she? What possible use does she have for them now?'

'Don't put yourself through this, not today. Please. Maybe in a few weeks . . .'

'She won't be any less dead then.'

Reaching up he swept his hand roughly across the top shelf of the wardrobe. Something fell out. He bent down and picked it up. His mother's Best Straw. He held it in his hands, the brim sharp against his palms. He could feel his knees shaking. A tear slid down his cheek.

'Oh, Oscar,' Phyllis said. Cupping the side of his face with her hand, she wiped the tear away very gently with her thumb. Oscar closed his eyes. He put his hand over hers, pressing it to his cheek. Then, standing on tiptoes, Phyllis kissed him lightly on his other cheek. He could feel the warmth of her breath against his skin.

'I'm so sorry,' she murmured.

Oscar inhaled the clean smell of her hair. Somewhere in the house he could hear his mother clattering dishes and singing to herself.

> As I walk along the Bois Boolong, with an
> independent air,
> You can hear the girls declare, 'He must be a
> millionaire.'
> You can hear them sigh and wish to die,
> You can see them wink the other eye,
> At the man who broke the bank at Monte Carlo.

Oscar let go of Phyllis's hand. Instead, he gently cupped the back of her skull, feeling the smallness of it, the way the curve of it fitted into his hand. Her eyes were palest grey but very bright, like water reflecting the sky. She did not say anything. She did not need to. She just looked up at him, all of her and all of himself held like water in her clear light eyes. Her hands crept up to encircle his neck, her thumbs smoothing the hair above his ears. Oscar thought of perfect numbers, which are the same whichever way you look at them, because they are the sum of all the whole numbers that divide them, and all the time in the kitchen his mother sang 'The Man Who Broke The Bank at Monte Carlo'.

Closing his eyes, he kissed her.

The peal of the doorbell startled them both. They pulled apart like two people waking up, blinking at each other in the half-light. Without her in his arms Oscar felt unbalanced, unsteady on his feet. Phyllis started towards the door but he caught her hand. Her mouth was like a crushed flower, the edges blurred from kissing. He pulled her towards him again. There was another long ring on the doorbell, then the round shape of Mrs Mulley's face sliding into focus in blue and red as she pressed her nose against the etched stained glass of the front door.

'We have to let her in,' Phyllis murmured.

'Not yet,' he implored, but she had already slipped from his arms. She opened the door. Mrs Mulley bustled in, a grip in one hand and a basket with a cloth over it in the other. Her hat was dark with rain.

'I was wondering if you was even in, what with the hall light off and all.' She took off her hat and shook it. 'If you'd've told me straight off it'd take me that long there and back I'd never've bothered. Half an hour I must've waited for the bus, and others in front of me twice that to judge by the queue of them, and when it finally came it was that crowded I wasn't sure the conductor'd even let us on.' And she sighed, subsiding inside her wet coat like a punctured tyre.

'Well, you're here now,' Phyllis said and she took the old woman's basket from her and led her down the corridor towards the kitchen. Oscar leaned against the wall, closing his eyes. He was so tired. Without Phyllis's arms around him he could feel himself dissolving, the particulars of skin and bone and hair evaporating into a veil of dust no more substantial than his own shadow.

'I'm going to go.' Oscar opened his eyes. Phyllis was already wearing her coat. In one hand she carried her upside-down hat, her gloves curled up in the crown like nestlings.

'No,' he said and he wrapped his arms around her so tightly that she dropped her hat. The gloves fell out. She pressed her face against his chest. He held her closer, his fingers finding the shallow dents between her ribs, crushing her against him, pressing his lips to the smooth red cap of her hair. He could feel the warmth of her, the angle of her chin against his chest. Bending his head, he groped for her mouth like a blind man but she turned her face away.

'I have to.' Ducking out of the circle of his arms, she picked up her hat from the floor. She turned it in her hands, brushing imaginary dust from the brim.

'I don't understand.'

'I know. That's just it, don't you see?' She looked up at him abruptly, her gaze helpless and fierce at the same time. 'Oscar, you've just lost your mother. You want someone to cling to, a lifebelt to keep you from going under. I understand that, of course I do. It's just that . . . it can't be me. Not this time. I'm sorry.'

Jamming on her hat she fumbled with her gloves. He reached out, catching her sleeve, but she pulled her arm away. She tugged at the wrists of her gloves, interlacing her fingers to push them down over her hands.

'It's my fault,' she said. 'I don't know what I was . . . I mean, God, you're so young, barely more than a child. I should never have . . .' She pressed her gloved fingers against her mouth, her face stricken. Then she shook her head. 'I'm sorry.'

'Don't say that. And don't go. Please.'

'I have to. I'm sorry. This . . . it was a mistake.'

'Not for me.'

Phyllis squeezed her eyes tight shut. 'It doesn't work, you know. Using other people like morphine or aspirin or something. It might feel like it helps, for a bit anyway, but it doesn't. It only makes things worse.' She hesitated, her hand on the latch of the front door. 'I'm sorry,' she said again, very quietly.

The door closed behind her with a neat click. Oscar stood in the hall and let the emptiness fill him like a bottle.

In the kitchen doorway Mrs Mulley cleared her throat. 'Miss Melville won't be long, will she? Only I've supper almost done.'

'She's gone.'

'Gone? Gone out, you mean? Well, what time's she coming back?'

'She's not.'

Above his head the house creaked, the timbers stretching, and water gurgled in the pipes. If he

227

listened hard enough, he thought, perhaps he would hear his mother coming down the stairs.

Mrs Mulley sighed. 'I just wish she'd said, that's all,' she said, wiping her hands on her apron. 'I'd not've gone and done her a potato.'

CHAPTER 16

'I 'm impressed by your intrepidity, Miss Shackleton,' Mr Cardoza said as the waiter poured the champagne. 'I thought of sending a dog sleigh for you.'

'I wish you had. The train was Arctic.'

'I had to think of the dogs. The tundra is one thing, the New Forest quite another.'

'You're not fond of the New Forest?'

'Fond of it? I'm not at all convinced it exists. I don't believe in the country.'

Neither do I, Jessica thought. From the moment she had stepped out of the train into the smoky screech of Charing Cross Station she had felt thrillingly alive. The raw wind and the coal stink and the heaped-up banks of dirty snow had only exhilarated her further. She had walked along the Strand with a swing in her step, revelling in the honks of motor cars and omnibuses, the shriek of trains, the deafening clang of a speeding fire engine. Her mood had been so gay that she had even smiled at the blue-lipped soldier shivering outside the hotel with his wretched face and pinned-up sleeve, and dropped a sixpence into his tray of bootlaces. For all the luxurious hush of the Savoy Grill she could feel it still, the filthy relentless vitality of London coursing through her.

She did not say that to Mr Cardoza. 'You mustn't say that,' she admonished him. 'Every time you say that, a little field dies.'

Mr Cardoza grinned. It flattered and unnerved her, the way he looked at her, his amused eyes holding her gaze. Boys of her own age snatched looks, their eyes ducking away from yours as though they had stolen something and were afraid of being caught. Also they stared at your breasts. Mr Cardoza did not ogle her. He just looked at her steadily, a smile playing on his lips, as if he could see inside her head and what he saw amused and delighted him. When he lifted his glass, smiling at her over the rim of his glass, she was tinglingly aware of the surface of her skin, the waxy weight of lipstick on her lips, the movement of breath in the back of her throat.

'I don't believe in the country,' he said. 'I don't believe in the country.'

'Now look what you've done. That's the whole of the New Forest coated in tarmacadam.'

'And without even breaking a sweat. If only the Irish were so efficient. Give me a week and you'll live in London without even having to move.'

'You shouldn't make promises you can't keep.'

He laughed. 'You don't have a place in town?'

'We did. It's been sold.'

'A pity.'

'It's a disaster. Before the War, my mother would have lain down her life for that house. Now that she only cares for the Other Side, she wants to bury me alive in the country. When I die of boredom I shall haunt her relentlessly.'

'So you don't believe in the country either?'

'I want to live.'

'Amen to that.'

After the precipitate departure of the Yorkshire Melvilles, Lettice had written to Eleanor. She had thanked her for her kind hospitality and begged her to know that Evelyn had every sympathy for their pain and distress.

> If his words seemed monstrous it is only because the facts themselves are monsters. Evelyn is no more than their unhappy messenger. He has said again and again that he would not be in this position for all the world but, since what is done is done and cannot be undone, he must act as he has always acted, with honour. We can wish and wish but the truth remains the truth, however cruel and unjust, however bitter, as you, dear Eleanor, know only too well.

Eleanor read the letter in the morning room. When she had finished she tore it in half once and then again and dropped the fragments on the tea tray. It was easy enough to piece it back together.

Jessica posted her reply that afternoon. She said she was sure Lettice would understand that her mother was still too upset to write. Things had been very difficult for both of her parents in recent months and particularly for her mother, what with all the awful business with Mrs Waller. Without that comfort, without even the comfort of a grave to visit, it was not surprising that she had come to regard Ellinghurst as a kind of shrine.

However, Jessica could not help wondering whether, if Lettice were able to arrange an introduction to one of Sir Oliver Lodge's mediums in London, if Eleanor were once again able to make contact with Theo on the Other Side and with someone who could be trusted, it might help reconcile her just a little to a future without Ellinghurst. She did not want her mother to know she had written, of course, it should be Lettice's idea, that was the whole point, but if there was anything Lettice could do, it might help to repair a little of the damage. Certainly it could do no harm. The same afternoon, she telephoned a bookseller in Southampton and ordered a second-hand copy of *Raymond* for her mother.

It was easy enough to be first to the post. Her mother never came down before breakfast. She undid the string, careful not to tear the paper. The book was inscribed on the frontispiece: *With deepest sympathy, from Muriel.* Jessica took out the bookseller's bill and put it in the fire. Taking the sketch of the sleeping man that Guy Cockayne had sent her from her pocket, she slipped it between the pages. Then carefully she tied up the parcel again and put it back with the rest of her mother's letters.

She refused to feel uneasy. Eleanor had given her no choice. She had no intention of lying, not directly. And it was hardly even a lie, was it, to create an atmosphere, an environment for belief? It was like a wild flower meadow. A farmer could offer the land but what grew there was a matter for the wind and the bumblebees and the nature of the soil. Eleanor would believe what she chose to believe. It was not a crime, to give a grieving mother hope.

It turned out that Eleanor already had the book. Her copy was fat with turned-down corners, the spine worn. Some of the pages were coming loose. She brought it down to the morning room, holding one next to the other, then opened the newer copy.

'But I don't know a Muriel,' she said, frowning. She turned the pages but the sketch did not fall out. Jessica had to leave the room. She was afraid that if she stayed she would give herself away.

The next day the letter came from Cousin Lettice. Eleanor returned the letter and the book to her. It had never occurred to Jessica that Eleanor would presume the book was a gift from Lettice. For two days she was in despair. Then Lettice telephoned. She told Eleanor that she quite understood if she did not want an introduction to Sir

Oliver, but that she did not like to be accused of buttering her up. Whoever had sent the book to Eleanor it was not Lettice.

She returned the book. This time, when Eleanor opened it, she found Guy's sketch. After that it was easy. Sir Oliver and Lady Lodge invited Eleanor and Jessica to lunch with them at their flat near Sloane Square, after which they would meet anonymously with a Mrs Leonard at her home in Maida Vale. Mrs Leonard, Sir Oliver explained, had been engaged exclusively for three months the previous year by the Society for Psychical Research, during which time she had conducted sittings with seventy of their researchers. The resulting report had demonstrated solid and scientific evidence of spirit communication.

Jessica declined the luncheon invitation. She hoped that the Lodges would not think her rude, but, having given the matter consideration, she felt that Eleanor would find it easier to speak freely without her daughter present. Jessica would be happy enough entertaining herself at an art gallery or doing a little shopping. It meant she had to go to the sitting, of course. There was no way out of that. Without the sitting there was no reason to go to London and without going to London there was no possibility of lunch at the Savoy. Sometimes, when opportunities presented themselves, you had to seize them with both hands, however high the price.

★　★　★

Mr Cardoza leaned back in his chair, his fingers steepled against his mouth, and smiled at her. She smiled back. Following the maître d' to their table, she had looked at the sleek men like seals and at their elegant, slender companions with their cigarettes and their ruinously expensive dresses, and she had wished she had not come. She had felt clumsy and provincial and about fourteen years old, a schoolgirl taken out by her uncle as a treat. She did not feel like a schoolgirl now. In the glow of champagne and cut-glass chandeliers and Gerald Cardoza's amused attentiveness, she scattered light like a diamond.

'So let me guess,' he said. 'I'm a school friend. No. An old governess.'

Jessica's smile flickered. 'Do you have a hanky tucked in your sleeve and breath that smells of licorice?'

'Or am I Victoria and Albert? I've the gravitas for royalty, don't you think? And I'm always happy to eat for two.' His smile was droll, teasing. Jessica frowned and took a sip of champagne. She had always hated being teased. The champagne went down the wrong way. She tried not to cough.

'You're not suggesting I lied to my mother?' she said stiffly.

'Didn't you?'

'Of course not,' she lied.

'So she allowed you to lunch with me? Without a chaperone?'

'I'm not a child, Mr Cardoza. I do as I please.'

'Is that so?'

'It most certainly is.'

'I see.' He smiled. It was plain that he did not believe her. 'And what exactly do you please?'

'Apart from champagne?'

'Apart from that.'

'I want you to give me a job,' she said. She had surprised him. The realisation emboldened her. 'When we met at Mrs Carey's funeral you said your magazines for women were hopelessly old-fashioned. Maiden aunts, you called them. You said that it was time the old frumps were scared out of their stays.'

'Did I indeed?'

'You did.'

'And what has that to do with you?'

'I want to do some scaring.'

Mr Cardoza laughed. 'You're not serious?'

'Oh but I am. I am a very serious young woman.' She looked at him. 'You're not suggesting I might have had another reason for lunching with you, are you?'

'It never crossed my mind. So tell me, Miss Melville, what experience do you have of magazines?'

'None whatsoever.'

'How compelling.'

'I thought that was the whole point. A completely new approach.'

'I suspect it's not quite that simple.'

'I'm a quick learner. And I would be fearfully grateful.'

His eyes flickered.

'Truly,' she said softly, holding his gaze. 'I would hardly know how to thank you.' She expected him to say something. Instead, he went on looking at her as though she were a sculpture he was examining or an exhibit in a glass case. Then he picked up his drink and drained what was left.

'Unfortunately I'm only the proprietor,' he said. 'The editors choose their own people.'

'But you employ the editors.'

'In a manner of speaking, yes, but—'

'So you could encourage them, couldn't you? If you wanted to. It's just I can't help thinking it might be rather fun. If I were here in London, and not stuck in the back of beyond.'

She leaned in towards him, her chin resting on the flat of her hand. Mr Cardoza went on studying her. He did not smile. There were yellow flecks like crystals of coffee sugar in his brown eyes. Everything about him was fixed, distinct, the broad lines of his jaw and brow, the squares of his fingernails, the deep creases in his cheeks and between his eyebrows. She thought of the gawky, self-consciously chivalrous Hampshire boys who could be manipulated like chess pieces and she knew she was playing with fire. Her skin prickled as she waited for him to lean closer, to say something she might not know how to answer. Instead, to her confusion, he laughed.

'You know something, Miss Melville?' he said. 'You may have the body of a pedigree Persian but your instincts are pure alley cat.'

Still laughing, he raised a hand to the waiter. Jessica was abruptly aware of the hum and rattle of the restaurant around them, the proximity of the other tables. She had the uneasy feeling that she had made a fool of herself. She stared at the tablecloth as she waited for Mr Cardoza to ask the waiter for the bill, to make some excuse about an appointment he had to keep. Instead, he asked for more champagne.

'I'll be drunk,' she protested but he only smiled and held out a brimming saucer. She took it. Very lightly, almost by accident, he brushed the inside of her wrist with the back of his fingers.

'A toast,' he said. 'To the future.'

'To the future,' she echoed, taking a sip. Her nose prickled with the fizz of it, her skin too. 'Whatever it may hold.'

CHAPTER 17

She was late. As she hurried up the steps the frigid air clung to her cheeks, thick with her own exhalations and the sour tang of fog. Beside the front door there were several bells, each one labelled with a number. She rang them all, one after the other. She could hear the music of them, somewhere inside the house.

A man opened the door. He wore a battered tweed jacket and a vague frown, half hidden by his spectacles.

'Mrs Leonard?' she asked and he nodded and led her down a long, narrow hall that smelled of gravy and furniture polish and through a door at the end to a small parlour. Her mother was already there, standing at the window. The glass caught the reflection of her face, a pale oval floating like a moon against the grey sky. She did not turn around as Jessica unbuttoned her coat.

'You're late,' she said.

'Sorry.' Jessica sprawled in a chair. 'No taxis.'

It might have been true. Since the War, Mr Cardoza said, taxis had been scarcer even than decent chocolate. In the confined space of a taxi cab the lines of him were even more definite. He sat with his legs apart, his gloved hands resting on his thighs as they made their way around Trafalgar Square and up the Mall towards Buckingham Palace. Jessica crossed her legs away from him, her face turned towards the window, a warning not to touch that only heightened her awareness of the nearness of his upper arm, the light brush of the hem of his cashmere coat against the side of her knee. When the elderly engine coughed it jolted them both. Jessica held the strap above the door to stop herself from falling against him. She wondered what she would do if he tried to kiss her, and if he was wondering the same thing.

Then abruptly, at the corner of the park, he asked the cabbie to pull over.

'I'm afraid this is where I get out,' he said. 'I shall be in touch. About the job.'

'I'll look forward to it.'

He smiled at her. Then, taking off his hat, he leaned forward and kissed her very lightly at the corner of her mouth. It was the kind of kiss an uncle might give his niece, yet somehow it was not that kind of kiss at all. His chin was soft and sharp at the same time.

'My God, but you are lovely,' he murmured, his mouth close to hers.

'Am I?'

'Lovely enough to make a fool of a wise man.' She thought he might kiss her again. Instead, he settled his hat on his head and got out of the cab.

He leaned down, one hand on the open door. '*À bientôt*, Miss Clematis.'

'*À bientôt*, sir. I should call you sir, shouldn't I, if I'm going to work for you?'

'I'd prefer Your Excellency. But Gerald will do.'

'Isn't it a little soon for that?'

'Do you think so?' The way he looked at her made her flush. Drawing a note from his wallet he gave it to the cabbie. 'Warrington Avenue. And take care of her. Goodbye, Miss Jessica Melville.'

'Goodbye, Ambassador.'

As the taxi coughed and leaped away from the kerb Jessica turned, watching him through the back window until the cab lurched, picking up speed, and he was gone, lost between the dappled trunks of the plane trees.

Mrs Leonard did not look like a medium. She looked like somebody's aunt. She wore a silk blouse with a paisley shawl, and sensible low-heeled shoes. Her hair was neatly pinned. She asked them if they wished to introduce themselves or if they preferred to remain anonymous. Her accent was educated but she did not pinch out the words in shiny little beads from the front of her mouth like other women of her class. Instead they flowed from her steadily, gently, like a slow-moving river. She asked if they would like some tea.

'No tea,' Eleanor said, clutching her hands in her lap like a grenade.

'Are you sure?' Mrs Leonard said to Jessica. 'It's no trouble.'

'I'm quite all right, thank you,' Jessica said, though actually now she thought about it she did rather want some tea. The champagne from lunch was starting to give her a headache. She wondered if Mrs Leonard was psychic as well as sensitive or if she could just smell the wine on her breath.

Mrs Leonard showed them to a small walnut table in a corner of the room and drew the curtains, putting on a dim lamp that softened the edges of the furniture and thickened the air to a yellowish soup. She explained that, once the sitting had begun, she would allow herself to pass under the control of her spirit guide. Feda, she said, was a distant ancestor of hers, the Hindu wife of her great-great-grandfather who had died in childbirth when she was only thirteen years old. Feda was not the girl's real name but a shortening of it, derived by Mrs Leonard from the letters brought forward when Feda had first started to come through. Since then Feda had always referred to herself by that name.

While Mrs Leonard was in trance, it would be Feda's voice that they heard. Mrs Leonard herself would know nothing of the words spoken through her, either during the sitting or afterwards. It was the responsibility of the sitter to speak directly to Feda and through her to the spirits for whom she was communicating. It was easiest, Mrs Leonard said, to imagine it as a meeting between friends,

242

the friends who had gone over and the friends on this side. When she asked if they had ever sat before Eleanor did not answer. In the yellow light her face looked sallow, the shadows beneath her eyes as dark as bruises.

'Trust in Feda,' Mrs Leonard said gently. 'With her agency we shall reach those you seek on the Other Side. In the Spirit World there exist what I can only describe as Enquiry Bureaux, where those who are anxious to send messages to their loved ones on earth make contact with those spirits who have grown proficient at coming through. Occasionally these are people they, or you, knew when they lived in this world. Mostly they are strangers. Do not be afraid. They wish you no harm. They come through because they want to help you.' She smiled at Eleanor, then turned to Jessica. 'You are not afraid, I think. But you are uncertain. You have doubts.'

'With respect, a great many people have doubts about what you do.'

'Jessica! Mrs Leonard, I apologise, my daughter—'

'Your daughter is right. My sitters are often doubtful. They have many questions and I am glad of it. Scepticism provokes productive investigation, provided of course that the sitter maintains an open mind and a sincerity of purpose. I would ask you only to remember that the seance, like the scientific laboratory, has conditions that must be respected. Disruptive conduct is not only unhelpful, it can be very dangerous. Ask as many questions

243

as you need but do so, I beg you, with courtesy and respect. Feda wishes only to help you. She will do her best to seek for you whatever proofs you require. Is there anything else you would like to ask me?' The intensity of her gaze made Jessica squirm. She shook her head.

'Very well, then. Shall we begin?' Mrs Leonard bent her head, putting her hands together. 'Let us pray.'

Jessica pretended to close her eyes, watching the medium through the blur of her eyelashes. As she intoned the words in her clear quiet voice a change came over Mrs Leonard's face, the skin slackening over the bones. Eleanor's face was clenched with concentration, her eyes squeezed tight as a child's.

'Amen.'

There was a silence. Then a faint hum began to vibrate in Mrs Leonard's throat. Her lips were slightly parted, her head tipped back. She was quite still and yet she quivered with sound, like a strummed guitar string. Very slowly her head began to move from side to side, her mouth making the shapes of words. She did not speak. Her mouth began to move faster until, throwing back her head, she raised herself almost out of her seat, her hands stretched into stars.

Suddenly she froze, her mouth open, inhaling a long shuddering breath. She held the breath a long time before releasing it but, as she exhaled, all the tension seemed to drain from her body. Her shoulders loosened and her fingers curled and, as she settled back into her chair, the frown on her face gave way to blankness, and then to a childish grimace.

'You know, it isn't fair to push in, not like that. You have to wait your turn.'

The voice was high, a child's voice. There was petulance in it but laughter too. There was a whispering, as though the child were talking to someone just out of sight.

'I have to!' the child protested. And then in a different voice, the singsong voice of children in schoolrooms, she said, 'Good afternoon, ladies.'

No one spoke. Then Eleanor leaned forward. 'Is that you, Feda?'

'Yes, Feda. Feda is here.' Again there was whispering. 'Feda can't see your face. Stop laughing.'

'Is there . . . is there someone with you, Feda?'

'Yes. Raymond is here. The girl too.'

So that was her trick, Jessica thought. To start with someone half-familiar and then reel out the line. She shook her head, impatient with the shiver at the back of her neck.

'The girl?' Eleanor asked.

'Raymond's sister. With the long yellow hair. She has been here a long time, much longer than Raymond. Raymond takes care of her now.'

'Does Raymond have a message for us?'

The room was warm and very airless. The headache tightened around Jessica's temples. She could hardly bear it, the pitifulness of Eleanor's hope, her credulity. She wanted to scream, to turn on

245

all the lights, to shake Mrs Leonard awake and keep on shaking her until her teeth rattled. Think of London, she told herself. Think of nightclubs and champagne and driving motor cars and falling in love. Instead she thought of Mr Cardoza, the touch of his lips at the corner of her mouth. The uneasiness in her stomach made her feel faintly sick.

'There is someone else here,' Feda said. 'I can't see him well; he is not as solid as Raymond. I think he has not been over long, or not yet learned to build himself. It is not easy, Feda knows, it takes time. But he is very eager. He won't wait, though I tell him he must.' She giggled. 'Don't joke, this is serious.'

'Who is with you, Feda?' Eleanor whispered.

'A young man. Feda doesn't think she has seen him here before. But then Feda sees so many people. He is waving his arms. He is saying something but Feda can't hear. Stop it!'

'My darling, is that you? Oh, Feda, please, I beg you. Tell me who it is.'

'He is trying to build up the letter but it is hard for him. He shows me N or M, he cannot keep it straight. Or perhaps it is W? What do you mean, can I read? If you are mean to me I shan't help you, so there.'

'M,' Eleanor breathed. 'M for Melville. Oh, Feda, tell me what he looks like.'

'He is tall, not too tall, though. Brown hair. Well-built, not heavy or thick-set but strong. He has

246

brown eyebrows too and a straight nose, a good-sized mouth, not full but not thin either, a nice mouth. There are dents on the sides of it, from laughing. His face is oval. His hair falls over his eyes but he pushes it away with his fingers.' Again she giggled. 'Cut it, then, if it provokes you so.'

It was a lucky guess, Jessica was certain, but she could not help thinking of Theo then, the impatient way he had of jabbing at his hair.

'It was here.' Blindly the medium pressed the flats of her hands against her chest, then moved them down towards her stomach. 'Or here? Sudden, he says it was very sudden. Stop it, stay still – I can't see his eyes, he keeps closing them. He's teasing me.'

Eleanor was weeping silently, the tears rolling down her cheeks.

'He is still not built up but Feda feels like she knew him. From before. He must have been waiting here for you. He cannot say how long, time slips here, it is hard to count. He is laughing with Raymond, both of them laughing. He likes to laugh.'

'Theo, darling, it's you, isn't it?'

The medium clapped her hands together in delight. 'He says right first time.' Then she yelped, wriggling in her seat. 'Theo is tickling Feda. He's laughing. And crying a little too. You are! He says he can't believe he has come through at last. He tried, he says he tried to reach you but he never had the strength.'

'My darling, darling boy—' Eleanor's voice cracked.

'Theo says don't cry. He is mended now. Nearly as good as new.'

'And happy? Are you happy, my darling?'

'He is nodding. He says when he first waked up he was sad, it was dark and cold and there were so many lost boys, so much pain and wretchedness, and he was afraid, but now it isn't dark, it is summer every day and he is happy. He misses you terribly but they are all together, the lost boys. Another family. And they are always laughing.'

'Tell me what it's like, where you are.'

'He says he wishes you could see it. He says it's like home, roses, huge roses and wood pigeons calling and green meadows where the grass is so long you can lie down without anyone seeing you. They play football and swim in the river. Like being a child again. Except for the brandy. Now he's teasing Feda, he says she's not allowed, but Feda doesn't care, so there. Feda thinks brandy is horrid.'

So did Theo, Jessica thought. And Theo played cricket.

'He says he has been trying to come through by himself. But though he tries and tries he flounders.' She stumbled on the word and frowned. 'What's "flounders"? I thought it was fish!' There was some whispering and then she gave a shriek. 'Oh! Theo has a dog, a big dog, brown, too big for Feda. It's jumping up, Feda doesn't like it. But Theo says not to be afraid. He says it's kind. Something P, Feda can't quite catch it. Patch? Pug? Is it a pug dog?'

'Jim Pugh's dog?' Eleanor pressed her knuckles against her mouth. 'You've found it? Oh darling, I'm so glad. Remember how you loved that wretched thing?'

'He didn't!' Jessica cried. She could not help herself. 'He never liked it. And anyway it wasn't brown. It was white.'

Feda let out a peal of laughter. 'Should Feda say so? Out loud? Theo says he knew it, he knew you would be like this. He's laughing. A party? A party when you were small, too small maybe to remember, but Theo remembers. Poor conjuror, he says. Like the Spanish Inqui – not fair, too difficult for Feda.'

Jessica frowned but she did remember. A Christmas when she was four or five, a magician hired to entertain the children. Handkerchiefs all tied together and a bouquet of paper flowers and a real live rabbit in a top hat. She had held the hat upside down, feeling inside its lining for the trick.

'He says this isn't magic, not this time. He says to ask him something.'

'Like what?'

'Anything. Something only he knows.'

Jessica stared at the table. Then she looked up. 'Who am I?'

There was more whispering, a burst of childish laughter. 'Theo is teasing Feda. He doesn't give it clearly. He is bringing a letter, Feda can't make it out. Is it M? Now he has more. He is spelling something out. Mess? Feda's making a mess? He is laughing and Raymond too, but it isn't funny. Stop it or I won't try again. Be serious. So not M? Stop laughing. Mess is not a name. Jessica. You're Jessica.'

Jessica closed her eyes. Her hands were shaking.

'Messica,' Eleanor breathed. 'Miss Messica Jelville.'

'He is fading,' Feda said. 'There is a noise, a rushing noise, it is like the air going out of Feda, like there is a hole through my stomach. It is not Theo's fault, he did not know he did it. Feda is giddy. Like a merry-go-round.'

The medium whimpered, pressing her hands to her head. Then, very quietly she folded her hands in her lap and bowed her head.

Eleanor was weeping. Beside her Mrs Leonard took several slow deep breaths, in and out. Jessica bit her lip, trying to steady the thumping of her heart. The silence went on a long time. Then Mrs Leonard opened her eyes.

'He came?' she asked Eleanor softly.

Eleanor nodded, smiling over her handkerchief.

'He was strong enough to come through plainly?'

'As though he were in the room.'

Mrs Leonard nodded. 'I'm glad. And you?' she asked Jessica. 'Did you find the answers you sought?'

Jessica shrugged. She wanted to get out of that airless room, out into the street where the raw wind smelled of coal and blew away the past that clung to her like cobwebs. She waited in silence as Mrs Leonard turned on the lights and her mother made an appointment for another sitting the next week. She knew she should be glad. Mrs Leonard was her golden goose, the Trojan horse from whose belly she might besiege London and lay it waste. But all she could think of was Messica. By her sides her fingers stretched and curled, sifting the air for the dust of him.

When Mrs Leonard opened the parlour door a creamy ball of fluff bounded in. She picked it up. It snuffled happily in her arms, its tongue lolling like a pink petal.

'This is Ching,' she said. 'She is always excitable with new sitters. So many strangers in the house at once, of course. And here is my husband with your coats and hats. Thank you, my dear.'

Outside it had grown dark. The street was clogged with fog, curls of yellow-grey like wisps of sheep's wool snagged around the street lamps. Jessica crossed her arms tightly across her stomach, hugging herself close. Beneath her fur hat her mother's eyes shone.

'Oh, Jessica,' she sighed, squeezing Jessica's arm. 'Do you see now? How death does not part us? He was there with us, just the same as ever.'

Her breath made ghosts in the air. Jessica looked away. 'Was he?'

'How can you even doubt it? The initial M for Melville, Jim Pugh's dog, the party with the magician. Messica Jelville. Who knows of that but us?'

Jessica did not answer.

'For God's sake, what else must he do?' Eleanor cried. 'What manner of hoops must he jump through before you accept that he's still with us? That he is not gone?'

Jessica closed her eyes. She could feel the press of it at the back of her throat, the sharp point of all the terror and grief she had swallowed and never acknowledged, not just for Theo but for them all, all those thousands and thousands of laughing young men who had never come back. *So many lost boys.* What good did it do, to think about them now? The War was over. The guns were silent. The battlefields swarmed with armies of Chinese coolies, paid to salvage what remained of Flanders from the mud and bones. Already, they said, the flowers were beginning to come back. Why then would anyone want to make themselves remember? Was it not unbearable enough to lose them once, without losing them again by appointment every Thursday afternoon?

The fog tasted of sulphur and rusted metal. She thought of Mr Cardoza and of the other soft-palmed, soft-bellied old men in the Savoy Grill stroking the stems of their champagne saucers with their fat fingers, fingers that had never held a gun, fingers that would beckon and prod and paddle the flesh of girls who should have been kissing their slaughtered sons, and she wanted more than anything to be in Hampshire where the air was

252

clear and smelled of gorse and lichen and the salt
lick of the sea.

What was gone was gone. There was no getting it
back, however hard you wished.

CHAPTER 18

Scientific experiments did not always deliver the expected results. This, Mr Beckers said, was why experiment and not theory was the engine of science. The facts were the facts, whether you could explain them or not. In 1911 Ernest Rutherford had aimed a beam of high-speed radium alpha particles at a sheet of thin gold foil. If atoms were diffuse spheres of electrical charge then most of the alpha particles should have passed straight through the foil; a few might have been slightly deflected. Instead, some of the alpha particles ricocheted straight back. It was, Rutherford was later to remark, like firing a 15-inch shell at a piece of tissue paper and having it bounce back and hit you. Rutherford realised that the atoms in the gold foil contained a tiny but very powerful concentration of positive charge that repelled the positively charged alpha particles.

He had proved the nuclear structure of the atom.

Oscar thought about Rutherford's experiment a great deal in the weeks after his mother's funeral. He had known when she died that she was gone for ever. There was no God and no aether, no ectoplasm or survival, despite the sensational stories in the popular newspapers, the first-person accounts of levitations and manifestations and conversations with the dead, the spirit photographs and the scientific proofs. The dead were not gathered on the Other Side, transmitting their messages of love and reassurance like radio waves for mediums to receive. At Rhyl, while they waited to be demobbed, he and several of the other officers from the Royal Engineers had occupied themselves with constructing primitive crystal sets on which they picked up a ghostly blend of voices, the dots and dashes of Morse code, and the crackling hum of static. Sometimes there were shrieks. It seemed like a kind of magic, a door opening to worlds concealed behind worlds, except that it was not. It was quite simple, once you got the hang of it. Electronic transmitters converted sound waves into electromagnetic waves and the crystal set converted them back into sound. It was beautiful and fascinating but it was not magic. There was no transmitter for the dead. The dead were gone.

And yet his mother was not gone. She slipped in under the doors, through the cracks in the window sashes. Sometimes in the evenings, sitting by the parlour fire, he heard the click of her key in the lock of the front door, the rustle of her skirts as she stepped into the hall, bringing with her a faint eddy of coal dust and cold pavement. He heard her voice in the garden from an upstairs window, the echo of her laughter as he walked down the kitchen passage, the clatter of her feet on the stairs while he shaved. Once, returning to the house, he even heard her playing the piano. The music stopped as he opened the door. He heard the squeak of the old piano stool, the click of the lid closing. But when he opened the door to the back parlour the room was empty, the air flat and undisturbed, the piano stool where he had left it, pushed up against the bookshelf. She wasn't there. And still she was, often.

He supposed he was glad, sort of. He wondered how long she would stay.

The house was not his. When Oscar said there must be some mistake the solicitor frowned unhappily and peered at his papers.

'No mistake,' he said. 'The house is owned by a Mr – where is it? – a Mr Alfred Phillips. You have until June to vacate the premises. Your mother didn't . . . goodness. I had rather assumed . . . no, well. I'm awfully sorry.'

A solicitous solicitor, Oscar thought numbly. His mother would have liked that. His name was Pettigrew. Mr Pettigrew explained that the rent had been met while his mother was alive by the earnings from an insurance policy that provided for her in the event of her husband's death. The policy had also yielded a small monthly stipend, payable until his mother's death.

'So that's it?' Oscar said. 'There's nothing?'

'Nothing? Heavens, no.' Mr Pettigrew was meticulous, matter-of-fact. Once all disbursements had been met his mother's assets comprised an account at the bank with a credit balance of eighteen pounds, nine shillings and four pence, along with her effects. Oscar inherited the contents of the house to include his mother's jewellery, the two gold poesy rings and her ruby earrings and the diamond brooch in the shape of a feather. In addition there was a second bank account, taken out by his mother but held in Oscar's name. The credit balance of that account was twelve hundred pounds.

'The funds are placed in a trust to allow you to take up your place at Cambridge,' Mr Pettigrew said. 'Four hundred a year would be sufficient, I understand, if not exactly generous. As the trust's executor, I am charged with the management of the fund. I recommend a monthly allowance. It is easy with a capital sum to convince oneself one is richer than one is.'

Oscar stared at Mr Pettigrew. Twelve hundred pounds was a small fortune.

'She said there was money for the University,' he said, hardly able to take it in, but Mr Pettigrew only smiled vaguely and put the file of papers on his desk. An envelope with Oscar's name typed on it in capital letters was clipped to the cardboard cover. Oscar wondered what was in it and why Mr Pettigrew did not give it to him. Perhaps it was his bill. He wondered how much of the twelve hundred pounds would go to Mr Pettigrew. Even solicitous solicitors did not work for nothing.

Mr Pettigrew closed the folder. 'I think that's everything. Unless you have any questions?'

Oscar shook his head.

'My involvement will continue until the funds of the trust are fully disbursed, by which time you will be twenty-one and at liberty to direct your own affairs. I shall look forward to meeting you again then. Of course, if you should need anything in the meantime . . .'

'That's it?'

'I think so.'

'But what am I supposed to do with everything?'

'I don't quite follow you.'

'The books. The plates. The furniture. We have a piano. What am I supposed to do with the piano?'

Mr Pettigrew looked stricken. 'I can arrange for someone to come. A valuer. If you'd like. Or there's storage, of course. Small items of value such as your mother's jewellery can always be kept here, in our safe, if you prefer.' When Oscar did not answer he patted the folder with both hands. 'No, well, no need to decide now. Just let us know.'

Oscar shook the solicitor's hand dazedly and went home. It was silent when he walked in and very cold. He lit a fire. Then he sat down. He could not think what else to do. It was March. The next time anyone expected him anywhere was October.

*   *   *

Phyllis sent him a postcard. The picture was a photograph of the British Museum, its austere courtyards deserted. On the back she wrote that she was leaving for Egypt to visit the excavations at the Valley of the Kings. She did not say who she was going with or when she would be coming back. She hoped he was well. There was no room on the postcard to say anything else. She signed it *P*. Oscar tucked the postcard into the frame of the mirror on his chest of drawers, writing side out. Whenever he brushed his hair or looked for a pair of socks he touched the P with his finger.

Time passed and the P grew smudged. The days smudged together too. Oscar knew he should be planning, packing tea chests. Instead, he lay on his bed. Spring was coming and the pale sun stretched its long fingers through the windows and traced patterns of lace on the dirty glass. Sometimes he heard his mother in the kitchen, rattling the drawers. He walked to the end of the street and bought bread and milk and cheese and thought of Phyllis kneeling in a desert as old as time, her eyes screwed up against the harsh African sun, her fingers with their bitten nails sifting the hot dust for fragments of the past.

He should not have kissed her. He knew that. A kiss like that was not the start of anything. It was a place to hide. He could remember almost nothing of that day, except how much he had wanted to kiss her and keep kissing until the world was no wider than the space between their faces, the circle of her arms. Afterwards when he thought of kissing her he could not summon it, only the gleam of the fire on her hair, the cup of her hands around her whisky glass. It did not turn his insides upside down. It held them steady.

He thought about going away. He wished he knew where he wanted to go. In a bookshop near Waterloo he purchased a second-hand guide to the Alps. He looked at the pictures of mountains and edelweiss and placid-faced cows and he thought how beautiful they were and how little they had to do with him.

Instead, he went to the library. He had read all the books they had on physics so he read the newspapers instead. There was unrest in Egypt. The Egyptian people wanted independence, an end to the British protectorate that had been supposed to last only the duration of the War. They staged a campaign of civil disobedience. The British exiled the leaders of the movement and ruthlessly suppressed their demonstrations. British soldiers patrolled the cities. Thousands of Egyptians were killed, but the violence only fanned the flames of nationalism. There were strikes and riots, attacks on railway lines, on colonial buildings, on ordinary British citizens. The newspapers talked of revolution.

Oscar took the postcard out of the frame of his mirror. He put it in his pocket. He thought perhaps it might be safer there. He thought of Phyllis in the Tiled Room with her chin on her knees, by the fire with her whisky, in the hall with her head against his chest, and he thought that if anything happened to her he would not be able to bear it, not because of the kiss which had not been his to take, but because she was kind and clever and finally going to University, which was what she had always wanted, and because when they talked it was not like a chess game but like one of Ernest Rutherford's experiments, simple and familiar and absorbing and utterly unexpected all at the same time.

He did not know if she was caught up in the troubles. He did not know if she was hurt or if she had come home. The not knowing itched at him like lice. He thought of writing to Jessica but could think of no pretext for a letter. Instead, he wrote to Sir Aubrey.

> I wanted to thank you. For as long as I live I shall never forget the extraordinary kindness you and your family have shown to my mother and to me. Without you this time would mark only an end. Instead, it is also a beginning. I take up my place at Trinity in October and hope one day that somehow I shall be able to repay you for all you have done. I think often of my many happy times at Ellinghurst and should be glad of news of the family if you have time to write.
> Affectionately, Oscar
> P.S. I hope you like the photograph.

The photograph he chose was one he had taken on his last visit. He had asked Jim Pugh to stop on the curve in the lane just as the castle came into view. It was not the prospect in all the paintings, the broad sweep of lawn rolled out in front of the castle like a carpet. From the lane the swollen summer trees obscured all but the tallest towers, encircled in the crook of the high north wall. Oscar had knelt in the verge, tilting the camera up so that the slanting evening sun tangled in the thickets of feathery grass. In the photograph it looked like the house was hidden deep in the forest, like an enchanted castle in a fairy story. Above the towers the mackerel sky was streaked with light.

He received a reply two days later. It ran to several pages, the first two outlining in detail Sir Aubrey's plans for extending the castle's fortifications, in particular the construction of an immense castellated wall from the south of the house almost to the stables. The new drive would require motor cars to pass through a new barbican gateway to the north and on around to the gatehouse.

> The wonderful photograph you sent me has spurred my resolve. How is it that so many fail to see what you capture so delightfully, that the house is not one house but many, each angle and viewpoint and fall of light offering a fresh pleasure? This way visitors will make almost a full circle of the house

before they arrive. A composition so artfully conceived must be appreciated in the round.

It was not until the final paragraph of the letter that Sir Aubrey mentioned the family.

> Phyllis is presently in Luxor, Thebes as was, before beginning her studies in archaeology at London University. The news from Egypt is alarming but she assures us she is a good distance from the troubles and quite safe. I would rather she were safe here in Hampshire but it would seem that the days when a daughter heeded her father are long gone. As for Jessica, she has her heart set on a job in London as assistant to the editor of a magazine which she claims will lead to great things. An archaeologist and a magazine journalist. It is hardly what one had imagined but then what is, I suppose, any more?

A fortnight later Oscar read in *The Times* of the spread of Egyptian unrest to the countryside, the bloody violence and burning of villages that had resulted in hundreds of Egyptians dead. Again he wrote to Sir Aubrey. He expressed interest in the new fortifications, in the progress of Sir Aubrey's book. He asked if Jessica was in London and if he might call on her. He enclosed another photograph, taken beneath the gatehouse arch one afternoon when he sought shelter from a thunderstorm. The ribs of the vaulted arch were reflected in the puddles and the sky was almost black. As he slid the photograph into the envelope he thought of the fair he had once gone to with his mother, where a gypsy woman in a ruffled dress had called out to passers-by to cross her hand with silver in exchange for their fortune.

The newspapers are full of Egypt, he wrote. *I do hope Phyllis remains unaffected by the troubles.*

When Sir Aubrey replied he spent several pages detailing the conversations he had had with architects, the difficulties of finding skilled stonemasons. He included several sketches made in cross section. It was not until the penultimate paragraph that he mentioned Phyllis. *The work sounds hard and hot and frightfully tedious but it is plain that it fascinates her. She is very busy.*

Oscar's days by contrast were desultory. He drifted through the London streets as the spring weather gave way to gales, wild squalls that whipped rain into needles and shrieked in the chimney pots. On the Common the wind ripped the branches from the trees, their new leaves curled tight like tiny green fists. In the library Oscar read books about the Valley of the Kings, the magnificent decorated tombs of the pharaohs, filled with the treasures they would need in the afterlife, and the strange discovery just before the War of a humbler sepulchre containing the bodies of sixty soldiers, killed in a fierce battle four thousand years before. At home, one evening, he sat alone in the parlour and pretended to tell his mother about what he had read but talking out loud only made him feel foolish and he kept forgetting what it was he meant to say. He muddled the dates and the dynasties, his tongue stumbling over the unfamiliar names. He told the empty room that it would have to read the book for itself. It was not his story to tell.

Then one windy April morning, turning the pages of the newspaper, Oscar's eye was caught by an article near the bottom of the page. Ernest Rutherford, the newly appointed Cavendish Professor of Physics at Cambridge University, was resisting attempts by the government to confiscate his supply of radium, on loan from the Vienna Academy of Sciences, as enemy property.

The jolt was like an electrical shock. He felt it in the soles of his feet, in the roots of his hair. It was forbidden to deface the newspapers in the library but he tore out the article anyway and put it in his pocket. All that day as he walked, he touched the scrap of newsprint in his pocket and the electricity surged and crackled under his skin. At home in Clapham he looked around him at the dirty windows and the piles of dirty cups and the clothes discarded on the floor and he wondered if they were his things or if the confusion had been made by someone else. He felt as though he had been asleep for a long time.

That evening he wrote to E. Willis, his college tutor at Trinity, asking if he might be permitted to matriculate not in October as planned but in two weeks, at the start of the Summer Term. He said that he knew that there were rules but that he was not sure he could wait any longer, that he had waited much too long already.

Upstairs the wind whistled in the chimney. It sounded like somebody laughing. He thought of taking the letter to Cambridge in person, of going to Liverpool Street Station and getting on a train and refusing to leave until they agreed to let him start, but he thought they might think he had gone mad. There was something of madness in him. He hugged it to him, not wanting to let it go. When he posted the letter it made a faint clang as it fell, like a bell ringing.

It was April but that night it snowed. The house was filled with a flat white light, with a silence dense as cotton wool. In the kitchen the drawers were undisturbed, the spoons lying quietly in their stacked embrace. The piano was dumb. There was no dark head resting against the wing of the Chesterfield, no humming or laughter or patter of footsteps on the stairs. He opened the wardrobe in the hall, buried his face in the soft folds of her coat with its astrakhan collar. The coat still smelled of her, faintly, but she was not there.

Mr Willis wrote back from Cambridge. He was sorry but there was no question of a place for Oscar until the beginning of the Michaelmas Term. He enclosed a reading list, hoped Oscar would use the intervening time wisely, and looked forward to seeing him in October.

Oscar sold his mother's coat. He sold the rabbit fur stole and the peacock scarf. He sold the piano to Miss Nicholson who lived around the corner with her brother, and his mother's brass bedstead to a man with a cart. The things he could not sell he gave away. At night he lay in bed and stared at the ceiling. The little black men did not come. There was sadness in it, but there was stillness too, and peace.

When all the drawers and the cupboards were empty, and the books nearly all in boxes, he made enquiries about boarding houses in Cambridge. There were several rooms available, including an inexpensive attic in a house on Chesterton Road which offered, the landlady said, pleasant views over the town. The landlady's name was Mrs Piggott. Oscar wrote to confirm that he would take the room with immediate effect.

He took the letter to the post box at the end of the street. When he got home, he lit a fire in the back parlour and settled himself in his armchair, a cup of tea on the floor by his feet. There was a pile of books on the fender stool. He leaned down and took one off the top. It was one of his mother's, Emily Dickinson's *Poems*. Oscar thought of the poem his mother had asked for again and again when she was ill:

> *Hope is the thing with feathers*
> *That perches in the soul,*
> *And sings the tune – without the words,*
> *And never stops at all.*

The book had been opened so often on that page it fell open when he held it. He put the letters from Cambridge inside and, closing it, put the book on the arm of his chair. The book was small and the corners of the letters stuck out. From time to time as he sipped his tea, he touched the corners of the letters very gently with the pad of his thumb. From time to time too, he looked up over at the Chesterfield and smiled, so that she would know he was thinking about her, that he had not forgotten that she was there, even when she was gone.

CHAPTER 19

The flat was in an imposing mansion block in Maida Vale, five storeys of red brick adorned at its eastern end by a pair of turrets, each topped with a pale green cupola. The turrets made Jessica think of home. The flats were very respectable, the agent said, and popular with widows as well as businessmen who had to be in London during the week. The one he showed them had three bedrooms and two rooms the agent insisted on calling receptions. He pointed out the liveried porters, the landscaped gardens, the latest plumbing and electrical amenities, including electric bells and a tradesman's lift. He stressed the advantages of an accommodation that was less than ten years old, that might conveniently be managed with only one servant.

Jessica walked with Eleanor to the end of Elgin Avenue. Mrs Leonard's street was no more than a short walk away. Perhaps in time Mrs Leonard would allow Eleanor to sit more frequently. It would be an advantage to be close by, just in case. In London too Eleanor could continue her acquaintance with Sir Oliver Lodge and his wife, perhaps with other like-minded people. When Eleanor demurred, Jessica urged her to think of the meetings she could attend, the lectures on spiritualism put on by the Society for Psychical Research. Jessica had done her own research and she did not mean to give up. The flat cost one hundred pounds a year, with an additional forty pounds for a maid. Jessica's salary as assistant to the editor of *Woman's Friend* was twenty-five shillings a week.

Twenty-five shillings turned out to be a quite extraordinarily small amount of money. Even a room in a ghastly hostel like Phyllis's cost the best part of twenty shillings a week once breakfast and dinner were included, and heaven only knew what they would be like. Baths were threepence extra. By the time she had paid for lunches and bus fares all the money would be gone, and that was before she had bought stockings or soap or lipstick or had her laundry done. There was her dress allowance on top, of course, but it was still not nearly enough.

Her first thought had been to plead with Gerald for an increase in salary. Five pounds a week might just do it, she thought. Since that first time at the Savoy they had had lunch together on two more occasions. She told her mother she was attending job interviews, which she almost was, she supposed. When he told her about the job he presented her with a box, beautifully wrapped in ribbon. Inside was a gold wristwatch. He said that the editor at

Woman's Friend was a stickler for timekeeping. Afterwards they walked together down to the river and in the deserted Embankment gardens she had let him kiss her. Close up his face was loose on the bone, the thin skin punctured with thousands of tiny black dots where he had shaved, and beneath the expensive spice of his cologne she could smell, very faintly, the stale mouse-nest whiff of old people. She was glad it was expected that you closed your eyes. Desire slackened a man's features, caused his eyes to hood, his mouth to soften. When it was Rudolph Valentino in the flickers, it gave you the goose bumps. Gerald just looked drunk.

She kissed him back. It was polite, like writing thank-you letters. She did not mention her pay. As things stood, it was Gerald who petitioned, who sought her favour. She did not ask for the outlandishly expensive lunches, the champagne, the presents in their beribboned boxes. If he chose to give them she owed him nothing in return, or nothing more than a kiss or two. There was something a good deal more businesslike about the negotiation of a salary. Payment in exchange for services. He would expect more than a kiss for five pounds a week.

Jessica could not live in London alone. The flat had many advantages, Eleanor conceded, but Jessica was only nineteen, too young to live without the care of an adult. She required a chaperone, and

Eleanor herself would not be there often enough to provide such care. Jessica pleaded with her but her mother was implacable. A maid–cook was in no way an adequate substitute.

Jessica stormed out of the house in a fury of rage and self-pity. She stamped down the drive and out onto the lane. She walked for a long time, her rage cooling to despondency. All her carefully laid plans had come to naught. She was stuck in Hampshire for ever. She would grow old and ugly and so desperate that she would be forced to marry the unspeakable Mervyn who would write her excruciating limericks and kiss her with his dead-fish lips. Or worse, the unspeakable Mervyn would marry one of the ghastly girls who giggled every time he went near them at parties, and Father would die, and she would be forced to become Cousin Lettice's companion or governess to the Yorkshire Melville boys, like Jane Eyre only without Mr Rochester. She thought wildly of writing to Guy Cockayne, of begging him to rescue her for Theo's sake. She had not heard from him for months, not since the end of the War, but she supposed his regiment would have a forwarding address.

She was going mad. Her parents were sending her mad. Father would die and she would not be Jane Eyre at all but Bertha, the crazy cousin however many times removed, raging in the attic as around her the rain came through the roof, drip-drip-drip into the tin buckets like a ticking clock. At the turning to the village she passed Mrs Briggs from the bakery, walking briskly in the other direction. Jessica hardly recognised her without her apron on. She wore a coat with something dead on the collar and a bonnet that would not have looked out of place in one of Grandfather Melville's photographs.

'Off to see your old Nanny, are you?' Mrs Briggs said cheerfully. 'She will be glad to see you.'

Jessica stared at Mrs Briggs. Nanny. She could not think why she had not thought of it before.

'Nanny,' she said delightedly. 'That's it. I'm going to see Nanny.'

Nanny hated London. She hated flats. She said that there was a reason that the better class of servant refused to work in them, that flats harboured infectious diseases, that they were a French invention and no one should have to live like the French. It was Nanny's firm belief that the French were dirty, that they never bathed but only dabbed at themselves with the corner of a wet towel. She said that only the French would imagine it respectable to have bedrooms on the same floor as the drawing room. But when Jessica cried and threw her arms around Nanny and said that it was all that she wanted in the whole wide world and that it would not be for long, only a year perhaps, and what would Nanny do with none of them at home anyway and no one to visit her, and that if she would only agree to come it would make Jessica the happiest girl in the whole wide world, and

273

besides Jessica would come home to Ellinghurst every weekend and Nanny could come too or she could visit her niece, she had a niece in Essex, didn't she, or was it Middlesex, the one with the husband who owned a draper's shop, because if she agreed to come to London Father would pay her and there would be money for travelling and everything, she knew that Nanny would do what she had always done. She would put her arms around Jessica and shake her jowls and tut, and Jessica would breathe in her familiar smell of talcum powder and boiled milk and know that everything was going to be all right.

Three weeks later Pritchard drove Nanny and Jessica to the station. They had very little luggage. Their boxes and trunks had gone ahead. When the porter had brought up their suitcases Jessica helped Nanny unpack. She stroked the new dresses she had purchased in Bond Street, the suit with its nipped-in jacket and narrow skirt. Jessica had winced when she saw the price tags and had the breathy saleslady send the account to her father. A miserly salary was no reason for the assistant to the editor of a London magazine not to look the part. Besides, you never knew who might turn up while you were busying yourself in your office and insist on taking you out to lunch. When they had eaten the supper the maid had left for them Nanny went to bed.

Jessica stood alone in the middle of her drawing room, her newly cut door keys in her hand, and she danced. It was a gleeful goblin kind of dance, a Rumpelstiltskin dance, except that unlike Rumpelstiltskin Jessica had got what she wanted most in the world and she had no intention of losing it. Somehow, she thought, leaping and twirling in delight, she had spun straw into something remarkably like gold.

It was all rather jolly at first, having a job, waking to the jangle of an alarm clock and gulping a cup of tea standing up while pinning one's hair and applying a hurried dash of lipstick. Even the trolleybus, crowded with bleary-eyed passengers, moved with a jolting purposefulness that filled Jessica with anticipation. The spring mornings were sunny, the sky a freshly washed blue, and the broad streets of Maida Vale were crowded with people hurrying, their heads down, all of them with somewhere urgent to get to. In her elegant new clothes, her hair swept up in a loose chignon beneath a dashing little hat, Jessica felt like a butterfly, suddenly free of the chrysalis of childhood. She smiled at the other girls on the trolleybus. They did not smile back. They ducked their heads, suddenly intent on tickets or gloves or the handle of a handbag. Their shabby coats were the colour of moths.

The offices of *Woman's Friend* were located at the top of a tall building in Bloomsbury. The building had seen better days. The paint in the stairwell was peeling, the carpet damp and malodorous.

There was no lift. On Jessica's first day she opened the door, expecting a reception area, and instead almost fell over a desk wedged in what appeared to be a corridor. Behind the desk a girl was banging at a typewriter. There were no windows in the corridor, which turned sharply behind her, and her desk lamp cast a reluctant circle of light. It might have been the middle of the night.

The cramped conditions were a result of budget cuts which required the magazine to share the premises with two of their sister publications, *Sewing Circle* and *Nursing Digest*. Desks were pushed into every corner, often so close to one another that there was barely room to squeeze between them. Jessica's at least had a slice of window, a three-inch-wide vertical offcut of smeared wire-glass tucked into the seam of a plasterboard partition. It was plain from overheard snatches of conversation that the other girls bitterly resented the new girl bagging such a prize, but no one said anything to her. They smiled at her carefully and said that if there was anything she needed she only had to ask. They offered her toffees when they handed round a bag. But there was a wariness in their manner, a formality that was not there between the rest of them. Gerald had told Miss Cooke, the magazine's editor, that Jessica was the daughter of a friend of his. There was no reason for them to disbelieve him. But she saw the way the other girls looked at her, noticing her dresses, her good handbag and expensive shoes. However much anyone pretended, she was not one of them.

On her first day they asked her if she wanted to come with them for lunch. The Busy Bee was a dingy-looking teashop tucked into a corner of Gower Street with grimy windows and curtains bleached into stripes by the sun. It smelled strongly of dust and sugar and stale fat. The girls sat at a greasy table in the corner and discussed whether they could possibly run to tinned peach melba or if it would have to be the usual sardines on toast. The table was too low. Jessica kept knocking her knees against it. Peggy said it was because the proprietress ground the table legs to make soup. Jessica poked at a poached egg that glared up at her like a watery eye and tried not to breathe through her nose.

'It's not exactly the Ritz,' Joan said, 'but there's nothing better for ninepence. I should know. I've tried them all.'

Jessica did not go to the Busy Bee again. There was a little French restaurant close to the British Museum with white-aproned waiters and a deliciously lemony sole meunière. She did not tell the other girls. They watched every penny and were always talking about money, about cheap cobblers and when museums were free and how to mend laddered stockings so they could do another turn. When Jessica had first seen a copy of the magazine she had told Gerald it was dowdy. Shop girls might not have much money, she said, but everyone wanted glamour. She talked about film stars and fashion plates and gossipy pieces about

277

society weddings and parties on the French Riviera, but Gerald only laughed and said that the readers of *Woman's Friend* would not know the Riviera from a hole in the ground. By the time she had been at the magazine for a week Jessica was quite sure that the same was true for the girls that wrote it. It was not just the Riviera. They wore the same dreary clothes day after day and they never seemed to launder them, or even bathe. On warm days the smell of unwashed bodies was almost overpowering.

Miss Cooke did not bother to glance through Jessica's envelope of cuttings. She pushed it to one side, and opened a copy of *Woman's Friend*.

'You'll be doing this,' she said, turning the magazine round for Jessica to see.

Fireside Chat occupied a double-page spread towards the back of the magazine. The girls at the magazine called it the agony column. Readers wrote in to the magazine's agony aunt, Mrs Sweeting, seeking her advice on all manner of problems, and the magazine published her replies. A widow with a kind heart, Mrs Sweeting had considerable experience of life's vicissitudes. A portrait of her in pen and ink smiled cosily above a curlicued banner that declared her the Voice of Understanding. So affectionately was she regarded that from time to time she even received letters from gentlemen enquiring, in the most respectful of terms, whether Mrs Sweeting might consider entering into a correspondence of a rather more personal nature.

Such letters were returned to their senders with a polite note asking them not to write again. The rest were divided into two approximate categories: practical questions about how to wash corsets or renovate a bathtub, which got the left-hand page, and *cris de coeurs*, which got the right. The letters themselves were not published, only the replies, but Mrs Sweeting often quoted sympathetically from the distressed appeals of *A LONELY GIRL* or *TIRED OF LIFE* before offering advice. This, Miss Cooke informed Jessica, was the secret of Mrs Sweeting's success. Readers appreciated her counsel; some doubtless even took it. But there was comfort of a much deeper kind in the assurance that, however wretched their lot, there were other readers out there whose sufferings were much greater than their own.

'You wish me to assist Mrs Sweeting?' Jessica asked.

'Assist her? You're to be her.'

'I don't understand. Is she ill?'

The editor snorted. Then she looked at Jessica. 'You're serious.'

It shocked Jessica more than she cared to admit to learn that Mrs Sweeting did not exist and never had done. The portrait had been the publisher's idea. He said that people liked to put a face to a name, especially when they were lonely. Until recently the agony column had been shared out among the girls who had dashed off replies when they could snatch a moment, but since the War the postbag had more than doubled. The publisher was talking of more pages.

'Which would be fine if they weren't all exactly the same,' Miss Cooke said briskly. 'Too much work, not enough money, dashed dreams of home and hearth. Do this job for six months and you'll be reciting them in your sleep. Magazine goes to press last thing on Tuesdays. I'll need your pages by Monday afternoon. Ask Joan if you need any help.'

Jessica spent the rest of the afternoon reading past issues of the magazine and trying not to be terrified. What on earth did she know about nourishing meals for one or how to get lipstick marks out of a blouse? It was Mrs Sweeting's romantic counsel, though, that made Jessica want to give her a good smack. The agony aunt's answer to everything consisted of sympathetic mumblings of the 'Bear up, dear sister' variety twinned with a frankly preposterous belief in the beneficence of destiny. It was nothing short of wicked, Jessica thought, to peddle the fictions that most men really preferred plain girls to pretty ones and that good things came to those who wait. As for the blatantly fallacious assertion that Cupid's bow and arrow waited for everyone and it was much too soon for a thirty-two-year-old woman to give up on finding happiness in love, it made Jessica want to laugh out loud.

That evening when she left the office she went to a bookshop on Tottenham Court Road and bought, on the recommendation of the sales assistant, a book by Agnes M. Miall entitled *The Bachelor Girl's Guide to Everything – or The Girl on Her Own*. There were surely no practical problems, she reasoned, that could not be solved between Miss Miall and Nanny. As for the romantic side of things, it was simply a matter of using some common sense. The readers of *Woman's Friend* needed help, not half-witted humbug.

CHAPTER 20

The restaurant at the King Club was small and dark and eye-wateringly expensive. Jessica adored it. The best tables were the booths, half-circular scoops set into the wall, their curved red banquettes like luscious red mouths. When the band started up at midnight, the banquettes were crowded with laughing revellers, drinking champagne and perching on one another's knees. Dancing never started till midnight anywhere. It was lucky that Nanny slept like a walrus. She never woke when Jessica tiptoed in in the small hours.

'I have a guilty secret,' Jessica confided. 'Shall I tell you?'

'Guiltier than never having seen *Iolanthe*?'

Jessica rolled her eyes. She had told Nanny that she had been invited to the operetta by the parents of a friend from work. It was only with difficulty that she had dissuaded Gerald from telephoning, pretending to be the girl's father. It irked her slightly, the entertainment he derived from her deceptions.

'I'm going to murder Mrs Sweeting,' she said.

'Death by drowning in a mixture of vinegar and bicarbonate of soda.'

'A taste of her own medicine?'

'An act of mercy. In the name of all the wretched factory hands and shop girls across the land. Plus when it's all over she'll be absolutely spotless.'

'She won't take it lying down.'

'Oh, but she will. She takes everything lying down.'

'My type of widow.'

Jessica laughed. She wished it did not shock her when Gerald said things like that. It was so provincial to be a prude. 'I'm sorry to disappoint you but Mrs Sweeting is pure as the driven snow, and a hundred times more bothersome. There, there, dear, bear up. Work is a tonic and patience is a virtue and platitudes are two a penny, and three on Saturdays.'

'Do I gather that Miss Cooke won the day?'

'She says if she publishes my answers people will think Mrs Sweeting has had a stroke.'

Gerald laughed.

'It's just such utter nonsense,' Jessica protested. 'How can anyone say that Mr Right comes to those who wait when the only thing Mr Right really wants is a gay girl in a pretty dress who laughs at his jokes and likes dancing?'

'Isn't that what Mr Wrong wants too?'

Jessica smiled, despite herself. The waiter brought wild strawberries, the first of the year. They were tiny and dazzlingly red. A single berry, she thought, would probably pay for a week of lunches at the Busy Bee.

'Did I ever tell you I can read fortunes?' Gerald said.

'I thought you just earned them.'

'Show me your hand.' He ran a finger lightly across her palm. 'This one's your life line. See how long it is? You'll live to be a hundred and ten.'

'Older even than you, then.'

'No one's older than me.'

'This line's deeper, though. It must be my telephone line. Or my clothes line.'

Aghast, Gerald put his hand over hers. 'Heavens, how terribly awkward. A gentleman never looks at a lady's clothes line.' His thumb caressed the side of her hand. She smiled at him. Then she froze. Under the table, she could feel his other hand slide over her knee. She crossed her legs.

'Gerald,' she remonstrated but he only smiled and shrugged.

'Don't blame me,' he said. 'What else is Mr Wrong to do when faced with a gay girl in an excessively pretty dress?'

Later, in the lavatory, she sat and leaned against the watered-silk wall, her head swimming with champagne. Above her a voluptuous naked lady reclined in an elaborate gilt frame, one hand cupping her breast, the other tucked between her legs. Jessica shook her head at her disapprovingly as she reached for the lavatory paper.

'And where is your Liberty bodice, young lady? You'll catch your death.'

She had never meant to let things with Gerald go so far. She had expected to make other friends by now, to be going to parties. She had thought the girls at the office would know people, that she would run into girls from school or from Hampshire, that her mother would introduce her to the London friends she had known before the War. She had expected a mantelpiece thick with invitations, evenings at the theatre, dancing in nightclubs. Of course she let Gerald take her out to dinner. She was nineteen years old. Why on earth would she go home every evening like the other girls at *Woman's Friend* and read detective novels and drink soup made from a cube when she could be dancing and drinking champagne? Gerald took her to heavenly places and, though sometimes she did rather wish that he knew people and could introduce her, she was also glad they never met anyone she might ever see again. The only friend Gerald seemed to have in London was a man called Ludo Holland, who was almost as old as him. Jessica liked Ludo. He was amusing and kind with a steadiness about him despite his ever-spinning carousel of actress girlfriends, but he was not someone she would ever bump into again. When the time came, she would leave it all behind and no one would be any the wiser.

And the time would come. The Season had begun and London was busy. It was just a matter

285

of a few introductions. After that the whole thing would snowball and the parties would start and she and Gerald would go back to the way it had been at the beginning, occasional expensive lunches and an admiration that might almost pass for avuncular. Until then, she sighed, sliding up her camiknickers, and fumbling unsteadily for the chain, until then there was no possibility of doing without him.

'So I shall just have to be clever, shan't I?' Jessica said, smiling tipsily at the lady in her gilt frame. The lady stared back at her with her shiny fish eyes and said nothing. Her white breasts were oddly childlike, with tiny scarlet nipples like glacé cherries. Jessica tutted at her, shaking her jowls like Nanny.

'Put something on, dear,' she said sternly, and went back to the dining room.

After dinner they went downstairs to dance. The nightclub was crammed. Ludo was already there, sitting at a corner table with a girl he introduced as Minty. All the other people seemed to know each other. She watched them, a raucous, restless, rackety crowd that rose and settled between tables, as noisy as rooks. Jessica thought she saw Lady Diana Manners in a corner, deep in conversation with a rakish-looking man with a patch over one eye.

Ludo had sprained his ankle. There was a stick propped up against the banquette. 'No dancing for me,' he said.

'Then why did you come?' Gerald asked and Ludo looked sideways at Minty in a way that made Gerald grin and shake his head. Ludo said that he had read in the *Daily Mail* that jazz music was contaminated with the primitive rituals of negro orgies and corrupted the young.

'You young have it all your own way,' he complained and he kissed Minty until she giggled and pushed him away. Gerald danced with Jessica and then with Minty. Minty had blonde hair and scarlet lips and a skirt edged with a fringe that showed her knees when she danced. She was a very good dancer.

'What have you done with Gerald?' Ludo asked Jessica as they watched them. 'That kind of energy would be undignified in a man half his age.'

Jessica laughed. 'I think you're jealous.'

'You could hardly blame me.'

She rolled her eyes at him. 'It seems to me you're not exactly miserable as things are.'

'Appearances can be deceptive.'

'Can't they, though.'

Ludo grinned. Taking a cigarette case from his inside pocket he extracted two and lit them, handing one to Jessica. 'My mother once sent my sister's old doll to the Doll Hospital. Do they have such places any more? Perhaps they don't. Anyway, my sister had loved that doll half to death, its hair all fallen out and the paint on its face rubbed away. It came back with bright yellow hair and these glassy blue eyes that seemed to bore straight into your soul. I thought my sister would be heart-broken, it looked nothing like it had before, but she absolutely adored the thing. It put the fear of God into me.' He shook his head, tapping the ash off his cigarette. 'After Christabel Gerald was in such a funk. For years. Nothing anyone did could shake him out of it. But recently, well, it's like he's been sent to the Doll Hospital. The old Gerald or near enough, but all brand new and shiny.'

'Does he put the fear of God into you too?' she teased. Gerald had never mentioned a Christabel. But then Gerald never mentioned anyone at all.

'God, yes. I'm considering a repaint myself, just for revenge.'

A little after two o'clock in the morning she asked Gerald to take her home. He was in high spirits, his gestures exaggerated by drink. He had a new motor car, a low-slung sporty thing which he drove at great speed and with much crashing of gears. Jessica wanted to ask about Christabel. Instead, she stroked the plump leather arm rest.

'A friend of my mother's used to have a motor like this,' she said as they roared up Park Lane. 'A white Alfonso XIII.'

'Beautiful machines. Did he ever take you for a spin?'

'He preferred my mother. I once caught them kissing in the garden. Eleanor just laughed. She said everyone had to have some fun now and again or they forgot they were alive.'

'Hard to argue with the principle.'

'I was eleven. The next day I took my mother's flower scissors and scraped them all the way down the side of that shiny white car. They must have known it was me but they never said anything. They said he had scraped it on the gate.'

Gerald took the turn to Edgware Road without braking. The tyres shrieked.

'Please, *pas devant la petite voiture*,' he said. 'You're making her nervous.'

'Then she'd better hope you're on your best behaviour. It's only wicked men who get the scissor treatment.'

When they reached Elgin Avenue Gerald did not pull up outside Biddulph Mansions. He stopped on the corner, where a cluster of plane trees blocked the light from the street lamp. There was no one about. His left hand caressed the gear lever. When it moved to Jessica's leg it was almost as though it had slipped there by mistake. Jessica picked it up and put it back on Gerald's lap. In the light of the street lamp she could see the veins like dark worms beneath the thin old-man skin.

'What did I say about being good?' she said teasingly. 'Goodnight, Gerald.' She leaned over, pecking him on the mouth. He caught her as she pulled away, his hand cupping the back of her head, his tongue pushing between her lips.

'There's good and good,' he murmured. 'Now that's what I call very good.'

Half-lifting himself out of his seat he kissed her again, his lips still soft but his tongue insistent, twining itself around hers. One of his hands was on her thigh, the other on her ribs beneath her breast. She tried to squirm away from under him but the car was too small, he took up all the room. His tongue choked her. She could not breathe. Her hands on his chest, she pushed him away. The street was deserted but Jessica was still glad it was Maida Vale and miles from anywhere where someone might know someone who knew her.

'You're a bad, bad man, Your Excellency,' she protested. 'I have a horrible feeling you mean to corrupt me.'

'Corrupt you?' He smiled, his hand sliding up to nudge her breast. 'Isn't it a little late for that, my little alley cat?'

'I don't know what kind of girl you think I am but—'

A car swung past them, its headlights brief and dazzling. Horrified, Jessica pushed Gerald roughly away. She could feel him looking at her but she did not look back. She stared out of the windscreen at the car as it drove up the street, smoothing her skirt over her knees.

'I'd like to go in now, please,' she said tightly. Outside Biddulph Mansions the car slowed, its brake lights like red eyes in the darkness. Then it stopped. Jessica watched as a chauffeur in a peaked cap got out and walked round to open the passenger door. She felt sick. She wondered if they had seen her, if they knew who she was. A blonde woman in a fur climbed out, followed by a man.

The woman was laughing. Instinctively Jessica ducked her head, a hand up to shield her face. Gerald snorted.

'Of course,' he said. 'The morality patrol.'

Jessica waited until the man and the woman had gone inside. Then she crossed her arms. 'I want to get out.'

'I see.'

Jessica waited but he did not open his door. 'Well?'

'Well, what?'

'Well, aren't you going to let me out?'

'I suppose so. In a moment.' He looked at her sideways. Then, his hands on the steering wheel, he shook his head, exhaling a bitter soundless laugh.

'What?' Jessica demanded.

'I was just thinking of that creature who declared she would die in captivity.'

'I don't know what you mean.'

'You told me that, do you remember? The first time I met you. That afternoon, it wasn't just that you were lovely. You had such audacity, such – verve. You meant to squeeze life for every last drop of juice that could be got from it, and if other people didn't like it, well, who ever gave a damn for what other people think? You were going to get what you wanted and the rest of the world could go hang. You were going to be free. God, it was wonderful. Intoxicating.'

'Just because—'

'Ludo laughed when I told him.' His voice was soft, as though he were talking to himself. 'He said I shouldn't believe a word of it. He said upper-class girls were all the same, constipated by convention and lousy with etiquette. He said before I knew it I'd be being dragged to tea with your mother.'

'My mother would rather die,' she said tartly but he only shook his head.

'You see? So much promise. I told Ludo he was wrong about you. That you were nothing like those ridiculous debutantes, that you were bold and original and spontaneous. That you were . . . irresistible. Was I the one who was wrong?'

He smiled at her and his smile was so sad that she let him kiss her after all. He kissed her gently at first and then harder, mashing his mouth against hers, and she closed her eyes and kissed him back, her mouth open and her tongue entwining itself with his, allowing herself to be carried along on the wave of it. His hands sought her neck, her breasts. She did not push him away. The more she kissed him the more she was the person he believed her to be, audacious and insolent and extraordinary. When at last it ended she was breathless and hazy and faintly triumphant.

'My God,' Gerald murmured, 'you are irresistible.' And Jessica's heart turned over and she wondered if she might not be a tiny bit in love with him after all. She kissed him again.

'I do really have to go in,' she murmured. This

time he did not protest. He walked her to the front door. As she fished her key from her bag he kissed her on the neck. Then he seized her around the waist and spun her round in a pirouette. She laughed, rolling her eyes at him. In the harsh glare of the porch light his hair shone silver and the lines in his face were thick and black. He looked as old as the hills.

'Go home, Gerald,' she said, and she gave him a little push with her hands. She could still hear him laughing as he climbed into his car and roared away into the night.

CHAPTER 21

It did not take long for Oscar's days in Cambridge to acquire a pattern. Despite, or perhaps because of, his irritation with Oscar's early arrival and at a loss as to what to do with him, Mr Willis had reluctantly agreed to allow Oscar access to the Wren Library, a privilege usually granted only to members of the College. Every morning after breakfast, Oscar gathered his notebooks and his folders and walked over Magdalene Bridge and up Trinity Street to the cobbled sweep in front of Trinity's Great Gate, on top of which, in the eighteenth century, the University's first astronomical observatory had been built. Every morning he stepped through the archway with its heavy oak door and walked across the great grand sweep of Great Court, past the fountain and the chapel and the Great Hall, and through the arch to Nevile's Court.

Every morning it took his breath away. It was on the stone flags of the north cloister that Isaac Newton had stamped his foot to time the echoes and determined the speed of sound. Oscar set his feet into the dents worn by centuries of feet and in the sunlit air the weight of history turned slowly, like columns of dust. The court had been designed by Christopher Wren. With its pale Italianate façades and its elegant colonnades it was perhaps the most beautiful place Oscar had ever seen and yet it was not its beauty that struck him the first time he saw it or its elegance but its immeasurable gravity, and the foolishness of the unintentioned pun had filled him with a rush of happiness like helium that almost lifted him off the ground. It was a joke that would have amused his mother.

Every morning he read and every afternoon he walked. He always went the same way, across Trinity Bridge and along the Newnham Road towards Grantchester. It was the sunniest May anyone could remember and on the Backs the warm afternoons were bright with chatter and laughter and the slow dip and splash of punts. Girls were not permitted on the river without a chaperone but they spread blankets on the grass banks, their parasols bright as butterflies. There were wicker picnic baskets and wind-up phonographs and bottles of champagne cooling in the river on lengths of string. Couples danced together on the lawns. The music drifted on the breeze, insistently gay, insinuating itself into Oscar's feet.

He did not stop. He did not even take photographs. His head was too busy with the books he was reading. The book list Mr Willis had given him covered the first part of the Natural Sciences Tripos. Oscar read them all, not only physics but chemistry and biology. When a subject caught his attention he turned to the bibliographies and read more. The librarian was helpful, at least until Oscar enquired about subatomic physics. Then he produced a single slim volume by a Trinity Fellow, Mr James Jeans, published before the War. That, he said apologetically, was all that they had. Oscar knew better than to ask why they owned none of the books by German scientists. Instead, he read Mr Jeans.

Mr Jeans' book was filled with incomprehensible equations but his central theory was clear. For years, in his work with black body radiation, he had attempted to accommodate his results within the parameters of classical mechanics. Instead, he had found them persistently in contradiction. Mr Jeans was obliged reluctantly to conclude that there was, underlying the most minute processes of nature, a system of mechanical laws quite different from the Newtonian laws upon which physics had been built thus far. But even if those laws could be identified, even if a complete set of equations to support them could be conceived and proven, the mathematics defied physical interpretation. Any attempts to explain or picture the mechanisms involved, Jeans stated baldly, led only to a state of hopeless confusion.

The phrase was like a fragment of meat caught between Oscar's teeth. It nagged at him. *A state of hopeless confusion.* Quantum theory explained subatomic physics but the human brain could not imagine it. But if something could not be imagined, then how could it possibly be true? As he strode on out of town, matching his thoughts to the metronomic tick of his heels against the stone, it occurred to him to wonder whether intellectual energy, like radiation, was also quantised, that it too was delivered in packets of predetermined size, proportional to the circumference of the brain, the length of the walking stride. Perhaps, he thought, if he could look inside his head, slicing off the top like a boiled egg, he would see the electrons of his thoughts circling the nucleus of his brain, compelled by the unfathomable laws of the hidden universe never to diverge from their preordained orbits. Perhaps, he thought, it was why they only ever seemed to take him in circles.

And still he read and walked and thought, each day in the same order. No one paid him the least attention. No one stopped at his desk or tipped their hat to him on the stairs. Even the porters, whose job it was to know everyone, hardly seemed to see him as he passed through Great Gate. Oscar did not mind. He felt light, divested of the awkward conspicuousness of his body, his whole self rolled up and contained inside the safe box of his skull. When, on the rare occasions he walked through the college in the afternoon, the place was hectic with undergraduates, laughing and shouting and waving tennis racquets with a noisy enthusiasm that smashed up the air into bright shards, but in the mornings, when the courts were deserted and magnificent and everyone in the University was deep in study, it seemed to him that the hush of the library was alive with a static hum, a symphony of thinking, as in every carrel and corner of the ancient buildings worlds grew and opened and held their silent faces up towards the light.

It startled him then when, cutting through Whewell's Court one pink evening, Oscar was accosted by a group of men drinking claret out of tooth glasses. Behind them, in a ground-floor room, a party was in full swing. Through the open window Oscar could hear the clamour of voices, the crackly jaunt of ragtime on a gramophone. The owner of the rooms had moved his furniture into the stairwell and the narrow space was a jumble of club chairs and tables and footstools with tapestry seats. An ashtray and a half-empty bottle of wine balanced precariously on the upturned feet of an ottoman.

'Do we know each other?' one of the men asked. To Oscar's confusion he realised that he had somehow stopped walking and was gaping as though they were an exhibit in the zoo.

'Sorry, I . . . I don't think so,' he muttered.

'You're quite sure? You're not a member of the Quinquaginta, are you?'

Oscar shook his head.

'Good God, Ferguson,' one of the other men laughed. 'Your tactics get baser by the day.'

The man called Ferguson only grinned. He had

298

dark hair and a wide smiling mouth and he leaned against the wall with one leg stuck out and his arms crossed over his chest as though he had been leaning there all his life. His left cheek, which faced the wall, was rubbery with scar tissue. The stretched skin tugged at the corner of his left eye, pulling it down so that it looked as though he was winking. Where his ear should be there was only a hole, marked by a shiny nub of purple flesh.

'Then what are you waiting for?' he said to Oscar. 'For a two-bob sub you'll find the door to Paradise thrown open and all the heavenly angels there for your delectation. Though, of course, you'll have to bring your own. The Quinquaginta may be a thoroughly modern kind of joint but we do cling to some vestige of decency. So, can I sign you up?'

Oscar stared at Ferguson helplessly. 'I'm sorry but I have no idea what the Quink – what that is.'

'Where have you been all term? The Quinquaginta is only *the* dance club in Cambridge. Other men may tell you it's all about the Vingt-et-un but believe me, besides the Quinquaginta, the Vingt-et-un's like a maiden aunt at a funeral.'

'The maiden aunt's mother,' a third man drawled. 'With bunions.' He was much younger than the others, short and scrawny with the raw bones and shiny red pimples of a schoolboy. Above his scarlet silk cravat his Adam's apple bobbed like a fishing float.

'I'm sorry,' Oscar said, 'but I don't dance.'

'Don't dance?' Ferguson protested. 'What madness is this? How else are you going to get pretty girls to fall into your arms?'

'Certainly not by letting them see me dance,' Oscar said. He meant it seriously but Ferguson only laughed and held out his hand.

'I'm Kit Ferguson.'

'Oscar Greenwood.'

'This reprobate is Jay Girouard and this is . . . Wilkinson, is it?'

'Winterson,' the schoolboy corrected. 'Geoffrey Winterson.'

'Girouard lives on this staircase, when he's sober enough to find it,' Ferguson said. 'Do you want a drink?'

Without waiting for an answer he took a dirty glass from the window sill and sloshed some wine into it. Oscar hesitated, then took it.

'Thank you,' he said.

Despite their age the men were all first years. Ferguson had come up in January, Girouard in April. Girouard joked about being older than the dons but only Winterson mentioned the War. Obliged to relinquish his commission on account of weak lungs, he had gone straight to Cambridge after Highers the previous October. He wore his extra term like a medal.

Oscar was glad when Winterson declared himself thirsty and went in search of wine. He was even gladder when he discovered that Girouard was reading Natural Sciences and Ferguson Mathematics which, at Cambridge, included the study of theoretical physics. After that he did not have to worry about thinking of things to say. He had a second glass of wine and talked about the photoelectric effect and whether light was a particle or a wave or, as Einstein would have it, somehow both at the same time. It was only when the party was breaking up that it occurred to Oscar to mention that he was not actually at the University. Ferguson laughed.

'So you're here but you're not here,' he said. 'The Prof won't like that. He hasn't much time for theoretical physicists.'

The Prof was Ernest Rutherford. According to Ferguson everyone called him that, even his wife. Oscar grinned.

'He's quite safe here,' Ferguson added ruefully. 'As far as this place is concerned quanta are just some dubious foreign nonsense, like spaghetti or Fauvism. What matters is the Maxwellian tradition and the study of strains in the aether.'

'But they teach it, don't they? Quantum theory, I mean.'

'Apparently there's a new fellow at Christ's who means to teach a course next year,' Girouard said.

'Only to you lot,' Kit said. 'Not to us. It's all right for you to be misled. You're nothing but mechanics with your magnets and your cathode tubes and your columns of observable facts. Us

301

mathematicians are the vestal virgins of the University. We must be chaperoned by Larmor at all times for fear that our purity be corrupted by sticky-fingered wops.'

'We're not allowed to have tea with them without the door open and all four feet on the floor at all times,' Girouard said.

'He's right. Look, I've got to go but come and find out for yourself. Monday, four o'clock. And bring cake. Nobody's allowed without cake.'

'Another of Larmor's rules?'

'If it were it would be the only one I agree with. Great Court, M staircase. Room One on the ground floor.'

'You're a scholar?' Oscar asked.

'Not exactly.'

'But I thought only scholars got rooms in Great Court.'

'Actually, it's scholars and cripples. Don't look so stricken. Who wouldn't give their left leg for a room on Great Court? I'll see you on Monday.'

There was a walking stick propped against the stairs. Oscar had not even noticed it. Ferguson took it and levered himself away from the wall. His left leg did not bend. He had to swing it in a stiff half-circle to bring it forward like a pendulum. As he manoeuvred his way out of the crowded stairwell his foot struck a spindly-legged table, sending it flying.

'Pick on someone your own size, Ferguson,' someone shouted.

Ferguson grinned.

'In the battle of the wooden legs, all enemies are equal,' he said. 'That one was mine.'

CHAPTER 22

Oscar never did join the Quinquaginta. He could not comprehend why Kit Ferguson liked dancing, a pursuit he considered both tedious and alarming, and he had no interest in meeting girls. But he liked Kit. From time to time, on the way back from his walks, he bought cakes at the bakery on Magdalene Lane and went to Kit's rooms in Great Court for tea. Sometimes Girouard was there and Oscar did not stay long. Girouard vibrated with a kind of hectic restlessness, as though the air he breathed might at any moment run out. His gaiety brooked no possibility of refusal, except when he was suffering the aftereffects of some party or other, when he liked to sprawl on Kit's sofa with his feet propped up on the arm, drinking Kit's sherry and complaining about people Oscar did not know.

When it was just Kit they talked about physics.

Like Oscar Kit was baffled and entranced by the quantum hypothesis, but when he quizzed his lecturers they deflected his questions. They insisted that quantum theory remained far from inevitable, that many British mathematicians remained unconvinced by its hypotheses. When Kit protested to his supervisor, Mr Lopez sent him away with a journal containing an article by Sir Oliver Lodge. The piece, 'On Continuity', had been delivered as a presidential address to the British Association for the Advancement of Science. In it Lodge rejected as unworkable the theories both of quanta and of relativity.

'It would be funny if it wasn't so depressing,' Kit said. 'Here lies classical physics, one foot in the grave, and who do they wheel in to resuscitate it? A fucking Spiritualist. A man who refuses point blank to accept that when something's dead, it's really bloody dead.'

It came as a great comfort to Kit when Sir Oliver Lodge began a lecture tour of England and the newspapers denounced him as a mountebank and social menace, a peddler of nauseating superstitious drivel to the weak and the credulous. The innate conservatism of the Cambridge faculty exasperated Kit. Cambridge would never accept the quanta, he said, just as they would never admit women to full membership of the University, even though the arguments against both were in tatters. The Trinity fellows would continue to shuffle like superannuated penguins across the lawns of Great Court, their top hats tipped over their eyes, and thank God, who being British was mercifully a moderate, dependable sort of chap and not prone to excitability, that at least in these ancient courts of learning time had the common decency to stand still.

305

'Kropotkin gave up on revolution in England after the 1881 Congress,' Kit told Oscar. 'He said that England was a country impermeable to new ideas. He knew you could turn everything upside down, tip every last assumption out onto the floor and trample them into the dust, and the English would only sigh and put the kettle on and put everything carefully back the way it was before.'

That was the thing about Kit. He talked about physics and history and philosophy and music and the headlines in the newspapers as if they were all part of the same conversation. Everything interested him. He was as opinionated about Sherlock Holmes and Charlie Chaplin as he was about the music of Schoenberg or the poetry of Pound. Oscar thought that if he lived a thousand years he would never know as much as Kit. He also could not help wondering why Kit wanted to know so much about so many different things when there was still so much to learn about physics.

'Except that's not true,' Oscar countered. 'A year ago elements were immutable. Then Rutherford starts firing alpha particles at nitrogen atoms and, hey presto, he's turned it into oxygen and changed the way we look at the world for ever. Even the Cambridge penguins admit that.'

'Actually, one or two are asking whether he hasn't just discovered alpha particles with longer ranges.'

'All right. So some of them are beyond hope.'

'Besides, the Prof may be doing extraordinary work but when it comes to theory he's as bad as the rest of them. The other day someone asked him what he made of Einstein's General Theory and he said he considered it a magnificent work of art, irrespective of whether it is valid. It was as damning a piece of praise as I have ever heard. More tea?'

'Please,' Oscar said. He watched as, with one hand on the table, the other on the arm of his chair, Kit levered himself to standing. His leg jutted at an awkward angle. As Kit righted it a spasm of pain crossed his face, pulling down the bad side of his face so that it looked like he was winking. He bit his lip, pressing his fingers hard into the top of his left thigh.

'Are you all right?' Oscar asked.

'Cramp. Stupid bloody thing. To get cramp in a leg that isn't even there. Happens to everyone, apparently. A doctor told me that Nelson was a martyr to the muscle paralysis in his right hand which dug his fingernails into the palm of his hand. Except, as every schoolboy knows, he didn't have a right hand, not after the battle of Santa Cruz de Tenerife.' Kit closed his eyes, kneading the flesh beneath his trouser leg. 'I feel like Captain fucking Ahab.'

'Who?'

'You haven't read *Moby-Dick*? What are you, a bloody scientist or something? Jesus fuck fuck fuck.'

His face creased with pain, he leaned into his false leg, then forced himself to straighten up. When he carried the teacups over to the table they chattered like teeth against their saucers. Oscar knew better than to try and help him. Kit never talked about the War. It was Girouard who told Oscar that he had been wounded at Messines. Oscar had remembered the tremor of excitement that had run through his school when they heard the news of the triumphant offensive at the Messines Ridge. The Allies had tunnelled under German lines and laid a line of more than twenty mines beneath the German trenches. When the mines were detonated, the explosion was so loud that Lloyd George had heard it in Downing Street.

'So Rutherford doesn't like theoreticians,' Oscar said as Kit limped back with his tea. 'That's hardly news. And I'm not sure he doesn't have a point.'

'Et tu, Brute?'

'What?'

'Never mind. I just never thought you'd turn out to be one of them.'

'Of course you did. You know quite well I don't understand at least half of what you do. But even if I did it's just . . . what Rutherford does in the lab is real. The mathematics only works when it relates to the facts, when it creates connections that make sense of what we know. Take Einstein's theory of light-quanta. All right, so light is emitted in quanta when electrons jump from one energy state to another. All the experiments support that. But if you accept Einstein's equations you also have to accept that the time of transition and the direction in which the light-quantum is emitted is entirely random. Beyond probability it's impossible to predict exactly what will happen. Doesn't that bother you?'

'So the theory has weaknesses. It needs refinement.'

'It's not a matter of refinement. His equations reject the basic laws of cause and effect. If Einstein is right, where and when an electron exposed to radiation will jump off is down to free will.'

'Free will?'

'Well, what else would you call it? Once you've eliminated causality, free will is all you have left.'

'Or something else. Something we don't yet understand.'

'So you're saying you accept Einstein's theory?'

'I hardly understand it. But I want to accept it, yes.'

'Even though it makes no sense?'

Kit shrugged. 'When did the really important things ever make sense?'

Sir Aubrey continued to write to Oscar, care of Mrs Piggott. His letters were long, composed over several sittings. He had abandoned the idea of the new fortifications, there were complications Oscar did not quite grasp to do with engineering and Godmother Eleanor, but he was working again on his book and was actively seeking a publisher. He

309

planned several new chapters on Henry, his brother, and the ways Ellinghurst had inspired his pioneering work with X-ray spectra. He said that it was Oscar's letters that had started him thinking about Henry's work. During his graduate studies in Manchester, Henry's supervisor had been Ernest Rutherford.

Sir Aubrey came to Cambridge to meet Rutherford at the end of May. He took Oscar to lunch at the University Arms Hotel. The dining room had a jaunty commercial air, its furniture glossy with the faux-solidity of the brand new. The two levels were divided by the barley-sugar spirals of a shiny mahogany balustrade. Behind Oscar, on a matching mahogany table, a huge fern burst from its brass pot like a great green fountain. Its fronds licked the back of Oscar's neck.

Sir Aubrey looked old. He was old, old enough to be Godmother Eleanor's father rather than her husband, but he had always been old in a bluff, impervious way like a house or a mountain, weathered on the outside. Now he was thin, his collar too large for his scrawny neck. His grey hair was thin too, showing the pinkness of his scalp, and the backs of his hands were purple-spotted and roped with veins. They shook a little as he drank his soup.

His conversation, by contrast, was as hectic as a child's. He asked Oscar about Cambridge and whether he had taken any photographs recently but his questions were perfunctory and it was plain

310

from his eagerness that he only really wanted to talk about Ellinghurst. Oscar longed to ask after Phyllis but he could not see how to ask without interrupting. Instead, he listened as Sir Aubrey seethed to himself about the lack of agricultural innovation in England. When Oscar enquired after the family he talked not of Phyllis but of Henry. He told Oscar that Rutherford had offered Henry a fellowship at Manchester but that Henry had returned instead to his research at Oxford, despite the University's refusal to grant him financial support. 'So you see,' he said drily, 'I have been a patron of physics a long time.'

'My tutor says that your brother was one of the truly great.'

Sir Aubrey smiled. He said that Henry had had little truck with his own reputation, believing himself to be no more than a part of a greater scientific whole. A skilled scientist might contribute his own brick to the collective construction, Henry had argued, but, if he did not, it hardly mattered. Before long someone else would do it in his place. 'You, perhaps,' Sir Aubrey said.

'If only, sir. But the mathematics—'

'We Melvilles have always been Oxford men but I can't blame you. The Cavendish has a fine reputation. Cambridge, though. *Hail, ye horrors, hail! ye ever-gloomy bowers,/ Ye Gothic fanes and antiquated towers,/ Where rushy Camus' slowly winding flood/ Perpetual draws his humid train of mud.* Do you know the poem? Thomas Gray. Fewer than a thousand lines of poetry in his lifetime but still one of the most admired and influential poets of his age. He and Henry would have liked one another, I always think. Of course, Gray had mixed feelings about Cambridge, and not just because of the weather. You should be careful, you know. The Fenland damp is very bad for the chest.'

'I am quite well, sir.'

'I'm glad, I'm very glad. And the teaching is good?'

'As I said, sir, I don't matriculate until October.'

'Of course. I forget you're so young.' Sir Aubrey shook his head, staring out over the dining room. 'I was already twenty when Henry was born. Older than you are now. He was more like a son to me than a brother. Another son.' He was silent. Then he looked at Oscar. 'I wondered if you might like his books.'

Oscar stared at Sir Aubrey. 'His books? But, sir—'

'Violet, his widow, is moving abroad and offered them for the library at Ellinghurst. I would rather you had them. I should like to think of you following in his footsteps. Placing your brick on top of his.'

H. J. G. Melville's books. Oscar's eyes shone. 'Sir, I don't know what to say.'

'You scientists never do.'

They drank their coffee in the lounge. Sir Aubrey's feverish energy had evaporated and he slumped in his chair, his pouched eyes rimmed with red. When Oscar rose to leave he roused himself, pressing Oscar's hand between his own.

He told Oscar that if he ever needed anything he only had to ask.

'And come and see us, won't you? Come and bring your camera. I long to see what you find next. And Jessica is home every weekend.'

'Thank you, sir. I should like that.'

'We would not want you to forget us. We are all very fond of you.' He sighed, shaking his head. 'It got my grandfather too, you know. Cancer.'

'I didn't know.'

'No, well, no one talks about it, do they? It embarrasses them. Filthy bloody disease. An unspeakable instinct for the finest people. Like the War. It's only the cowards and the charlatans who come home.'

Oscar walked back across Parker's Piece towards town. It was a breezy blue afternoon, high clouds scudding across the sky. He thought perhaps he might go to Ellinghurst. He could hardly begrudge the time when Sir Aubrey had been so generous. Henry Melville's books! For that he would listen to any number of stories of Melvilles long dead. Besides, Ellinghurst was glorious in June. In Egypt, Sir Aubrey said, it was too hot for excavations by the end of May.

In two weeks Phyllis was coming home.

At the pillar box on Magdalene Street he saw Kit. He was talking to a girl in a spotted dress. She held a bicycle by the handlebars, its basket piled high with books. Oscar turned, hoping to slip by unobserved.

'Greenwood, you snake, aren't you going to say hello?'

Reluctantly Oscar turned back. Kit grinned. 'I don't suppose you know each other, do you?'

The girl shook her head. She had an upturned nose and a mass of pale brown hair swept up into a makeshift bun. Balancing her bicycle precariously against her hip she put out her hand.

'How do you do?' she said.

'Frances Kellaway, Oscar Greenwood,' Kit said. 'Frances is a friend of Latham's.'

'Peter was at school with my brother,' Frances explained.

Oscar looked blank. Kit rolled his eyes at Frances. 'Please excuse him. He knows perfectly well who Peter Latham is and he is delighted to meet you. It's just that he likes to pretend that his mind is on higher things. That way he looks brilliant and ducks any obligation for good manners.'

Frances laughed.

'Frances is at Newnham. English Literature,' Kit said to Oscar. 'I have a hunch that her mind really is on higher things, only unlike you she is much too polite to show it. Look, I've got to go. If I'm late for another of Lopez's supervisions all hell will break loose.' He smiled at Frances and kissed her lightly on the cheek. 'I'll see you tonight, then.'

Frances watched as he limped away, swift despite his stiff-legged gait. Her eyes were soft, her pale cheeks flushed with pink.

'It was nice to meet you,' Oscar said.

'Yes. You too.' She lingered as Kit disappeared through Magdalene gate. Then she smiled at Oscar. 'Are you going my way?'

They walked together up Bridge Street, Frances pushing her bicycle.

'So have you and Kit been friends long?' she asked.

'We met at the beginning of term.'

'He seems to know everyone. All the girls, at any rate.'

'Well. He likes dancing.'

'I know. It seems so unlikely, doesn't it?' She looked over her shoulder towards Magdalene as if she hoped to catch a glimpse of him. 'He's so clever and brave. And funny too, of course. I think half of the girls I know are a little bit in love with him.'

Oscar did not know what to say to that.

'Will you be there tonight?' Frances asked. 'At the Quinquaginta?'

'I don't dance. It's an act of kindness, I promise you. I've two left feet.'

'Me too. Kit doesn't believe me. He says he has no left foot at all and if he can dance, anyone can. That it's simply a matter of not thinking too much.' She laughed the same uncertain laugh. 'I've never been terribly good at that.'

'"We're fools whether we dance or not, so we might as well dance."'

'I'm sorry?'

'It's a Japanese proverb. Or so Kit claims.'

'Is it? How dispiriting. Or cheering. I'm not sure.'

'I wouldn't worry. Knowing Kit he probably made it up.'

'You make him sound like a rotter.'

'Sheer jealousy. You wait until you've known him a bit longer, then you'll understand. Attack is our only line of defence.'

Frances laughed, her bottom lip caught between her teeth. She was not a particularly pretty girl but she had a pretty smile. Outside Trinity they said goodbye. Then she got on her bicycle, tucking up her skirt so it did not catch in the chain. Oscar had started towards Great Gate when she called after him.

'He's not . . . that is, I mean, I'm not being an idiot, am I?'

He turned. 'What?'

'It's only . . . never mind. Sorry. Sorry.'

Wobbling a little, she bicycled away down Trinity Street. Oscar watched her back wheel disappear around the bend, then turned back towards the college. Above him Henry VIII gazed out coldly from his niche in the stone gate. At some point the previous century an undergraduate had scaled the gate and replaced the royal sceptre in his hand with the leg of a wooden chair. The joke had stood for over fifty years.

'Handy to know they keep a spare,' Kit had remarked once. 'In case of emergencies.'

Oscar ducked through the oak door and crossed

Great Court. The afternoon sun caught the windows of Kit's rooms, making him squint. He wondered if, instead of thermodynamics, Kit was thinking about Frances Kellaway with her pretty smile and her two left feet. He could not imagine it somehow. Girouard teased Kit about girls but Oscar had never known him serious about one. He was not sure that Kit knew how. It would require him to be serious about himself, at least for a moment, and Oscar was not sure he knew how to do that either.

He felt a twinge of pity for Frances with her tentative laugh and her longing lighting up her face like fluorescence. So much was written about the wonder of love, books and books crammed with words, but what purpose did any of it serve, except to create an idea of the world that was not real? A poem was no different from a scientific theory; the sheer beauty of it might take your breath away, but if it failed to observe the facts it was worth nothing. Discontinuity was inherent in radiation phenomena. Falling in love with someone did not mean that they loved you back. Those were the facts, whether you could explain them or not, and all the elegant expression in the world could not make them different.

CHAPTER 23

After nearly a month the novelty of working had worn thin. It was exhausting getting up early, wearisome waiting at the stop for the crowded trolleybus. As it jolted along the familiar route Jessica stared blankly out of the dirty window at the familiar dingy diorama, the figures scurrying along the pavements like wind-up toys. She thought how heavenly it would be to have a car, the passengers in the bus gaping at her as she roared along Marylebone Road. Gerald had held to his promise to teach her to drive. Twice before dinner, he had taken her to the Outer Circle of Regent's Park and let her take the wheel. He said she was a natural. She wished Theo could have seen her. Gerald said the car could do eighty miles an hour on a straight road and even in the Park the speed was exhilarating. In the mornings, though, like Cinderella, the car was a distant memory. When it rained the other passengers smelled of wet dog. On warm ones they smelled meaty, like gravy.

It was worse in the office. The sun beat down on the roof, heating it up like a greenhouse, and though they pushed the windows open as far as they would go on their rusted hinges, there was no breeze to stir the soupy air. Jessica's slice of window was painted shut. She pushed her chair back against the wall to avoid the aggressive strip of sunlight that moved across her desk every morning, imprinting its shape in purple on the underside of her eyelids and shrivelling the milky surface of her tea. She was tired of *Doubtful* and *Betty-Blue-Eyes*, tired of reducing diets and vinegar face washes and sponging black lace with tea.

'We should be like Spaniards,' Joan said, 'and keep the curtains permanently drawn all summer.'

'Except there aren't any curtains,' Peggy pointed out.

'There must be some old blackout blinds somewhere.'

'Blinds? I bet Ethel just tarred the windows, the old cheapskate. This is *Woman's Friend*, after all.'

'*Disculpe, signorina*! That's *Amigo de la Mujer* to you.'

There was supposed to be no talking in the office but Joan and Peggy talked all day, snatching their conversations in fragments in the narrow spaces between the clattering typewriters and Miss Cooke's withering glare. The exchanges reminded Jessica of a toy Theo had had when he was small, a wooden box with coloured pegs sticking out of it and a hammer to hit them with. If you hit a peg hard enough it went in and another one popped out. You never knew which colour it would be.

They called Miss Cooke the Bottlewasher. It startled Jessica that two girls could be like that together, like boys were, good-humoured, undemanding, slipping effortlessly from practicality to intimacy and back again and never taking offence, always on the edge of laughter. At school friendships had been whispery, clammy things, heavy with secrets. The girls had hunched their arms around their friends just as they had hunched their arms around their papers during examinations, defying anyone to peek. They had divided into pairs like lovers and held hands and put notes in one another's satchels and wore two halves of the same pendant around their necks. Joan and Peggy were the same with everyone, even Jessica. It was just that they were more so with one another.

Jessica could not imagine how they stayed so cheerful. There was always too much to do. She had hoped to persuade the Bottlewasher to let her go early on Fridays but Miss Cooke only said that there was plenty more for Jessica to do if she had spare time. She gave her articles to proofread, snippets to cobble together about cold cream and custard powder and the countless children of the royal family. On a particularly sweltering day, with Doreen off with the flu, Jessica was instructed to do the horoscopes. She rather enjoyed it. There was something cheering about ordaining the future. She read Joan's out. Joan was a Capricorn. According to Jessica's predictions the colour blue would prove lucky for her in the week ahead. The next day she came to work with a blue scarf knotted around her neck. She told Jessica she had borrowed it from a girl in her hostel.

'You'd better be right,' she said. 'I hate blue. And it itches like the devil.'

Gerald was a Sagittarius. Jessica wrote that it was a week for those born under the sign of the archer to count their blessings and not take loved ones for granted, but either she was wrong or Gerald did not read *Woman's Friend*. On Monday he telephoned her at work, pretending to be a French friend of her mother's visiting London, and, in an execrable accent, told her that he was going away for a few days on business. He promised to telephone when he got back.

Without their evening to look forward to, the days dragged. Eleanor came to London to see Mrs Leonard on Wednesday as she always did. She told Jessica that Theo had been glad to hear that Phyllis was coming home. She said he had talked about Guy Cockayne, about his visit to Ellinghurst.

'He said it meant so much to him, for us to know his friends from that time,' she said. 'He said they were another family to him.'

'Perhaps we should ask Guy to dinner,' Jessica suggested. 'If that's what Theo would like.'

'Perhaps we should.'

She gave her mother the last address he had sent her, care of a firm of solicitors in the City, and recalled with a prickle of anticipation his narrow hands, his pale poet's face. Part of her had always

321

imagined marrying a friend of Theo's. She had watched them out of her bedroom window on summer evenings, playing croquet or drinking cocktails on the terrace, and wondered which one was hers and when she would be old enough for them to know it. Guy Cockayne was different from those boys with their tennis racquets and their easy laughter, but she still thought of him sometimes, when she was alone. There was something complicated about him that drew her. And he had loved Theo. She loved him a little already, just for that.

The next night, which was Gerald's night, she took a long bath and read a magazine while Nanny played Solitaire, clicking her tongue at the cards. In Mayfair and Belgravia the newly minted debutantes would be putting on their evening dresses. Before the War girls had been presented individually in the Throne Room but a four-year backlog rendered such a system unworkable. Instead, the King and Queen held garden party courts with the girls presented *en masse* and in ordinary day clothes. In the photographs on the society pages they clustered together awkwardly under their hats, like guests at a fête. Jessica thought she recognised one or two of them from school. She wondered if they had got any better at dancing since the days when they had pushed her around the school gymnasium, their damp hands clutching hers. She tried not to envy them the balls. She had asked Theo once if balls were dreamy and he had laughed and said only if she meant the kind of dream when things repeated themselves over and over and, however hard you tried, you could not run away or make yourself wake up.

Theo would have adored the places Gerald took her to, the Grafton Galleries and the Embassy Club and Morton's in Soho. At the Grafton there was a negro band and everyone was rich and beautiful and determinedly, recklessly happy. Jessica adored the club's old-fashioned proprieties: the cakes from Gunter's, the obligatory gloves, the demure layers of tissue paper obscuring the paintings of nudes on the walls were all part of a sly joke, an arch pretence of innocence that, when the band played syncopated jazz and the floor was crowded with dancers pressed together in the tango or moving their hips suggestively in the shimmy, was both soothing and deliciously absurd.

Gerald disliked the Grafton. He said that there was no point in a nightclub that did not serve alcohol, that if he wanted cakes and sandwiches and iced coffee he could go to tea with the vicar. He particularly detested the violently pink concoction they called Turk's Blood that was the speciality of the house. In his day, Gerald said, Turk's Blood was a proper drink made with red Burgundy and champagne.

Gerald liked the secret places, the cellars and the sleazy side doors where you had to ring the doorbell with a special code to be let in. He liked the Seven Souls and the Lotus and the Vampire Club, where there were men in lipstick with powdered faces and women in suits and ties, and the band was led by a negress with a gravelly voice who performed in a white dinner jacket and top hat and sang the popular songs with lewd lyrics of her own invention. He liked Rector's, a dingy basement on Tottenham Court Road where decanters of whisky were provided in the gentleman's cloakroom and the band, dressed in firemen's helmets, came down from their places to dance like madmen among the crowd.

Jessica supposed she liked them too. You could like things and not like them at the same time. She disliked the taste of cigarettes but she loved the way they made her feel, the enigmatic curl of the smoke around her face, the cool dismissive act of exhalation. When she smoked she felt like Theda Bara, exotic and mysterious. And the music was thrilling. When the band played the reckless rhythms of 'Livery Stable Blues' and 'Tiger Rag', she had to dance, to surrender to its mad exuberance until nothing mattered but the trombones and the motor horns and the cowbells and the frying pans beaten like drums, pounding like a score of hearts in her chest. Then the champagne and the music echoed in her bones and her teeth and shimmered beneath her skin, and she was someone else, someone wild who would die in captivity. In the flat unsparing stare of daylight, she thought of Gerald's hands, his creased old man's skin, and the recollection of what she had let him do could make her squirm. But in the darkness, under the plane trees, with the champagne and the music still resonating inside her, she wanted him. She wanted him to want her. She pushed his hands away but she waited for them to come back. She wanted them to come back. Her body arched and her breath quickened, just like his.

She did not ask Gerald about Christabel. She did not want to be the kind of girl who cared about that sort of thing, but she did not like not knowing either. One night, alone with Ludo Holland at the table, she asked him.

'He hasn't told you?'

'I haven't asked. I don't suppose it's any of my business.'

Ludo took a drag of his cigarette. 'She was his wife,' he said. 'She died. A motor smash. Three years ago.'

Jessica stared at him. 'He was married?'

'Very. It was a bad time.' He tapped the ash into a dirty glass. 'But then it was a bad time for everyone.'

When Gerald returned to the table Jessica put her hand on his, sliding her fingers between his, and kissed him.

'What's that for?' he asked but she only shook her head and kissed him again. She had never given a thought to his life before her. He did not seem the kind of man anything bad would ever happen to. She felt very tender towards him and at the same time faintly appalled. He was a widower. It gave him depth, the shadow of poignancy darkening his reckless gaiety. It also made him seem older than ever.

★　★　★

When her father telephoned the flat Jessica demanded to know what was wrong. Her alarm made him irritable. He told her brusquely to be quiet and listen, that he meant to be up in London the next Thursday and that he wished to have dinner with her and Phyllis.

'Phyllis is home?'

'She arrives tomorrow.' He ignored Jessica's protestations that Thursdays were not convenient. He said that he would prefer to have dinner in the flat where they would be able to talk privately, without interruption.

Jessica supposed it was something to do with Ellinghurst. Ever since Cousin Evelyn had delivered his verdict she had tried not to think about what would happen to the house when Father died. It was one thing having Lettice and her grub babies at Ellinghurst, quite another selling it as a school. At least the Yorkshire Melvilles were family. If they lived at Ellinghurst it would still be their house, or nearly theirs. She would visit them when she wanted and everything would be almost the same. But a school? There would be lessons in the Library and Prize Giving in the Great Hall. When she thought of hordes of screaming ten-year-olds rampaging along the corridors it made her feel sick.

The maid agreed to work an evening shift. Jessica left the food to her and Nanny. Her father never noticed what he ate. She asked Nanny to arrange for whisky and gin to be delivered, to make sure there were candles and flowers and wine and a fire laid in the dining room. She told Nanny to have the bill sent directly to her father.

Gerald was put out when she told him she would not be able to see him but Jessica only laughed and told him he was not the only one with other business to attend to.

'And no, it isn't any of your business what my business is,' she said and she smiled into the receiver at his silence on the other end of the line. The pleasure of piquing his jealousy made up just a little for two whole weeks without dancing or drinking champagne.

Phyllis was the first to arrive. Jessica hugged her.

'Welcome home,' she said. 'How was Egypt?'

'Interesting. Hot. Where's Nanny?'

'I sent her to the flickers. She wanted to see you but Father insisted. Private business and all that.'

Phyllis peered out of the window at the row of new houses going up further down the street, the distant green of the market gardens. 'Nice place,' she said.

'You could live here too if you wanted.'

'I don't think so.' She lifted the lid of the piano, ran her finger down the keys. 'I thought you said this block was all businessmen and widows.'

'It is . . . mostly.'

'Which category does the woman who lives across the landing fall into?'

Jessica shrugged. 'How would I know? I've never met her.'

It was not quite a lie. They had never been introduced. But Jessica saw her sometimes, a blonde in nail polish and scarlet lipstick, sliding into the Rolls-Royce that waited outside the building. Once, late at night, as Jessica struggled with her key, the door of the other flat had opened and a grey-haired man in evening dress had come out. He had stopped to light a cigarette on the landing but, when he raised his eyes and saw Jessica, he had put his hand to his cheek like a horse's blinker and hurried away down the stairs.

'I'm not sure Nanny would approve,' Phyllis said. 'She appeared to be going out in her nightgown.'

'Definitely a businessman, then.'

Phyllis smiled and Jessica smiled too. She looked at the clock on the mantel. Father would be here any moment. She had butterflies. 'Drink?' she said.

Phyllis drank whisky. Jessica had gin. By the time their father arrived Jessica was a little giddy. They talked about his train journey and the closeness of the weather and ate soup and veal in a white sauce. It was not until the maid had served the apple Charlotte that Father cleared his throat and said that he had something to say. Jessica buried her face in her wine glass, letting the fumes dance in her head.

'Cousin Evelyn has made his position very clear,' Sir Aubrey said. 'Should he inherit Ellinghurst he will sell. I have stressed to him repeatedly his duty to family, to history, to the ties that have bound the Melvilles to Ellinghurst since the reign of

Charles II but to no avail. He cares only for money. For profit.'

He raised his hand, silencing Phyllis's protest. After long consideration, he said, he had come to a decision, one which he had now had the opportunity to discuss with the estate's lawyers. Throughout its history, the house had passed from father to son, and, once, in the eighteenth century, to a nephew, there being no direct male heirs. But while this arrangement was a cherished tradition, it was not enshrined in law. There were no legal restrictions on the inheritance of the estate. The current baronet might bequeath it by will as he chose.

'This has been a difficult and painful decision,' he said. 'The Melville baronets reside at Ellinghurst. That is and has always been the proper order of things. I had always hoped – I had expected – that it would continue to be so. But Evelyn gives me no choice. His inheritance would be a catastrophe. The house must go to one of you.'

Phyllis and Jessica exchanged looks.

'I have turned it over and over and it is the only solution. You would have to be married, of course, that goes without saying. It would be advantageous if there was money. There are . . . pressures on the estate. None, however, are insurmountable. You will raise your sons at Ellinghurst and they shall inherit in their turn. The Melville line will continue.'

'Except they wouldn't be Melvilles, would they?' Phyllis said. 'Not if we were married.'

'They could be. The law allows for it.'

'You would expect our husbands to change their names?'

'There have always been Melvilles at Ellinghurst.'

Phyllis considered her father. Then, quietly, she began to laugh. Jessica stared at the table. The wine and the gin had muddled her head. She could not think straight. She could not understand why Phyllis was laughing.

'I must say, Father, it's quite an offer,' Phyllis said. 'Marry my daughter, give her all your money and take her name, and in exchange you get a crippling mortgage and a house of dubious architectural merit. How could any right-thinking man resist?'

'Phyllis, for God's sake,' Jessica said. 'Can't you let Father finish?'

'Why? What could he possibly add that could make this plan of his anything but entirely preposterous?'

'I think you should at least listen to what he has to say.'

'Do you indeed?' She shrugged, holding up her hands. 'All right, then. Go on. I'm all ears.'

Even Jessica in her confusion had to admit that her father's proposal was unconventional. Whichever of his daughters married first would inherit the house on Sir Aubrey's death. Entailments would prevent it from being sold or devised by will. It would instead pass directly to that daughter's male heirs or, if she had none, to the male heirs of her sister. Whoever inherited the estate would be required under the terms of the entailment to adopt the Melville name.

'So it's a race?' Phyllis said. 'Even better. A fight to the death. Or should that be debt?'

'I am sixty-six years old,' Sir Aubrey said stiffly. 'I shan't live for ever.'

'Don't say that,' Jessica protested.

'I'm sorry, Jessica, but we must face facts. Decisions have to be made.'

Phyllis considered her father. She was no longer laughing. 'Very well. Since we are facing facts let me add a few of my own. I mean to be an archaeologist. I don't intend ever to marry and I have absolutely no desire for children. I don't care how many legal documents you draw up, I will never live at Ellinghurst or take any responsibility for its future. I will not be enslaved by the legacy of my forefathers. I have my own life to lead. Is that fact enough for you?'

'You're young,' Sir Aubrey protested. 'Wait until you fall in love.'

'I'm not so very young, Father, and I have already been in love. If that changed anything it was only to make me surer than ever.'

'And what about your duty, your obligations as a Melville?' he demanded.

'I'm sorry for the servants, the tenants, of course I am, but I cannot be held responsible for them. Times change.'

'So you would throw away three hundred years of history?'

'I couldn't do that even if I wanted to. Nothing changes the past.'

'But Ellinghurst is in our blood. It's who we are.'

'No, Father,' Phyllis said, 'it's a house. An impossible, impractical house. I'm sorry.'

Sir Aubrey's hands tightened into fists. With deliberate dignity he turned away from his oldest daughter. 'Jessica?'

'I . . . I don't know. I mean, I love Ellinghurst, you know I do. But it's a lot to take in.'

Sir Aubrey folded his hands together, his face expressionless. Then, silently, his shoulders shaking, he bowed his head.

It was an exquisite relief when the maid came in and Sir Aubrey cleared his throat and patted his nose with his handkerchief. Gratefully Jessica suggested coffee in the drawing room. Not long afterwards Phyllis left to catch her bus. She said she had to get back before the hostel locked the doors. Sir Aubrey and Jessica drank their coffee in silence. At Ellinghurst the last of the light would be fading from the rose-gold sky, the air soft with the scent of roses and cut grass.

'I will think about what you said, Father,' Jessica said. 'I promise.'

There was another long silence. Jessica could hear the maid moving about in the kitchen. 'What does Eleanor think?'

Sir Aubrey frowned at her, baffled. 'Eleanor? Whatever does this have to do with your mother?'

CHAPTER 24

The story was called *The Winds of Romance* and concerned a shop girl and a mysterious dark-eyed sheik. Jessica tried to fix her attention on the lines but the words swam on the page. Instead, she stared out of her slice of window. The wires in the reinforced glass turned the white sky to graph paper and distorted the lines of the chimney pots, making them ripple like flags.

After her father had gone back to his club she had stayed awake a long time, drinking what was left of the wine and thinking about Ellinghurst. Phyllis was right, even if she was right for the wrong reasons. Her father's proposal was ridiculous, ridiculous enough to be faintly alarming, but not because of his expectation that they would both marry. There was nothing remotely unreasonable about that. Unlike Phyllis, Jessica was normal. She had no intention of ending up a spinster. It was all very well dabbling at *Woman's Friend* while she was nineteen, it was a lark, an adventure, something to shock her mother with, but she could no more imagine working for the rest of her life than she could imagine flying to the moon. Work was not for ever, not unless you were a failure at everything else. Jessica would fall in love. She would have a heavenly husband, heavenly sex, with any luck plenty of heavenly money. Heavenly children too, she supposed, in time, though she could not quite imagine it. Of course she would. Unlike Phyllis, she intended to be happy.

But Phyllis was right about the other part. Even a millionaire quite *boulversé* with adoration would hardly leap at their father's proposition. To take on Ellinghurst and the burden of death duties, to raise their children as Melvilles, a cuckoo in his own cripplingly costly nest? Jessica loved every stone of Ellinghurst but even she could see that it was no Chatsworth. An American heiress might be lured by the promise of dukedoms and Van Dykes but a neo-Gothic castle with a rotting racquets court and a thirteen-storey tower built of unreinforced concrete? Even the ghostly endorsement of Christopher Wren could not turn that into a convincingly silken purse.

And yet, for all that, it would be wonderful. Jessica had never imagined she would have to leave Ellinghurst, or not completely. It would still be her home, even when she lived somewhere else. It would always be where she belonged. London was wild and gay and intoxicating but when she imagined herself happy she imagined herself at Ellinghurst, in the clear green water of the lake or sprawled on the lawn in the sunshine, listening to the wood pigeons and the distant thwack of tennis balls. In her imagination she walked through the arched rooms and every hinge, every handle, every slope and glance of light was as familiar as her own body.

And Theo was there, not in her mother's extravagant memorial or even in his old bedroom, which Eleanor still refused to clear out, but in the worn treads of the stairs, the scuffs on the paintwork, tucked up inside the too-small coats and lined-up boots in the old pantry. The previous weekend, Jessica had gone out to the old greenhouses and amidst the boarded-up windows and the broken pots she had found Grandfather Melville's old bath chair. Mould grew grey maps on the cushions and the damp wicker sagged but when she sat in it and her fingers closed around the arms, she was ten years old again, her heart in her mouth and her hair streaming out behind her, terrified and exultant, conscious only of the chair's careering jolt and the soaring joy of Theo's approbation.

So much had been lost already. The thought of never again going to Ellinghurst, of the pieces of their lives there, so many generations of lives, being pulled apart and packed into lorries to be split up and sold, it was unbearable.

She went home for the weekend reluctantly, apprehensive of being cornered by her father, of being pressed. She did not think she could endure it if he cried. Phyllis was no help, of course. She had work in London, she said, and could not come home. On Saturday morning Jessica rose late and dressed slowly, keen to avoid her father at the breakfast table. It was both a surprise and a relief when Eleanor told her that Mrs Maxwell Brooke and Marjorie were coming to lunch. It was a long time since her mother had had guests at Ellinghurst.

'I didn't know you still saw Mrs Maxwell Brooke.'

'I don't,' Eleanor said. 'She invited herself. Out of the blue. She said Marjorie was dying to see you again.'

'Really?' Jessica looked bemused.

'She was absolutely insistent. There was nothing I could do to stop her.'

Jessica had not seen Marjorie Maxwell Brooke since before the War. She had written after Theo died, of course, but by then Eleanor and Mrs Maxwell Brooke were no longer friends. Jessica had never written back. Of all the girls who had trailed after Theo Marjorie had been the most irritating.

'You know she's in love with you,' she had said to Theo once. 'She keeps your photograph in the drawer of her bedside table and kisses it every night before she goes to sleep. And she practises her signature. Mrs Theodore Melville inside all her exercise books, over and over.'

Actually, she did not know that for certain but she was sure it was true. It was what the girls at her school did when they mooned after boys and Marjorie was easily as silly as they were. She had hoped to make Theo shudder. Instead, he laughed. To Jessica's bafflement he had never minded Marjorie, even though she was not pretty in the least and had a laugh shrill enough to bring on neuralgia.

The Maxwell Brookes arrived promptly in time for sherry at twelve thirty. Mrs Maxwell Brooke had darker hair than Jessica remembered and a good deal of gold jewellery. As for Marjorie, the lankiness of adolescence had hardened into angularity, sharp juts and knobs that her expensive wool dress did little to soften. She had cut her hair. The bobbed style was impeccably fashionable but it was not becoming. It emphasised the thinness of her nose, the pointed spade of her chin. The bones of her wrists were as prominent as knuckles.

Marjorie was a debutante. She was twenty-three. Mrs Maxwell Brooke talked breezily of the court balls that were expected at Buckingham Palace once a final Treaty of Peace had been signed.

'You're not out yet, are you, dear?' she said to Jessica. 'We had rather hoped Phyllis might be one of Marjorie's girls but she isn't, is she? Certainly we've not seen her, though we've kept our eyes peeled. Goodness, but there are a lot of them. Planning a ball is perfect headache.'

Jessica looked at Marjorie. 'A ball,' she said. 'How thrilling.'

At lunch Mrs Maxwell Brooke talked to Sir Aubrey about Ellinghurst. She was very gay. Her grandfather had known Grandfather Melville and she told a long and rather muddled story about a gun Grandfather Melville had invented for him to shoot wasps. 'It was frightfully dangerous,' she said. 'But a marvellous way of deadheading the roses.' When she laughed her bracelets rattled like castanets.

After lunch Father went back to the library. The women drank coffee in the drawing room. Eleanor told Mrs Maxwell Brooke about Theo's memorial.

'I should love to see it,' Mrs Maxwell Brooke said. 'Wouldn't you, Marjorie?'

'Why don't you go with Eleanor?' Jessica suggested quickly. 'Marjorie and I will come later. We've so much to catch up on.'

As soon as they were gone, Jessica turned to Marjorie. 'I'm so glad you came. I've been meaning to look you up in London. I'm there too, you know.'

'Yes, your mother said. She said you were working for a magazine. It sounds frightfully glamorous. I bet you have queues of admirers?'

Jessica thought of Gerald and of Guy Cockayne who had still not answered Eleanor's letter. She wondered, not for the first time, whether the firm of solicitors had remembered to forward it on. 'Hardly queues,' she said. 'It's just a relief to be in London at last and not dying of boredom out here.'

'Really? I'm always so glad to come home.'

'Come on. You must be having the time of your life. All those balls.'

'I suppose so.'

'You don't sound very sure.'

'No, I mean, of course. It's fine. It's lovely. Very busy.'

Jessica slid her a sideways glance. 'I wondered if perhaps you might like to come to supper with me one evening. I should so like it if we could be friends.'

'Really?'

'But of course. Theo was very fond of you, you know.'

Marjorie stared down at the cup cradled in her bony hands. Then, abruptly, she clattered it into its saucer. 'I still can't believe he's gone. I keep thinking—' She shook her head. 'I'm sorry. It's just . . .'

'I know.'

'I thought he was wonderful. We all did. Terence was just saying the other day that of all the boys . . . well . . .' She forced a smile. 'You remember Terence Connolly? He stayed here once or twice with his parents before the War.'

'I remember.'

'Mother hadn't heard from them for years. They went back to America. But when Terence enlisted Mrs Connolly wrote and asked if he could look us up while he was over here. She said we were the only English people she could think of to ask. We saw a good deal of him before he was posted.

Now he's waiting to be demobbed. The camp's only in Surrey so he comes up to London when he can.'

'Marjorie, you dark horse. So you and Terence Connolly . . .?'

Marjorie blushed. 'Heavens, no. Goodness. I mean, he's awfully nice but an American, can you imagine? Mother would have sixty fits.'

After that she would not talk about the Season or parties. She asked Jessica about her work and about Phyllis and whether there was still a tennis court at Ellinghurst. When Eleanor and Mrs Maxwell Brooke came back from the memorial Mrs Maxwell Brooke told Marjorie it was time to go home.

'Thank you, Eleanor, for a delightful afternoon,' Mrs Maxwell Brooke said, kissing her cheek. 'Promise you'll lunch with us soon. In July, perhaps, when the Season's over and things are a little less hectic. Goodbye, Jessica, dear.' She turned to leave, Marjorie behind her. Then she turned back. 'Just one other tiny little thing. I don't suppose you would have an address for Oscar Greenwood, would you?'

'For Oscar?' Eleanor said, puzzled. Behind her mother Marjorie stared at her shoes.

'It's just that I happened to hear that he's in London now and we thought it might be rather fun to catch up. The children were all so close, weren't they, growing up? I was so very sorry to hear about Sylvia, by the way. Aubrey told me. Too ghastly. It must have been a terrible blow.'

'Thank you.'

'Anyway, and it was only a passing fancy really, I thought, given that the poor child must be at a loose end, that he might find it entertaining to accompany Marjorie to a dance or two. I have to confess, I find it a shocking imposition, this new habit of inviting "Miss Maxwell Brooke and Partner". One should simply refuse, I mean, one might as well ask a girl to bring her own sandwiches, only one doesn't want to be awkward, no girl wants a reputation for being difficult, and, well, we thought young Oscar might find the whole thing rather a gas. So if you did have an address . . .'

'Oscar's not in London,' Jessica said.

'But I was sure I heard—'

'He's in Cambridge. Not that he'd come, even if he was. Oscar doesn't like dancing. Or parties. Or other people much, for that matter.'

'I think that's rather up to him, don't you, dear?' Mrs Maxwell Brooke said. 'Well, it's not as though Cambridge is Timbuktu. It can't be more than an hour or two on the train and we'd be more than happy to cover his ticket. Might you have an address for him there, Eleanor, dear?'

'Aubrey does, certainly. Remind me to ask him, Jessica.'

'Or perhaps he wouldn't mind being disturbed now? While I'm here? I shouldn't want you to have to go to all the bother of telephoning.'

Eleanor hesitated. Mrs Maxwell Brooke smiled at her blandly.

'Very well,' Eleanor said. 'Jessica, run and ask your father for Oscar's address, would you?'

Jessica did not run. She walked quite slowly. She could hardly get over it, the sheer brass neck of Mrs Maxwell Brooke. *Marjorie was always so fond of him.* What a lot of rot. Marjorie had always been too busy mooning after Theo even to notice that Oscar existed. It was Jessica who had been made to play with him and listen to his queer nonsense, Jessica and Oscar who, to Jessica's fury, had been lumped together as 'the little ones'. What possible right did Mrs Maxwell Brooke have now to swan in and help herself to Oscar like a film star selecting a bonbon? Well, she was in for a disappointment. Oscar loathed dances and he would never give a fig for bony Marjorie. Oscar loved Jessica. Mrs Maxwell Brooke could whistle until her lips wore out but that was the way it was. There was no changing Oscar. He was like the chemistry experiments they had done at school: understand them or not, they always came out exactly the same way.

Oscar belonged to Jessica. He always had.

Her father was sitting in a chair when she knocked on the library door. She wondered if he had been asleep. When she asked him for the address he pointed her towards a pile of letters on a table by the window. They were all from Oscar. She wondered why Oscar was writing to her father but she did not ask. She wrote down the address and walked slowly back to the Great Hall.

Mrs Maxwell Brooke held out her hand. 'Thank you, dear,' she said.

Jessica fingered the piece of paper. 'I had forgotten Oscar and Marjorie were such friends,' she said.

Mrs Maxwell Brooke went on smiling. 'I've always said to Marjorie that there is no bond stronger than the bonds one forges in one's youth. Childhood friends are friends for life.'

'Marjorie and I were just saying the same thing. So you'll invite Oscar to Marjorie's coming-out ball?'

'If he is in town, then I'm sure—'

'What fun. All of us together, it will be like old times.'

Mrs Maxwell Brooke's smile flickered uncertainly.

'Marjorie tells me you've invited Terence Connolly too,' Jessica enthused. 'Phyllis will be thrilled. It's been years since—' She broke off, a hand to her mouth. 'Oh, heavens. You do mean to invite Phyllis and me, don't you? I just assumed . . . Please tell me I haven't put my big old foot in it? Here, this is for you.' Eyes round with innocent mortification, she held out the paper with Oscar's address on it. Mrs Maxwell Brooke took it.

'Of course you girls are invited,' she said grimly and on her wrists her bracelets rattled like gold teeth.

The Maxwell Brooke car crunched away over the gravel.

343

'Thank heavens,' Eleanor said. 'I thought she'd never leave.'

Jessica watched her mother climb the stairs, leaning on the banister like an old woman. There was a bowl of white roses on the hall table. She drew one out and sniffed it. It smelled very sweet. Then one by one she pulled out the petals and dropped them on the floor: *worships me, adores me, just wants me for my body.* The suit of armour watched her with its slit-eyes.

'What are you looking at?' she asked. She laughed. Then, taking its cold hand in hers she stood on tiptoes, kissing it on its metal beak. Her laughter echoed inside the empty metal shell, making her laugh even more.

Cinderella was going to the ball.

CHAPTER 25

On the last Saturday in June an aeroplane flew across the Channel from Paris to Buckingham Palace with a letter for the King. The delegates to the Peace Commission had signed the Treaty of Versailles and ended the state of war between Germany and the Allied Powers. Germany would no longer be permitted to keep a navy or an air force and a cap would be placed on her army, restricting it to no more than one hundred thousand men. Territories that had provided the country with revenue from iron, coal and steel were to be removed from her control. Meanwhile, she would be expected to foot a bill of nearly seven million pounds in reparations, to include pensions to England's war widows. It was said that when the German representatives, who were last to arrive, were ushered in to the gilded glitter of the *Galerie des Glaces*, nobody stood. The Germans sat white-faced, their eyes on the frescoed ceiling, as one by one the Allied delegates affixed their signatures to the treaty. Afterwards, they were escorted hurriedly from the room before the air echoed to the sound of a gun salute and

President Wilson, together with Lloyd George and Clémenceau, stepped out onto the terrace to the tumultuous cheers of the massed crowd. It was five years to the day since the Archduke Franz Ferdinand had been assassinated in Sarajevo.

In the afternoon Oscar walked. He walked to St Ives and sat outside the village pub, a pint of beer in front of him, his hat tipped back and his face turned up to the sun. He wished he could talk to Kit. The world felt a long way away and very small, as though he was looking at it through the wrong end of a telescope.

He had thought he would be glad to have Cambridge back to himself. After the hushed intensity of the summer examinations there had followed the wild bacchanalia of May Week, a whirl of pleasure, of parties and picnics and drifts of women swooping and settling around town like colonies of gaily-coloured birds. Oscar found it difficult to work, to think. The college was giving a May Ball and, as Oscar negotiated the ranks of arched white jasmine and potted palms that blocked the entrance to the Porter's Lodge and watched from the window of the Wren Library as the workmen banged up the tents in Nevile's Court and laid the wooden floors for dancing, he felt for the first time as though he had no place there.

A van brought the books from Sir Aubrey. There were several boxes. Oscar lugged them one by one up to his attic room and made a wall of them beside the desk. When he unpacked the first box he asked Mrs Piggott to take a photograph of him sitting with them piled on his desk and sent it to Sir Aubrey with his next letter. He did not go to the library. Nor did he see Kit, though once by the river he glimpsed him leaning on the parapet of Trinity Bridge with a girl in a pale blue dress. He studied at Chesterton Road, puzzling over Henry Melville's pencilled marginalia and doggedly working his way through Mr Willis's syllabus. Mrs Piggott complained, she said she did not run the kind of house where gentlemen lounged about in their rooms all day, but at least from up there Cambridge looked almost the same as it always had, the canvas tents no more than glimpses of white between the spires and the leaded roofs. He was glad when the women took flight and the tents came down and all that remained of them were divots in the velvet lawns.

It was the last day of term when he ran into Kit in Trinity Street.

'Where the devil have you been?' Kit said. 'We thought you must be dead. Either that or locked into some abandoned cellar at the Cavendish with nothing but alpha particles to keep you going through the Long Vac.'

Kit was going down the next day. He was to spend a few weeks with Girouard in France and the rest of the summer at his family's estate in the Highlands.

'You'd adore it,' he said to Oscar. 'Shooting and

347

Scottish dancing and a deep distrust of cleverness in all its forms.'

'It sounds like Army training.'

Kit laughed. 'The food's not much better, either. You'd better come to tea this afternoon. It might be the last decent meal I have for months.'

Oscar bought rock buns at the baker's on Bridge Street. By that time in the afternoon they were all that was left. The woman behind the counter put them in a brown paper bag, then held the bag by its corners and flipped it over to close it. The bag made him think of his mother. When they had bought cakes when he was little she had drawn mouse faces on brown paper bags with black noses and long black whiskers and black centres to their twisted brown paper ears. He was still thinking about his mother when he came out of the shop and walked straight into a girl walking the other way, dropping the bag on the pavement.

'Goodness, I'm so sorry,' the girl said, ducking to pick it up, and as she handed it to him Oscar realised it was Frances, Kit's friend. He had not seen her since the day they had met outside Magdalene. 'Oh, hello,' she said.

'Hello.'

'Oscar, isn't it? We met once. With Kit Ferguson.'

'I remember.'

'I hope your cakes aren't spoiled.'

'Rock buns. The fall will have done them good. Softened them up a bit.'

Frances smiled awkwardly, fiddling with a button on her sleeve.

'So, are you well?' Oscar asked to fill in the silence. 'You look well.'

'I'm . . . yes. It's awfully warm, isn't it? Though I suppose one shouldn't complain. Not after all that rain last month.'

'I suppose not.'

'And how are you? How's Kit?'

'Kit? Well, I think. I've hardly seen him.'

'I thought he might be away.'

'Just busy, I think. Examinations and May Week and everything.'

'Yes. Yes, of course.' She forced another smile. 'I should let you get on. Those rock buns won't eat themselves.'

'It was nice to see you.'

'You too.'

'Should I send Kit your . . .?'

'Regards? Yes, of course. Send him my regards.'

Kit's room was bare, the emptied shelves patterned with dust. Most of his belongings had been packed away in tea chests. He had to rummage in one to find a teacup for Oscar.

'I just bumped into Frances,' Oscar said.

'Who?' Kit unwrapped the cup from its newspaper, wiping it on his sleeve.

'The girl you introduced me to outside Magdalene that time. Newnham. English Literature. Surely you remember. She remembers you. She sent her regards.'

'Oh God, her. The one with the hair. I took her to the Quinquaginta. Only once, mind. It was like dancing with a malfunctioning marionette.'

'I liked her.'

'Bad luck, old chap,' Kit said, sloshing tea. 'I don't think you're her type.'

'Actually, that's not—'

'Don't blame yourself. There's a particular sort of girl that throws herself at cripples. The grislier the better. We saw them in the hospital all the time and not just the nurses either. Complete strangers sometimes who'd written to Matron asking if they could visit, and always with this look in their eyes, this voracious pity as though there could never be enough wretchedness to go round.'

'And Frances was like that?'

'One of the worst I've ever seen. Every time she fixed me with those moony bloodhound eyes another little bit of me died.'

The next day Kit went down and Oscar had Cambridge to himself. It was very warm. Without the hectic spill of undergraduates shouting and stirring up the air the creamy courts and cloisters of Trinity lapsed into a kind of drowsing reverie, a half-waking dream in which time did not flow forward steadily like a river but progressed in lazy whirls and eddies, turning back on itself. Then, in the shadows and the squinting glare of light, it was Isaac Newton who stood there still, the echo of his stamped foot quivering between the sun-warmed colonnades, or Francis Bacon in his doublet and lace ruff, while Oscar passed unseen like a faint breath of wind, as insubstantial as a ghost.

The Cavendish was closed, at least to undergraduates. Sometimes he saw Rutherford walking in the street, alone or deep in conversation with one of his research students. In fourteen weeks Oscar would be attending his lectures. It felt like a very long time to wait. He walked through the hot afternoons, to Grantchester and Madingley and St Ives, but it did not stop the restlessness, the itch in the soles of his feet. He took out the guidebook he had bought to the Alps and turned the pages, imagining walking in the mountains, measuring out the grandeur of the great peaks footstep by footstep, the clear mountain air easing his rusted brain like engine oil. He investigated trains, modest *pensiones*. He told himself that it was the greatest luxury of all, to travel alone.

Then, returning from his walk in a world at last at peace, he found a letter from London. He recognised the handwriting. He tore it open reluctantly, wondering when Mrs Maxwell Brooke would finally accept defeat. She had already written three times to ask if he might accompany her daughter to dances in London and, undeterred by his refusals, sent him an invitation to her coming-out dance. It was so long since they had seen him at Ellinghurst, she had written each time, and they were dying to hear what he was up to. She hoped he remembered Marjorie with as much fondness as Marjorie remembered him. Oscar did not remember Marjorie at all. Each time he had politely but firmly declined. It was becoming a tiresome waste of stamps.

'Anything nice?' Mrs Piggott asked, pretending to busy herself with the vase of dried flowers on the hall table. Oscar did not answer. He glanced to the bottom of the letter.

> Do think of coming if you can. We received your reply but I know how plans change, particularly for a young man of your age, and I wanted to write and say again how delighted we would be to see you if you could come. It would mean a great deal to Marjorie. The Melville girls will both be there, of course, and Terence Connolly. You remember Terence, don't you? It will be like old times.

Phyllis was home.

The Melvilles' flat was on the third floor of a mansion block with green turrets. When he rang the electric bell there was a pause. Then a voice trumpeted through the brass speaker with such volume he stepped backwards.

'Well, you found it then,' Nanny shouted. 'Are you going to stay down there?'

'I thought—'

'Wait in the lobby. You've a taxi cab, haven't you?

It's not right, of course, a respectable girl doesn't go to her first—'

The line crackled and went dead. A moment later the glass door buzzed. Oscar pushed it open. The lobby had a low ceiling and a thick carpet that muffled sound. Oscar sat down to wait on a flimsy chaise near the stairs. His legs did not want to stay still. He jiggled his knees and watched the gilt hand above the elevator door tick as it lumbered upwards. On the third floor it stopped. Oscar heard the door clank open. His stiff collar pinched. He put a finger inside it, turning his head from side to side to ease the pressure of the stud against his throat. The gilt hand shivered and began to count back down.

There was a grinding of cogs and then a soft clunk as the lift reached the ground floor. Oscar stood. The doors opened but the woman who stepped out was not Phyllis. She wore a silver dress covered all over with shiny silver beads and a feather in her startlingly blonde hair. Her lips were scarlet. She looked Oscar up and down, her head on one side. With a sigh the lift began grudgingly to grind back upstairs. Then slowly she touched the tip of her tongue to her scarlet lips and smiled.

'Please tell me you're my birthday present,' she said.

Oscar reddened. 'I'm sorry, there must be some—'

'I'm teasing you, darling. I haven't been nearly good enough this year for a present like you.' She laughed, wrinkling her nose. 'Still, you can wish me a happy birthday if you like.'

'Happy birthday.'

'You're not going to give me a birthday kiss?'

Oscar hesitated. Then reluctantly he stepped forward and touched his lips to her cheek. She smelled of something powerful and expensive that made him want to sneeze.

'Twenty-one again,' she said. 'One might almost consider it a miracle.'

She sauntered across the lobby towards the front door. When she walked her hips shimmered and the beads on her dress hummed quietly together, like bees. At the door she waited expectantly. It was a moment before Oscar realised she was waiting for him. He hurried across the lobby and opened the door. She smiled up at him, touching his cheek with one scarlet-nailed hand. Behind Oscar's taxi cab a chauffeur in a peaked cap waited beside a shiny black car.

On the other side of the lobby the lift clunked noisily to a stop. Oscar turned, dropping the door behind him. The metal cage slid open.

'Hello, Oscar,' Jessica said.

She stood in the mouth of the lift, one hand on her hip. Her dress was a draped swathe of rose silk-satin that clung to her bosom and hips and curved upwards at the front to reveal an underskirt of pale rose chiffon. The sleeves of the dress were made from the same chiffon, pale cobwebs that clung to her bare shoulders. Her lips and cheeks glowed, flushed with pink, and in her honey-coloured hair she wore a diamond tiara. Behind her Nanny stood four-square in a dress of black bombazine.

There was no Phyllis.

'Out,' Nanny said to Jessica impatiently, flapping her hands. 'Before this thing crushes us both half to death.'

Oscar tried to smile as Jessica pecked him lightly on the cheek. She wore the coquettish expression of a film star on a cigarette card.

'Phyllis isn't coming?' he asked. The disappointment was like hands pressing down on his throat. It made his face feel stiff. He tugged roughly at his too-tight collar. He could not think why he had come.

'She's meeting us there. Why soak in delicious French bath oil when you can shiver in three inches of tepid water for threepence? I truly think Phyllis believes that if she enjoys herself even a little bit she'll explode or turn to dust or something. I can't imagine why she's bothering to come at all.' Jessica turned slowly, showing off her shimmering silk ankles, the white smoothness of her startlingly exposed back. 'So. What do you think?'

Relief made Oscar generous. 'You look lovely.'

She did look lovely. He could see it quite plainly, just as he could see that a painting was beautiful or a flower, but it did not touch him in the least. He stepped forward and kissed her cheek. On her chin, powdered over but still distinctly visible, there was a tiny pimple. It was red with a yellow centre, as though a tiny yellow worm was burrowing upwards from beneath the skin.

'Lovely is as lovely does,' Nanny said briskly. She smelled exactly as Oscar remembered her, of boiled milk and talcum powder. 'Now, where's this taxi of yours?'

As they drove Jessica pressed her lips together, touching her palms together in silent applause, the excitement rippling over her like water. For all her loveliness there was something childish about her, as though the dress and the face and the hair were just an elaborate dressing-up costume. When Oscar thought of how he had ached for her, the intensity of his infatuation, he felt only bafflement and a faint smudge of shame.

'What?' Jessica said.

'Nothing. I didn't say anything.'

She smirked, smoothing her dress over her hips. 'I suppose you've been to heaps of these dances now, haven't you? Now that you're Marjorie's beau. Don't look so innocent. We know you've been escorting her to balls all summer.'

Is that what Phyllis thought? Not that it mattered what Phyllis thought. Oscar frowned, shaking his head. 'But I haven't been to one.'

'Her mother didn't ask you?'

'She asked me. Several times. I don't know why. I never went.'

Jessica laughed. 'Poor Mrs Maxwell Brooke. I did warn her.'

'I hardly even remember Marjorie.'

'But you're here tonight.'

Oscar shrugged awkwardly. 'I wasn't going to. But there was nothing much going on in Cambridge and I just thought . . . you know.'

'I know.'

The evening sun was bright. Jessica put a hand up to shield her eyes as she looked out of the window. In the Park people strolled arm in arm beneath the trees. It was hard to believe that she and Phyllis were sisters. Everything about her was on the outside, Oscar thought, lit up loud and bright as a funfair ride. He wondered what it felt like to be her, inside her head. The spot on her chin seemed to be getting bigger.

She turned her head, catching him looking. A tiny frown puckered her brow.

'One thing, Oscar,' she said. 'It's nice to see you and everything but you have to promise not to be a bore and trail after me all evening. It's not my job to look after you, all right?'

'All right.'

'All right.' She nodded. Then she glanced at him sideways, her hand drifting up to cover her chin. 'Don't be upset. You have to let me be myself, that's all.'

'I'm not upset.'

'Of course boys don't like to show their feelings. Not like girls.'

'I'm not upset, truly.'

'Good. Well, that's good then.'

They travelled the rest of the way in silence, Jessica gazing out of the window, her cheeks sucked in and her chin thrust out as though she were posing for a photograph, while from beneath its crust of powder her tiny pimple glared at Oscar with its sour yellow eye.

The dance was in a house in Belgravia, rented for the occasion. Oscar climbed the stairs behind Jessica and a wheezing Nanny, taking care not to tread on Jessica's train. When they reached the ball-room a man in a red livery took their cards and announced their names as they entered. The room was beautiful, a jewel box of elaborate gilt-and-white plasterwork with a flower-strewn frescoed ceiling and gilt-framed mirrors reflecting the light of two exquisite crystal chandeliers. Everywhere there were huge gold vases filled with white flowers. At the end of the room the orchestra sat on a raised stage hung with white silk. They played softly, the music curling like smoke above the chattering guests.

A waiter offered a tray of champagne. Oscar took a glass and moved forward into the room, looking around him. He could not see Phyllis. As the band struck up a foxtrot a girl beside him in a green dress stood on her tiptoes.

'Which one is your cousin?' she hissed at her friend, large in lavender.

'Over there. With the glasses.'

'Oh. All right. You'll introduce me, won't you? You promise?'

The lavender girl sighed. 'You mustn't bother him to dance, though. He says he wishes he'd never learned, he's such a slave to it these days. He hates it when girls push themselves on him.'

'Jessica Melville?' A round-faced girl in silvery lace clutched Jessica's arm. Jessica looked at her in confusion.

'I thought it was you! Lucinda Allingham. From school? What a nice surprise. Are you out? Only I've not seen you all Season.' She smiled at Jessica and then at Oscar. 'I don't think we've met. Jessica, aren't you going to introduce us?'

Jessica stared past Lucinda at the crowded room. 'Oscar Greenwood, Lucinda Allingham.'

Lucinda smiled at Oscar and held out her hand. 'How do you do? And how do you know Marjorie?'

'I didn't realise we were so early,' Jessica said, craning her neck.

'Early?' Lucinda said. 'Actually, I think you're one of the last.'

Jessica frowned. 'But I don't understand. Where are all the men?'

Oscar had not noticed it before but now that he looked he saw that there were only a handful of men among the clusters of ballgowns that crowded the room. Several, grey-headed and bespectacled, were plainly fathers, enduring the proceedings with ill-concealed boredom as their thick-waisted wives talked avidly together. Some were boys, Oscar's age or even younger. The few in between were spaced around the room, black-coated candles

359

around which the girls gathered like moths. One, shorter than the girls who leaned in towards him, was bald as an egg but for a few soft hairs like a baby's that gleamed gold in the light of the chandeliers. Another sat in a chair, his crutches propped against the table beside him. One leg of his trousers was pinned up over a stump. He stared into the middle distance as several girls fussed around him, fetching drinks and cushions. There were perhaps ten girls to every man.

A raw-faced youth clapped Oscar on the shoulder.

'Not dancing, Greenwood?' he said. It was Geoffrey Winterson. When Oscar introduced him to Jessica and Lucinda, he ignored Lucinda and asked Jessica to dance. She hesitated, then, shrugging, allowed him to lead her onto the floor.

'So you're at Cambridge,' Lucinda said. 'You must be fearfully clever,' but before Oscar could think of a reply a gaggle of girls clustered around them.

'Cinders, there you are! I'm sorry, are we interrupting?'

'This is Oscar Greenwood,' Lucinda said and she tucked her hand into the crook of Oscar's arm. 'He was just about to ask me to dance.'

'Actually, I—'

And suddenly there she was. He did not notice what colour she was wearing, only the pale grey of her eyes, her soft uncertain smile.

'Hello, Oscar.'

'Phyllis,' he said. 'You came.'

★ ★ ★

It was impossible to talk to her. He tried several times to make his way through the crowd towards her but each time Marjorie's mother headed him off, tucking her arm in his and steering him towards someone he simply had to meet. She introduced him as Marjorie's dearest childhood friend and insisted he dance, not only with Marjorie but with several other girls who smiled bravely as he trod on their toes and whose names he forgot as soon as the music stopped. Over their shoulders he glimpsed Phyllis as she nodded and smiled politely at Marjorie's friends and elderly relations. For a while she sat with Nanny. She did not dance. The light from the chandeliers gleamed on her shingled head. A little before eleven, she touched him on the elbow. The girls around him exchanged looks as she murmured that she had a headache and was going to go home.

'Not yet,' Oscar said. 'I've hardly seen you.'

'Well. You've been busy.'

'At least let me see you into a taxi.'

Outside, among the sleek cars parked along the kerb, several cabs idled.

'Cab, sir?' a liveried footman asked. Oscar looked at Phyllis.

'How's the head?'

She smiled guiltily. 'Miraculously a great deal better.'

'It's a beautiful night,' he said. 'We could walk a little. If you wanted.'

They walked together, side by side, in and out

of the soft pools of lamplight that lined Elizabeth Street until the last strains of the orchestra were swallowed up into the night. She did not look at him or take his arm but all down his left side his skin was electric with the closeness of her. It was very warm. In the velvet sky the crescent moon sprawled on its back, trailing veils of cloud.

'I'm sorry if I dragged you away,' Phyllis said.

'Don't be. I mean, you didn't. I was glad.'

'You didn't want to stay?'

'Not even a bit.'

'But you were in demand. You danced with everyone.'

'It wasn't really dancing.'

'It looked like it to me.'

'Do you know Newton's third law? For every force or action there is a reaction of equal magnitude in the opposite direction. I didn't dance with those girls. We simply kept one another from falling over.'

Phyllis laughed and Oscar's heart turned over. She had always laughed like that, in gulps like sneezed hiccups. Until that moment he had not known he had forgotten.

'When did you get back?' he asked.

'A week ago. Ten days.'

'I thought your father said the excavation season ended at the end of May.'

'I stayed on.'

'To work?'

'Not really. I just wanted to stay.'

362

There was a silence. For the first time it occurred to Oscar that perhaps Phyllis had met someone else. That she was in love or, worse, engaged to be married. Of course she was. A girl like her would have no shortage of admirers. She opened her mouth to say something else and he was seized by a sudden urgent longing not to know. Not yet.

'So,' he blurted, 'what exactly were you excavating?'

'We were looking for a tomb. The tomb of the boy-king Tut-ankh-Amen.'

'And did you find it?'

'No such luck. Poor Mr Carter. He's the archaeologist leading the excavation. It was his third season in the valley, three years of digging with nothing but the foundations of a few mud huts to show for it. He was very gloomy by the end. He's sure the tomb's there but his patron is losing patience.'

'This boy-king is important, then?'

'Actually, he's rather obscure. We know almost nothing about him.'

'So why does he matter so much to your Mr Carter?'

'Because we know almost nothing about him.'

Oscar smiled. He wondered if Mr Carter was the reason Phyllis had stayed in Luxor an extra month. 'It must be disheartening,' he said. 'Digging for nothing.'

'Disheartening and dusty and dull dull dull. Until suddenly it isn't and the world stands still and you'd happily have dug ten times as long for one tenth of the joy.'

Oscar thought of Mr Rutherford and his research assistants crouched in the dark in the cellar of the Cavendish Laboratory in front of a brass chamber filled with nitrogen, counting the scintillations on a zinc sulphide screen. 'Like physics,' he said.

They turned the corner onto Buckingham Palace Road. Between Victoria Station and the dark-choked trees of Grosvenor Gardens there was a taxi stand with a green cabman's shelter, its gas-lit windows fogged with steam. A cab waited at the rank. The driver leaned against the bonnet, smoking a cigarette. The smoke clung to the warm night air like cobwebs.

'Are you tired?' Oscar asked softly. 'Do you want to go home?'

Phyllis shook her head. Crossing Eccleston Bridge they walked through Pimlico towards the river. The houses that lined the narrow streets were tall and dark behind their high iron railings, as secretive as books.

'I'm sorry, though,' Oscar said. 'It must have been disappointing.'

'It should have been, I suppose, but it wasn't. Not in the least. I mean, we didn't find the tomb, of course, but . . .' She shook her head. 'Never mind.'

'Tell me.'

'It doesn't matter.'

'It does to me.'

She ducked her head. 'I found . . . it sounds so stupid. But I found . . . life.' She smiled at him awkwardly. He did not smile back. There was a

364

stone in his throat. He hated Mr Carter with all his heart.

'Life,' he said.

'Everyone thinks that archaeology is the study of dead things. I think that's partly what drew me, at the beginning. That everything about it had been dead for thousands of years. There is nothing so utterly dead as an Egyptian mummy. Have you ever seen an embalmed body, unwrapped, I mean? It's like a faggot of bones. The skin is brown, set hard. It stinks of resin. It's the starkest, most sombre thing you ever saw. Even when it isn't behind glass in a museum it's impossible to imagine it breathing or laughing or eating. It was how I felt too, for a while. I felt I belonged with them, the grim, melancholy, shrivelled people whose great bequest to history was the solemn honouring of their dead.'

'And now?'

'Now I see I had it all wrong. All that deadness, the dogged cataloguing of bones, that's not archaeology. They're part of it, of course, an archaeologist needs bones, just as an accountant needs ledgers or a physicist needs . . . whatever physicists need, but the ancients were no more piles of bones than we are pieces of meat. Before they died they lived. The ancient Egyptians most of all. They were so blithe, so joyful. They danced and they feasted and they told stories and they sang songs, wonderful songs. They've found some of the songs during excavations but the truth is they never died. You still hear them when you go into the villages, these

365

sweet explosions of melody bubbling up like springs. And the tombs! There was one tomb I visited where the walls were inscribed all over with these extraordinary carvings, gazelles leaping as the sun came up and wild duck and butterflies and songbirds wheeling in the sky. It sounds silly, I know, but it was as if the artist had not just carved animals and birds into that stone but happiness. The sheer joy of living.'

'It sounds wonderful.'

'And it's not even the past. That's the thing. One day at the excavations, a labourer raised a millstone. It was thousands of years old. Later that afternoon a farmer came and asked if he could have it. To use. His was broken and he needed a new one. Nothing's changed. The women still grind corn in their doorways in exactly the way they do in the tomb-paintings, and the little boys have the same shaven heads with the little tuft of hair left for decoration, and the singers at weddings still put their hands behind their ears when they sing, and the dancing girls with their kohled eyes shake the same tambourines they shake in the Pharaonic reliefs. There is an epitaph the ancients often carved in the tombs of their dead: *Thou dost not come dead to thy sepulchre, thou comest living*. It is almost as if they are all borne along by the present, only the present is not the tiny slice of time we allow it to be but a great rolling river, deeper and broader than we can begin to imagine. Does that sound ridiculous?'

'Just because we can't picture something doesn't mean it isn't true.'

'I thought scientists weren't allowed to say things like that.'

'These days they are.'

They had reached the river. They leaned on the stone wall, gazing down at the inky water, the gleaming mud of the pebble-studded flats. The stone was rough with lichen and warm as skin. The tide was coming in. Oscar could taste the salt on the faint breeze. Above the smudge of trees along the Embankment the gas-lit clock-face of Big Ben hung in the sky like a harvest moon.

'You sound happy,' he said.

'I think I really am. For the first time in my life there's a place for me; I finally know what I'm for. It's different for you, you've known that all your life.'

Oscar shook his head. 'Not really.'

'You have. You just don't realise it because you don't know how it feels not to know. I didn't know, not for a long time. I thought I went to Egypt to dig but really I went because I didn't want to feel. I wanted to forget. It was only when I was there that I finally understood that remembering is all we have. We hurtle through life scarcely catching our breath and then when it's over everything gets thrown away, all of it, important or foolish, fine or squalid, swept up and thrown out, emptied out into some midden of forgetfulness. We think it's that or live for ever in the shadow of death. But we're wrong. We have to remember as the Egyptians

367

remember, joyfully, by grinding their corn and telling their stories and singing their songs. That's how we raise them from their tombs.'

Oscar was silent. Behind her an electric tram drew a brief vivid streak of light across the dark bow of Vauxhall Bridge. Then it was gone.

'I'm sorry,' Phyllis said. 'I shouldn't have . . .'

'You should. It helps. To talk about it.'

'You must miss her very much.'

'I do. I keep thinking of things I want to tell her.' His mouth twisted. 'Perhaps I should be telling someone else. Telling her stories and singing her songs.'

'Perhaps you should.'

He turned his head. She looked at him steadily, her face pale in the darkness.

You're the one I want to tell, he wanted to say. *Only you*. Instead, he leaned on the wall, gazing out over the coal-chip glint of the river. 'I thought you were going to tell me that you were getting married,' he said.

'Married? Why on earth would you have thought that?'

He shrugged. 'I don't know. I suppose I was afraid you might have met someone in Egypt. You know. Fallen in love.'

'Well, I didn't.'

'You're sure? Not Mr Carter or an Egyptian farmer or a . . . a lost boy-king?'

Her laugh was very quiet, barely more than a breath. He turned towards her. For a moment they looked at one another. Then, taking her hands, he pulled her towards him. The clouds had cleared and the night sky was dizzy with stars. Oscar felt small and very steady, as though at this moment he and Phyllis were the exact centre of space-time, the tiny nucleus around which all the universe's electrons sketched their orbits. When he took her hand she did not protest. The skin of her palm was rough and calloused. He touched the callouses one by one, learning them by heart. Softly, Big Ben sounded out the quarter hour.

'I'm sorry,' he said. 'About the last time. I meant to tell you that before.'

'It was my fault. I should never have—'

'You were right. That time. I'm not sorry now.'

'No.'

'Promise me you won't run away again.'

'In these shoes? I couldn't if I wanted to.'

'I knew I liked them. You should wear them always.'

Phyllis smiled, her face tipped up towards his. In the darkness her eyes gleamed pearl-grey, like the sky just before the dawn. Bending down, he kissed her. He kissed her, his mouth matching hers, and the trams and the river and the moon and the stars blurred and spun all around them like the pictures from a magic lantern, light and shadows, and the only thing in the world that was real was her, her mouth against his mouth and her fingers in his hair. The faster an object travels the slower time passes.

On the lighted face of Big Ben, the minute hand trembled, holding its breath.

CHAPTER 26

Marjorie Maxwell Brooke was a perfect fool and so was her perfect fool of a mother, Jessica told herself as the trolleybus rattled down Marylebone Road. She supposed they had not set out to have the most disastrous ball of the Season but it had not prevented them from running away with the prize. Jessica did not need to have gone to any of the other balls to know that. If she had only worked for a proper magazine, she thought, and not a stupid rag for factory girls and drapers' assistants, she might have made a story of it, *A Debutante's Cautionary Tale*. There was nothing anyone could do to mitigate the catastrophe of the previous evening but next year's debs should at least be allowed to learn from the Maxwell Brookes' mistakes.

Rule 1: Do not under any circumstances hold your dance at the end of the Season unless you wish it to resemble the winter sales, and the only merchandise still on the shelves items in peculiar colours or with unflattering

370

necklines or that on closer inspection turn out to have buttons missing and snags in the silk. The bargain-hunting atmosphere will bring out the worst in the girls present and result in an unseemly snatch-and-grab. Do not mistake this lunatic behaviour for success. In the cold light of day those girls with the slightest glimmer of sense will immediately apprehend the unsuitability of their purchases and return them for a full refund.

Rule 2: In the absence of eligible men, find more eligible men. Do not invite schoolboys, mentally defective relatives, American ex-servicemen with an exhaustive knowledge of English cathedrals, men less than five feet four inches tall, Mummy's boys with speech impediments whose only topic of conversation is the girl who has just thrown them over and without whom life is not worth living, or slack-jowled business associates with wandering hands. All of these undesirables will conspire to fill the dance cards of your most appealing guests upon their arrival and ensure that if there is a single attractive man in the room [see Rule 1, above] he will leave before they have had the opportunity to make his acquaintance.

Rule 3: If one of your female guests has graciously provided an introduction to one of the few acceptably handsome men present, do not conspire to ensure that he is too busy all night with your daughter's fat friends to dance with her.

Rule 4: Do not, moreover, expect your guests to dance to an orchestra last employed during the Napoleonic Wars unless you have failed to follow Rules 2 – 3, in which case dancing of any kind will already be a wretched and joyless experience.

Rule 5: Offensive, ill-mannered and foul-mouthed gentlemen to be forbidden entry. Should they attempt to humiliate the guests, they should be humiliated in return, preferably publicly and with the greatest conceivable ignominy. Rotten eggs recommended.

She had spied him immediately, a tall athletic-looking man of perhaps twenty with thick, dark hair and a mocking smile that made her think of the film star Leonard Fairbanks. He looked restless, despite the smile and the girls that clustered around him, weary and bored. Disregarding the name scribbled on her dance card, Jessica had squeezed through the crowd towards him. As she passed him she knocked his drink with her arm, splashing him with champagne.

'What the . . .?'

'I'm so awfully sorry,' she said, smiling up at him contritely. 'How terribly clumsy of me.'

His face shrivelled. 'For Christ's sake,' he hissed and he pushed past Jessica, his elbow catching her roughly in the ribs. In her confusion Jessica redirected her smile at a raw-skinned youth of perhaps fifteen with a prominent Adam's apple and a starter moustache who was leading a girl in a pink dress out onto the dance floor. The boy winked.

'Patience, patience,' he muttered as they passed. 'Wait your turn.'

The thought of it still made Jessica's insides turn over in mortification. She had fled to the cloak-room, resting her head against the cool glass. It was only when she opened her eyes that she saw the girl on the chaise longue. She was wearing a pale green dress that almost exactly matched the eau-de-Nil silk of the cloakroom walls and reading a book. Their eyes met in the glass. Neither of them said anything. Jessica washed her hands care-fully and dried them. She smoothed her hair, ran lipstick over her lips, neatening the corners with her little finger. Then, taking a deep breath, she opened the door. The clamour of the party rushed in like floodwater. Behind her the girl in the pale green dress smiled faintly and raised her book.

'Come back soon,' she said.

By the time the trolleybus reached Regent's Park it was crowded and stiflingly hot. Miss Cooke looked pointedly at her wristwatch as Jessica slunk through the door. Joan was hunched over her desk. She did not look up as Jessica squeezed past.

'How was the ball?' she asked. They all knew about the ball. Jessica had gone to the hairdresser at lunch time and for the rest of the afternoon had been unable to talk or think about anything else. It made Jessica squirm to remember it.

She tried to laugh. 'Actually, it was a nightmare.'

Joan frowned at the typewritten sheet on her desk and pencilled a sharp cross in the margin. 'Bloody hell,' she said. 'Sorry, what was that?'

'It doesn't matter.'

At her desk Jessica shuffled paper and stared out over the cross-hatched sky. The office was sweltering. A trickle of sweat ran down her spine and into the waistband of her skirt. She wrinkled her nose. Was that smell her? She put her wrists to her face and inhaled, but the sharp whiff of her own underarms was stronger, cutting through the bergamot and oak-moss of Chypre by Coty. She was turning into one of *Woman's Friend*'s unwashed Bachelor Girls.

Mechanically she began to open letters.

I try to stay cheerful but I can't help thinking any girl who says she wants to stay single all her life is only fooling herself. My sister suggested that perhaps the emigration scheme

She dropped the letter, tore open another.

But since he came back he says he doesn't love me any more. He says he's met another girl. He says it's for the best, that however hard he tried he could never be the sort of chap I wanted him to be, that we'll both be better off

A third. The envelope was pale blue, the address written vey neatly in green ink.

Not being married and seeing very little hope for it now, my friend and I long to put our small talents to other use. Would you know of any books on how to make paper flowers?

Jessica put her hands over her face. She told herself the things she had wanted Joan to tell her: that she was a silly to worry, that she was beautiful and there was someone out there just waiting for her to come along, someone more wonderful than she could possibly imagine, and till then she had to remember what Theo had always told her: that coming-out dances were ghastly and debutantes were drips, and that anyway there were plenty more fish in the sea.

She did not believe herself any more than she would have believed Joan.

That night Gerald took her to a little Russian place near Berkeley Square where they ate caviar and drank oily cocktails that made Jessica's head swim. Gerald was in a frenziedly good humour. He told Jessica about a scientist he had met whose laboratory was developing a machine to broadcast pictures just as the wireless broadcast sound. He talked very fast about mirrors and cells and the electronic retina. Jessica did not understand very much, except that the images would somehow be sent by telephone. Gerald said that he was going to invest. He ordered champagne so that they could celebrate. Afterwards they went on to a new club in Soho. It seemed that Gerald had invested in that too.

The entrance was tucked down a narrow alley, the door unmarked and unlit. They had to ring a bell to be allowed in. Downstairs Gerald was greeted by a man with hooded eyes and a purple mouth like an overripe plum. All around them the walls of the basement were covered with murals of gods. Jessica gaped. The gods had gold wings and flowing hair entwined with flowers and absolutely no clothes on. From between their smooth white thighs jutted huge erect phalluses.

'The Erotes,' Gerald told her as they followed the man to a corner booth. 'The Greek gods of love and desire.'

Ludo Holland was already there with a girl called Freddie. He said she was an actress. Jessica smiled and nodded and tried not to look at the walls. Right behind Ludo's head a god's phallus stuck up like a unicorn's horn. The god was sprinkling something from a cup onto a lady straddling a bull. She had her head thrown back and her mouth open. The hair between her legs was luxuriously curly and on her bare breasts the nipples stood out like light switches. Jessica swallowed her shock and tried to be amused. How daring and marvellous to throw over the fusty old rules and traditions, to spit in the eye of prudence and propriety. Theo would have loved it. On the tiny dance floor one girl wore leather chaps like an American cowboy, another a diaphanous black slip through which her brassiere could quite clearly be seen. Girls danced with girls, men with men. A black man danced with a white girl, so pale Jessica could see the blue veins in her arms. A man in bare feet and a purple silk coat danced by himself. What better antidote to Marjorie's unspeakable dance? She pictured Lucinda Allingham in her rustly silk taffeta, the rictus of horror on her round face as she took in the tumescence of the gods. The thought made her laugh out loud.

Gerald's mood grew wilder, his vivacity sparkling the air like salt. Jessica let herself be lifted and carried by the tide of him. She felt reckless, greedy for his gaiety, his desire for her. She drank and danced, too much of both, the cacophonous jazz careering through her in riotous swoops and runs, and in the half-dark of their booth she sat on his lap and let him kiss her. It exhilarated her to know the power she had over him. They laughed and drank and from time to time Gerald went away and came back and there was a glitter to him, like sunlight on water. He danced with Jessica and with Freddie and, when they pleaded exhaustion, with a girl with cropped hair and a shimmery backless dress with a fishtail like a mermaid. His hand pressed the bare skin of her back.

When, with a wild crescendo, the music exploded to an end the mermaid put her arms around Gerald's neck and kissed him on the mouth. Gerald's hand slid down her back. Then he pulled away, murmuring something in her ear that made them both laugh. Still laughing, he came back to the booth and slid in next to Jessica. His face glistened with perspiration, the hair around his temples oily with it. He drained his champagne glass thirstily, then leaned over towards her. She thought he meant to kiss her. Instead, he bit her sharply on the neck. It hurt. When she cried out he laughed more. Under the table his legs twitched with restless energy. The music started up. Immediately he seized her hands.

'Dance with me,' he said.

'Aren't you exhausted?' she protested but he only laughed and pulled her into the whirling vortex of dancers, spinning her around until Jessica was dizzy with it.

She did not recognise him at first. He was sitting at a table on his own in a dark corner half-hidden by the bar. He was not in evening clothes. He wore a soft-collared shirt like an artist's smock open at the neck and an unknotted silk scarf. The costume made Jessica think of Lord Byron. It was only when he struck a match to light a cigarette and she saw his face, his full mouth and high cheekbones, that she realised it was Guy

Cockayne. He had grown a moustache. It suited him. She watched his elegant fingers as he dropped the match in the ashtray and put the cigarette to his lips. His hair had grown longer. It fell over his brow just as Theo's had once, so that he had to push it out of his eyes. In the dim light of the nightclub he looked pale and very handsome. He leaned back against the banquette, his long legs twisted in an elegant knot, and something inside Jessica turned over.

The dance seemed to last for ever. Guy Cockayne smoked his cigarette and stared into the bottom of his drink. Jessica watched him over Gerald's shoulder, willing him not to leave. He did not look in her direction. When at last the music stopped Jessica went back with Gerald to their table. Ludo and Freddie were smooching, her legs crossed over his. When Gerald nudged him with one elbow Ludo slid Freddie along the slippery banquette but he did not stop kissing her. Gerald rolled his eyes and upended what remained of the bottle of champagne into their glasses.

'I have to powder my nose,' Jessica said, reaching for her evening bag. In the cloakroom she hurriedly smoothed her hair and reapplied her lipstick. Her cheeks were flushed from dancing, her eyes bright. She looked pretty. Behind her the walls of the tiny cloakroom were painted with black and white zigzags. It was like being inside a migraine head-ache. Butterflies prickling her stomach, she pushed open the door and went out.

Guy had his back to her as she squeezed around the overcrowded dance floor towards his table. There was another man at his table. The other man leaned towards Guy, striking a match for his cigarette. Jessica hesitated, momentarily disconcerted. Even in the dim light of the club it was plain that Guy's companion was not quite proper. His moustache was too narrow, his oiled blond hair too short at the sides. His suit was the cheap regulation kind issued to privates on demobilisation. It was ill-fitting, too wide in the lapels, the chalk stripe too loud. He held his cigarette like an Irish labourer, pinched between finger and thumb. She could not help wondering what someone like Guy would want with a man like that.

It was in a sort of trance that she watched Guy put his hand on the weasel man's thigh, his long fingers splayed. The man moved closer. Guy's hand slid upwards. He touched the man's chest, his neck. Then, sliding his fingers into the man's hair, he pulled him towards him. Jessica saw the weasel man's lips part, the glint of his pointed tongue as it pushed into Guy's mouth. The music stamped and banged in Jessica's head as she stared, rooted to the spot. The weasel man put his hand between Guy's legs and he jolted, rising slightly out of his seat, his mouth opening as though he would eat the weasel man alive. Their tongues writhed together, coiling and twisting. Then the weasel man pulled away. He stood and Guy stood too, so abruptly he knocked over a stool, and, with the weasel man leading, they pushed their way out of the club.

Man's love is of man's life a thing apart, Jessica thought dizzily. *'Tis woman's whole existence.*

She told Gerald she wanted to go home. When he protested, declaring her a bore, she pleaded a migraine headache and said that she would be quite all right if only he could see her into a taxi cab. She was glad when he did not insist on taking her home. The thought of him pawing at her made her feel sick.

She let herself into the flat. Dawn was breaking and, to the east, the paling sky burned pink and gold. The pink was the colour of Guy Cockayne's tongue. She could not stop the pictures from flickering in her head, fragments of film run too fast. She had always laughed at the men in their lipstick at Dixie's. They seemed so absurd, like pitiful versions of the boys dressed up as girls in Theo's school plays. She had not thought of what they did together, the disgusting things they did together. The thought of Guy and the weasel man, writhing together in a car under the plane trees—

Suddenly Nanny's bedroom door opened and Nanny was standing there. She wore a plaid dressing gown that Jessica recognised from her childhood and an elasticated net over her hair. Her face was crumpled with sleep. She crossed her arms. 'Exactly what time do you call this, young lady?'

Jessica took one look at Nanny's grim expression and burst into tears.

381

'Why do men have to be so . . . beastly?' she sobbed and she let Nanny take her into her arms and rock her, just as she had when Jessica was a little girl.

A week later, on a damp grey Saturday, she went with the other girls from the office to the Peace Parade. Somewhere in the crowd were Nanny and her niece, up from Essex for the day. Nanny had looked forward to it for weeks. There would be bands and merry-go-rounds and folk dancing in the Park and, in the evening, a huge firework display. It made Jessica uneasy. She was not sure Theo would have wanted to be remembered that way. She went all the same. She was glad that the girls had asked her. She was glad too that she did not have to go home.

She had always loved Ellinghurst in July, the trees in full leaf, the borders riotous with stocks and lupins and delphiniums and shock-haired dahlias, the grey walls of the battlements billowy with blue campanula. The bees humming in the dropping roses and the sun-warmed flags of the terrace under bare feet and the mossy cool of the woods and the dappled green lake with its darting dragonflies, the bow of the old rowing boat nudging drifts of yellow irises and bulrushes like fat cigars. In July the schoolroom was locked and inside the magic circle of the castle walls time drowsed like a sun-drugged cat.

She longed for it, staring out of her slice of window at the padded white sky, but she did not go home. Instead, she walked beneath the dusty plane trees along the Grand Union Canal. Beneath the iron railings the pavement was green with goose droppings. The last time she had been to Ellinghurst was the weekend after Marjorie's ball. The garden was extravagantly abundant, almost wild, the hedges choked with honeysuckle, the path through the woods knee-high with feathery grass. Her father said it was impossible to find men who wanted the work, that the War had made them greedy. He was in a fractious mood, his voice querulous. His hands shook as he spread his toast. For the first time Jessica saw that he was an old man.

She told him she would ride while he worked but he said that there were things to discuss. He demanded to know what she had done about arrangements since they had last met. What about Marjorie Maxwell Brooke's dance? Who had she met and what were their prospects and how soon before things were more settled? She realised, did she not, that there was not a great deal of time?

He gave up eventually and went to the library but, when she walked through the garden less than an hour later, she saw him signalling to her from the window. She pretended not to see. It was only a few minutes before he appeared on the terrace. He said he wanted to ask her opinion about a point in his book, something about the dance floor Grandfather Melville had invented for the Great Hall that was sprung and mounted on wheels to permit it to be easily moved, but when she asked why he was asking her he did not go back to the house. Instead, he sat next to her, gazing out over the sloping garden.

'It's all here,' he said. 'Don't you see? Everything that means anything.'

All that day and the next he sought her out, in the morning room and by the lake and in the shade of the beech trees at the bottom of the lawn, until she thought she would go mad with it.

'I'm trying, Father,' she said and she glared at him to keep herself from crying. 'I'm trying.'

She wanted to talk to Eleanor, to have her intercede on her behalf, but she knew it would not do any good. Her parents barely spoke to one another any more. Eleanor did not come down for breakfast. Her father ate his lunch in the library. At dinner they spoke through her, as though only she understood both of their languages. In the past when they had gone through periods of not speaking to one another their antagonism had charged the air around them like a thunderstorm, the silence crackling with static. It was not like that this time. There was no tension, no awkward atmosphere. They had simply ceased to see one another. When one of them entered a room to find the other there neither of them said anything. They did not exchange glances or sigh or tut under their breath. The one at the door simply turned around and went somewhere else. That was the thing about Ellinghurst. Even with two thirds of the rooms shut up there was always somewhere else to go.

★　★　★

384

Despite the drizzle the streets were packed. Crowds filled the pavements and spilled out over the streets, bringing the traffic to a standstill; they stood on bollards and boxes and walls and railings; they squashed onto balconies and hung from lampposts and out of open windows, throwing handfuls of biscuits and damp confetti, roaring and clapping and singing at the tops of their voices. The noise was deafening.

Jessica followed Peggy as she squirmed through the crush towards Trafalgar Square, nearly losing a shoe when someone trod on her heel. Nelson's Column was wreathed in garlands of flowers. Packs of children sat on the backs of Landseer's lions and on their heads, kicking their heels against the lions' muzzles. The front of the National Gallery was festooned with Union Jack flags.

Jessica stood on tiptoes. She could just see the caps of the troops as they marched up from Whitehall where a monument had been erected as a symbol of remembrance, a huge wooden box like an upended coffin where the troops would salute the dead. Peggy said they had called it the Cenotaph, which was Greek for empty tomb. It was the kind of thing Phyllis would know. Perhaps Phyllis was here in the crowd somewhere, thinking about Theo, remembering or trying to remember. She had hardly seen Phyllis since she came back from Egypt. She never came home to Ellinghurst. She said she was too busy in London with her work, that she had years of books to catch up on if she was to be ready when her University course began in September. Jessica knew she was avoiding their father. She came to the flat one Wednesday evening when Eleanor was in London but, when Jessica tried to talk to her about it, she murmured evasively and changed the subject. All through dinner she was vague and preoccupied and as soon as it was over she left.

'I don't know what's wrong with that girl,' Eleanor said. It was not until her mother had gone to bed and she sat alone looking out over the dark castellated chimney pots of Little Venice that Jessica realised that Phyllis was happy. Her smile clung to the air in the drawing room like Alice's Cheshire Cat.

If anything the crowds were thicker in the Mall. The wide road was lined with wooden obelisks painted white. They looked like flower trellises but perhaps they were tombs too. On and on the men came, battalion after battalion through the drifting rain, marching up towards the Palace. Fifteen thousand, Peggy said. Fifteen thousand men who did not die. Around Jessica everyone was whooping and waving flags and programmes and souvenir paper handkerchiefs printed with flowers. One squealing troop of girls had Union Jack flags wound around their heads like turbans.

'We love you, boys!' they shrieked as the machine men filed past, square after perfect square. 'We love you!'

Beside Jessica a man stood with a small boy on

his shoulders. The boy was wearing a forage cap so much too big for him that he had to hold it up with both hands. A Japanese officer passed on a dancing black horse, his battalion marching behind him. Over his shoulder he carried a white flag with a scarlet sun. The boy turned his head to look and she saw the badge. A crown and tiger in a wreath of laurel leaves. The Royal Hampshire Regiment. Theo's regiment. She thought of Guy's sketch, the cap badge picked out in meticulous detail, then pushed the thought away.

'Nice hat,' she said to the little boy.

The boy eyed her and kicked the man's chest. The man looked sideways at her, his eyes blood-shot and unfocused. He smelled of spilled beer.

'Tigers,' the little boy said.

'Hampshire Tigers,' she said and she had a sudden vivid memory of Theo in his uniform, not blithe as he had been on the day he left, his cap tipped back on his head at an angle calculated to exasperate Father, but home on leave that Christmas when he was always drunk. Scotch-tinted spectacles, he had told her, with a laugh that did not sound like his. But what was like him, by then?

'Three and a half days,' the man barked suddenly. He was very drunk. Jessica tried to move away from him in the crush but he swung round to glare at her, the boy swaying on his shoulders. 'If all the dead men had marched, this fucking circus would have taken three and a half fucking days.'

★　　★　　★

There were fireworks that night, ten thousand rockets fired from Constitution Arch in Hyde Park. Peggy and Joan went to watch them. Jessica went home.

The flat was dark. Nanny was still out with her niece. Jessica closed the curtains but she could still hear the bangs. When at last she drifted into an uneasy sleep she dreamed she was back at Marjorie's dance, in the eau-de-Nil bathroom with its marble basins and its oval looking-glasses and its lamps that were gold goddesses, holding up glass spheres of light. The pale girl in the pale green gown was curled on the watered-silk chaise as she had been then, except this time it was not a book she held in her lap but knitting, a khaki scarf that grew longer and longer, curling like a tapeworm around Jessica's ankles. Jessica stood at the looking glass, the rim of the marble basin cool under her hands, but it was not her own reflection that she saw staring back at her but the girl on the chaise, her unblinking pale green eyes as blank as sea glass. She did not say anything. She just went on knitting, the needles clicking unnoticed in her fingers as she looked at Jessica with her rose silk dress and her honey-coloured hair and the desolation in her as loud as the roar of the sea inside an empty shell.

Every man you might have married, her glass eyes said, *is already dead.*

CHAPTER 27

For the rest of Oscar's life he never knew a place in the world as beautiful as Cambridge in the summer of 1919. It was as if the nerves in him had been magnetised, irresistibly drawing sensation to his eyes, his lungs, his brain, his skin, until the intensity of it was almost too much to bear. He walked along the familiar streets in a daze of seeing, overcome by the greenness of the lawns and the blueness of the sky and the perfect pewter gleam of the cobbles beneath his feet, struck time and again by the loveliness of things he had somehow never noticed before: the round glass panes in an overhanging upper window like bottoms of bottles, the splintery grey grain of a warped medieval lintel, the straining neck and gripping claws of a pockmarked gargoyle clinging for dear life to a narrow ledge, its mouth stretched wide and its veined wings raised and half-opened, ready for flight. He had not thought the world so full of ordinary marvels. He stopped often, the business of the day forgotten, captivated by the repeating pattern of coiled Chelsea buns on a tray in a baker's window or a cat asleep in a puddle of sunshine, his ears translucent pink, his long whiskers as dazzling as the filaments of electrical light bulbs. On warm evenings, when the tourists had packed up their guidebooks and their picnic baskets and the tethered punts drowsed four deep in the shallows beyond Clare Bridge, he read by the river in the shade of the horse chestnut trees as the filigree light danced on the underside of the pale stone bridge and behind him, like an alchemist, the chapel of King's College turned the evening light to gold.

Sometimes the hot weather caused thunderstorms, the air crackling with electricity. Then, as the clouds massed on the horizon, purple as bruises, and the horizon darkened to pencil shading, the obscured sun cut through the clouds in brilliant columns of light. A lifetime before, or perhaps only a few weeks, crossing Waterloo Bridge, he had tried to explain Rayleigh scattering to Phyllis, the dispersion of light by molecules in the air smaller than the wavelength of the light. He told her that it was because of Rayleigh scattering that the sky was blue and sunsets pink and orange.

'The ancients thought sunsets proved the existence of God,' Phyllis said. 'Do you think anyone believes in God any more?'

'No one I know.'

'I wish I did sometimes. It would be a comfort, wouldn't it, to believe in something bigger? Something more than just us.'

'You don't have to believe in God to believe in that.'

'But what?'

'The universe.'

'The universe?' Phyllis made a face. 'But that's like believing in the British Empire or the motor car. It's just . . . there.'

'It's not like that at all. It's like God. Well, almost.'

'How?'

'You really want me to explain?'

'More than anything.' The way she said it made his heart turn over.

'All right,' he said. 'I believe that the design of the universe determines all things to exist, that it obeys its own inexorable laws to cause effects that we understand only dimly but which underpin every aspect of every particle in every solar system in space. I don't understand how and even if I was five hundred times cleverer than I am I probably never would, but I also understand that it doesn't matter. I don't have to know how it works to believe it, to be in awe of its mysteries, its beauty and complexity. Of the unimaginable intelligence that created it. I'm not in awe of motor cars. The rudiments of the internal combustion engine are actually pretty easy to grasp.'

'Says you.'

Oscar grinned. 'My mother always said we'd do better if we stopped worrying about believing in God and believed in other people.'

'Even if you don't know how they work?'

'Then most of all.'

The bridge was crowded with people hustling towards the railway station, girls in belted mackintoshes, blank-faced businessmen with bowler hats and rolled umbrellas. A jostle of anonymity and yet every one the central character of their own story, hoping and dreading and striving and suffering and wanting to be happy. Oscar hoped they were happy. He wanted to open his arms, to laugh out loud so that the happiness that swelled inside him might be scattered on the air and carried like spores into people's lungs, their blood. He had not known that about happiness, that it would feel like there was so much to spare. He leaned against Phyllis, entwining his fingers with hers.

'I believe in something else as well,' he said.

'And what's that?'

'I believe that once in a blue moon things happen that you never dreamed of, that you never even knew enough to hope for.'

'The hand of Fate?'

'There's no such thing as Fate. But sometimes, just sometimes, there's sheer dumb luck.'

He meant to return to Cambridge the morning after Marjorie's dance. Instead, he stayed in London. He took a room in a cheap hotel behind Marylebone Station. The hotel was called the Majestic. The plaster on the façade was peeling and the carpet in the narrow hallway was dark with stains. Every day he told Phyllis that he would go back to Cambridge that evening but as the sun slipped lower, angling through the chimney pots and setting the summer trees on fire, he missed one train after another until he gave up pretending and said that one more night would not hurt. By the third evening the proprietress sighed when he pushed open the door. She had copper hair and long overlapping teeth smudged with lipstick.

'Don't tell me,' she said, hauling her ledger out from beneath the desk. 'You missed the last train.'

When she had reentered his name in the register she gave him his key and the suitcase he had left with her during the day.

'Room Five. Again.' She sucked on her long teeth. 'I don't know what line of business you're in and I don't suppose I want to. Whatever it is, though, it wouldn't hurt to buy a clock.'

He stayed in London for nearly a week. He drifted through those first days as though he was in a hot air balloon, aware only of Phyllis beside him and the sudden rushes of joy like gusts of wind that tipped him sideways, giddy with exhilaration, the city beneath him as tiny and inconsequential as a toy. In the end it was Phyllis who gently suggested it was time he went back to Cambridge. London was her city, her days earthbound, moored by her work. She was taking lessons in Arabic and ancient Egyptian hieroglyphs from an Egyptologist at the British Museum. She would not miss them, she said, not even for him.

He waited for her in a dingy café near the museum, spinning out a cup of tea. The professor gave her exercises to work on between lessons. Several times that week she brought her books to the Park and studied while he sprawled next to her, waiting for her to be finished. Absorption puckered the skin between her eyebrows and pressed the pink tip of her tongue against her teeth. The urge to touch was too great for him then, but though she smiled at him distractedly or touched her fingers to his, he knew that she did it to please him, that her attention in that moment was all for the feathers and the snakes and the indecipherable squiggles and dots of the Arabic abjad, and that it was one of the reasons that he loved her.

He loved her. He knew it quietly, with a certainty that startled him and yet was somehow no surprise at all. His love for her was a part of him and perhaps always had been, marbling the muscular tissue that moved his ribs and raised his diaphragm, diffusing every tiny alveolus in his lungs. He could feel the constriction of it, like the squeeze of a hand, whenever he took a breath. He could no more stop loving her than he could stop his own heart.

They agreed Phyllis would visit Cambridge the following Sunday. Oscar worked, partly because Phyllis had said he must be longing to get back to it but mostly to make the time pass. He attempted geology, a subject he had never studied before, but it stifled him, the stolidity of it, the leaden creep of imperceptible change.

Instead, he thought about Einstein. It seemed impossible, somehow, that a single scientist, working alone, had developed a theory of Nature that encompassed the whole history of the universe, that described the state of matter and geometry everywhere and at every moment in time. In the science journals his critics questioned Einstein's conclusions and argued against the mounting mathematisation of modern physics, the tendency to abstract and increasingly abstruse theory building without regard to the principles of common sense. While Oscar had a basic grasp of the principles of special relativity, or hoped he did, the general theory bewildered him. He wished Kit was in Cambridge. He had told Phyllis he accepted the limitations of his own intelligence but it was not quite true. He could hardly bear to think that the future might be closed off to him, that his own intellectual shortcomings would keep him from gaining even the most passing glimpse of this new and hidden world. If Kit were here perhaps he would be able to explain it in a way that Oscar understood.

The mass of an object or system is a measure of its energy, and if a body gives off the energy E in the form of radiation, its mass diminishes by E over c^2 where c is the speed of light. The speed of light is a constant and space and time are relative. The span of a year, a yard, changes dependent upon the position and velocity of the observer. It defies reason. And yet when you are in love and waiting, you know only too well that every minute is an hour, and the sixty miles to London stretches and shrinks, the reach of a hand and, abruptly, the breadth of a boundless sea.

A year later it was Sunday. He was waiting for her on the platform when the train pulled in. She wore a wide-brimmed hat and a white dress with green stripes. He took her to the river, to the horse chestnut tree. They sat on the bank on his outspread jacket, looking down into the water. It was not awkwardness that kept them from speaking but its opposite, a deep absorbed settling that had no purpose for words. He held her hand in his, his skin alive with the silent music of her. She no longer bit her fingernails.

Later, when the tourists came, they rented a rowing boat. He told the boatman that she was his sister. She leaned against the cushions, smiling at him as he rowed them splashily upstream towards Grantchester Meadows, his shirtsleeves rolled to the elbows, and he wondered if it was possible to be happier than he was at this moment, his arms aching, his palms rubbed raw by the rough wooden oars. Silvery fish darted in the trailing weed and the banks of the river were foamy with meadowsweet.

'We could stop,' she said.

'We're not there yet.'

'Then at least let me help.' Setting the boat rocking from side to side, she stood and twisted herself around to sit next to him. He slid to one side to give her room, feeling the warmth of her hip next to his, her hand on his arm as she steadied herself. 'One each.'

Her stroke was oiled, easy, the oar dipping into the green water like a hand.

'My father taught me,' she said. 'He said it was a good way of getting away from people.'

She told Oscar that her mother was going to Flanders. According to Eleanor, it had been Theo's idea. In a recent sitting he had grown agitated, repeating a single name over and over again. The name had not come through clearly. Edwin, the spirit guide said, or perhaps Eamon, she could not be sure. The next day Eleanor had received a letter from Mrs Coates. The two women had not seen each other since the terrible events in Bournemouth, though they had continued to write. Tucked inside the letter was a cutting from *The Times*. A French officer was offering private tours of the battlefields. Mrs Coates said that she had already written to him to make enquiries. Perhaps, she thought, if she could see the place where her boy had passed his last days, she might find some peace. She asked if Eleanor might want to go with her.

Eleanor cried when she got the letter. Mrs Coates' son's name was Alwyn.

'It's not just the awful tenuousness of it,' Phyllis said and she stared out towards the bank, her oar lifted from the water. 'How will going do anything but make it worse? It's like some terrible vision of Hell out there. And it's not safe. The ground is packed with unexploded shells; they go off all the time. People get hurt, killed even. But she won't listen. When I said she'd only get blown to bits she looked at me with this expression on her face as though there was no point in even talking about it, that I couldn't possibly understand.'

'And your father? What does he say?'

'He says it's her business. I don't think he cares any more what she does.'

'I'm sure that's not true.'

'Are you?' She pulled in her oar, letting it rest in the rowlock. 'I saw him this week, you know. In London.'

'How was he?'

'I don't know. He didn't see me. He was helping a woman out of a taxi. She did this weird pirouette as she stepped out onto the pavement, like a chorus girl or something, and then he kissed her.'

'Are you sure it was him?'

'They were only as far away as that tree. I don't know how they didn't see me too. I just stood there, frozen to the spot, gaping at them.' She looked at Oscar. 'It was Mrs Maxwell Brooke.'

Oscar did not say anything. He reached out and took her hand, sliding his fingers between hers. She shrugged.

'I don't know why I care. It should be better, shouldn't it, knowing that they're just as bad as each other?' She tried to smile but her eyes were bright with tears. She blinked. 'Sorry. So stupid.'

'Not stupid in the least.' Leaning over he kissed her very gently on the corner of her mouth. She turned her head away, pulling her hand free of his.

'I'm sorry,' he said. 'I didn't mean . . .'

She wiped her eyes on her sleeve. Then, cupping his head with both hands, she kissed him so hard that he no longer knew where his mouth ended and hers began. When at last they pulled apart he was dizzy, dazzled, the glitter of the sunlit river patterning his eyes. Her eyelashes were paler at the ends than at the roots and in the grey of her eyes there were hazel flecks like freckles. She caught his hand and kissed it. 'Ouch,' she said softly, touching her lips to the blisters.

'Aye, there's the rub,' he said.

She laughed. 'Rub-a-dub-dub, three fools in a tub, and who do you think they be?'

'You and me and . . . just you and me. Two fools in a tub.'

'I suppose we'll just have to manage without the candlesticks.'

'We'll have meat and bread,' he said. 'We can eat sandwiches by moonlight.'

'With a runcible spoon like the owl and the pussycat.'

'All right but I have to warn you, I shan't dance.'

'Not even with me?'

'Not even with you. You need to preserve your energy.'

'And why is that?'

'To row me home. You do know you're rowing me home, don't you?'

'You . . .!'

Leaning over Phyllis seized a cushion from the bench and tried to thump him with it. He twisted away, setting the boat lurching from side to side as he snatched a cushion of his own and held it out in front of him like a shield. She pushed it away, laughing, pressing her cushion against his face and her laugh was so infectious it made him laugh too and she let her cushion fall and leaned against him, still laughing, the boat rocking beneath them as though it was laughing too.

CHAPTER 28

London at the height of summer was dead. The grass in the Park was yellow and the trees drooped, heavy with dust. On Marylebone Road the buses coughed out exhaust smoke, hazing the air blue. When Jessica took off her blouse at the end of the day there was a grey line around the collar and the fabric was speckled with smuts.

Gerald had gone away. Some friends had taken a villa on the water at Lake Como. A palazzo, Gerald called it, which made Jessica think of Nanny. Nanny would have considered palazzo to be showing off. She was glad when he did not ask her to come with him – the Italian lakes were for old people and invalids, people who liked to take a little air in the afternoon in their bath chairs – and at the same time faintly perturbed. She knew he knew the girls at *Woman's Friend* were entitled to only one week's holiday each year, that Jessica would have to wait until the other girls had taken theirs. She still wondered if he was growing tired of her. She wondered, too, if the friends at Lake Como had known Christabel.

'Tell me about her,' she asked him once but he only shook his head and said that it was not something that he talked about. He did not seem angry with her for asking. That night he danced as wildly as ever but, when he kissed her goodnight, there was something hungry in his kisses that was deeper than desire. It touched her and frightened her, to sense the need in him. He was not supposed to need her nor she him, or not like that.

He told her he would be back for her birthday.

'Twenty years old,' he said. 'I thought maybe a bath chair?'

At weekends she went home. There was nothing else to do. Phyllis never came. She said she was busy with her work and that she could not spare the time. She did not seem very sorry about it. For the first time Jessica wondered if Phyllis had met someone and if she had if she would marry him after all. She was not sure if the thought of Phyllis being the one to inherit Ellinghurst made her mostly glad or mostly sorry, but the thought of her in love made Jessica feel hollow inside. She told herself the man was very likely a professor or some other dusty exhibit from a museum, shrouded in tweed and ink stains and with a near-sighted squint, but it did not cheer her. Sometimes in her lunch break she walked up to the Park where Phyllis's college was or down Gower Street towards the British Museum, hoping to catch a glimpse of her, of the two of them together. She never did. The walks left her hollower than ever, angry with herself and angrier still with Phyllis who had so callously abandoned her.

Her mother was as bad. In August Eleanor cabled to say that she had decided to remain in France another month. Without her there was no one to occupy the downstairs rooms. The new housemaid, a thick-ankled girl with a thick local accent, scurried around every morning dusting and plumping the undented cushions but the air still felt stale and disused. Jessica walked through them, fingering things, adjusting ornaments on shelves as though her touch might bring them back to life. The evenings were too warm for a fire and the huge grates were empty, neatly blacked. Even the flowers looked stagey, as though they were made of silk. The rooms reminded Jessica of Hampton Court where Nanny had taken them during holidays in London when they were small.

'Imagine it,' Phyllis had said wide-eyed to Jessica. 'Henry VIII actually walked on these floors and sat in these chairs and slept in that bed.'

'And did big jobs in that chamber pot,' Theo added, making Jessica giggle, but it had not made it any easier to picture Henry VIII. To her the rooms with their rotting upholstery had felt as dead as the Tudors.

Her father kept erratic hours, often working through the night and retiring to bed just as Jessica came down for breakfast. He ate on trays in the library, scattering crumbs amidst his papers. He refused to let anyone in to clean. He had purchased a camera and each week he sent rolls and rolls of film to be developed in Bournemouth. The photographs were returned in brown paper packages that piled up unopened on the library floor. Her father said that they were for the book. One Saturday morning when a delivery arrived, Jessica asked if she might look. She thought it might be rather nice to have some pictures of Ellinghurst at the flat in London but when she opened one of the envelopes she frowned.

'Like this,' Sir Aubrey said, turning the photograph round in her hand and she saw that it was a tassel, carved in wood.

'Do you know where that is?' he asked and when she shook her head he insisted that she came with him, there and then, to the Great Hall where he showed her the festoons of ropes and flowers carved into the back of the two great chairs that flanked the doorway. At the base, behind the tapestry seat, was the tassel.

'You see?' he said, visibly distressed. 'No one sees.'

He said he meant to photograph everything, that he owed it to the house to be meticulous. He showed her several other pictures and demanded that she identify them: a hinge with a three-pronged design from the inner door of the gatehouse, a leaf carved into the gallery balustrade, a six-petalled flower which she swore she had never seen before but which her father said was the repeating pattern in the ironwork of the vent under the billiard table.

She grew accustomed to walking into a room to find him there, his lens pressed up against a cornice or the catch of a window like a child outside a toy shop.

He no longer quizzed her about London or the people she had met during the week, not since the time she lost her temper and said that she did not know how she was supposed to meet people when he and Eleanor had never made the least effort to introduce her to anyone proper.

'I told you from the beginning you had to let me come out,' she cried. 'I told you but you wouldn't listen.'

Her father had not rebuked her for raising her voice. Jessica wondered if he had even heard her. He had a way of vanishing into himself in the middle of conversations these days, his expression softening to blankness until a sharp word recalled him and he blinked at her, his neck stretching out like a tortoise waking from hibernation. Sometimes she wondered if he might be going senile.

He must have heard her, though, because after that he stopped asking. At first she was relieved, but as the weekends passed it frightened her, that he too might have given up. Then, on the last weekend of August, he told her that he had asked the Maxwell Brookes to lunch. When Jessica asked why, he said that she must be tired of the two of them rattling about in the house alone.

'Honestly, Father,' she protested. 'I'd rather solitary confinement than the Maxwell Brookes.

405

Can't you put them off?' But he only shrugged and said that the arrangements had already been made. The prospect of having to talk about Marjorie's ghastly party, to dredge up something flattering to say about it, made Jessica cringe. She had done her best to push the recollections of that evening out of her head but now she found them insinuating themselves back into her head, the girl in the cloakroom, Leonard Fairbanks and his unconcealed disgust, the shock of walking in to that beautiful ballroom and seeing nothing but girls, crowds of desperate girls where the wonderful young men she had yet to meet should all have been. If Marjorie tried to talk about it, she thought, she would simply walk out and leave them to Father. It was him who had asked them, after all. It was his responsibility to entertain them both.

It was something of a relief, then, when Mrs Maxwell Brooke came alone. Marjorie, she said, settling herself like a hen on an egg, was at a weekend house party. 'We met Lady Sarah in London during the Season. A dear girl and such a good family. I only hope Marjorie is making the most of it.'

They talked during lunch of Ellinghurst and the arrogance of English publishers. Mrs Maxwell Brooke was sympathetic. She seemed to know a good deal about it. She asked Jessica about her job, wrinkling her nose girlishly as if the subject was not only outlandish but faintly obscene and,

406

provoked into defensiveness, Jessica declared that in her opinion all girls ought to work, at least for a bit; that everyone should know what it was like, out there in the real world.

'Oh my,' Mrs Maxwell Brooke said, glancing meaningfully at Sir Aubrey.

It was a beautiful day. Sir Aubrey told the maid to serve coffee on the terrace.

'I'll leave you ladies to it,' he said and Mrs Maxwell Brooke nodded at him and tucked Jessica's arm into hers. Her upholstered bosom nudged the back of Jessica's wrist.

'Don't look so alarmed, dear,' she said as she marched Jessica briskly outside. 'Your father thought it might be a good idea if you and I had a little chat. He's anxious about you. Of course he is. This job of yours and the flat. Maida Vale. I mean, really. It is quite clear that your mother has been most . . . distracted.'

'My mother has had a very difficult time.'

'Of course she has. You all have. It's been perfectly horrid. But one must think of the future. Of your future. There is a great deal at stake.'

Jessica frowned. 'What are you talking about?'

The coffee was already set out on one of the tiled tables Eleanor had had brought back from Italy. Mrs Maxwell Brooke lifted the silver coffee pot and poured out two cups. 'My dear, your father has taken me into his confidence. He is anxious and not without reason. You are a Melville and that privilege brings responsibilities. If your mother refuses to meet those responsibilities then someone else must do so on her behalf. Cream and sugar?'

'Just cream.'

'A girl in your position must be brought out. How else can she possibly make a suitable match? I only wish I could help Phyllis also, poor child, but your father says the damage there is already done and I'm afraid he might be right.' She sighed theatrically, shaking her head. 'The War may be won but we have paid a very high price for victory.'

'So I'm to come out after all?'

'It is a little unorthodox, I know, but something must be done. The prospect of another gruelling Season again next year, well, it is hardly something I relish, but I cannot stand by. I will not let your father down after all he has endured. Besides, it might be rather fun for you and Marjorie to attend some parties together, if she should find herself at a loose end. She could show you the ropes.'

'So you would act as my . . . my mother?'

'It might be rather jolly, don't you think?'

'And what about Eleanor?'

'Your mother has made her bed, my dear. Now she must lie in it.'

Jessica supposed she should be glad that her future was finally to be settled. She was glad. The Season might have its longueurs, all those grisly girls' lunches and tedious tea parties, but what other way was there really of meeting anybody? By the following spring the War would be almost forgotten. All the men would finally be demobbed and the world would go back to normal. As for the ghastly Mrs Maxwell Brooke, she had to admire her father's tactics. He knew as well as Jessica that Eleanor would never permit Mrs Maxwell Brooke to get her hands on her daughters. It was no more than a threat, a warning shot to bring her mother back to her senses. She had not reckoned her father so cunning.

She would have to give up *Woman's Friend*, of course. It had been fun but it had only ever been a temporary arrangement. Like Gerald. They had served their purpose. She had got what she wanted. Everything was just exactly as she had planned it. She could not understand why victory did not feel more triumphant.

She told Nanny that one of the girls from the office was throwing a dinner to celebrate her birthday. Gerald insisted on sending an invitation, *Mrs John Roylance, At Home*, with Jessica's name inscribed in careful copperplate. He sent his car for her. His chauffeur would not tell her where they were going.

They drove to the Savoy. Gerald was waiting in the American Bar. He was thinner than she remembered, his face burned brown from the sun. It made the hair at his temples look very white. He kissed her cheek and ordered champagne cock-tails. He jiggled his leg restlessly as he waited, his fingers drumming the table. When the waiter brought the drinks Gerald took them from the tray before the man could place them on the table. He handed one to Jessica.

'Happy birthday,' he said.

Jessica touched her glass to his and sighed happily, watching the sugar cube fizz in the bottom of the glass. The cocktail was the colour of old gold. 'I can't tell you how much I've missed you,' she said.

Gerald drained his glass. 'You know what they say about absence.'

'Not you, silly. I was talking to the champagne.'

She had barely drunk half of hers when he ordered two more. Then, reaching into his pocket, he produced a long thin box of scarlet leather, tooled in gold. Jessica eyed it excitedly, her bottom lip caught between her teeth.

'Open it,' he said.

She glanced around the crowded bar. It was a very public place to receive an expensive present. 'Do you think we should wait till dinner?'

'Open it.'

She hesitated. No one was paying them the least attention. Turning a little so that her face was in shadow she undid the gold latch and gasped.

'Do you like it?' he asked, lifting the diamond bracelet from its silk nest. She held out her hand so that he could fasten the clasp around her wrist.

'Oh, Gerald,' she sighed and she leaned forward to kiss him, admiring the bracelet over his shoulder. 'It's divine.'

'Diamonds suit you.'

'They do, they really do.' She frowned, puzzled, as he stood. His second drink was already gone. 'Are we going?'

'Not just yet. There's just something I have to do. I won't be a moment. Oh, and this is for you too.' He reached into his pocket and brought out another scarlet box. It was smaller than the other and square. He put it on the table. 'Open it while I'm gone.'

She sipped at her drink as he squeezed through the crush towards the lobby, her eyes sliding back again and again to admire the new bracelet. The diamonds glittered, bright flashes of fire. The box on the table was the right size for a ring. Could it possibly be that he meant to propose? The idea was absurd, they neither of them had the least interest in marriage, they were supposed to be having fun, but at the same time the thought sent a tremor of excitement through her. She could never marry Gerald, could she? She looked once more at the bracelet, turning her wrist from side to side. Then, biting her lip, she opened the second box. Inside, folded very small, was a piece of paper. She took it out. There was something inside the paper, something round, hard. Her heart stopped.

Her fingers trembling, she unfolded the paper. She felt nothing, only the dizzy sense of a hole opening inside her, ready for whatever it was she was about to feel to rush into.

The ring was a plain gold band. She stared at it and then at the piece of paper. Gerald's handwriting was cramped and spiky, a few words huddled in the middle of the page.

His Excellency
At Home
Room 116
Dinner 9 p.m.

She put the ring back in its box and put the box in her evening bag. She waited but he did not come back. At a quarter past nine she took the ring out of her bag. Slipping it onto her wedding finger, she went into the lobby.

'Perhaps you could telephone up to my husband in room 116,' she said to the concierge, 'and ask him to come down?'

The concierge eyed her left hand as he spoke. The ring was yellow and very shiny, like a curtain ring. Then he replaced the receiver. 'Your husband asks if you would join him upstairs, madam. Do you have any additional luggage?'

Jessica waited for another five minutes. She watched the elaborate doors of the elevators open and close. There was no sign of Gerald. Several of the hotel guests glanced at her quizzically as they passed. Jessica knew quite well that a well-dressed young girl alone in a hotel lobby at this time of night attracted attention. She knew that Gerald knew it too.

'At last,' he said when he opened the door.

'You deserted me,' Jessica said.

'In a very good cause, I assure you. Come in.'

'I don't know—'

'Dinner is ready.' When she still hesitated he took her hands and pulled her inside. The room was a drawing room with oil paintings and watered-silk walls and a marble-topped table crowded with orchids. There were doors on either side of the room, both of them closed. At least one of them, she supposed, was a bedroom. Long windows led out onto a balcony where a table had been laid with candles in silver candelabra. A waiter in white gloves stood beside a trolley laden with silver dishes. The candles guttered a little in the evening breeze.

'Happy birthday, darling,' Gerald said. Jessica hesitated. She could feel the throb of the unseen bedroom like a pulse from behind its panelled door. She looked at the waiter and then at Gerald. 'Ambassador,' she said.

The balcony looked out over the river. Beyond the trees the black water was brilliant with moonlight. They ate oysters, the first of the season, plump and silky and heady with the scent of the sea, and drank champagne. The waiter moved around them unobtrusively, disappearing into the drawing room between courses, but his presence reassured Jessica. Slowly she allowed herself to relax. Gerald was in ebullient spirits. He had purchased an aeroplane, he told her, and begun

413

flying lessons. His stories were hair-raising and entirely preposterous. He told her his teacher was a Russian émigré, an aristocrat who had fled the revolution with only the diamonds in his pockets. He was also teaching Gerald to speak Russian. Gerald said that there was no point in reading Pushkin unless you could read him in Russian.

'When will you have time to sleep?' Jessica joked but he only shook his head and said that he had wasted enough time already. They ate scallops and lobster and tiny paupiettes of sole in a sauce of cream and dry vermouth. When the waiter prepared crêpes Suzette, the blue and gold flames leaping and dancing against the dark sky, she clapped her hands together in delight and the diamonds on her wrist flashed. Gerald watched as she ate slowly, luxuriously, licking the rich syrup from her spoon. She smiled at him as the waiter slid her plate away, folding her hands under her chin. She could feel the hard circle of the ring against her jawbone. One day, she thought, when she was married she would live like this, in a suite with orchids and a telephone beside the bath.

'Where next?' she said. 'We don't want to waste time.'

'You don't like it here?'

'I love it. But I want to go dancing.'

'Haven't you had enough of dancing?'

'I'm twenty. No one has had enough of dancing when they're twenty.'

The waiter cleared the last of the dishes. Gerald

nodded at him and slipped a note into his gloved hand. The trolley rattled softly as he pushed it across the drawing room, closing the door to the suite behind him.

'So,' Gerald said, leaning over the table. He slid his fingers between hers. Jessica bit her lip. She felt giddy with wine and apprehension. It was like a carousel whirling too fast. She could not think how to make it stop.

'Gerald . . .'

He smiled, dipping his free hand into his pocket. 'Another present.'

She shook her head. 'I don't want any more presents. I want to dance.'

'Too bad. Sit.' She hesitated, half out of her chair. 'Sit,' he said again and he put a small silver snuff box on the table between them. It was oval with a clasp shaped like a hand. Inside, instead of snuff, there was a little heap of white powder and, tucked inside the lid, a tiny silver spoon. Gerald dipped the spoon in the powder. Putting it to one nostril he shut the other with the ball of his thumb and inhaled sharply. He tipped his head back, his fingers pressing either side of his nose, and closed his eyes. When he opened them again he smiled at her. His eyes glittered. He held the spoon out to Jessica.

'Your turn,' he said.

She knew what it was. Since the scandal of the chorus girl who died, the newspapers had worked themselves into a frenzy about the drug mania gripping London, a murky underworld of Chinamen and opium dens, of needle dancers and snow snuffers. They muttered darkly about dope fiends, an epidemic of depravity and vice. The chorus girl had died in a room at the Savoy. Jessica shook her head.

'No, thank you,' she said.

'Trust me, you'll adore it. It's like champagne without the hangover.'

'Isn't it against the law?'

'Only if you get caught. Don't be a bore, darling. It's your birthday. Everyone should break the law on their birthday.'

He was smiling but she recognised the notch between his eyebrows, the challenge in his eyes. He meant to make her do it. She thought of the Allenburys cocaine pastilles Nanny had given them when they had sore throats, the pretty blue-and-gold tin decorated with flowers. Eleanor had sent morphine and cocaine lozenges to Theo at the Front. The chemist in Mount Street advertised them in *The Times*. They were said to be good for the nerves.

'If I do it do you promise we can go dancing?'

'We can do anything you want to. It's your birthday.'

She hesitated. Then she took the spoon. The hit was sharp, corrosive, as though she had snuffed scouring powder. Her eyes watered. She swallowed, tasting bitterness at the back of her throat. The inside of her nostril felt numb.

'It doesn't taste as nice as champagne,' she said,

wrinkling her nose. Gerald smiled. He scooped another tiny spoonful and held it out to her.

'Now the other side,' he said. As she snorted he licked his finger and, dipping it into the powder, rubbed it against his gums. He closed his eyes, pressing his lips together. Then, opening them, he held out his hands. 'Shall we dance?'

'Without music?'

'I'll sing. It'll be marvellous.' Throwing back his head, he began a falsetto warbling so tuneless Jessica could not help but laugh. When he seized her around the waist, she did not resist him. Singing at the top of his voice, he spun her round the room until she was dizzy and breathless with laughter and filled with a sudden reckless exhilaration that fizzed in her toes and the roots of her hair. She kicked off her shoes, feeling the thick plush of the carpet under her stockinged feet.

'Another,' she commanded but Gerald pulled her close and pressed his mouth to hers. She pushed him away.

'Another,' she insisted. 'I'm dancing and so are you.'

'Let's dance in here,' he said and, catching her by the hand, he pushed open one of the drawing-room doors. The lamps were lit, the curtains drawn. The bed was enormous, the corner of the sheet turned back invitingly, like a hitched-up skirt. She turned, the elation shrivelling inside her, pulling her hand from his. He caught her from behind, his hands encircling her waist.

417

'Darling,' he murmured, his breath hot against her neck. She tried to pull free but he did not let go.

'You said we'd go dancing,' she protested.

'You'll like this kind of dancing better.' He slid his hands upwards, his fingertips finding her breasts, his mouth moving over the nape of her neck. The press of his tongue made her shiver, despite herself. 'Do you know how long I've waited to do this? My God, you adorable creature, you've been driving me mad.'

'I . . . I can't.'

'But you want to, don't you? You want to.' And she did not answer because she did want to, not in her head but in the nerves that crackled and flashed like fireworks through her body, electrified by his fingers, the warm insistence of his tongue. Her heart was racing. She could hear the voice in her head telling her to stop but it was so faint and far away and her body so thrilling and present and alive, and anyway what did it matter, she was in a hotel room alone with Gerald, whatever the damage it was already done, and she could not stop him now, not even if she wanted to, not without a terrible scene, and the evening had been perfect, with the exquisite dinner and the diamond bracelet, oh God, the bracelet, and after all wasn't life for living, and . . .

And then she was lying on her back on the silk counterpane and her dress was pushed up around her waist and Gerald's mouth was on her stomach and his fingers were sliding up between her thighs and under the silk of her French knickers.

'Oh,' he murmured, tugging at the buttons of his trousers. 'Oh God.'

When he thrust himself inside her the pain was like a punch, sending her reeling back to herself. She stared at the ceiling as he strained on top of her, bracing herself against the bruising ram of him, over and over. It seemed to take him a long time. Then, with a cry, he pulled out of her, his shrivelling erection pulsing pale slime onto her thigh. The sight was disgusting. She turned her head, the weight of him sprawled across her like a big game trophy, and wondered if she looked different, now that she was no longer a virgin.

CHAPTER 29

Some day, Oscar supposed, summer would end but, as he drifted dreamily through that sun-drunk August, it did not seem that way. Phyllis came to Cambridge every Sunday. She said it was too hot to be in London. They lay together on a blanket beneath the shaded canopy of a weeping willow, watching the patterns the sun made on the feathery leaves above them. The shimmer of the river pierced the low branches, casting trembling stripes of light across their bare feet. The tree was ancient, its trunk several feet across. Bent low, the tips of its leaves trailing in the water, it formed a green curtain that concealed them completely. Sometimes they heard laughter from the water, the dip and splash of other rowers passing by, though few made it so far upriver. They left their own boat a little downstream, tied to a post slippery with moss. They had no desire to attract attention.

Beneath the willow the grass was sparse. They brought a picnic rug and the cushions from the boat and a wicker basket unwieldy with books. Oscar rigged up a contraption made of string so that they could trail bottles of beer in the water to keep them cool. Phyllis liked beer. She drank it from the bottle, the foam sometimes spilling over her chin. They ate sandwiches, feeding the crumbs to the curious moorhens who peered at them from beneath the willow's fringed hem, their scarlet beaks pulled up over their faces like Venetians at a masked ball. Phyllis told Oscar about the Egyptian gods, about Osiris and Isis and their jealous brother Set. He tried unsuccessfully to explain Einstein.

She always brought her books. She read them under the tree, her head resting on his stomach. She did not stop when he protested. She kissed him and said she had lost too much time already. She told Oscar to bring books of his own but he read hers instead. It made him feel closer to her. Once he read that the ancient Egyptians had been the first to wear rings on the third fingers of their left hands as a symbol of love because they believed that particular finger contained the *vena amoris*, a vein or nerve that ran directly to the heart. The idea charmed him but when he showed it to Phyllis she only laughed.

'A rumour started by a seventeenth-century English lawyer,' she said. 'Citing unidentified ancient sources never since substantiated. The Egyptians knew nothing of the circulation of the blood and their rings were intended to appease the gods, not their husbands. But then isn't that what lawyers do, take something magical and reduce it to matrimony?'

She brought him little presents too, things he had not seen since before the War: bananas from Jamaica, French nectarines, a bar of melting Belgian chocolate. They ate it slowly, luxuriously, licking the sweetness from their fingers. He was not surprised then when, on the third Sunday in August, she produced a brown paper package from her bag. It was the size of a short, very fat cigar. He smiled. 'What is it?' he asked.

'Happy birthday.' He looked at her, then at the package. He felt sick. He had never told her about his mother's lie. He had never told anyone. 'Open it.'

'You shouldn't have—'

'Open it.'

Reluctantly he tore open the brown paper to reveal another layer of wrapping, newspaper, slightly yellowed. The newspaper was in Arabic.

'Like Pass the Parcel,' he joked and he tried to hand it back to her but she only raised an eyebrow and shook her head. He hesitated. Then he pulled away the newspaper. Inside was a small clay figure, shaped like a mummy. Though its body was crudely formed, beneath its grey headdress its face had been painstakingly shaped and painted in ochre. Its chipped clay lips were pursed and its heavily kohled eyes gazed out at Oscar with undisguised suspicion. On its whitewashed chest it bore a column of hiero-glyphics painted in black, at the top an eye, then below that an upended T and finally a shallow curve with a dot at its centre. The curve was thicker at one end than the other where the paint had been smudged. A black line topped with a half-circle was painted along one side of its body.

'She's a *shabti*,' Phyllis said. 'A servant for the afterlife.'

Oscar cradled her in his hand. She fitted almost exactly into his palm. 'She's beautiful.'

'She's probably Seventeenth Dynasty. At that time nearly everyone was buried with one or two, some with hundreds and hundreds. They believed that the dead passed on to the Field of Reeds and that everyone would be expected to work together to cultivate it. The *shabti* was the servant who would do that for you. Look, here's her hoe.' She pointed at the painted line. 'The hieroglyphs are the spell put on her so that she would answer for her master or mistress when they were called to work. *Shabti* means answerer.'

'Where did you find her?'

'In the souk in Luxor. The hawker had a biscuit tin full of them. He was rather disappointed I chose this one, he was angling for something grander, but I liked her. She looks so furious, doesn't she? As though she's been tricked.'

Oscar laughed. 'Who can blame her? Bewitched into doing someone else's hoeing for all eternity.' He touched the *shabti*'s face with one finger. 'She's wonderful. Too wonderful to give to me. You should keep her.'

'Too late. She'll only answer to you now.' Phyllis closed his hand over the *shabti* and kissed him. Her lips were soft and warm. 'Happy birthday.'

All he wanted was to kiss her back, for ever and ever. Instead, he sat up, looking down at the *shabti*. She glared at him balefully. He took a breath and held her out to Phyllis. 'I don't suppose you could wrap her up again and give her to me in April?'

She did not interrupt him as he explained. She lay on her stomach, her chin propped on her hands. When he was finished she kissed him. Then she took the *shabti* and put her in her bag.

'April's a nicer month for a birthday,' she said. 'More like a beginning.' Later, staring up into the leaves of the willow, she said, 'Do you think ours will be the generation that finally stops being ashamed of sex?'

It was she who undressed him, in the end. She was gentle, determined. She paid no heed to his assurances that she did not have to, that he was content to wait. She unbuttoned his fly and took him in her hand and, when he thought that he would explode with the ecstasy of it, she slid her leg over his, straddling him, and guided him inside her. He gazed at her, wordless, breathless, as she pushed herself upwards and arched her back, throwing her head back in a silent shudder of pleasure.

Afterwards, as they lay together, their legs tangled, he said that he was sorry, that next time it would not be over so quickly.

'I know,' she said and, twisting onto one elbow, she kissed him, her fingers finding their way between his shirt buttons to stroke his stomach, and immediately he felt himself hardening again, his bones melting like candle wax. She kissed him very slowly. Then she took his hand and placed it between her thighs.

'Like this,' she said and he knew then that he was not the first. Later, when he asked her, she said it had been during the War. She was not sorry. She had loved him, or thought she had. He had not loved her. It was not possible to love someone, she said, when you were very unhappy. The idea of Phyllis in another man's arms tortured Oscar. Alone in Cambridge on the long hot nights, he imagined her with him, their bodies entwined in the moonlight. He could see the curve of her breasts pressed against his chest, the proprietorial arc of his arms.

He knew it was his own fault for asking. He had thought that knowing would help, like turning on the light and seeing that the monster behind the door was only his dressing gown hung on a hook. Instead, it only made the monster more real.

Then, as though someone had turned a switch, the summer was over. The deep blue sky turned grey, blotting out the sun. The temperature dropped. Two days later snow fell. It was not yet October. Cambridge was muffled, blanketed in white. Below Jesus Lock the river froze. The Silver Street boatman lifted his punts from their jetty and put them into winter storage. He said the cold would crack their hulls.

The first Saturday after the snow Oscar went to London. They went to the British Museum. Afterwards they sat in a stuffy tea room near Liverpool Street Station, watching the steam condense on the windows. He held her hand under the table. She told him she had been to see a doctor and obtained a Dutch cap. She had worn a ring, invented a story about her husband struggling to find a job. Oscar was startled by her candour, her resourcefulness. Phyllis only shrugged. They could not risk a baby. Outside, labourers were working to rebuild the part of the station destroyed by German bombers in 1917. The piles of sand and bricks were iced with snow, like cakes. He held her tight as he kissed her goodbye. He wanted to ask her what she had done with the ring but he was afraid she might think it a stupid question. Through her swaddling of scarves and jerseys he could hardly feel the shape of her.

The next Saturday the railwaymen came out on strike against an attempt to cut their wages. The strike paralysed the railway system for ten days. In Cambridge Oscar slept with both his jerseys on and his overcoat spread out over the blankets. In the mornings, there were patterns of ice on the inside of the window and, on the water in his washstand jug, a skin of ice like the milk skin on a cup of tea. Without the means to transport it coal piled up outside pits across the country. Mrs Piggott said darkly that they might as well be in Russia. She took to double-locking the front door at night, in case of trouble.

It was the longest Oscar and Phyllis had gone without seeing each other since Marjorie's ball. Every morning Oscar scoured the newspapers for the latest news of the strike. He did not care about the railwaymen's wages, the necessity of an eight-hour day. He just wanted them to go back to work. In the end the Government capitulated first. Oscar took the first train out of Cambridge. When he arrived in London he went straight to the hotel behind Marylebone Station. A place like that did not stretch to scruples. The proprietress with the copper hair was behind the desk. She grinned when she saw him, showing her long teeth.

'Don't suppose you got the time, do you?' she said.

She gave him the key to Room 5. The electric fire was on a meter. Even with it fed the room was icy. They lay tangled together under the blankets in the narrow bed, only the tip of Phyllis's nose showing as she told him excitedly about her lectures, her tutors, a proposed expedition to Malta to join the excavation of a Neolithic temple. Her term had just begun.

'You're going away?' Oscar asked, disconcerted. The room was more dismal than he remembered. There was damp on the ceiling and scabs of mould along the splintered skirting boards.

'If I can raise the money. It's horribly expensive. They only tolerate students because we subsidise the digs.'

When she said she was waiting for the right time to ask her father, he knew that she was serious. Phyllis hated her dependence on her father, the obligations it brought. She lived as thriftily as she was able, impatient for a time when she would be in a position to support herself. She was matter-of-fact about Ellinghurst passing to distant cousins. She said there were advantages to the ancient injustice of primogeniture, that houses like Ellinghurst were nothing but prisons, bulwarks of stone and history that shackled their heirs, confining them to the same purposeless lives for generations.

'Father could have been a distinguished scholar,' she said. 'He took one of the highest Firsts in Greats of his generation but when he was offered a fellowship, he refused it. He said he couldn't live in Oxford, that his place was at Ellinghurst. He threw his life away.'

'Perhaps he thought Ellinghurst was more important.'

'Then that only serves to prove my point. The Bolsheviks are right. Private estates should be the property of the whole people, and not just for the good of the workers. For the landowners, too. To set them free.'

'And exactly how free would you be without your father's money to support you?'

'This isn't about the money. It's about living a life that matters, that means something, not the one ordained by an accident of birth. We only get one chance, Oscar. We can't waste it.'

She was impatient, hungry for life, for learning. She raged against the injustice that women, when they married, were required to resign from careers in teaching and the civil service but she was baffled, too, by the eagerness of her contemporaries for marriage.

'How is it that society has succeeded so triumphantly in convincing my sex that we are pitiful, thwarted half-women until we are joined with a man, when in fact it is marriage that denies a woman a self of her own, that robs her of her freedom and her independence and forces on her a form of legal home confinement? Don't look at me like that, you know quite well it's true. A man's marriage is one part of him, a woman's must be her whole life.'

'It doesn't have to be like that, surely?' Oscar protested.

'One of the other girls came in to lectures last week with a ring on her finger. I looked at that ring and all I could think of was those marks farmers paint on their sheep. A big inky splodge that says, "This one's mine". Of course she only came in to show it off, she had already withdrawn from the course.'

'Perhaps she loves him,' Oscar said quietly but Phyllis only frowned.

'Even if she does,' she said, 'how can that possibly be enough?'

Phyllis did not hanker after a home. She had no interest in the domestic life and no desire to be tied down. The thought of motherhood oppressed her. Imagine, she said, the drudgery, the boredom, the wretchedness of a life without solitude, without the time and the freedom to study, to travel. It incensed her that, even as Parliament prepared to pass into law an act that would finally lift the bars that prevented women from entering the professions, when even Oxford and Cambridge, those bastions of obscurantism, teetered on the edge of granting women full admission, permitting them at last to gain the degrees for which they had studied and been examined, intelligent women continued to subscribe to the fiction that children were the crowning achievement of their lives. The purpose of life was not mindlessly to breed. It was to examine, to question, to try to understand. A single life was so brief, so full of possibility. Who in their right mind would squander it rocking a cradle?

It did not seem to occur to her that Oscar might not feel the same way.

The next day he returned to Cambridge to matriculate. Kit was already there. He had a new leg, a futuristic-looking contraption built from a copper-aluminium alloy. It was much lighter than his old leg and he moved on it almost gracefully but it did not stop the cramps.

'Still, better than German jawbones, I suppose,' Kit said, and when Oscar looked blank he shook his head and limped over to the bookcase. He

430

scanned the spines, then pulled out a book in a worn green cloth cover which he tossed onto Oscar's lap. Oscar turned the book over, glancing at the title. *Moby-Dick* by Herman Melville. He had never heard of it.

'Just read it, would you?' Kit said. 'It'll save an awful lot of time.'

Oscar took the book back to his room and forgot all about it. His days were busy, crowded with lectures and supervisions, including, once a week, a lecture from Rutherford himself. Oscar was always the first undergraduate to arrive in the Maxwell Theatre on that day, taking his place in the front row of the stacked wooden seats, but Rutherford was invariably there before him. A heavy-set man with a round face and thick pepper-and-salt moustache, he wore an old-fashioned black suit with a waistcoat and a pocket watch that he studied as the men filed in. He looked like a bank manager.

At midday precisely Rutherford snapped his watch shut and slid it into his waistcoat pocket. The silence was sudden and intense. Rutherford did not speak. Instead, he drew a few loose pages of notes from the inside pocket of his coat and glanced over them. When he was finished he folded the notes and slid them back inside his pocket. Then he clasped his hands together, the tips of his thumbs against his lips. As if pulled by invisible threads, every one of the undergraduates in the theatre leaned forward a little in their seat.

431

The Prof had no time for obfuscation, for answers that tied you in knots. Academic philosophy bored him. Theory, he said, was another word for opinion. What mattered were the facts. A simple experiment, using simple apparatus and directed by the disciplined imagination of an individual or, better still, a group of individuals with different points of view, was capable of producing striking and conclusive results beyond the imagination of the greatest philosopher or mathematician.

'Theorists play games with their symbols,' he liked to say, 'but we turn out the real solid facts of Nature.' His lectures included frequent experimental demonstrations, as well as a copious stream of diagrams and photographs that served as experimental records. In experimental science, he said, the great discoveries came not from sophistry or pretension. They came from observation, from seeing with one's own eyes not how one presumed or imagined or hoped things to be but how they truly were.

His students puzzled over this. They argued that physics was not as simple as the Prof liked to suggest, that the complexity would not just go away because he wanted it to. They said that there was a fine line between simplicity and lack of imagination, which was another kind of stupidity. Some claimed he had a chip on his shoulder because he was a simple man himself, a colonial from New Zealand whose father had worked in a flax mill. They also complained that he ignored the syllabus. They said it would be his fault if they failed their examinations.

Oscar took no part in these conversations. He never lingered after lectures in the courtyard. He liked to be by himself then, so that he might feel it humming in him, Rutherford's joy in a good experiment and the thrill of believing, for as long as he could make it last, that all that was required to understand the great mysteries of the world was honesty and a faith in possibilities, whatever they might yield.

There were some older men among Oscar's fellow freshmen, conscripts who had had to wait their turn to be demobilised. Mostly, though, they were boys just out of school. They felt very young to Oscar, though they were perhaps only a year or two his junior. He saw little of them. As for *BUTTERWORTH D*, whose name was painted next to Oscar's at the bottom of the staircase and with whom he was supposed to share rooms, he appeared not to exist. There were mutterings of a deferment. Oscar let his books spread across the two small bookcases and piled his papers on the spare second desk. One misty November morning he returned shivering from the Baths in his dressing gown to discover that the man's name had been removed from the noticeboard at the bottom of the staircase. All that remained of *BUTTERWORTH D* was a ghostly shadow of black letters beneath the fresh white paint.

He had never dared risk it until then, but the next Saturday at tea time, as the dusk gathered like sweepings in the narrow Cambridge streets, he smuggled Phyllis back to his room. They made love in *BUTTERWORTH D*'s single bed.

'Two fools in a tub,' Oscar said and Phyllis laughed and kissed him. Later, wrapped in blankets, they toasted crumpets in front of the fire. Phyllis glanced at the books piled on the floor. A flicker of surprise passed over her face.

'Is this yours?' she asked, extracting *Moby-Dick*.

'A friend lent it to me. He said I had to read it.'

'You should.'

'You've read it?'

'A few times.'

'Oh, good. Then you can just tell me what happens and I don't have to read it myself.'

Phyllis opened the book, slowly turning the pages. 'Don't you want to?'

'I don't read novels.'

'That's not true. You read *The Time Machine*.'

'You remember.'

'Of course. I read it too, after that.'

'Did you?'

'You made it sound interesting.'

Oscar brushed his lips against her bare shoulder. She smiled vaguely, absorbed by something on the page.

'It's strange, isn't it?' he said. 'To think of before. When you were just . . . you.'

434

Phyllis did not answer. She bent her head, her face softening as she read. Oscar kissed her neck, then her ear. She leaned away from him a little, her eyes on the words. Gently he reached out and took the book from her.

'Not now,' he murmured, dropping it behind him on the floor. As he bent to kiss her he saw her glance at it. The hesitation was no longer than a breath before she turned, her body arching up to meet his. He found the book several days later, pushed out of sight beneath the narrow bookcase. He was supposed to be preparing for a supervision but it was no longer so easy to work in his room, not now she had been here. He picked up the book, turning the pages as she had, wondering which passage had caught her attention. The chapter was set out oddly, like a play. He frowned at it. Then he turned back to the beginning and began to read.

A week later he sat with Kit at breakfast. It was early, a little after seven in the morning, and Trinity Great Hall was almost empty, the silence broken only by the muffled clatter of plates from the kitchen. Above them the vast diamond-paned windows were turning from black to a streaky yellow-grey. Oscar ate his eggs absently, *Moby-Dick* open on the table by his plate.

'Bloody hell,' Kit said. 'They've only gone and bloody done it.'

Oscar did not answer. He did not want to talk

435

to Kit. He wanted to be beside Ahab and Starbuck aboard the *Pequod*, watching Moby-Dick rise up in the water, the corpse of Fedallah lashed to his side in a tangle of harpoon ropes.

'Aren't you going to ask me what they've only gone and bloody done?'

'Later,' Oscar said, his eyes on the page. As the great whale turned and swam away from the *Pequod*, Starbuck turned to Ahab. *'Moby-Dick seeks thou not. It is thou, thou, that madly seekest him!'*

'Not later, Ishmael. Now.' Ignoring Oscar's protests, Kit placed the folded newspaper over the open book. 'Right there.'

Reluctantly Oscar followed Kit's finger. Under the headline *REVOLUTION IN SCIENCE, NEW THEORY OF THE UNIVERSE*, the paper reported that a team of British astronomers had travelled to the island of Principe off the west coast of Africa to photograph the recent solar eclipse. Their results had been presented at a joint meeting of the Royal Society and the Royal Astronomical Society in London. By plotting the positions of the background stars visible near the perimeter of the darkened sun, the scientists had proved that, in the gravitational field of the sun, light bent not as the laws of Newtonian science would suggest but in precise accordance with Einstein's theory of general relativity.

When interviewed, the President of the Royal Society admitted to finding parts of Einstein's theory opaque. He also acknowledged that, to support his assertions, Einstein had offered three experimentally quantifiable cases as proofs. The first, relating to the motion of the planet Mercury, had already been verified; the second, the angle of light deflection around the sun, could now be considered confirmed. Although there remained uncertainty about the third, which concerned the spectrum of light emanating from the sun compared with the light of laboratory sources, one thing was beyond doubt: the Einstein theory had now to be reckoned with. Human conceptions of the fabric of the universe would never be the same again.

'Well?' Kit demanded.

Oscar put down the paper. He thought of those nights during the War when he had sneaked out into their tiny garden after his mother was asleep to stare up at the familiar patterns of the constellations. In Clapham on those clear nights space was constant and absolute and so, with the blackout, was the darkness. Now space was curved and light did not travel in a straight line and at night the street-lamp dazzle of London threw an orange veil over the sky, hiding the stars.

'You know what this means, don't you?' Kit said. 'Not only has the miraculous Mr Einstein changed physics for ever, he may just have achieved the great miracle of changing Cambridge University. They'll have to teach us this stuff now. I've got to go but come for tea. We can celebrate. The King is dead, long live the King.'

With one hand on the table, the other on the

back of his chair, he levered himself to standing. When Kit was in pain the bad side of his face seemed to shrink, pulling down the corner of his eye. It looked like he was winking.

Alone Oscar gulped the last of his tea. The trickle of undergraduates had thickened to a steady stream and the rumble of their chatter bounced and echoed beneath the vast vaulted ceiling, combining with the clatter of cutlery and the chink of cups and saucers like the tuning up of an orchestra. Oscar thought of Ishmael who set sail with Ahab in pursuit of the great whale, not like Ahab because he was in the grip of an obsessive hatred for the beast but because he was curious and he itched for the sea.

'And the great flood-gates of the wonder-world swung open,' Ishmael said and Oscar felt it too, the magnificence of the future as it rose from the depths of unknowing and made a snow hill in the air.

CHAPTER 30

Eleanor cabled three times from France that autumn, each time delaying her return for several weeks. Nanny's niece had gone to take care of her daughter who had had a baby and Nanny sometimes stayed in the flat at weekends. Jessica could have stayed too, if she had wanted, but to her surprise she realised she wanted to go home. She was glad to get away from London, from Gerald. She only took a little cocaine, just enough to tip her into gaiety, but sometimes she had difficulty sleeping and on Fridays she was often short-tempered and jittery. The ache in her as the headlights of the car swept round the turn to pick out the great stone gates was as sharp as homesickness. She drank tea in front of the fire and read the books she had read as a child. Sometimes she rode Max. She was too big for him and he was getting old. She let him canter on a loose rein, pulling him up when he started to wheeze. In the cold air his breath made clouds that caught in his eyelashes.

She took pleasure from solitude, from the safety of sameness. It perplexed her that her father, who had only ever regarded guests as an unwelcome interruption, was suddenly intent on company. Several times he wrote to Oscar in Cambridge, inviting him to stay. When Jessica asked why he said that it was a kindness, that Oscar had nowhere else to go. He said that a house like Ellinghurst did not suit being empty.

'He's your guest if he comes,' Jessica warned him. 'I gave up nurse-maiding Oscar Greenwood years ago.' But Oscar never came. He had commitments to the University and too much work to do. Instead, he wrote letters which Sir Aubrey left on the hall table for Jessica to read when she came home. To her surprise he was a lively correspondent, though when he wrote about science she could hardly understand a word he said. Sometimes he enclosed newspaper cuttings or photographs he had taken.

'He has Theo's old camera,' Sir Aubrey told her. 'The Brownie, do you remember?'

Jessica remembered. Knowing that the camera had been Theo's made her look at the photographs more closely. The snaps he sent were mostly of Cambridge but occasionally he sent pictures of Ellinghurst he must have taken during the War: the bust of Socrates distorted through the mullions of the library window or the deserted stables with Max staring out disconsolately over his half-door like a lone drinker at a bar. There were never any people in Oscar's photographs but it seemed to Jessica that there had been, that the stillness he captured had not had time properly to settle but rippled like the surface of a pond into which someone had thrown a stone.

She did not try to explain the feeling to her father. Her father had recently purchased his own camera, a considerably more sophisticated model than Oscar's Brownie, and she did not want to encourage him into another of his disquisitions on the art of photography. His pictures were also of Ellinghurst, taken from every conceivable angle and intended as illustrations for his book, but though they were carefully competent they had none of the simple intimacy of Oscar's snapshots. Once Oscar sent a picture of the Tiled Room in the tower, taken through the arch of the open door, and when her father showed it to her Jessica thought of that raw afternoon when the boys from Theo's regiment had come and Oscar had looked at her as though she was as much of a miracle as water into wine, and she had not wanted to give it back. When she asked her father if she might keep it, he hesitated only slightly before nodding. She told him she liked the idea of always having a piece of Ellinghurst in her handbag.

Oscar was not the only person Sir Aubrey invited frequently to visit. Most Saturdays that autumn Mrs Maxwell Brooke joined them for lunch. She did not bring Marjorie. She told Jessica that there were house parties every weekend during the pheasant shooting season, that Marjorie was always dashing from one county to another. It was not

441

true, she said, all the doom and gloom people liked to spout about the War having changed the world for ever. Little by little, and not a moment too soon, things were finally going back to the way they were before.

'I wonder if you might not think of shooting here again, Aubrey?' she said. 'The shooting parties here were always marvellous,' and there was a little notch between her eyebrows as though she were doing calculations in her head.

Jessica could not help but notice how successfully Mrs Maxwell Brooke had insinuated herself into the space left empty by Eleanor. She was shrewd, of course. Although it was plain that Saturdays were not the only days she visited, there was no suggestion of impropriety. She was careful always to ask Jessica if she might speak to Mrs Johns about some trifling domestic issue or other and, when Jessica expressed surprise, she confided that both Eleanor and Aubrey had lent unfailing support in the dark times after the death of her own husband years before, that she could not think how she would have managed without them. It was a privilege, she said, to have some small opportunity to return their many kindnesses. A man like Aubrey, she said, should not have to bother himself with the everyday responsibilities of running a household.

'Ellinghurst is a great blessing and a great burden,' she said. 'It is not right that your father should have to bear it alone.'

'I'm sure Eleanor will be very grateful for all you've done,' Jessica said sweetly and she took some pleasure in the flicker that crossed Mrs Maxwell Brooke's face. She supposed Mrs Maxwell Brooke was lonely with Marjorie away all the time but there was no point in encouraging her. Soon Eleanor would be home. She wondered what Mrs Maxwell Brooke would do then, whether she would disappear or try instead to reprise the role she had played so eagerly before the War, of Eleanor's principal admirer and acolyte.

On 11 November, at the eleventh hour of the eleventh day of the eleventh month, the country marked the first anniversary of the Armistice with a Great Silence. The hour was marked by a burst of rockets fired upwards into the sky. As the blasts echoed through the grey mist of the morning, every passenger train on the railways, every clattering goods train and shunting engine, shuddered to a halt. In every city buses and lorries and taxis stopped where they stood, their engines stilled. Beneath the pavements of London the Underground trains waited motionless in their tunnels and the ships in the Channel stayed their course. As the explosions faded and the chiming bells of clocks and churches fell silent, all sound ceased. Men pressed their hats to their stomachs and bowed their heads. Kneeling children pressed the palms of their hands together. In the offices of *Woman's Friend* the girls stopped typing and put down their pencils and closed their eyes. For two long minutes everyone remembered.

No one wanted to break the silence. It extended awkwardly, fading into a rustle of paper and clearing throats. For the rest of the day the mood in the office was sombre. Joan and Peggy hunched over their work, the frantic clatter of the typewriters another kind of silence. Later, as she put on her hat, Jessica caught sight of Miss Cooke sitting in the cubicle of her office. She was crying silently, knuckles white against her face.

Eleanor was home. The day after the Great Silence she came to London to see Mrs Leonard. Afterwards she and Jessica had supper together at the flat. To Jessica's surprise, she did not immediately launch into an account of the sitting, the things Theo had said to Feda. She asked Jessica about her work and listened to the answer. There was a new quietness about her, a composure Jessica did not recognise. She wondered if it was over at last, if in France Eleanor might finally have put her grief to rest.

'You look well,' Jessica said.

Eleanor was silent, her eyes on her lap. She picked up her napkin and patted her lips with it. Then, folding it neatly, she laid it beside her plate. She was going back to France. With the help of her French guide, she had found a house close to the village of Fontaine, some miles north of Arras. The village had been badly damaged by German shells but work was being done and the inhabitants had begun to return. Beside the ruins of the village church, piled with rubble and broken pews, there was a small cemetery, a tangled plot of perhaps one hundred graves. Theo was buried there. She had visited his grave every afternoon; as the shadows lengthened she had felt the boys gathering around her, their faces pale in the gloom and their laughter like the distant wind in the trees.

In the mornings she had walked across the devastated landscape where the fighting had been. It was there, among the shattered trees and mounds of mud that marked Theo's last days that she had finally found peace. She was no longer separated from him by not knowing. Once she saw a woman digging wildly with her hands in the mud, scrabbling for something, anything to hold onto. Many of the boys could not be found. She knew she was lucky. There were gangs of Poles clearing the battlefields, rolling away the barbed wire, filling the trenches. The blasted tree stumps were being dug up and new saplings planted in their place. Eleanor had wished she could stop them. The wasteland of cratered mud, devoid of shape, of sense, of the dogged persistence of life, was Theo's true memorial, the horror of loss made manifest.

One day, she said, life would return to those ruined fields. It was hard to imagine, harder still to bear. But she meant to be there then, too, as the first tentative shoots pushed through the mud. It was Theo's place. Every leaf, every flower and

445

blade of grass that sprang from that earth was a part of him. She belonged there, where he was.

The greed of her grief was gone. In its place was something calmer and more stubborn. She would leave soon, she told Jessica, as soon as things could be arranged. She asked for Jessica's blessing, and hoped some day that she and Phyllis might come and visit her. She did not intend to return to England. Whatever became of Ellinghurst there was no longer a place for her there.

'You're leaving Father?' Jessica said, stunned.

'We have agreed to live apart. It is better that way.'

'I see. Poor Father.'

Eleanor's jaw tightened. 'Oh, yes, poor Aubrey. I suppose you know he wants a divorce?'

'A divorce?'

'Of course I've refused. The scandal . . .'

'The scandal, of course. You've always worried so terribly about scandal.'

'It's quite impossible. It would break Theo's heart.'

'Theo's?'

'You know why he wants a divorce, don't you? So he can marry that ludicrous Verity Maxwell Brooke. It seems the War was very good to Verity.'

Jessica glared at her mother. 'And why not, if she makes him happy?'

'Happy? Oh, please. Don't be naïve.'

'Remember that time in the garden with the revolting Mr Connolly? You said everyone had to

446

have some fun now and then or they forgot they were alive. Or was that rule just for you?'

There were two red spots in the centre of Eleanor's cheeks. 'You think I'm the one who began this? Your father was never faithful to me, not even at the start.'

'You didn't exactly suffer in silence.'

'He broke my heart.'

'My heart bleeds for you.'

'God but you're a heartless little bitch, aren't you?'

'And who do you think I got that from?'

'You're right. You're your father's daughter. Cold through and through.'

She left the next morning before Eleanor was up. By the time she came home her mother was gone. She bathed and dressed and snapped at Nanny when Nanny said she looked tired and wouldn't it be better if she did not go out for once. It was not just Eleanor. That afternoon Joan had cornered her in the ladies' cloakroom. She hoped Jessica would forgive her presumption, she would not ask, not normally, only there was a job going at *Perspective*, a job that might almost make up for two wretched years of knit-and-purl at *Woman's Friend*, the kind of job that hardly ever came up and then only ever went to men.

'It's the old boys' club, you see,' Joan said. 'Members only. But then I thought, you know, since you and Mr Cardoza are friends . . .'

The way she said friends had made Jessica's insides turn over. When Joan pushed an envelope into her hand and said that she understood if it was inappropriate but if there was any way, any way at all, Jessica had muttered something about Mr Cardoza being really a friend of her mother's, and fled. She had spent the rest of the afternoon trying not to think about who else might know.

She did not know any more what she felt about Gerald. Since that night in the Savoy she felt both more tender towards him and more uneasy. She found herself thinking about him at work, wondering what he was doing and if he was thinking of her. Sometimes, at night, she took the diamond bracelet from the sleeve of the folded-up sweater where she had hidden it from Nanny, and put it on and tried to imagine what it would be like, to spend a lifetime with a man like Gerald. It was not so crazy an idea. Hadn't Ludo confided that she was the first girl since Christabel that Gerald had truly cared for? He was witty and rich and generous and he adored her. Often, it was true, he drank too much or disappeared to the cloakroom with his snuff box. Then his moods grew wilder and, though he grew more wild in his affections too, his vivacity often tipped over into imperiousness and he was cruel to her, mocking her for being prissy, a debutante wet blanket. She tried to lighten her mood to match his but it was not easy to keep up. Sometimes, she thought, there was something almost grim about his feverish pursuit of amusement. It did not seem to make him happy. In the early evenings, before he had begun seriously to drink, he as good as admitted it. He had begun, a little, to talk about the future. The previous Thursday, he had said something about the Riviera in June.

'Imagine it,' he said. 'No more filthy foggy London. A shaded terrace overlooking the sea. Pine trees and bare feet and freshly picked figs for breakfast. Wouldn't we be happy?' And she had smiled at him and thought that really they might be. London was not good for him, she could see that. He had had a cold for weeks. His eyes were pouched and bloodshot, his voice hoarse, his nose streaming. He did not seem to be able to shake it off.

That evening they went to the King Club for dinner. They drank a good deal and she tried to be gay but she knew she did not fool him. She feared he might think her dull. Instead, he took her hand and asked her what was wrong.

'It's nothing,' she said but he only shook his head.

'Not to me,' he said, so she told him about Eleanor and her father. She thought he might laugh, or turn it into a joke. Instead, he listened gravely, watching her over the rim of his glass. It was easy to talk to someone who listened like that.

'She doesn't love him,' Jessica said. 'She never has. But she won't let him go.' And he kissed her fingers and said that it was unbearable, the damage people did to one another in the name of love.

'But sometimes they save them too,' he said, and the way he looked at her squeezed her heart into a fist. She let him kiss her outside the restaurant where anyone might see, and in the car she put her hand on his leg. He reached down to take it in his, sliding his fingers between hers, and she rested her head on his shoulder, inhaling his expensive leather and cedar wood smell.

'Where are we going?' she asked.

'Himeros.' Himeros was the club with the murals. Jessica thought of Guy Cockayne and shook her head.

'Not there, not tonight,' she pleaded but Gerald was adamant. He said he was meeting someone. Jessica presumed he meant Ludo but when they got to Himeros there was only the man with the plum mouth. He showed them to a corner table where there was already a bottle of whisky and a bottle of champagne in a bucket of ice. The band was in full swing and music filled the tiny space, blotting out speech, blotting out thought. Jessica could feel the thump of it like a pulse in the walls, in the floor beneath her feet. The gods with their erect phalluses seemed to be thrusting in time. She sat down reluctantly as the man put his mouth to Gerald's ear and said something she could not hear. On the table next to theirs a girl was performing the splits, her dress hitched up to her thighs. Her legs were bare, her toenails a vivid shiny vermilion.

Gerald slid into the booth beside her, pouring

himself a half-tumbler of whisky which he downed in a single swallow. He poured another. Then, taking the snuff box from his pocket, he opened it. He did not bother with the spoon. He pinched some powder between his finger and thumb and, tipping back his head, thrust them into his right nostril. Jessica gaped at him.

'What are you doing?' she demanded, her mouth close to his ear. 'People can see.'

He shrugged at her as though he could not hear and took another pinch, his eyes closed against the hit. Jessica pushed the box out of sight behind the whisky bottle. He blinked, his fingers smoothing out the sides of his nose. 'Don't you want some?' he shouted.

When she shook her head he shrugged again and gulped his whisky. 'It might do you good.'

'I'm fine as I am.'

'Then God help us both.' The derision in his face was like a slap, only she hardly had time to register it because Ludo was there and a girl Jessica vaguely recognised although she could not remember her name, and they were sitting down and Gerald was pouring drinks and shouting something that made Ludo laugh and then he was pulling her to her feet and into the whirling vortex of the dance floor and the heaviness in her lungs gave way to breathlessness and the music coursed through her head like a river in full spate, bearing the thoughts away, and when at last it exploded to a crescendo Gerald was whooping and kissing

451

her and she kissed him back because she knew he had not meant to hurt her and she was no longer sure if it had even happened the way she thought it had anyway.

Gerald did not bring out his snuff box in front of Ludo. He did, however, pay several visits to the cloakroom. Jessica did her best not to notice. She drank champagne steadily, doggedly, disregarding the headache that pushed up from the nape of her neck and spread like a flower opening over the back of her skull. It was late when they finally left, staggering up the stairs into the dirty black dregs of the night. In the yellow light of the street lamp Gerald's face had the grey pallor of wet clay and his eyes were red, the pupils punched into them like holes. Beside the car he pulled Jessica towards him, crushing his mouth against hers. Kissing him made her tongue feel numb.

'You're a wicked girl, did you know that?' he mumbled. She tried to pull away but he held her around the waist with one hand, fumbling at the fly of his trousers with the other.

'Gerald, for God's sake,' she whispered but he only caught her by the wrist, pressing her hand against his crotch. She recoiled, expecting the insistence of his erection, but instead he was soft.

'Come on,' he said hoarsely and he closed her fingers around him, palpating them so that she was almost kneading him, his hips grinding against her like a dog, but still he did not harden.

'Please, Gerald, not here.' She looked over his shoulder, terrified that someone would come out of the club and see them.

'For fuck's sake!' Abruptly he pulled away, wrenching the car door open. 'Get in.'

'Gerald—'

'Frigid fucking bitch!' he hissed. Behind the wheel he stabbed at the ignition switch on the dashboard and stamped his feet. The engine roared. Wrenching at the hand brake he threw the gear lever and jammed his foot on the accelerator. The car made a sudden leap forward, jerking Jessica back against her seat. She clutched at her arm rests as Gerald accelerated. His fly was still open. She could see the white cotton of his drawers.

'For God's sake, Gerald, slow down,' she shouted above the scream of the engine, but Gerald only glared through the rain-smeared windscreen and pressed the accelerator. The tyres squealed as he swerved onto Park Crescent, pitching Jessica against the door. The empty-eyed houses stared unblinkingly as he gunned the engine. The car leaped like a horse across Marylebone Road and shot towards the black mass of the Park.

'Stop!' she cried, her voice shrill with fear.

She was not sure what happened next. She thought perhaps a black car pulled out of a side street. Afterwards, when she closed her eyes, she could see the twin beams of its headlamps, the rain coursing through the rotating tubes of

453

light like streams of silver fish. Certainly the car swerved, its tyres squealing, so that the back half swung out like an opened door, and there was the sound of car horns and screaming, her own screaming, she thought perhaps, but coming from a long way away, and a pall of smoke slung like a wet sheet across the road.

Then the sheet parted and he was standing there, not smiling but gesturing impatiently, pushing his hair away from his brow with the heel of his other hand just as he always had.

Theo.

'Come on,' he said. 'Quickly or we'll miss it.'

She stared at him. 'It's you,' she said.

'Who else would it be? Come on, Mess, what are you waiting for?'

'Don't call me Mess. You know I don't like it when you do that.'

'So? It's what you are. Look at yourself.'

Jessica looked down at her lap but she could not see anything. Where her body should be there was just smoke and darkness and the blare of car horns and screaming, coming from a long way off.

'What a mess, Miss Mess,' Theo murmured. It sounded like the beginning of a song or maybe a limerick. 'What a messy bloody mess.'

'I'm sorry,' she said and she was crying, crying all over, tears pouring through her hair and down her arms and dripping from the tips of her fingers. Theo pulled at the car door but he could not open it. His hair was very long, longer than she

454

remembered. It fell over his eyes. The ends of it caught in his eyelashes. He did not push it away.

'It's stiff,' Jessica said. 'You have to pull really hard.' And she put her hand out towards him but her hand was glass and so was the window, cold and hard, and he was on the other side and his mouth was moving and she could not hear what he was saying and her face was glass and her tears too. If she listened she could hear the high-pitched chime they made as they shattered.

'My own Mess,' he said, his voice suddenly very close, and he leaned through the window and the glass did not smash but flowed around him like water and he took her in his arms and she thought he was going to embrace her and she wanted to weep with relief but instead he pulled at her, jerking her neck and jolting a shock of pain through her skull. She cried out. He let her go and immediately he started to fade, the outline of him blurring and swirling like smoke.

'Stay with me,' she cried and she snatched at him, her fingernails like claws, and for a moment he was there, a part of her, and quite gone, both at the same time.

When she came back to herself again she was no longer in the car. Her head floated on her neck like a balloon, dizzy with rushing sparks of light. She closed her eyes. Someone was beside her. He was crying.

'Theo?' she murmured.

Theo did not answer. Jessica blinked blearily. It was dark. The wind tossed in the dark shapes of the trees and scattered the rain in furious handfuls. She saw wet pavements, a narrow white pillar, the car, half-mounted on the pavement. It was twisted at an awkward angle like a broken arm, its bonnet crumpled against a lamppost. In the circle of lamplight the road was bright with rain and broken glass.

She shivered. Her feet were wet, her stockings too. When she turned her head the pain made her giddy. She closed her eyes, swallowing nausea. When she opened them again she saw Gerald sitting beside her. He had his hands over his face. His shoulders shuddered as he wept into his palms.

'Are you hurt?' she asked. Her voice did not sound like her own.

He bent his head lower, his back convulsed with sobs as he rocked backwards and forwards, emitting a ghastly high-pitched keening like an animal caught in a trap. She leaned towards him but at the same time something in her recoiled. She could not quite bring herself to touch him.

'Gerald, what is it?' she said. 'Are you hurt? Please, Gerald, you're scaring me. What is it?'

His back heaved, once and then again, as though he were being violently sick. Then, with a frightful moan, he turned, burying his face in her lap, his arms clutching her around the waist. She stiffened. She could feel his tears soaking into the pale silk-chiffon of her dress. She prayed it was not blood.

She would never get blood out without Nanny noticing, she thought, and immediately hated herself for thinking it.

Her head throbbed as she made herself stroke his back. She knew she should call an ambulance. She would have to ring on someone's doorbell and they would ask her who she was, who Gerald was. What possible explanation did she have for being alone in a car with Gerald in the middle of the night? The police would come, they would take a statement. Gerald had been driving recklessly. If he was summoned to go up in front of a magistrate it would get into the newspapers. People would know she had been there. Her name would be published. She hated him then, for his carelessness. She could feel the panic rising in her like smoke.

'It's all right,' she said through gritted teeth. 'Everything's going to be all right,' but he only wept harder. His sobs were an agonised howl, wracking his body, the breath torn from him in painful shudders.

'For God's sake, Gerald,' she said. 'You have to tell me what's wrong.'

He raised his head. His eyes were red, swimming with tears, his face smeared with snot, but she could not see any blood. 'Help me,' he whimpered.

The fear then was like acid in her bones. He had sustained internal injuries, perhaps he was dying. If he died, the scandal . . . but she could not think that. He was dying. She could not abandon him. 'I'm going to go for help,' she said.

He shook his head, clutching at her like a child. 'Don't leave me.'

'I have to. We need to get you to a hospital.'

'I don't need a hospital. I need you.'

'I know but if you're hurt—'

'But I'm not hurt,' he moaned and his face crumpled, tears spilling down his cheeks. His shoulders shook. 'Not a scratch. Not a fucking scratch.'

She looked at him. 'I don't understand.'

He twisted to look at her, clutching at her coat with his fists. 'I can't do this any more. Don't let me do this any more.' His eyes were wild with pain and distress. 'Don't leave me. Please. Marry me. Marry me, darling.'

She gaped at him, the disgust hardening in her throat.

'Marry me,' he pleaded, his voice cracking. 'Oh God, don't you see? You're the only one who can save me.'

A taxi cab swung into the street, catching them in its headlights. Jessica raised a hand against the glare as the cab slowed and pulled over. A gentleman in the back lowered the window.

'Has there been an accident? Do you need help?'

Jessica waited for Gerald to say something but he only buried his head in her coat. 'Please,' he whispered.

Jessica wanted to slap him. Instead, she smiled her most charming smile. 'You are kind and I know we must look like the most awful vagrants, but this

is actually our house. Our housekeeper is just telephoning the police but we thought it best for my
husband to sit here for a moment, just to get over
the shock. We'll take him in presently. Such bad
luck, a dog ran out in front of us, he had to swerve
to avoid it. The lamppost rather got in the way.'

'Indeed. Well, so long as you're both unhurt.'

'Quite unhurt, thank you. The dog, too, I'm glad
to say. One just hopes it will look both ways next
time it crosses the road.'

The man smiled. Then, touching his hat, he
settled back into the cab. Jessica watched its tail-
lights disappear around the corner and thought of
Theo, asking her what she was waiting for. Pushing
Gerald away, she stood up.

'I'm sorry,' she said. Sliding off her glove she
unclasped the diamond bracelet from her wrist
and held it out to him. He did not take it. He
stared at her, tears shining in his bloodshot eyes.
Carefully she laid the bracelet on the step beside
him. 'Goodbye, Gerald.'

'Don't leave me,' he pleaded, holding out both
hands. 'You can't leave me. Where are you going?'

She bit her lip, gazing up the lamplit street. In
the shadows near the Park she thought perhaps
she saw someone move. She knew he would not
come back. She looked at the crumpled car and
then at Gerald. Lightly she touched her fingertips
to the bruise on her forehead and winced.

'It's time I went home,' she said.

CHAPTER 31

The weekend before she left for Malta Phyllis came to Cambridge for a whole weekend. It was the first time she had managed such a thing. A friend of hers at Bedford College had put her in touch with a cousin who was in her third year at Newnham. Exasperated with the college's draconian chaperonage rules, the cousin and her sister, a year younger and also at Newnham, had persuaded their parents to rent them a house in Grange Road beyond the reach of the authorities. As long as she did not mind the sofa, Phyllis was welcome to stay the night.

Oscar went with Phyllis to leave her suitcase. Irene Howard was a tall lean woman in a fisherman's sweater and tweed trousers.

'Just put your things down anywhere,' she told Phyllis. 'I'm afraid it's a bit of a mess.'

The hall was narrow and as crammed as a junk shop. There were bicycles propped against the hall wall and tea chests brimming with crumpled newspaper and piles of books and hats and gramophone records and opened letters and, up the stairs, pairs and pairs of empty shoes, like an invisible queue.

Beside the laden coat stand there was even a battered Indian totem pole with outstretched wings and a malevolent expression.

'Handsome, isn't he?' Irene said. 'I swapped him for my uncle's skeleton. Not his actual skeleton, obviously. That would have been unfeeling. The one he had as a student doctor. He used to dress her in pearls and fur coats and stand her in his window to spook the neighbours. She was our chaperone all last year. Dear Mrs Mandible. She was an utter Gorgon.'

Irene and Beatrice were throwing a party. Irene had Oscar help her move the table and a sofa to make room for dancing. 'You will come, won't you?' Irene said as they left and, to Oscar's dismay, Phyllis agreed that they would. They walked along the river, the bare trees black against the dirty snow of the sky, and he thought of the hours that they should have had, the hours that now were no longer theirs, and he hunched his shoulders, his hands deep in his pockets.

Phyllis did not notice his silence. She breathed on her mittened fingers to warm them and talked gleefully of the sculptures that the dig had recently uncovered, scores of images of the human figure from small clay models to full-size statues carved from the local limestone.

'Some of them are so detailed they show quite plainly the style of dresses that the Bronze Age women would have worn,' she told him, her voice crackling like static in the frozen air.

461

Further downstream an old beech tree had fallen across the path, its roots in the air like an outstretched hand, its leafless branches raking the water. Phyllis stroked its grey flank. Then, finding a foothold, she clambered up onto it, lichen chalking green marks on her skirt. For a moment she stood looking down at him, her hair bright beneath her woollen hat, her cheeks flushed pink from the cold. Oscar wished he had brought his camera. Not that Phyllis would have let him take a picture. She hated having her photograph taken. She always hid her face when he tried, or turned away. The few photographs he had of her he had stolen when she was asleep. The pictures moved him, stirred him even, but they discomfited him too. For all the intimacy of the pose there was something closed about her sleeping face, something he could not reach. He was jealous of the places she went to in her dreams.

Laughing, her arms held out like wings, she walked away from him along the slippery bark towards the water.

'Be careful,' he called after her as she neared the bank but she did not hear him. She picked her way along the tree until she stood in the cleft of one of the high branches. She was much higher now, high above Oscar and the black rush of the water. She threw her head back, her mouth open, her arms held above her like a pagan priestess, a silhouette against the dead white sky. She shouted

462

or perhaps she sang. Oscar did not know. The wind whipped the sounds away before he could hear them. He watched her, waiting for her to turn and make her way back to him.

The party was crowded, thick with smoke and music. People were dancing in the dining room and in the parlour. A man in a velvet coat swerved a bicycle through the crush, a laughing girl balanced on the handlebars. Someone had put a gown and mortar board on the totem pole. It eyed Oscar coldly as he squeezed past it. Kit was leaning against the parlour wall with a glass in his hand, talking to a tall girl wearing what appeared to be a pair of silk pyjamas. Beside her was a table set with a bewildering array of bottles. When Kit saw Oscar he gaped theatrically.

'Bloody hell,' he said. 'The mountain has come to Muhammad. Mix the man a drink, Bea, there's a good girl. While you're at it make it two. I need something for the shock.'

The girl in pyjamas was Irene's sister. She took a bottle of gin from an ice bucket on the table and poured a slug into a silver cocktail shaker, along with a splash of something from a green bottle.

'One of Bea's martinis and you won't know yourself,' Kit said. 'Or anybody else, for that matter.'

Irene squeezed through to join them. 'Hello, Kit, darling. You look ravishing as always.' Kissing him on the cheek, she intercepted the glass Bea was

463

holding out to Oscar, dropped an olive in it, took a gulp and, sighing happily, handed it back. The gin was oily, swirled with cold.

'Just making sure it's not poisoned,' she said. 'Be an angel, Bea, and fix one of those for Phyllis.'

'Where is she?' Oscar asked.

'Upstairs powdering her nose. She'll be down in a minute.'

Oscar sipped his drink as Kit asked Irene about the play she was rehearsing.

'Oscar and I shall come,' he said. 'We shall sit in the front row and scream like schoolgirls every time you make an entrance.'

'How lovely,' Irene said. 'Only according to Miss Clough it is improper for men to see girls in men's clothing. It's brothers and fiancés only.'

'Like Herod.'

'Like Herod, only less compassionate.'

Behind Kit Oscar saw Phyllis hesitating in the doorway. He waved and she smiled, her bottom lip caught between her teeth. Oscar's heart turned over.

'This is Phyllis,' he said to Kit. Still laughing Kit turned. The laugh caught in his throat. Phyllis stared at him.

'Phyllis,' he said.

'Hello, Kit.' The words came out squashed. She did not look at Oscar.

'Don't tell me you two know each other?' Irene said.

'We do,' Kit said.

'Drink?' Bea said, holding out a glass, but Phyllis did not take it. She just went on staring at Kit.

'It's been a long time,' Kit said softly. 'How are you?'

'I'm all right. You?'

'Pretty good.' He gestured with his glass. 'Legless as always.'

Nobody laughed. There was a silence. Irene took the glass from Bea and put it into Phyllis's hand. Phyllis blinked at it in confusion. Then Irene slid her arm through Oscar's. 'Come and dance,' she said. When he shook his head her arm tightened around his. 'Come on. Bea, come with us. It's a party, not a wake.'

Oscar looked helplessly at Phyllis but she only stared at her drink. Like a prisoner in irons Oscar allowed himself to be led away. He danced distractedly, heavily, his feet as clumsy as a clown's. Several times he trod on Irene's toes.

'Sorry,' he mumbled. 'Sorry.'

The gramophone record stopped, the needle skating over the shellac. Someone lifted it from the turntable, slid another from its sleeve.

'One more?' Irene said. Oscar shook his head.

'Sorry,' he said again.

She nodded. 'You might want to give them a minute,' she said gently.

Oscar went upstairs. He sat in a bedroom on a bed covered in people's coats. He was there for a long time. When he came down the party was still in full swing. People were dancing in the hall

465

and in the dark passage that led to the kitchen a couple were kissing. His heart flipped like a landed fish before he saw that it was not them. He could feel his hands trembling. Pushing past them more roughly than was quite necessary he stepped down into the kitchen. Someone had switched out the light. In the faint white gleam of the moon, abandoned glasses and bottles glittered like eyes. It was a moment before he saw her standing by the window, staring out into the darkness. She was alone. Slowly she turned to look at him. In her cupped hands she cradled a martini glass, half full. She held it out towards him. 'Drink?' she asked.

Oscar shook his head. There was a silence. Phyllis drank, emptying her glass.

'It was him, wasn't it?' he said at last. 'The man you loved. It was Kit.'

Phyllis put her glass on the counter and turned back towards the door. He could see her face reflected in the black glass, a pale oval with two holes for eyes. 'He was at Roehampton. In my ward.'

'Kit Ferguson.'

'Yes.'

'You said he didn't love you. That's what you said.'

'Yes. Because he didn't. Not the way I wanted him to, anyway.'

'And you? Do you still love him?'

'Oscar . . .'

Someone had turned up the gramophone. The music filled the kitchen, an old Joplin rag Oscar's mother had liked to play on the piano.

The contrariness of it, the intoxicating verve of the syncopations, had always made them laugh. He could hear laughter coming from the dining room now, the shiver in the wooden floor as they danced.

'I thought I loved him,' she said. 'I didn't know then what love was supposed to feel like.'

'Don't lie to me. I saw the way you looked at him. The way you looked at each other.'

'Oscar, stop it. You're being ridiculous.'

The music was sharp and insistent inside him, forming and reforming like patterns in a kaleidoscope. 'He gave you *Moby-Dick*, didn't he?'

'Actually, I gave it to him.'

Oscar thought of Ahab, dragged by the neck to the depths of the ocean by the whale, his tiny boat caught in the whirlpool of the sinking *Pequod*. 'Melville,' he said.

She shrugged. 'Eleanor's American friends were always giving us copies.' In the dining room someone was singing loudly along with the Joplin. There was laughter and cheering, a piercing whistle. Phyllis stretched a hand out towards him. He did not take it. She let it fall. 'Kit said you never told him you had a girl.'

'He never asked.'

They were both silent. With a final extravagant crescendo the rag came to an end. There was a roar of riotous applause.

'He said if I broke your heart he'd break my kneecaps,' she said softly.

'He broke yours.'

Phyllis's spine sagged. Oscar glared at her. Then something inside him broke open and, taking her in his arms, he clasped her against him, holding her so close that there was no room for anyone but her.

The next day, leaning on the parapet of Trinity Bridge, he asked her to marry him. It was a bitter morning with a sharp north wind. She huddled in her coat, her hands buried deep in her pockets. The tip of her nose was red with cold.

'You're not saying yes,' he said.

Phyllis stared down at the river. A pair of tufted ducks bobbed on the surface of the water. 'You didn't honestly think I would, did you?'

'I know it's absurd. I haven't a job or any money, I'll be an undergraduate for years. It doesn't make the least sense. Except that it does. It makes sense of everything. I love you, Phyllis.'

'Oscar . . .'

'You love me too, you can't tell me you don't.'

'This has nothing to do with love.'

'What else can it possibly have to do with?'

'Everything else. All the stuff that doesn't matter.'

'So you're saying no?'

'Yes. I'm saying no.'

'No, not now, or no, not ever?'

Phyllis bit her lip. 'Oscar, please don't. We've talked about this. I thought you understood.'

'It wouldn't have to be like you think. You could

still travel, still do all the things you want to do. I wouldn't expect you to give up your work.'

'How gracious.' She sighed. 'Oscar, I'm sorry but you know it isn't like that. Men marry and carry on with their lives just as before. Women become . . . wives. I love you. You know that. But I can't be a wife. I just can't.'

'Marriage is a prison.'

'Yes. For me.'

Oscar was silent. He stared at the metal bolts that studded the Mathematical Bridge. According to Trinity legend, the bridge had been designed by Isaac Newton to be self-supporting, its timbers holding together without the use of fastenings, only fellows of the University had taken it apart to see how he had done it and then been unable to put it back together. Like so many other stories, that one had turned out to be a lie.

'Why did you ask me?' she asked. She did not sound scornful or angry. She sounded sad. 'Why did you ask me when you already knew what I'd say?'

'Because I love you. Because I thought you loved me.'

'Not because of Kit?'

'Of course not.'

'Marriage is not a guarantee of happiness, Oscar. If anything it's the opposite. Look at my parents. Or yours.'

'We won't be like them.'

'No,' she said. 'We won't.'

469

Oscar held her gaze. Then he looked away. 'So that's it,' he said flatly.

'You make it sound like it's the end of something.'

'Isn't it?'

'Not if we don't want it to be. Can't we just go on the way we are?'

'And how long do you think we can do that?'

'For as long as we are happy.'

'In separate houses, separate cities, seeing each other once a week? It's not enough. Not for me.'

'Then I'm sorry. It's all I have to offer. For now. At least for the next few years.'

'And then?'

'I don't know. We could live in sin.' He stared at her. She shrugged awkwardly. 'People do it. Some aren't even struck down by thunderbolts.'

'Why would you even consider that?'

'Because I love you.'

'Just not enough to marry me.'

'Haven't you listened at all? Marriage has nothing to do with it.' She took her hands from her pockets and held them out to him. He hesitated, then he took them in his. She was not wearing her mittens. Her fingers were waxy with cold.

'I don't understand,' he said. 'I'm not asking you to keep house for me. Or even to have children if you really don't want to. I just want us together, properly. For ever.'

'Why? Are you afraid of the scandal?' She was mocking him. For a moment the light in him dulled, like a cloud passing over the sun, and he did not love her at all. He let her hands drop.

'Forget it,' he said.

It was too cold to walk. They went to a teashop. There was steam on the inside of the window and a group of young men loudly insulting each other and complaining of their headaches. Neither of them said sorry. When they had drunk their tea Phyllis said that perhaps it was best if she caught the early afternoon train back to London. Oscar did not protest. They took the bus to the railway station, Phyllis's suitcase on the seat between them. They did not speak. On the platform she kissed his cheek.

'I'll write when I get there,' she said.

She was leaving for Malta in two days. She would be gone for six weeks. He put his arms around her stiffly, wretchedly, and she stood inside his embrace. She did not take her hands out of her pockets. He tried not to think of her standing with Kit, her arms around Kit's neck. She looked good with Kit, in his mind's eye.

'All aboard,' the guard shouted.

'I ought to go,' she said. Oscar nodded. She did not turn around as she boarded the train. The guard walked down the platform, slamming the doors. Then he blew his whistle and, with a scream of wheels, the train pulled out of the station, shrouding Oscar in a cloud of steam.

CHAPTER 32

Jessica wrote to Gerald. She thanked him for all he had done for her, but after due consideration she had decided to hand in her notice at *Woman's Friend*. She did not think that she was cut out to be a journalist. She hoped he did not mind that she was also enclosing a selection of articles written by one of her colleagues who had recently applied for a post at another of his publications.

> She asked that I show these to you as a kindness to her. Having read them, I believe the kindness is all on her side. If there is anything precious to be salvaged from the wreckage of the last few years it is that women are more than daughters and wives and mothers, that we have a voice and a place not only in the home but in the world if we are only brave enough to stand up and speak out. Joan Pickard is brave, brave enough to speak the truth, however ugly or inconvenient. With your help she can be heard.
>
> Below is an address where you can write

to her. We may not be able to change the past but we can honour the present, as best as we know how. What other salvation is there?

She remained at the magazine for two more weeks. In the second week Eleanor came to London, en route for France. she asked if Jessica might be able to come with her to see Mrs Leonard the following morning and Jessica said she was sorry but she had to go to work. It was the closest either of them came to an apology.

Eleanor stayed at the flat for two nights. The second night Phyllis came to dinner. They did not talk much. There was not much to say. Phyllis was going away too, to a dig in Europe. She was quiet, withdrawn.

'What about Christmas?' Jessica demanded. 'What about Father?' And when Phyllis said that Father had given her his blessing, that he wanted her to go, Jessica retorted angrily that she was not sure Father even remembered who Phyllis was any more, that perhaps he had confused her with someone else. She wanted to argue but Phyllis would not stay long enough even to do that. She murmured something about a tutorial in the morning and, brushing her cheek against her mother's, slipped away before dinner was even finished. It seemed to Jessica that she was more present in the flat when she had gone than she had been all evening. Eleanor went to bed. Jessica sat at the table as the candles burned to stumps and stared out at the starless sky. The reflected flames gazed like cat's eyes from the dark glass, blinking yellow. She had never thought it would be her who would be the one to be abandoned.

She told Nanny that if a man tried to telephone she was to tell him Jessica was out. Nobody did. She supposed she was glad. Nanny patted her hand and said that London was no place for a young woman these days and that everything would be better once they were home. She hummed happily to herself as she moved around the flat and when she played Solitaire she slapped the cards down with a little gasp of triumph as though she had squashed a wasp. Her cheerfulness made the flat feel very cramped.

Instead, Jessica lingered at work. Lady Astor was standing for Parliament. The seat in Plymouth had been her husband's until his father's death propelled him into the House of Lords, prompting an emergency by-election, and if she won the forty-year-old American would be the first woman ever to take up a seat in the House of Commons. Joan and Peggy were petitioning Miss Cooke to include a piece about her candidacy in the magazine.

'She is a symbol of hope for women throughout the country,' Joan protested but Miss Cooke was adamant. There was no place for politics in *Woman's Friend*, even if the candidate was a twice-married divorcée who lived in one of the grandest houses in England. Joan was furious.

'The *Saturday Review* calls her candidacy a nursery romp and demands the disenfranchisement of Plymouth for frivolity and corruption and we can't even run a half-page on why women need women in Parliament?' she raged to Peggy and Jessica over lunch at the Busy Bee. 'What does the Bottlewasher think our readers are going to do, knit themselves into a revolutionary frenzy?'

'We should run a competition,' Peggy said. 'Crochet a Communist.'

Joan laughed, despite herself. 'Bake a Bolshie.'

'There must be a book on how to fold one out of tissue paper.'

'Dear Mrs Sweeting, can bicarbonate of soda bleach the stain of feminist sedition from my soul?'

Peggy stopped at the draper's on the corner for needles. She told Jessica and Joan not to wait. It was so cold in the stairwell that Jessica could see her breath.

'Did you ever hear anything back from *Perspective*?' she asked Joan as they climbed. Joan shook her head.

'I think that one bit the dust.'

'Surely there's still a chance? It's only been two weeks.'

'They would have written by now. They turn these things around awfully quickly.'

'I meant to say, I thought the articles you sent them were first-rate.'

'Thank you. And thank you for your help. I'm very grateful, truly.'

'Except that I wasn't any help, was I?'

'You were. You gave my work to Mr Cardoza. Didn't you?'

'Of course I did. It's just that my timing . . . well, it was pretty awful.'

'I don't understand.'

'Mr Cardoza and I, we're . . . we're no longer friends. I can't believe he would have done anything, you know, to spite me, I'm sure he wouldn't, but I'm just so sorry. I really hope it wasn't my fault, that I didn't mess things up for you. You deserved that job. You're a wonderful writer.'

Joan stopped so suddenly that Jessica almost cannoned into her. 'Is that why you're leaving the magazine?' she demanded. Her cheeks were pink from the cold and the climb. 'Because of Mr Cardoza?'

Jessica hesitated. 'I don't know. Sort of.'

'He didn't ask you to, did he?'

'No, of course not. I just thought maybe it might be time. You know. To stop.'

'To stop what?'

'Making mistakes?' Jessica offered with a weak laugh.

Joan did not laugh back. 'And it's not a mistake to give up this job?'

'I don't know. I don't think so.'

Joan was silent, one fist bouncing on the banister. Then, folding her lips together, she shrugged and went on up the stairs.

That afternoon, Jessica answered her last letter as Mrs Sweeting. In Plymouth the voters were going to the polls. It was getting dark and raindrops wriggled like tadpoles diagonally across the stippled glass of her window. The window frame was leaking. There was a puddle on the painted window sill, peppered with smuts.

> You say you have been walking out with your young man for the past six months but, although he takes you to the pictures and buys you chocolates and all your friends regard him as your sweetheart, he has never shown you the affection. Well, for the love of peace, Crushed Strawberry, stop being such a complete and utter wet blanket. What on earth are you waiting for? Either throw the cold fish over, and his violet creams with him, or fling your arms around him and kiss him for all you are worth. How else will you ever know if he wants to kiss you back?

They arrived back at Ellinghurst on the afternoon train. It was dark as they pulled up the drive, heavy clouds blotting out the moon. The house loomed above them like a cliff, its windows unlit. As they pulled up under the carriage porch Mrs Johns came out to welcome them. She told them that Sir Aubrey had been called away on business and would not be back until the next day. In the Great Hall Jessica removed her coat reluctantly. It was chilly, despite the roaring fire. The central heating was not working, Mrs Johns explained. There was a problem with the boiler or the pipes, no one seemed sure. She asked if Nanny meant to stay for supper but Nanny shook her head. She was eager to get back to her cottage.

Jessica ate supper alone. She did not bother to change. Afterwards she went upstairs. The hot water was still working, Mrs Johns explained, at least in the first-floor bathrooms. She would have a maid draw Jessica a bath. Jessica could hear the roar of the running water from the east wing corridor as she crossed the first-floor landing. She hesitated, leaning on the balustrade that overlooked the Great Hall. There were cobwebs on the vaulted beams, their loose threads drifting lazily in the updraught, and the suits of armour wore felted toupées of dust. Poor house, she thought, and she stroked the sleek wood of the balustrade. So much for Mrs Maxwell Brooke. It was time someone took things in hand.

She meant to go up to her bedroom and undress. Instead, she found herself walking down the passage that led to her mother's bedroom. Outside the door she hesitated, one hand on the porcelain knob. Then, turning it, she went in.

The room was empty, as blank as a room in an hotel. There were no books on the curved shelves, no ornaments on the mantel, no photographs in frames. Even the silver carriage clock was gone. The bed was shrouded in a heavy coverlet Jessica had never seen before. She sat at the dressing table, staring at her reflection in the three-sided mirror. The powder puffs and the silver-backed hairbrushes and the hairpins in their china dishes had all been cleared away. All that remained was a pale mark on the polished walnut, a ghostly circle left by a long-ago glass. Jessica touched the circle with one finger. She slid open the dressing-table drawers. The top one contained the small brass key to its own lock. Otherwise they were empty. The drawers in the chest were empty too, neatly lined with sheets of folded paper. When Jessica leaned down she could smell it, under the paper smell, the lingering traces of lavender.

In the dressing room there was a large brownish patch like spilled tea on the wall above the window. The wallpaper with its tendrils of ivy was bloated, peeling away at the seam. Jessica opened the wardrobes. The rails were cleared, the shelves that had once held Eleanor's rows of shoes quite bare. The wood inside the wardrobe was rough and raw-looking, marked with scuffs and, near the bottom, a scribbled mark in white chalk. The paper that covered the base was old and slightly askew. She squatted, smoothing it out, but the corner was awkward, as though the paper were folded too thick. She lifted it.

There was another piece of paper under the lining paper, folded several times into a square. She unfolded it. The paper was old, the creases so deep that in places the paper had split. It was engraved with the address of a club in Pall Mall.

Dearest E, I write in haste, already on my way home to you. Your letter – what can I say of your letter, except that it pierced my heart? Of course there is no one else. There has never been anyone but you. You are exhausted, I know, and wretchedly low in spirits as you always are in the first months, but such vile and baseless imaginings, such hateful threats? They are nothing but a torture to us both. You are my all, you and the little ones, and will be always. A

Her father returned the following afternoon. She heard the car, the sound of voices as Mrs Johns greeted him in the Great Hall. A gale was blowing in from the sea and, beyond the battlements, the trees tossed like ships against the darkening sky. She went down to meet him. He kissed her absently, his fingers plucking at the clasp of his briefcase, and disappeared to the library. He did not emerge for tea. Jessica sat alone by the fire in the morning room. She supposed there were things she should be doing, menus for the following day, a list of matters to discuss with Mrs Johns.

Instead, she flicked desultorily through old copies of her mother's magazines. The elegantly drawn plates advertising furs and French undergarments were a far cry from the small advertisements for

480

Triumph Female Pills and Phillips' Dental Magnesia that peppered the pages of *Woman's Friend*. She wondered which of the girls had been given her desk, who would become the platitudinous Mrs Sweeting in her absence and whether they would have to take on another girl, whether they thought of her when she was not there. She thought how glad Joan and Peggy would be that Lady Astor had won her seat in Plymouth by more than five thousand votes. 'We are not asking for superiority,' *The Times* had quoted her as saying, 'for we have always had that; all we ask is equality.' Jessica wondered if Joan had seen it or whether she should cut it out and send it to her at the magazine. She knew it would tickle her. It occurred to her too that they should definitely do a piece on Lady Astor's costume on her first day in Parliament. The historic hat. Even the Bottlewasher could not call that politics.

The house was very quiet as she went up to change for dinner. When she returned there was still no sign of her father. She waited in the drawing room but when the door opened it was only Mrs Johns. Her father sent his apologies but he had urgent work to do. Again Jessica ate alone. To her surprise she found herself missing the oppressive clatter of the maid in the kitchen at Maida Vale, the shuffle and sigh of Nanny playing cards. The meat was tough. She chewed at it until the gristly mass of it in her mouth became intolerable and she had to spit it into her napkin. She did not wait for the maid to clear her plate. She rose, asking for coffee in the drawing room.

'Two cups, please.'

She drank hers quickly. Then, pouring a second, she added sugar and took it to the library. She knew that the maid could do it just as well but she had had enough of being alone. She knocked and knocked again. When her father did not answer, she pushed open the door.

She did not see him at first. The leather chairs and the low tables and the lamps had all gone and, in their place, trestle tables, the kind that they had used for tenant parties before the War, were crammed in, end to end. Each table was heaped with books and boxes and ledgers and mountains and mountains of papers and envelopes and manila folders tied with string. Boxes filled the spaces under the tables and stacked the window seats, leaning drunkenly against the mullioned glass, and on top of the boxes the packages from the photographic developer in Bournemouth, hundreds and hundreds of them, heaped up like sandbags. Open books lay abandoned on every surface, bristling with paper markers or sprawled, spines broken, face down. Torn-up drifts of paper littered the floor. And everywhere, like bunting, fluttered scraps of paper covered in her father's scrawl, pinned to the edges of the trestles, the carved frames of the bookcases, the panelled window shutters.

'Father?'

'What is it?' His voice was muffled, impatient. 'What are you doing here?'

'I brought you some coffee.'

He stood and she saw him, tucked into a corner behind a mound of worn black ledgers. He was still wearing the tweed suit he had travelled in. Squeezing her way between the laden tables and the heaped-up boxes, she held out his cup. He frowned. Then, taking it, he swallowed the coffee in a single gulp. There was ink on his fingers and on the cuff of his shirt.

'Thank you,' he said, clattering the cup back onto the saucer.

'Have you eaten?'

'There's a tray somewhere.' He waved without looking up. 'I'll eat when I've finished.'

'And when exactly will that be?'

'Go to bed. I'll see you in the morning.'

'I could help you, you know,' Jessica said. 'With the book. If you wanted.'

'Right now the book is the least of my concerns. Go to bed.'

'Why? What's the matter?'

'The matter is that this damned Government is determined to break us. Taxes, rent controls, inflation. Land values going down the drain. Twenty-five per cent we pay, now, on estate income. Twenty-five per cent! And that's before death duties. How the devil do they think . . .?' He pressed his fingers to his temples, blowing out between his lips. 'It doesn't matter. Go to bed.'

'What are we going to do?'

He shook his head, forcing a smile. 'We'll manage. Between us we'll manage.'

'You mean, when I get married.'

'If only that were all it took.'

Jessica was silent. She picked up his cup and saucer, staring at the brown smear of coffee at the bottom. 'Are you really thinking of marrying Mrs Maxwell Brooke?' A frown like a twitch flickered over her father's face.

'Eleanor told me,' she persisted. 'Is it true?'

'It's an option I am considering.'

'Because of Ellinghurst?'

'It would certainly give us some breathing space.'

'And if Eleanor refuses to give you a divorce?'

'There are ways. I am talking to lawyers.'

'Wouldn't that mean a scandal?'

'Almost certainly.'

'And Mrs Maxwell Brooke? She wouldn't run a mile?'

'That's a risk one has to take.'

Jessica looked at her father. 'You would do all that? To keep Ellinghurst?'

'One hundred times over. Wouldn't you?'

She blinked. 'I don't know.'

'But I do. This house is in your blood, just as it's in mine. You could no more abandon it than abandon your children.'

'Except I don't have any children.'

'Not yet. But you will. And when you do they

will love this place as you and I do, in the marrow of our bones.'

'I have to find a husband first.'

Sir Aubrey smiled drily. 'That would be advisable.'

'Husbands are not so easy to find, you know. These days.'

'Perhaps you're just looking in the wrong place.'

The tears rose unexpectedly in her throat. She turned her head. 'I should let you get on,' she said.

At the door she paused. Her father's pen scratched noisily across the paper and his hair gleamed white in the circle of light from the desk lamp. 'You would tell me, wouldn't you, if there was anything else I could do?'

Her father was not listening. He turned a page of the ledger. Softly she closed the door.

CHAPTER 33

On the last day of the Michaelmas Term, Mr Willis left a message for Oscar in his pigeonhole. He asked that Oscar come and see him urgently. Instead, Oscar went to the Victoria cinema on Market Square. The afternoon feature was *South*, an account of Sir Ernest Shackleton's heroic and ill-fated attempt to reach the South Pole. Oscar watched as the grinning crew embarked on their expedition, waved off at the dock by a huge and cheering crowd. England had been at war with Germany for four days. In Antarctica the *Endurance* pushed through mile after mile of frozen sea, its glittering rigging festooned with icicles, its bow scything a path through the pack ice while all around icebergs loomed against the sky, vast white cities crowned with towers and spires. The sled dogs gambolled on the ice and the meteorologist played the banjo. It was magnificent and beautiful. Then the temperature dropped. Little by little, month after month and inexorably, the ice entombed the *Endurance* in its crushing grip. There was nothing Shackleton's men could do but watch. Oscar watched too, bleakly, as, powerless against the ice, the 350-ton vessel crumpled like a paper boat. The rudder smashed first, then the mast, snapped like a matchstick before a violent eruption of ice forced the ship high into the air. For a moment the ice held it aloft, a broken trophy, Ahab's *Pequod*. Then it was gone. Oscar closed his eyes, frozen and bereft. It was no solace to know that not one of Shackleton's crew had lost their lives. In the row behind him a couple kissed as though they were drowning.

Phyllis had written from London before she left, a short breezy letter wishing him a happy Christmas and sending him an address in Malta where he might write to her. Since then he had received two picture postcards, one of the Grand Harbour in Valetta and another of a man in a tall hat milking a goat. The weather was mild, the work interesting. She had visited the Caravaggios in St John's Cathedral. He stared at the black-and-white photographs, trying to picture her squinting in the sunlight by the blue Mediterranean Sea, or in whispering churches among the candles and the plaster Madonnas and the heavy smell of incense, but he did not write back. He could not think of what to say.

It was over. He understood that Phyllis had not said so, that on paper there was no reason why they could not go on exactly as they had before, but it did not change the facts. He thought of Rutherford behind his apparatus in the Maxwell

Theatre, his fingers tucked into the pockets of his waistcoat.

'As our friends the theoreticians would say . . .'

She did not want to marry him. It did not matter why. She did not want to marry him and that was that. He had asked and she had said no. The results were conclusive. The day after she went back to London Kit came to his rooms. Oscar heard him knocking but he did not answer. He waited for Kit to give up and go away. He did not want Kit's sympathy, his empty reassurances. She would have married Kit. The thought haunted him. He dreamed of it, Kit laughing and Phyllis in a hat with a little veil, her pale face tipped up towards his. When he woke his eyes burned and his throat was raw as though he had been shouting in his sleep, and he wanted to break things and to bury his head in his pillow until the world went black and nothing mattered any more.

He did not attend his last supervision of the term. He sat on his unmade bed and watched the minute hand of his watch move slowly around the face until the hour was over. He could hear the clatter of the bed-makers in the court outside emptying their buckets through the iron gratings, the shrill whistle of a tradesman's boy. He had an appointment with his tutor, Willis, but he did not go to that either. The next day a bad-tempered note from Willis insisted that Oscar come and see him urgently. Oscar did not answer it. He did not go to the library or to the last of

Rutherford's lectures. He heard the clocks strike one, a brief burst of voices on the stairs as men went down to lunch. Some time later there was a bang on his door. It was Kit. He had Girouard with him. He said that they would not leave until Oscar opened up. He said that if Oscar refused he would use his leg to break it down. Oscar did not answer. They banged for a while and then Girouard said something Oscar did not hear and they went away.

Later that day a note was pushed under Oscar's door. It was getting dark by then but Oscar had not switched on the lights. In the grate the embers of the dying fire winked and faded. Oscar looked at the note for a long time. In the grainy gloom of dusk it looked like it was floating. Then he rose, shivering as he crossed the room on icy feet. He had not realised he had grown so cold. The paper was torn from a notebook and folded several times. Oscar unfolded it.

When it's a damp, drizzly November in your soul it's high time to get to sea. If you haven't plans for Christmas how about the boundless oceans of Shropshire? K

He put the note in what remained of the fire. The paper blackened and shrivelled but it did not catch. When he pumped the bellows lacy fragments rose, drifting into the chimney like moths. The next day everyone went down and Oscar went to the cinema.

When he came back a light snow was falling. It settled across the silent court, a fine white gauze, unmarked by footprints. A single light burned above his staircase door. All the windows were dark. He took the letters from his pigeonhole and went upstairs, his feet echoing emptily on the stone steps.

One of the letters was from Sir Aubrey. Opening it, Oscar slid out the enclosed photograph and studied it. It was a new game of Sir Aubrey's, the photograph. Each one was of a particular detail at Ellinghurst, taken close up, which he challenged Oscar to identify. The first one was easy, the monkey bell push Sir Crawford had designed himself for the breakfast room, the bell a wooden apple gripped in the monkey's wrinkled old-man's mouth. Since then he had sent several photographs in every letter. He refused to tell Oscar what they were, even when Oscar admitted to being stumped. He said that, if Oscar thought hard enough, he would remember.

Oscar propped them up on his mantelpiece like invitations. One was of a stone bird with raised wings which Oscar was certain he knew but which he could not place. He had carried it in his pocket for a week, walking in his head through the house, before, in bed one night on the cusp of sleep, it came to him that it was a part of the carved mantel in the library. The pleasure of the realisation made him smile in the dark. The next day, in London with Phyllis, he had found the photograph still in his pocket and extracted it.

'Come on,' he had said. 'Do you recognise it?' but Phyllis did not want to play. She said that Oscar should not encourage her father, that he was quite obsessed enough with Ellinghurst without people egging him on. Oscar knew that their correspondence made her uncomfortable, even though she only shrugged when he asked her and said that what he did was none of her business. To reassure her he left his letters out where she could read them but she never did, even when he asked her to.

'Mostly I write about physics,' he told her. 'I've never mentioned you.'

'It doesn't matter.'

'Of course it matters. I wouldn't want to think I was going behind your back.'

'Well, are you?'

'No, but—'

'Then what I think isn't important.'

'But of course it is. It's what matters most.'

'Even if I am being entirely irrational?'

'Even then.'

'But why?'

'Because I love you.'

She looked at him then and shook her head. 'Except it's not love when placating the other person trumps what's right, is it? It's tyranny.'

He had played that conversation again and again in his head since the day on the bridge. Every time he sat down at his desk with a piece of paper to write to Phyllis in Malta he thought of it again and he put his pen down and put his head into his hands because there was nothing to say. Sound could not travel in a vacuum, however loud you shouted.

The photograph was of a geometric pattern, an eight-pointed star like a cross with two points at each end, surrounded by a honeycombed pattern, light against dark. In the centre of the star was an eight-leafed flower. From the blur of light in one corner it was plain that the surface of the pattern was glazed. Oscar knew it immediately. He pressed his fingers against his eyeballs, fiercely enough to make the darkness sparkle. Eyeballs were harder than people thought which was why the white, the fibrous outer layer of the eye, was called the sclera, after the Greek word *skleros*, meaning hard. Then, blinking, he put the photograph face down on the desk and unfolded the letter. The handwriting was slapdash, scribbled in haste or perhaps on a train. Oscar's eyes skimmed the page, hardly taking in the words, the acknowledgement that the previous photograph had indeed been a detail from a painted panel in the drawing room, the hope that this one might prove more of a challenge, the repeated entreaty to come to Ellinghurst for a weekend or perhaps even for Christmas.

It would mean so much to me and I know Jessica would be glad of the company. I told you, I think, that Phyllis is away in Europe, and it is awfully dull for her rattling around on her own.

The letter went on to several pages. Oscar did not read them. He looked at the plain back of the photograph on his desk. The pattern burned through the card, projecting itself like a film onto the back of his skull. It was one of the floor tiles from the octagonal room of the tower in the woods, the ones that Sir Crawford Melville had had brought back especially from India. He thought of Phyllis huddled on the bench the day that Theo's uniform arrived at Ellinghurst, her arms around her shins, the cuffs of her jersey pulled down over her red hands. When she had looked up there had been two marks on her forehead where she had pressed it against her knees. He thought of Theo standing under the beech trees, the smoke of his cigarette smudging the dusk like chalk dust, and it was Theo who seemed real then and Phyllis the apparition, so that when he reached out for her in his imagination his hands slipped right through her and she faded, diminishing as he watched until all that was left of her was an ache in the air, tender as a bruise.

The next morning, there was a brisk knock on his door.

'Mr Greenwood?' Mr Willis said sharply. 'Mr Greenwood, I know you are in there. If I have to force the lock there will be a fine for damage to college property.'

Reluctantly Oscar opened the door. Mr Willis took in his dishevelled state, the chaos of books and cups and discarded clothes that littered the room.

'Alive, then?' he said.

'I'm sorry, sir. It's just I've been . . .'

The tutor shook his head wearily. It was plain that his interest in Oscar's health extended only as far as establishing that he was extant. In a tone that reminded Oscar of the public information films shown in cinemas during the War, Mr Willis informed him that the freezing weather had caused several pipes in the court to burst. A problem with the main required the paving to be dug up, making access to the staircases on Oscar's side impossible. Oscar had until the following morning to vacate his rooms.

'If you had come to see me when I first summoned you, arrangements might have been made to avoid disruption to your studies. As it is I am told there is nothing in college until next week. You have somewhere you can go, I hope?'

Oscar shrugged.

'Well, I'm sure you'll think of something,' Willis said wintrily. 'Happy Christmas, Mr Greenwood.'

Oscar sat at his desk for a long time after his tutor had gone, staring at the photograph of the tower floor. Later he walked up to Mrs Piggott's house on Chesterton Road. When he asked about the room she said she was sorry but she had another gentleman up there now, a travelling salesman. She offered him a cup of tea.

It was snowing again as Oscar walked back over

Magdalene Bridge, sticky flakes that clung to his coat and hat. The grey sky sagged over the college roofs and the river was oil-black. Ahead of him the black outline of a man pushed a bicycle along the narrow pavement. Oscar walked along the wavy line left by the tyre, the fresh snow creaking under his feet. In his rooms he packed a bag. The photograph of the tile from the tower was propped up against his table lamp. He picked it up, running his finger over the honeycombed patterns that encircled the star. He could not go, he knew that, it was impossible, and yet the urge to be there, where there was so much of her, where the air bore the mark of her like an imprint in snow, was so strong it was a kind of breathlessness. He opened Sir Aubrey's letter again. *It would mean so much to me and I know Jessica would be glad of the company.* For a moment he let himself imagine it, walking in to the Great Hall, sitting in the window seat in the library, on the circular bench in tower. Then, biting his lip, he turned the page.

I have been thinking a great deal of Thomas Gray these last weeks. Gray published fewer than one thousand lines of poetry in his life-time, afraid, he said, that they would be taken for the works of a flea. As a young man I marvelled at his humility. Now I find myself wondering if it was not cowardice that constrained him, fear of failure or, worse, of mockery. It is safer to do nothing than to do

something and fail. Gray died aged fifty-five.
How old must one be before one understands
that omission is the greatest failure of all?

Oscar put the letter into his pocket and picked up
his suitcase. At the door of his room he hesitated.
Putting the suitcase down, he went to the bookcase. It took him several minutes to find the slim
volume of poems he had read to his mother in
Clapham. He held it in his hand, one hand
smoothing the cover. Then, sweeping the Ellinghurst
photographs from the mantelpiece, he tucked
them inside the book and put them both into his
coat pocket.

At the Majestic Hotel the proprietress looked up
when he arrived. Her hair was no longer copper
but a dark purplish-red.

'And just what time do you call this?' she asked
drily as she hauled out her ledger. 'Alone, are you?'

He did not know why he had come. The room
was even worse than he remembered it. He did
not bother to get undressed. He pushed some
coins into the meter and huddled under the
blankets on the lumpy mattress, flooded with a
miserable gratification at the squalor of the room,
the prodigal agony of remembering.

It was very late when he finally slept. When he
woke he could not remember where he was. It had
snowed again in the night and the room was harsh
with light. His head ached and he was filled with
an obscure shame, like a drunk only half able to

remember the night before. He knew then that he could not stay. His clothes were crumpled, twisted awkwardly around his body. He smelled of trains and old dog.

He washed in the grimy bathroom at the end of the passage and changed into a clean shirt. He had to go away, somewhere where the air was clear and everything was unfamiliar. He would go to Europe, to the Alps. He would learn to ski. The improbability of the idea only added to his determination. He thought of the pictures in his book, the figures small as ants against the white majesty of the mountains, and then of Phyllis in bed, her knees a hump of blankets, her red head bent over her book of hieroglyphs. The bird with the human head was the glyph for soul, and the scarab beetle was said to push the sun into the sky at the dawn of every day. He wondered dully if there might be a time one day when not everything made him think of her.

He went back to Cambridge. He needed boots, a thick coat, books.

'Can't that wait?' he had said to Phyllis over and over as she read or scribbled in her notebook, his mouth tracing her jaw, her ear, the nape of her neck, his hand sliding wonderingly up her thigh, and she had only smiled and kissed him and moved the book where she could see it.

'You're next,' she always said. 'I promise.'

A wooden barrier had been erected across the arched entranceway, a painted sign nailed to its front: No Entry. Along the east side of the court a wide strip of paving stones had been lifted and stacked and several men were digging a trench. A pick sang as it struck rock. Oscar called out but the men only shook their heads and pointed to the sign. The barrier was secured with a heavy iron chain. When Oscar rattled it they shrugged and went on digging.

At the Porter's Lodge Oscar pleaded with the fat porter. 'I only need ten minutes. Just to fetch some things.'

'And you are, sir?'

'Greenwood. M staircase.'

'Mr Greenwood.' With a grunt the porter prised himself out of his chair and, peering at a rack above his head, extracted an envelope. 'This came for you yesterday. They said you'd gone down. No forwarding address.'

Phyllis, Oscar thought. As he fumbled with the envelope his head buzzed with static like a radio set and his fingers seemed to belong to someone else.

FATHER VERY ILL ASKING FOR YOU STOP
PLEASE COME URGENTLY JESSICA

CHAPTER 34

The proper name was cerebrovascular disease, Jessica said. A stroke, or rather two strokes. The first had been mild, though frightening enough at the time. They had been working in the library when suddenly his face had slackened, his eyes widening as though he was trying to focus. He slumped in his chair, his head falling sideways. He managed to tell Jessica that there was a pain in his head. Then the left side of his body seemed to crumple, his arms dropping at his sides, and he collapsed to the floor. By the time Dr Wilcox arrived he was conscious but disoriented and very dazed. It was not clear if he understood what the doctor was saying to him. The whole of the left side of his body was numb.

The next day he was tired and a little shaky on his feet but otherwise apparently recovered. His arm and leg moved normally and his speech was unimpaired. When Dr Wilcox urged him to rest he waved away his concern. He told Jessica that the doctor was an old woman who fussed over nothing. A week passed. Then two days ago he had taken his camera and gone out to the barbican gate. No one knew exactly what had happened or how long he had lain there before the gardener's boy found him sprawled on the path near the moat, one side of his face badly grazed.

It was nearly a day before he recovered consciousness. Even then he was very confused. The seizure had paralysed his left side. The left side of his face hung loosely on the bone, his eye pulled down to expose the wet red gum beneath, and his tongue lolled in his slack mouth, making his speech unintelligible. A nurse was arranged, a brisk woman with a starched cap and a starched manner. She called Sir Aubrey the Patient with a starched capital letter.

'I have no wish to agitate your father,' Dr Wilcox confided to Jessica, squeezing her arm, 'or you, my dear. But his condition is grave. He is weak, susceptible to secondary infections. To another seizure. If he has matters outstanding, affairs to be put in order, it might be advisable . . .'

Jessica glared, pulling her arm away. 'But you don't wish to agitate him?'

She cabled Eleanor and Phyllis and asked them to come home. She telephoned Mrs Maxwell Brooke who to her great relief received the news calmly and told Jessica that she would come when she could.

'Today's impossible, my dear. But perhaps tomorrow. I'll telephone.'

When she asked her father if there was anyone

else he wished her to write to, he jerked his head and mumbled something she did not hear. The nurse wiped the saliva from his chin with a white cloth.

'The Patient needs to rest,' she admonished, rearranging his useless left arm on the counterpane, but Sir Aubrey reached out with his good hand and caught Jessica's.

'Osk,' he managed.

'Oscar?' She frowned, unsure she had heard him right. 'Oscar Greenwood?'

His breathing was laboured. He tried to nod. 'Osk.'

She knew then that he did not expect to get better. She cabled Oscar with a heavy heart and wondered if she should telephone the lawyers. She was afraid her father might not have made the proper arrangements. He had never been practical. Eleanor had always said that for Aubrey meetings with the estate accountants were like going to sea, long stretches of mind-numbing boredom punctuated with flashes of blinding terror. It was one of the few jokes she made that made him smile. Besides, who knew what he might do for the satisfaction of confounding Cousin Evelyn?

Oscar arrived after lunch the next day. The nurse said that she was sorry but Sir Aubrey was not well enough for visitors. He had developed a temperature, a thick cough. She asked that they leave him to rest. Instead, they went for a walk.

It was very cold. Oscar buried his hands in his pockets.

'You haven't had snow here, then?' he asked and Jessica shook her head.

'Too close to the sea, Father always says,' she said. They turned to look at the house, grey against the low grey sky. 'Thank you. For coming.'

'Of course.' He hesitated. 'How bad is it, really?'

'Nobody seems to know. He's very weak. If there was another stroke . . .'

'So your mother and Phyllis, they're coming home?' The crack in his voice touched Jessica. 'I don't know yet. I've cabled them. I'm sure Phyllis will; I mean, she'd better. I don't know about Eleanor. Perhaps she'll turn out to have a conscience after all. Even without the wretched Feda telling her what to do.'

'Who's Feda?'

'She isn't anyone. Not any more.'

Oscar did not want to walk in the woods. They made their way down through the garden and across the moat towards the gatehouse. Oscar walked fast with a long stride. He was taller than she remembered, and more substantial. In her walking shoes her head barely reached his shoulder. It was hard to recollect the cringing little drip he had been as a boy, so painfully easy to cow that he might as well have worn a sandwich board begging you to torment him. He had a quiet confidence, a thoughtfulness that made him seem older than his years. At lunch, he had listened as

502

she talked about her father, properly listened as though he meant to memorise the words, and the knot that had tied itself tightly inside her had eased because Oscar was there too, and whatever it was that happened next she would no longer have to do it all on her own.

When they reached the gatehouse they stopped. Oscar touched the scowling face of one of the stone lions. Then he looked up at the coat of arms carved into the stone lintel of the archway.

'Heaven at last,' Jessica said.

'My mother used to say that every time we drove in.'

'Did she? I can't imagine you did. We weren't very nice to you back then.'

'You weren't very nice. The others were all right.'

Jessica smiled faintly. 'The others didn't know you existed.'

He was silent, gazing up at the lintel. She wondered if he was thinking of that afternoon in the tower, the afternoon that she put her arms around his neck and told him to kiss her. They had been barely more than children then but he had held her as though she was the only girl on earth. She wondered if she was still the only girl he had ever kissed.

They walked back along the edge of the rhododendron plantation towards the East Gate. Oscar was silent, lost in thought. The wind had sharpened and the clouds were dark and bruised-looking. Above the inky scrawl of the winter trees

Grandfather's Tower swayed like the mast of a giant ship.

'They'll knock it down, I suppose,' she said. 'They won't risk small boys throwing themselves out of the windows. Or lunatics, for that matter.' Oscar did not answer. 'Oscar?'

He blinked at her, confused. 'I'm sorry, what?'

'Grandfather's Tower. They'll demolish it, I suppose.'

'Who will?'

'Whoever buys the place.'

'The house is for sale?' His shock was unfeigned. Jessica shrugged.

'Not yet. But Cousin Evelyn thinks that houses like this are white elephants. And anyway he prefers Yorkshire. He's told Father he'll definitely sell. Poor Father, he couldn't bear it, he was trying everything he could, but he never thought . . .' She swallowed, trying to keep her voice matter-of-fact. 'If he dies, I mean, if he dies now, before Phyllis or I . . . well, then it will be a school or a hotel or a madhouse. A madhouse would be best, don't you think? At least there's a tradition of that. Grandfather Melville was mad as a March hare.'

'Jessica, I'm so—'

'Don't. I'm not sure I could bear it if you said anything kind.' She turned away from him, pressing her fingers to the bridge of her nose. 'Sorry.'

He put a tentative hand on her shoulder. She closed her eyes. It had been as cold as this that

504

afternoon in the tower, the tip of his nose icy against her cheek. Four years ago, almost to the day. She could still remember the way he looked at her when he finally stopped kissing her, his dark eyes wide with astonishment.

She turned back towards him, stepping closer, and leaned her forehead against his chest. The wool of his coat prickled her skin. He patted her awkwardly, like a dog, and she thought of Jim Pugh's old terrier, turning in ghostly circles on the dusk-clogged lawn.

'Hold me,' she whispered.

'Jessica—'

'Please,' she said and she closed her eyes, waiting for his arms to encircle her, for the ground to stop pitching, just for a moment, beneath her feet.

The motor car's engine coughed as it turned in under the arch of the gatehouse. Abruptly Oscar dropped his arms. Burying his hands deep in his pockets, he set off briskly towards the house.

'Oscar, wait,' she called but he only walked faster, his shoulders hunched against the cold. The car was getting closer. As it rounded the bend its headlamps illuminated the leathery leaves of the rhododendron. She turned, one hand raised against the glare of the lights, and stepped onto the verge to let it pass. It slowed. Mrs Maxwell Brooke wound down the window. In the car beside her was Marjorie, her pointed face framed by a close-fitting hat.

'Jessica, my dear, you're not off somewhere, are you? Don't tell me Mrs Johns forgot to say I had telephoned? We're here to see the poor patient.'

There was no sign of Oscar as Jessica showed the Maxwell Brookes into the Great Hall and rang for tea.

'None for me, dear,' Mrs Maxwell Brooke said briskly. 'We can't really stop. We absolutely have to be in London by seven at the very latest, but of course we couldn't bear to go without popping in. I suppose he's well enough for visitors?'

Brushing aside Jessica's demurrals she bustled upstairs, Mrs Johns in her wake. Jessica and Marjorie stayed by the fire. The thick-ankled maid brought tea and walnut cake. It was only when Marjorie lifted her cup that Jessica noticed the sapphire on her left hand. 'You're engaged,' she said.

Marjorie smiled awkwardly, holding her hand out. 'So it would seem.'

'Your mother never said anything.'

'It only happened the day before yesterday. It's why we're going to London, actually. We're lunching with his mother tomorrow.'

His name was Lionel Wilbraham. He was the older brother of a girl with whom Marjorie had come out, the much older brother, she admitted with a self-conscious laugh. He was thirty-five, an old man. He had been in the War until a gas attack left him with pulmonary tuberculosis; now he worked for the Ministry of Health. They had met at a weekend house party in Kent. He had arrived with another girl, she had assumed they were together. It had come as a complete surprise, at the end of the weekend, when he asked if he might telephone her. She had not thought he had noticed her at all.

'Your mother must be thrilled,' Jessica said.

Marjorie made a face. 'You know Mother. She'd have preferred a grouse moor. But she's relieved. She was starting to worry I'd be left on the shelf.'

'And at least he's English. He is English, isn't he?'

'Of course.'

'Poor Terence Connolly,' Jessica said and Marjorie flushed, her neck mottling pink as she took a slice of walnut cake.

Mrs Maxwell Brooke hurried back down the stairs. 'Marjorie, are you ready?' She looked at Jessica, one hand pressed to her chest. 'My dear girl, why didn't you say? I thought it was another of his attacks but he looks perfectly ghastly. His face! And he couldn't speak, couldn't get one word out.'

'He's better than he was.'

'The nurse would only let me stay a moment. She didn't want me in there at all, only I absolutely insisted. She says it's unlikely he will ever regain the use of his left side. That he'll be paralysed, confined to a bath chair.'

Jessica nodded numbly. Mrs Maxwell Brooke sighed, shaking her head as Mrs Johns helped her on with her coat. 'Jessica, dear, I wish I could do more but I'm sure Marjorie's told you her news? So you see, we absolutely have to be in London. You will promise to write and let me know how your father is, won't you? And of course, if there's anything I can do, anything at all. Your parents were both such a strength to me when Robert went. I don't know what I'd have done without them, truly I don't. Your mother is coming home, I presume?'

'I'm not sure. I've not yet heard.'

Mrs Maxwell Brooke pursed her lips as Mrs Johns opened the front door. The car was waiting under the carriage porch. 'And your handbag?' she chided Marjorie. 'Goodness, dear, I hope you don't mean to be so giddy when you're married. You'll drive that poor husband of yours to distraction.'

'Goodbye, Jessica,' Marjorie said. 'I hope your father feels better soon.'

'Thank you. And congratulations.'

Mrs Maxwell Brooke smiled at her daughter as she climbed into the car. Then, with a sympathetic frown, she touched her cheek to Jessica's. 'You'll let me know, won't you, if there's anything we can do? I can always send someone over from the house.'

'Thank you.'

'Take care of yourself, my dear. And have a happy Christmas. If you can.'

'We'll see you before then, surely?'

'I rather doubt it. It's to be a London wedding,

St Margaret's, so we'll be up and down from town like a pair of Jack-in-the-boxes. By April I shall be good for nothing but hibernation.'

'I'm sorry. The last thing you'll feel like by then is the Season all over again.'

A flicker passed over Mrs Maxwell Brooke's face. She opened her mouth to say something. Then she closed it again, resettling her handbag on her arm. 'Tell your mother to come home,' she said. 'In difficult times a mother's place is with her children.'

The tea was cold by the time Oscar came back into the Great Hall. He did not see Jessica curled up in a chair in front of the fire, a cushion in her lap. He stood in his coat and hat, looking up at the vaulted ceiling.

'Where have you been?' she said.

Oscar jumped. He took off his hat. 'I went for a walk.'

'You missed the Maxwell Brookes.'

'I'm sorry.'

'You're not sorry in the least.'

'Not really, no. How were they?'

Jessica shrugged. She looked at the fire, the flames curling around the apple logs like ribbons. When she were small Nanny had told her that if you looked very carefully you could see your future in a fire, but however hard she tried she had never been able to see anything but flames.

'How is your father?' Oscar said.

'A little better, I think.'

'Might I go up and see him, do you think? I'd like him to know I'm here.'

'Of course.' She uncurled herself from her chair but he shook his head.

'Stay where you are. You look comfortable. I know where I'm going.' His hat still clutched in his hands, he started up the stairs.

'You're allowed to take off your coat, you know,' she said.

'Ah.' He looked uncertainly at his hat, then put it on his head while he unbuttoned his coat and took it off, laying it over the banister. It slid slowly down the mahogany slope, catching on the carved eagle that topped the newel post. He took off his hat and looked at it again.

'Throw it,' she said. 'Go on. For old times' sake.'

Oscar threw it. The hat missed the eagle by several feet and skittered across the stone floor to land beside Jessica's chair. 'Close,' he said.

'To what, exactly?' Stretching out an arm, she picked it up. The brim was dusty. She brushed it, resting it on the cushion in her lap.

'Your turn,' Oscar said.

Jessica grinned. 'All right.' She threw it without thinking, without standing up. It was a clumsy throw, a loop entirely lacking in the skimming elegance of Theo's wristy flick, but to her astonishment the hat landed squarely on the eagle's head, coming to rest jauntily over one eye. She looked at Oscar in triumph. 'Bloody hell,' she said.

Oscar grinned. 'Theo would be proud.'

She grinned back. Theo had always pretended that the hat game was a fluke but the truth was he had practised and practised. She had watched him once from behind the banisters of the gallery, throwing Father's top hat again and again. By the time Nanny discovered him there were dents all over the crown.

'Old hats like this are old hat,' he had declared, quite unrepentant as she chivvied him up the stairs, and when Nanny said sternly that he could tell that to his father, he said that someone had to do it and that Nanny should be thankful he was willing to save her the trouble.

Oscar was gone for only a few minutes. When he came back downstairs his expression was sombre. The nurse was asking for her, he said. Her father's condition had worsened. She had asked Mrs Johns to telephone for the doctor. When Dr Wilcox came he gave Sir Aubrey something to help him sleep. He said he would come back in the morning.

Jessica and Oscar had dinner in the dining room. It was too large a room for two. They talked about Ellinghurst. It startled her, how many stories Oscar remembered, stories that she had forgotten or never properly listened to in the first place. There was a wistfulness in his dark eyes as he talked, the tenderness cut through with melancholy. She watched the shadows passing over his face and she felt a closeness between them, an intimacy borne not just of history but of understanding. Even when he fell silent there was no awkwardness. She knew how remembering swallowed the words sometimes, the dizzying way it opened the heart out like a flower and at the same time squeezed it like a fist. She knew it because it was just the same for her.

CHAPTER 35

The next morning Oscar woke early. He stood shivering at the window, watching the reluctant dawn stretch slowly over the castle wall. Mist clung to the sloping lawns and snagged in the branches of the winter trees. It had rained in the night. Beneath him the terrace was slick, dark as a lake.

In the Great Hall he tugged on his boots. When he had come down early as a boy there had always been a bustle about the house, hurrying maids with coal buckets or footmen with trays. Now it was deserted, the only sign of life a fire newly lit in the vast fireplace. It was as though the castle were just waking from an enchanted sleep, or slipping into one. Oscar hunched over the blaze as he pulled on his coat, closing his eyes against the shrivelling burn of the flames.

Though the rain had stopped the air outside was heavy with damp. It clung to his hair, seeped into the wool of his coat. He walked down across the muddy lawn and through the copse of beeches towards the iron fence that marked the boundary of the wood, listening to the rooks stirring in the trees. The fence was choked with ivy and brambles, the path overgrown. He had to lift the rusting gate from a tangle of weeds to push it open. By the time he reached the tower the cuffs of his trousers were soaked through.

He had thought the door might be locked. Instead, it gave way easily when he leaned against it. The windows of the Tiled Room were thick with grime and cobwebs so that the light was murky, like being underwater. One of them was broken. Ivy twisted through the jagged shards of glass and clung to the dirty tiles on the walls. The wooden seat that ran around the room had rotted in places. Several of the slats were missing. He stood there for a moment, remembering. Her hair had been longer then. She had worn a brown jersey and a green skirt and, around her neck, his woollen scarf with the stripes. Slowly he walked across the room, dry leaves whispering against his boots, and for a moment she was there, her arms wrapped around her shins, her cuffs pulled over her hands, her pale face gazing up at his. Through the dirty window the sky was the colour of her eyes.

The previous afternoon, unwilling to return to the house while there were visitors, he had walked up through the garden, following the castellated wall around the house to the kitchen gardens and the old stables. He had stopped at Theo's memorial and thought how municipal it looked with its polished black statue and its dome of shiny purple marble like burned skin, like one

514

of those civic amenities paid for by local councillors that accommodated drinking fountains and troughs for thirsty dogs. The rough-hewn battlements behind it served only to make its glossy neo-classicism more incongruous, more absurdly faux, but then everything about Ellinghurst was fake. It was not a medieval castle any more than Theo's memorial was a Greek tholos, but only a rich man's romantic pretence, complete with ready-made ruins. No arrows had ever been fired from the arrow slits. The portcullis had never been lowered against a marauding enemy. That Jeremiah had insisted upon a portcullis that could be lowered did not make the house any less of a folly. A giant and magnificent folly but a folly all the same.

Sir Crawford Melville had understood that. His tower was the most magnificent folly of all. He had not cared a jot for what posterity would make of it. He had built it because he wanted to, to see if it could be done. It had been his triumph, his legacy, the tallest structure of unreinforced concrete in all of England. And when he died he had had his ashes scattered from the very top because he knew that what mattered was not bricks and mortar but the loftiness of one's ambitions, the splendour of one's dreams.

Oscar reached into his pocket, taking out the photograph of the tile. Phyllis would come soon, today or tomorrow. By then he would be gone. Would she write and say that she was sorry she had missed him? Only if it were true but perhaps it would be, a little. Perhaps she would think of him, of the last time they had been at Ellinghurst together on a frozen day four years ago with the ghost of Theo pacing the beech copse and the stink of Flanders clinging to their hair.

She would not come to the tower. She would not walk, as he had walked, in the places where he remembered her, from the time before he even loved her. She would not miss this house when it was gone, or feel that with its loss a part of herself had been lost too. She was not sentimental, not like that. She had told him once she never understood why people clung so passionately to objects, why they invested such significance in tokens, theatre programmes or train tickets or the dried-out flowers from long-ago corsages. She could not see the point in keeping things. Things faded and crumbled to dust but the people that you loved became part of you, absorbed into the marrow of your bones, the soft pulp of your teeth, the cells of them dividing and dividing, altering you little by little and for ever. You could not lose them if you tried.

He knew what she meant. He even envied her. It was easier not to care about things, especially when they were not yours to have. When Jessica had told him that Ellinghurst was to be sold he had felt the shock of it like a slap. It had never occurred to him to think of Ellinghurst as an asset, a representation of monetary value just as much as a bank

516

note or a share in a company. It was simply a fact of life, Ellinghurst and the Melvilles, the house and the family indistinguishable, inseparable. Impregnable. The War had ripped open the earth like a sinkhole, sucking Theo down, but Ellinghurst would never fall. Encircled in its ivied walls, deep in its fairy-tale forest, the castle slumbered, and the paroxysms unmaking the world were nothing but a muffled rumble, a train passing far off in the distance. Bombs might fall, gas and shells and bullets choking and smashing, but at Ellinghurst the world continued the way the Melvilles wanted it to be, the way they had always pretended that it was. A fantasy bound in a folly. Oscar understood why it had made his mother so angry. It had not stopped him from wanting to pretend too.

When Oscar had stood by his bedside Sir Aubrey had tried to say something. The words had not come. Instead, he had begun to weep. As the nurse hustled him away Oscar thought of Phyllis who would weep for her father as she had wept for Theo, but who would never weep for Ellinghurst. A house was a house, until it was a prison. The thought that this might be the last time he ever came here was a stone in Oscar's throat.

He turned over the photograph. On the back, in pencil, he had written her a message. He knew she would never see it but he wanted to leave it here, tucked under the seat where they had sat together that frozen day four years ago and somewhere, in a narrow fissure of his heart, the seeds of her had lodged and tentatively begun to germinate. Since then the cells in his body had divided innumerable times, his skin sloughed off, his hair and nails grown through and out. He was not the boy he had been then, because of her.

The rasp of the door made him jump. He turned.

'I thought you'd be here,' Jessica said.

'It's not your father . . . he's not . . .?'

She shook her head and looked at the photograph in his hand. It was a pattern, slightly blurred, with a star at the centre. 'That isn't one of Father's, is it?' she asked, glad to change the subject.

Oscar nodded. 'He used to send them to me at Cambridge. It was a kind of game we played. I had to guess.'

'God, not you too. Bad luck. How did you do?'

'All right, I think. Some were impossible.'

'Like the hot air vent under the billiard table?'

'That was one?'

'I know. Who exactly crawls around peering under the furniture?' She rolled her eyes, frowning at the picture in his hand. 'What's that one, do you know?'

'It's the floor. In here.'

'Is it?' She pushed the leaves away with one foot. 'So it is. And you knew it?'

'Straight away.'

She smiled. In his shoes she would have lied. She

looked around the room, at the bench under the window where he had kissed her for the first time.

'Four years ago,' she said softly. 'It seems like a hundred, doesn't it?'

Oscar did not answer. He put the photograph back in his pocket.

'Theo always loved it out here,' Jessica said. 'He had his den here, remember, right at the top? He used to take me up there sometimes. One night when it was completely dark we lit sweetie papers and dropped them out of the windows. I thought I'd never seen anything so beautiful.'

She smiled, remembering the flames like fiery wings in the darkness. Theo had leaned right out of the windows to watch them fall, so far that she had tugged at his legs to pull him back inside. She had forgotten that. She had tugged at his legs but he had shaken her off impatiently, catching her elbow painfully with one heel as he swung himself into the black hole of the empty window arch. He sat on the sill with his back to her, letting his legs dangle down outside. She did not dare say anything. Instead, she watched as he leaned out, holding the slim concrete pillars that held up the lintels. Then abruptly he twisted round, bringing his legs inside. She thought he would finally climb down. Instead, he leaned backwards out into the night, his back arched into the cold black wind of the night.

'Look, no hands,' he said. 'I'm flying!' Then he let go.

'Catch me!' he screamed and suddenly he was hurtling through Jessica's head, not floating on the air like the lit sweetie papers or the scattered dust of Grandfather Melville, but falling, falling and smashing like an egg on the kitchen floor, and she had burst into noisy sobs and clutched at his legs and Theo had kicked out at her, hard enough that she let go, the scream huge in her chest, and she had thought he would fall then for certain but he had pulled himself back into the tower, his mouth tied in a knot, and said that if he had known what a baby she was he would have brought Phyllis instead. He had never taken her up to his den again.

'Are you all right?' Oscar asked. She looked tired, her golden lustre dull and tarnished. He wondered if it was anxiety for her father or for herself that knocked her off balance and robbed her of her old imperiousness. A girl like Jessica was not made to manage alone.

'You're cold,' he said. 'We should go back in.'

There was a cable on the breakfast table. It was from Phyllis, from the French border. She would arrive at Ellinghurst the following afternoon.

'You'll stay, won't you?' Jessica said, passing Oscar the telegram. Just the sight of her name like that, printed at the bottom of the flimsy sheet of paper, was enough to make his heart leap. He thought of her sprawled under the willow tree, pulling bottles of beer from the river like shiny brown fish, and in London bent over her books, the pages smouldering in the fierce heat of her focus. He thought of her on the platform at Cambridge station the last time, the way she had looked at him as though she was trying not to be disappointed in him, as though he was the one forsaking her. He thought of her walking through the front door into the Great Hall, a slight pale figure in a squashed hat, and the thought was a bruise in his chest, inside the circle of his arms. He was not sure that he could be here with her and not hold her.

'I don't know,' he said.

'Please.' Jessica touched his sleeve, her face turned up to his. He flinched, shifting in his chair. 'At least until Father's well enough to see you. He was so adamant that he talk to you. Phyllis won't stay, you know. She never stays.'

Oscar did not answer. He picked up his coffee cup and in his head the film played over and over, the car drawing up under the carriage porch, Mrs Johns opening the front door, Phyllis greeting her and hurrying into the Great Hall, the brim of her hat turning towards him as he stepped forward, but though he strained to make it out, he could not see her face. However many times he ran it back there was no more film, only a clatter of black and white as the reel spun to a close.

In the early hours of the morning, the nurse heard Sir Aubrey crying out. His temperature had risen sharply and, along with a shaking chill, he was seized with sharp chest pains. The dry cough that had troubled him for several days now brought up a greenish phlegm. He struggled to breathe. For the rest of the night he drifted in and out of a fevered sleep. When morning came she summoned Dr Wilcox who confirmed pneumonia. He prescribed aspirins for the headache and steam inhalations to ease the congestion in his lungs. Visitors, even Jessica, were prohibited.

When Jessica had seen the doctor out she went back upstairs.

'The Patient's sleeping,' the nurse said. She looked exhausted.

'Good. Then you should too,' Jessica said, ignoring the nurse's protests. 'I'll sit with him. If he wakes I'll ring the bell.'

When the nurse had gone she stood at the window watching the rain drift in gauzy veils across the lawn. She wondered if Oscar had gone for a walk or if he was somewhere in the house. She hoped he had thought to take an umbrella. Raindrops snaked down the window panes, fattening as they swallowed one another's tails. There was a cold draught where the window had warped. The paint was peeling from the rotting sash frames and clots of whiskery moss clogged the stone sill. Above the window the gutter dripped, streaking the wall with green slime. Little by little the house was surrendering, letting go.

Restlessly she opened her father's wardrobe, running her hand over the lined-up jackets, the silk ties like drying fishes on their racks. She looked at the photographs in their silver frames on the chest of drawers, Theo as a baby in a bunchy sailor suit, herself and Phyllis in matching summer dresses, Uncle Henry and Aunt Violet on their wedding day. Tucked into the frames were several snapshots of Ellinghurst. Jessica did not know if there had ever been a picture of Eleanor. Until his illness this room had been her father's private domain.

In the next room her father coughed violently, fighting for breath. Hurriedly Jessica pushed open the door. The curtains were drawn and the twilit gloom was warm and stale. The nurse had propped her father up so high he was almost upright and his head lolled back against the stacked pillows, his mouth slack. When he coughed the force of the convulsion jerked his body, his startled hand jumping on the counterpane.

Jessica poured a glass of water and held it to his lips but he did not swallow. The water ran over his mouth and down his chin. He coughed again, wildly, helplessly, his eyes bulging as though he were choking. Jessica fought the surge of panic that spiked her throat.

'I'll fetch the nurse,' she said but as she stepped away from the bed he caught her wrist. His eyes were imploring but, though his tongue moved stickily in his mouth, no sound came out.

'What is it, Father?' she asked, trying to keep her voice steady. With her free hand she reached for one of the neatly folded handkerchiefs on the bedside table and wiped his mouth. He spat, a slick of greenish-yellow streaked with blood. Then he let his head fall back onto the pillows.

He closed his eyes, his face softening, his fingers uncurling from around her wrist. His breath slowed. Jessica watched him sleep, her hand on his, soothed by the faint whistle of air in his lungs. The room was very warm. She leaned her head against the wing of the chair as the lassitude spread through her, softening her bones. Drowsily she closed her eyes.

She dreamed of Max. They galloped across the park, Max's sides heaving, his smoky breath wreathing his head. Theo was with them. At the bottom of the hill by the river they stopped and Max dropped his head, his lip curled as he ripped greedily at the long grass. Jessica let out the rein, her hands on the pommel of the saddle, and looked back up at the house. It was evening, summer, the sky a deep cornflower blue, and the low sun flamed gold in the windows. She raised a hand, shading her eyes from the glare.

'Theo?' she said but Theo was not there. Max raised his head, yanking the bit. His mouth was frothed with green. The sun in the windows grew stronger, licking upwards, golden-red. Above the towers the blue sky was black. She could hear it, louder and louder, the greedy crackling, the crash of beams. Max whinnied, a high sharp shriek like a scream. The house was on fire.

She woke suddenly, her mouth dry, her heart pounding. In the bed her father gasped, a shrill string of strangled whimpers as he fought for breath. Frantically Jessica pressed the bell, then ran to the door and flung it open, shouting for the nurse. When she hurried in, tying a freshly starched apron, Jessica was holding her father's hand. His lips were blue.

'For God's sake, do something,' she cried. The nurse pulled Sir Aubrey forward and, sliding her hands up inside his pyjama jacket, rubbed him vigorously on his back and his chest simultaneously. Sir Aubrey's eyes stretched. Then, with a violent convulsion, he coughed, splattering the blankets with vomit and phlegm.

Jessica held his hand as the nurse bundled up the dirty sheets for laundering. He lay jacketless in the half-stripped bed, his chest pale and sunken against the pillows, his bad arm slumped uselessly at his side.

'Poor Father,' she said shakily. He stared at her in exhaustion, his mouth hanging open. His tongue was furred with grey. 'You're not allowed to die, do you hear me? You have to hold on. For me and Phyllis. For Ellinghurst.'

Her father's good eye fluttered. His bad one, bloodshot and raw, stared sightlessly past her shoulder. His tongue pushed at his teeth. She leaned closer.

'What is it?'

His mouth made an O. 'Oss.'

She frowned helplessly. 'I can't—'

'Osk.' The effort of speaking made the tendons stand out in his neck.

'Oscar? Oscar's here, Father. He's here. When you're better you can see him.'

'You,' he echoed. He stared at her, his mouth straining, but the effort to shape words was too much for him. He closed his eyes, his head falling back against the pillows. Jessica ran her thumb over the back of his hand. The skin was papery, stained with blotches of purple. When the nurse returned with a clean pyjama jacket she stepped back from the bed, watching as she dressed him and fastened the buttons. He did not open his eyes. The nurse spread clean sheets over him, smoothing them flat. In the wide bed he looked hardly bigger than a child.

'He needs to rest,' the nurse said.

Downstairs Jessica thought about ringing for tea. Instead, she opened the front door. It had stopped raining. She stood under the carriage porch, breathing in the cold winter air. Then, crossing her arms tightly against the chill, she walked across the gravelled sweep towards the terrace. Away from the shelter of the house the wind was sharp, whipping her hair in tails across her cheeks. She tipped back her head, exhaling the stale strained taint of the sick room. Perhaps Oscar was working in his room. She wanted to tell him that her father had been asking for him. He would not leave then, surely, not until he was stronger. Perhaps he would even stay for Christmas. They could go on playing Father's foolish photograph games in rooms familiar as her own hands and telling the stories her father had told and his father before him. Phyllis knew those stories too but they had never interested her. She scratched in the hot foreign sand for the stories of strangers, arranging bones and broken bits of bowl into lives long lost, into crumbled gods and vanished kingdoms, and sloughed off her own past like a snake shedding its skin.

It was different with Oscar. Ellinghurst was not his house or his history, and yet it had marked him, inking him under the skin like a sailor's tattoo. She saw how he stood in front of the fire in the Great Hall, his hand absently stroking the head of the stone lion carved into the chimney-piece. When she told him that as a girl she had called the lion Rex and pretended he was her pet, he smiled and said that before he was old enough to know that the marble bust in the library was Socrates he had always addressed him as Mr Albus.

'It means white in Latin. I felt sorry for him because he was blind.'

He no longer blushed when she smiled at him. The awkwardness of adolescence had given way to something more reserved, not coldness exactly, he could never be cold, his boyish enthusiasms were too easily stirred, but something private and unreachable, as though the parts of him that might be broken had been carefully wrapped and put away. Sometimes she spoke to him and it was as though she had woken him from sleep, the way he jumped and stared at her as though she was not the person he was expecting to see at all.

She was glad, of course, that his adoration was no longer so excruciatingly blatant. The way he had gazed at her with those abject Labrador eyes of his, so apprehensive and yet so cringingly hopeful, it was no wonder those dogs were always getting themselves kicked. And yet back they wriggled with their eager smiles, tongues lolling and tails between their legs, unable to resist the lure of whatever scrap might be dropped from the table. That morning at breakfast she had touched his arm without thinking and he had frowned and pulled away. Perhaps he thought the gesture inappropriate with her father so ill upstairs, or perhaps he was not thinking at all, she could see from his face that he was preoccupied, but the frown had stung all the same. There had been a time, she knew, when her touch would have turned him upside down.

She still remembered the summer he came to stay before he went to training camp. He had barely been able to look at her, let alone speak, and yet he had not been able to stop looking either. She had come down the stairs in her new dress and the stunned expression on his face had made her want to laugh out loud. She had been so hopeful then, the future fizzing in her like champagne, all those wonderful young men just waiting to fall in love with her, and she had kissed him not because she cared for him in the least but because at that moment she could do anything she wanted and because the temptation to knock him for six was simply too strong to resist. She had kissed him and laughed and thought how adorable she was and what an utter goose he was to love her when he knew she would never love him back, not if they both lived to be a hundred.

She had not known then that people changed. Or, if they did not change exactly, that things happened that made them see that they were not quite the people that they had thought themselves to be. They shifted inside their skins, tugging, smoothing, finding a more comfortable fit. Oscar was like that. He had made a useless boy. He lacked entirely the careless ease, the blithe gift of living in the moment that had drawn children so inexorably to boys like Theo, but boys did not go on being boys for ever. Oscar had grown up. It suited him. She was not surprised her father was fond of him. They were alike, she thought, the kind of men people dismissed as weak and passionless because they talked less than they thought, and their passions ran deep inside the rock of them and not noisily on the surface for everyone to see.

Perhaps Uncle Henry had been like that too. At dinner Oscar had told her that one of his professors at Cambridge had supervised Uncle Henry's researches in Manchester before the War and immediately she had pictured him in the racquets court fiddling about with Uncle Henry's old beakers and flasks, adding his own burn marks to the scorches that scarred the floor. Theo had always mocked Oscar for being a swot and an egghead but it was not difficult to imagine him doing something extraordinary. That was the thing about scientists. They saw what no one else bothered to see or else they looked at something perfectly ordinary, something everyone looked at every day, and thought something no one else had ever thought. Theo had been clever at making the world bend to his will but Oscar's cleverness would change it. Because of men like Oscar things that had once seemed fantastical or insane were ordinary. Today you could fly to Paris in two hours in an aeroplane with reading lamps or talk on the telephone in New York to someone in San Francisco. And tomorrow? Tomorrow, perhaps, there would be time machines and space machines to visit distant planets and machines to work instead of people. Perhaps there would even be a machine that could save Ellinghurst from screaming schoolboys.

She shivered, suddenly chilled. It was much too cold to be out without a coat. Chafing her arms briskly with the palms of her hands, she crunched back across the gravel towards the house. She felt jolted, disoriented, as though she had tried to walk up a step that was not there. In her head she heard her father's voice. *Perhaps you're just looking in the wrong place.* Was that what he had meant her to see, monosyllabic little Oskar Grunewald with his skinny arms and his expression of wary trepidation, as though disaster was always just around the corner? The idea would have made Theo snort with contempt. But Theo was not here and Oscar was not Oskar any more. That day in the tower, the day the parcel had arrived with Theo's uniform and she had thought she would choke from the blackness inside her, she had put her arms around his neck and she had known, she had absolutely known, that he was the only thing at that moment that kept her from drowning.

Oscar Greenwood. It was ridiculous. There were, she told herself in Nanny's voice, plenty more fish in the sea. And yet, as she pushed open the door to the Great Hall, there was a stirring inside her like the first tentative beginnings of a fire, a lick of flame that could have been embarrassment or a long time since breakfast but which felt to her, at that moment, like hopefulness.

CHAPTER 36

He had hoped to slip away unnoticed but when he went downstairs Jessica was in the Great Hall, standing in front of the fire. Outside in the driveway Jim Pugh waited on the trap. His dog had been dead nearly a year but he still sat on the right-hand side of the box. Old habits were hard to break.

'I have to go to London,' Oscar said. 'I'll be back on the last train.'

Jessica looked disconcerted. 'What is it? Has something happened?'

'Not exactly. But there's something I have to do. Family business. You know.'

'Today?'

'I should have done it before. I'm sorry.' He buttoned his coat, then picked up his canvas rucksack, slinging it over his shoulder. 'I should go. I'll miss the train.'

'Pritchard would have taken you, you know,' she said.

She came out into the carriage porch to see him off. When the trap turned she walked out onto the gravel, watching them as they clattered down

532

the drive. He was glad when the drive curved and she was out of sight. It made London feel less far away. He wished Jim Pugh would whip up his pony. His leg jiggled up and down and on his knees his fingers tapped out a restless rhythm, like the rattle of a train.

That morning, when Jessica had gone up to her father, he had read the newspaper in the morning room. Captain Sir John Alcock KBE DSC, who in June had piloted the world's first non-stop transatlantic flight from Newfoundland to Connemara in Ireland, was dead. En route to Paris to demonstrate a new amphibian plane at an aeronautical show, he had crashed in heavy fog in a field twenty-five miles from Rouen. The news-paper declared his death an irreparable loss to aviation. He was twenty-six years old. Oscar stared at the grainy grey photograph of Alcock in his Royal Naval Air Service uniform. He did not look like a national hero, a celebrated knight of the realm. He looked like someone's brother, his gaze steady beneath the brim of his cap, a faint smile curving his lips.

Oscar let the newspaper drop to his lap. The house was very quiet. In the grate the fire shifted and sighed and the rain pattered gently against the window panes. It was only three days since the converted Vimy bomber in which Alcock and Brown had made their historic flight had been presented to the nation for exhibition at the Science Museum. Outside the gravel crunched as a car pulled across the sweep of the drive. The doctor, he supposed. He heard Mrs Johns calling out to someone, the brisk tap of her footsteps as she hurried across the Great Hall. Singing softly to itself, the grandfather clock counted out the hour.

A car door slammed. The front door was open. You could hear it if you listened, the shift in pitch as the outside came in. Tomorrow, he thought, another car would come. The gravel would crunch and the cold wind would rush through the open door, only this time it would be Phyllis who stood on the threshold, Phyllis who stepped into the hall, foreign with the city smells of coal smoke and trains.

'A pot of tea?' Mrs Johns would say, brandishing Phyllis's coat and hat at the maid to take away, and Phyllis would shake her head and wonder why it was that Mrs Johns never remembered that she did not like tea and she would turn to Jessica and kiss her cheek and say that she was sorry it had taken her so long and how soon before she could see their father, and Jessica would nudge her and say, 'Look who's here,' and she would turn, a tiny frown between her eyebrows, and her pale eyes would meet his and it would be like Rutherford's experiment with the alpha particles, a glance that should pass straight through him would strike him instead at the centre of himself, full strength, like a cannonball.

The doctor's shoes rang against the flags as Mrs Johns hurried him across the Great Hall and Oscar thought of Rhyl with its cobbled training square, the Welsh air echoing with the metalled clatter of men who would never come back, and then of Phyllis on the cold grey platform at Cambridge station, her heels brisk against the granite as she walked away from him into another life, and it was as though a door inside him had been thrown open. He sat up, his hands clasping the arms of his chair.

Phyllis did not want to marry him. So what? What did marriage matter? Marriage was not love. It was nothing more than paperwork, the cataloguing of a collaboration by curates and clerks, for love perhaps, sometimes, but often for profit or advancement or to appease polite society. Marriage is not a guarantee of happiness, Phyllis had protested to him once, but neither was it love's hallmark, its royal warrant. Marriage proved nothing. It changed nothing. It was not an honour to be bestowed on those who loved best. It was its consolation prize, a public ultimatum in lieu of a private pledge, an insurance policy for those who did not love enough, who called for vows witnessed before God and safeguarded in law because they did not trust one another enough to keep them otherwise. Phyllis was right. If their love was true, what need did they have of insurance, of the comfort of ceremony? She was his dearly beloved and he hers, witness to each other's troth, to the promises they made and made again each time they held each other in their arms. What choice did he have but to forsake all others? She was in him and of him, the breath in his mouth and the lift in his heart. She was his second self.

'As our friends the theoreticians say . . .'

His appointment was for five o'clock but it was nearly half-past by the time Oscar was shown into Mr Pettigrew's office. The solicitor waved at Oscar to sit and turned a page, tapping the papers with his fountain pen. He wrote something, then something else, and set the papers to one side. There were weary circles under his eyes.

'Oscar,' he said. 'And what can we do for you today?'

Oscar explained.

'I see,' the solicitor said, frowning faintly. 'Just the rings, you are sure? None of the rest of your mother's jewellery?'

'Not for now.'

Still frowning, Mr Pettigrew rummaged in a pile of bulging files and drew one out. It was very thin compared to some of the others. He untied the canvas tapes and opened it. The typed envelope with Oscar's name on it was still clipped to the cardboard cover.

'Would you consider it an impertinence if I asked why you want them?'

Oscar hesitated. Half of him wanted to tell Mr Pettigrew about Phyllis, her tenderness and her fierceness and her cool clear scruples, her obstinate refusal to be anything other than herself. The other

536

half was seized with a superstitious terror of saying anything out loud. He did not want to jinx it.

'It's a personal matter,' he said.

'I see.' Mr Pettigrew tapped the envelope thoughtfully. Then, sliding it out from its paper clip, he closed the file and retied the tapes. The file had GRUNEWALD printed in black ink on the front and underneath, in slightly smaller letters, GREENWOOD. Mr Pettigrew put it back on the pile. He looked at the envelope, nudging it slightly so that it lined up with the edge of his leather blotter. 'I assume you wish to take the rings with you?'

'Please.'

Mr Pettigrew nodded. Unlocking the top drawer of his desk, he took out a small bundle of keys. He closed the drawer. Then, opening it again, he put the envelope inside and turned the key. 'I'll just be a moment,' he said.

Oscar waited. He could hear the clatter of a typewriter, the buzz and thud of a bluebottle against the window pane. He tapped his fingers restlessly on the desk, impatient to get back to the station. It was nearly two hours until the train but he was already afraid he would miss it, just as he was afraid that the hours would never pass, that time, already sluggish, would stick and set like glue, trapping him in a permanent paralysed present where tomorrow never came. He looked at his file on top of the pile and wondered what was written in it and if the contents were his to read or if Mr Pettigrew would consider them confidential. The dusty office air was sour with ink and damp carpet.

When Mr Pettigrew returned he held what Oscar recognised as his mother's silk pouch in one hand. He half-rose from his chair but the solicitor sat down again behind his desk. Unlocking his drawer he replaced the bunch of keys and took out the envelope. He tapped it on the desk. Then he put it on the blotter and placed the pouch on top. He rubbed his jawbone, his fingers rasping faintly against his late afternoon beard. Then, sitting up a little straighter, he cleared his throat.

'It is, of course, no business of mine what you do with your mother's rings,' he said. 'They are your property to dispose of as you will. However, the terms of your mother's will place me in an awkward situation. I have here a letter from your mother. She left instructions for it to be given to you in the event of your marriage. I thought to inform you of this part of her bequest at our last meeting but there was at that time a great deal for you to take in, you were distressed, quite naturally, and I deemed it more politic to wait until the occasion of our next meeting, at which time I assumed the estate would formally be wound up. I had not anticipated, had never frankly dreamed, that there was any possibility that a situation of this nature would arise while you were still at the University. And perhaps I am indeed mistaken, perhaps your interest in these rings does not in fact signify an intention to embark on an engagement, and given the particulars of your circumstances I must confess to hoping that it does not, I would be remiss in my responsibilities to you as a minor if I did not urge you towards caution, to look before you leap, as it were, you are young still and in no position to support a wife, but if it is indeed your intention to marry, and you are of course within your rights to do so, the trust as it stands will continue to yield an income for some thirty months to come, albeit hardly one on which one might contrive to meet one's obligations as a husband, and I can only suppose that if you are decided upon such a course of action you have given the matter a great deal of thought and carefully considered the consequences, then I would be remiss too if I failed to act on your mother's instruction.'

He paused for breath. Then, leaning forward, he placed both hands on the envelope. 'So, you see, I am afraid I am obliged to ask you. Do you mean to propose marriage?'

Oscar looked at Mr Pettigrew and then at his lap. He wished his mother was with him now so that he could explain. She would have been glad about Phyllis, he thought. She had always liked her. She would have understood, too, why Phyllis did not wish to get married. Perhaps she would have understood better than Oscar. There was a poem by one of the Brontë sisters, he could not remember which one, that his mother had always loved, something about not walking in paths of high morality but where my own nature would be leading, where the grey flocks in ferny glens are feeding, where the wild wind blows on the mountainside. His mother was steadfast and brave and ashamed of the lies she had told, the hypocrisy of her post-dated respectability. She believed in honour but in instinct too, in impulsiveness and defiance and throwing caution to the wind. She would never have wanted him to choose convention over the call of his own heart.

He missed her. He had forgotten how much. He thought of her propped up in her chair in the window of her bedroom in Clapham, her shawl around her shoulders, writing him a letter about love. He looked at Mr Pettigrew and nodded.

'I do,' he said.

The train was late and almost empty. Oscar had the third-class carriage to himself. The nervous waves of agitation that had buffeted him all day had finally given way to a still and shining calm. As the train sped through the darkness he took the silk pouch from his pocket and shook the rings out into his hand. They gleamed in the shaded light, spilling gold onto his palm. His mother had told him once that the ivy leaves represented fidelity, eternity. As a plant, she said, ivy was tenacious and strong. It advanced slowly but its binds were unyielding, it could not be stopped. Its leaves were always green.

When Mr Pettigrew had unclipped the letter with Oscar's name typed on it from Oscar's file he had proceeded to open the envelope. For a bewildered moment Oscar thought that the solicitor intended to read it to him. Instead, he shook out another envelope which he gave to Oscar. The second envelope was cream. Oscar took it, the grain of the paper familiar against his fingertips. For as long as he could remember his mother had always used the same writing paper, which she bought from a tiny shop near Battersea Bridge where the proprietor was Italian and kept a jar of almond biscotti for children on the polished counter. On the front she had written, *To my dearest Oscar, on this happiest of days.* Her hand was still bold, despite the shake in her fingers.

He put the envelope in his pocket. He did not open it. It was not just the lingering shadow of superstition that stopped him, the old terror of the jinx. It was the recollection of his mother's quizzical eyebrows raised above her spectacles, the warning hand on his shoulder as he reached for a biscotti that had yet to be offered. She had trusted him to wait. He did not mind misleading Mr Pettigrew but his mother was a different matter. For all her playfulness and laughter, her standards had always been exacting, her scruples strict.

He picked up the smaller ring, his mother's, running his thumb lightly over its surface. In places, where the leaves were raised, their tips were blunt, worn soft. Unlike ivy, gold was soft and malleable. It acceded easily to those who worked it, as ornament, as currency, as medicine, as symbol of love. As the ring caught the light he thought of the dappled green patterns made by sunlight dispersed through the leaves of a willow tree by a river, the dazzling glitter of reflected water falling in bright lozenges on bare skin, the dark red gleam of a bent head. Sometimes when she roused herself to sit, her mouth swollen and blurred with kisses, her rumpled hair stood up from the back of her head, charged with static and the evening sun, and sometimes, when the clouds were low and bruised with rain, the red was almost brown and her grey eyes had a greenish tinge, like lichened stone. What colour would they be in Egypt, beneath the harsh Egyptian sun, or among the fallen grey tombs of a thyme-scented Mediterranean hillside?

He closed his hand around the rings, feeling them press twin circles into his palms. Tomorrow he would take her to the top of the tower, all 385 steps up, and there, where the winter wind whipped in from the sea to howl in the glassless windows, he would ask her to not marry him, to live together with him after her own ordinance in whatever unholy estate she desired for as long as they both should live. She would say yes – wouldn't she? Then he would slide his mother's poesy ring onto the finger of her left hand and hold out his hand so that she could put his father's ring on his. When his parents married they had moved the rings to their right hands according to German tradition. He and Phyllis would wear them always on their left. They would symbolise a promise of a different kind, the promise to go on promising, to live together forever in a state of beginning, their vows to each other accepted and unspoken.

He raised his hand to his lips, kissing the rings like a cardinal through the flesh and bone of his fingers. There were lights in the darkness now, a lorry's sweeping headlights, then the slitted eyes of curtained houses, smeared street lamps, the illumnated face of a municipal clock. The train slowed, its brakes screeching. It was nearly ten o'clock. Tomorrow. It was only two hours until it was today.

CHAPTER 37

J essica glanced at herself in the long mirror. She had changed for lunch into a dress she had bought in Bond Street when Gerald had first told her about the job, a breathtakingly expensive sheath of russet jersey by a French couturier whom the saleslady had declared *le dernier cri*. The dress was simple and elegant, cut on the bias. It had long sleeves and a demure neckline but the jersey moved against her when she walked, clinging to her hips, and the colour emphasised her creamy skin, the golden gleam of her hair.

Dr Wilcox had come again that morning. Her father was still feverish but his breathing was less laboured and he no longer coughed blood.

'Take heart, my dear,' the doctor had said, squeezing Jessica's elbow. 'Sir Aubrey has always been strong as an ox.' She had smelled his sour breath, the doggy whiff of his tweed suit. His ears were hairy and there were white flecks of loose skin like dandruff caught in the slack folds of his chin.

'If you don't mind, Dr Wilcox,' she had said icily, extracting her arm. 'I am not a pet to be pawed at.'

The doctor had left soon after that, his wattled neck a satisfactorily livid shade of purple. It made Jessica wonder why she had never said anything before. Peering at her reflection, she reached for her scarlet lipstick and unscrewed it. Then, hesitating, she put it back and picked up a second, a satiny pale pink. She smoothed it over her lips, then pressed them together, setting the colour.

The letter from Joan lay unfolded on her dressing table. It had come in the morning post. It turned out that Gerald had talked to someone at *Perspective* after all, that the editor had agreed to see Joan on the strength of his personal recommendation. Three interviews later they had offered her a job on the permanent staff. She was to start in the New Year.

> How can I ever thank you? I would offer to stand you lunch at the Busy Bee when you are next in London, if that were not more punishment than reward. I have a terrible feeling I may actually miss the place once I'm gone. Peggy tells me that's Perspective for you. Well, of course she does. There really is no help for her.

Jessica was glad for Joan. She did not let herself think about Gerald. That time was over, in the past. There was comfort, all the same, in knowing that he had done as she had asked him, that he was not so very angry with her after all. Perhaps he wondered about her sometimes, just as she sometimes wondered about him. She thought of Joan, her pencil scoring indignantly through another article about how to catch a man.

'Don't you ever want to marry?' Jessica had asked her once but Joan had only shrugged.

'You have to work really hard to find a husband these days. It's not the kind of work I'm interested in.'

Oscar was sitting in the Great Hall when she came downstairs, his fingers drumming his knees. When he saw her he stood hurriedly, almost knocking over the low table in front of him. 'How's your father?' he asked.

'A little better, I think. No worse, at any rate.'

'I'm glad.'

Jessica nodded. To her surprise she realised she was nervous. 'Why don't we go through to the drawing room? Phyllis will be here soon. I don't know about you but I could do with a drink.'

Oscar glanced again towards the front door. 'Not for me, thank you.'

'Well, keep me company at least. It's nicer in there. Sunnier. And no grimacing ancestors or medieval instruments of death.'

Oscar looked up at the halberds and lances and crossed pikes, at Jeremiah Melville who glowered at him furiously, clutching his stick. 'He doesn't seem to hold out much hope for the pair of us, does he?' He smiled, twisting his hands together nervously, stretching his fingers back from his palms. The pair of us. The words gave her courage.

'I do hope you'll stay,' she said. 'Just for a few more days. Having you here, it's been such a comfort for Father. For me, too. To have someone here to talk to, to share the anxiety . . . I know you're afraid that with Phyllis back you'd be in the way but you wouldn't, not a bit. The opposite, in fact. Phyllis is so pig-headed when it comes to Ellinghurst, pig-headed and unkind, she doesn't care if she upsets anyone, she just says exactly what comes into her head, and I'm not sure Father is in any state . . . well, there's no changing her, she's beyond hope, but at least if you're here she'll behave. People always behave better when it's not just family, don't they?'

He did not answer. Jessica heard the low growl of an automobile engine, the crunch of the gravel as it drew up under the carriage porch. Mrs Johns bustled through the Great Hall, tugging briskly at her cuffs.

'I'd be so grateful,' Jessica said but he was not listening. He watched, a lump like a half-swallowed mouthful in his throat, as Mrs Johns opened the door and said something and then suddenly there she was, framed in the stone arch of the door in her scarlet coat, almost exactly as he had imagined her, only slightly, startlingly different, as though it were her face that were wrong and not his recollection. Jessica crossed the hall.

'Thank God you cabled,' she said. 'We had time to replenish the whisky supplies.' And Phyllis laughed and kissed her sister's cheek and began to unbutton her coat and Oscar stepped forward and her hands dropped away to her sides and she looked at him and her lips parted and her grey eyes were dark around the edges, like clouds. 'Oscar.'

'Phyllis,' he said and it was like a word repeated too often, its shape strange and senseless in his mouth.

'I didn't know you were here.'

'Father asked for him,' Jessica said defensively. 'He came immediately. And thank God he did. You have no idea . . . the last few days. I'm not sure I could have borne them on my own.'

Phyllis nodded at Oscar, ignoring the reproof. 'Thank you,' she said. There was nothing in her tone to suggest they had ever met. Beneath her hat her hair was lighter than he remembered it. He wondered if it was the sun. It was winter in Malta. She took off her coat. 'How is he?' she asked Jessica.

'Better. A little. We hope. I've put you in the Chinese room, by the way. We're not really using the upper floors any more, not since all the problems with the plumbing. You've time to go up before lunch if you want.'

'I'd rather see Father.'

'You can't just turn up and barge in. He may be sleeping.'

'Still.'

Jessica glowered at her sister. Then, as suddenly as it had come, the anger was gone. She felt perilously close to tears. 'It's bad,' she said.

'I know.'

They looked at each other in silence. Jessica did not trust herself to speak.

'Come up with me,' Phyllis said softly, taking her hand, and they went together, leaving Oscar standing in the Great Hall, his heart loud in his ears and his hands like someone else's heavy at his sides beneath Jeremiah Melville's censorious glare.

All that afternoon Sir Aubrey drifted in and out of sleep. Phyllis talked at length with the nurse, and afterwards she walked with Jessica to the village to visit Nanny. They took a cake and a collection of postcards Phyllis had brought back with her from Malta.

'Nanny won't want to see those,' Jessica said, rolling her eyes. 'She detests abroad,' but Phyllis only smiled and said, 'Spare the rod and spoil the child,' which made Jessica laugh. Oscar was not sure why that was funny.

'Come with us,' Jessica said to Oscar but he shook his head.

'It's you she wants to see,' he said and Jessica did not contradict him. Alone in the house he went to the library. To his surprise the door was locked and, when he asked Mrs Johns if he might have the key, the housekeeper said that she was sorry but Sir Aubrey had asked that no one be allowed into the library but him, so Oscar fetched a book of his own from upstairs and took it to the drawing room. Jessica was right. Even on a dull day the imposing room was washed with light.

He settled by the fire but when he tried to read the words squirmed like tadpoles across the page and, instead of Lorentz transformations and the aberration of light, he thought of Phyllis at the lunch table, her chin propped on her hands, her shoulders turned away from him as she asked Jessica about Dr Wilcox, about the treatment for pneumonia, the possibility of another seizure. He had tried to keep his attention on his plate but like a tongue probing a sore tooth his gaze kept returning to the curve of her ear, the dusting of freckles like powdered chocolate along her cheek-bone, the soft down at the nape of her neck.

He had feared they might quarrel. Jessica and Phyllis were so unalike, not only in the way they looked but in what his textbooks would call their chemical properties, those qualities revealed by chemical reaction, by catalysis, by change, but instead he was startled by the ease between them, the careless abundance of shared references and private jokes. They slipped effortlessly from solemnity to silliness and back again, contradicting and consoling one another, their exchanges zigzagged with short cuts that made them hard to follow.

Like lovers, Oscar thought, silently helping himself to apple Charlotte he did not want. Since Phyllis had arrived she had barely spoken to him. Of course she had not. Her father was critically ill, possibly dying. It was a time for family. He dropped the spoon clumsily back into the dish. The maid straightened it and moved to offer the dish to Phyllis but Jessica leaned forward, pushing it away.

'Do you *want* to be the Greedy Girl?' she said disapprovingly to Phyllis who laughed and motioned to Doris to take the apple Charlotte away.

'Is she coming?' Phyllis asked and in the look that they exchanged there was no space for Oscar at all. He ate his pudding mechanically, the sweet crust clogging his mouth. The maid brought coffee. Jessica peered at the milk jug and said something about a skin and Phyllis cried, her shoulders shaking, and Jessica took her hand and they sat together, their fingers entwined, without saying a word.

It shamed him but he could not help it. It rose in his throat like smoke, the bleak sour fog of his schooldays. *Du allein.* Except Phyllis was not alone. She was not an only child as he was, nor an émigré, like his father, who could never go home. She had Jessica, her father, a place to belong to, to return to, a rope like the tether of a hot air balloon to reel herself in. He was not her only other. There were other people who would always love her as he did, without thinking, because the love was in their hair and their bones.

'One loyal friend is worth ten thousand relatives,' his mother had said and Oscar had believed her, of course he had. The two of them were the only real family they had left. His mother said that to understand the essence of humanity you needed only to study the ancient Greeks because they had known everything worth knowing, and, better still, they knew how to write it down. Since then Oscar had studied Poincaré and Lorentz and Bohr and Rutherford and Einstein. He had learned that it did not matter if people had believed the same things for centuries, for millennia. It still did not make them true.

He went upstairs and put the rings in a drawer with his mother's letter, underneath his socks. He would wait until it was over, until Sir Aubrey was better. When Sir Aubrey was better he would come back. They would look out over the tumbled moors of the New Forest and past the smudge of the sea to the wide sprawl of the rest of the world and they would draw the lines of their lives together, parallel and never quite touching, like railway tracks laid down to the horizon. He loved her. He would not ask for more than she could give.

It grew dark. He did not go down for tea. Later he heard feet on the stairs, snatches of conversation, the low rumble of a man's voice he assumed was the doctor. He did not want to go downstairs but he washed and changed and combed his hair, digging the teeth hard into his scalp, because love was selfless and what he wanted did not matter. Phyllis was not yet down. He accepted the glass of whatever it was that Jessica offered him and drank it too quickly as Jessica told him about

Nanny. She had knitted cardigans for both the girls which she insisted on them putting on there and then.

'Mustard yellow,' Jessica said. 'It's enough to make you miss the War.'

A sombre Phyllis came down just as they were going through to dinner. Sir Aubrey's temperature had soared. In his delirium he had mistaken Phyllis for his mother.

'Grandmother?' Jessica asked. 'Are you sure?'

'He called me Mama,' Phyllis said.

'Babies say Mama,' Jessica said. 'It's what you say when you can't say anything else. It doesn't mean anything. The only reason mothers have always called themselves Mama is to get in first.'

'Eleanor,' Phyllis said, rolling her tongue over the vowels like someone trying out a foreign language, and to Oscar's bewilderment both girls began to laugh helplessly, each attempt at recovery giving way to a new convulsion. They laughed until Jessica pressed her stomach and pleaded with Phyllis to stop.

'I'm sorry, Oscar,' Jessica said, wiping her eyes. 'You must think us mad.'

'Not at all,' he mumbled. 'It's nice to see you laughing.' He was glad Phyllis did not look at him. He was afraid she might be able to see inside his head.

At dinner Jessica asked him about Cambridge, his friends and his rooms and the photographs he had sent to Sir Aubrey.

'You should see them, Phyll,' she said. 'They're riddles, really. Like Father's. There's one that looks just like an angry face until you look closer and you realise it's actually a door handle. Where did you say you found that, Oscar?'

'St John's.' A side door near the Bridge of Sighs on a golden August evening. Phyllis had walked barefoot, swinging her shoes by their straps. He had photographed her feet, pale as fish in the trailing green weed of the river, and her wet foot-prints on the sun-warmed stone. Almost as soon as he had clicked the shutter they were gone.

Phyllis said little. She knew all his answers anyway. As soon as dinner was over she pleaded exhaustion after her journey and bid them both goodnight. She kissed her sister and brushed Oscar's cheek with hers.

'You'll have some coffee with me, won't you?' Jessica asked Oscar but he shook his head. His cheek prickled, electric with the touch of her. Jessica wore her long pearl necklace and a short silk dress with narrow straps like a film star's night-gown. Oscar thought of Phyllis's green-and-white striped summer dress, her squashed hat. *Worth me Best Straw*, he thought, and his heart ached.

Upstairs the bathroom door was locked. Jessica could hear the sound of water running. She banged on the door. 'Phyll?'

'What?' Phyllis's voice was muffled.

'Let me in.'

The door clicked and Phyllis opened it, her toothbrush in her mouth. She went back to the sink as Jessica crossed to the lavatory. Pulling down her knickers, she sat down. White foam spilled down the handle of Phyllis's toothbrush. She leaned forward to spit as Jessica wiped herself and reached up to tug on the chain.

'Budge over so I can wash my hands,' Jessica said, turning on the tap. Phyllis put her toothbrush under the flow. 'Wait your turn.'

Reaching for the soap she pushed her sister away with her hip. Phyllis flicked her toothbrush at her, spattering her with tiny droplets of water, and she made a scoop of her hand, splashing water over the front of Phyllis's nightgown. 'Now look what you made me do,' she said.

Phyllis took the hand towel from its rail and flicked it at Jessica's neck. Jessica laughed, ducking out of the way. Half-heartedly Phyllis dabbed at the wet patch on her nightgown. The starched white towel was thick and glossy, the Melville monogram embroidered on it in white thread.

'Are you all right?' Jessica asked, taking it to dry her hands. 'You hardly said a word all evening.'

Phyllis shrugged. She sat on the edge of the bath, the wet nightgown clinging to her thighs. The water made the white cotton almost transparent. Jessica could see the jut of her hipbones, the dark shadow of hair between her legs. She looked away, busying herself with her toothbrush.

'He's dying, isn't he?' Phyllis said quietly.

Jessica shook her head furiously. 'Don't say that.'

'When I saw him I . . . it's not him, Jess. Not any more. He's not there.'

'He's got a fever, that's all. It makes him confused. When that passes . . .'

'Does Dr Wilcox honestly believe it will pass?'

'He hopes. So should you.' Jessica swallowed, scrubbing ferociously at her teeth. Phyllis pleated the fabric of her nightgown between her fingers.

'Would I . . . would there have been time to talk to him? If I had got here sooner?' She looked up at Jessica tentatively. Jessica stopped brushing. If you had been here, she wanted to say, if you had ever bothered to come home, you could have talked to him whenever you wanted. Instead, she shook her head.

'Not since the second stroke,' she said. 'He hasn't really been able to speak since then.'

Phyllis bowed her head, staring at the bunched-up fabric in her fist. Jessica spat out the dental cream, then turned on the tap, rinsing out her mouth. She did not know how it was possible to feel so angry with Phyllis and so very close to her, both at the same time. Phyllis said something she could not catch above the noise of the water. She turned off the tap. 'What?'

'I said I stayed an extra day. In Malta. Two days nearly. There was this relief, this extraordinary relief quite unlike the others, they think it might prove as important a discovery as the fat lady statue. I . . . I waited. I wanted to stay.'

Jessica shook her head. 'Why are you telling me this?'

'I thought it was what mattered, this piece of stone that had been buried in a field for thousands of years. That it was somehow more important. I never thought . . .' She bit her lip. 'What if he had died before I got here? What if I had never had the chance to say goodbye?'

'He didn't die, Phyllis. He isn't going to, do you hear me? You have to stop saying things like that. It's horrible.'

'Saying things out loud doesn't change anything,' Phyllis said but there was something in the way that she said it that made Jessica think that she did not believe it either. They were both silent.

'Your feet are blue,' Jessica said.

Phyllis looked down. 'More lavender, wouldn't you say?'

'Nanny would call that showing off.'

'She would also tell us it was time for bed. Sleep, Jessica Margaret Crompton Melville, is a poor man's treasure.'

'And only thieves have important business after dark,' Jessica said, pulling the cord of the bathroom light, and in the darkness they smiled at one another, their eyes glistening with memories.

'I'd forgotten how full of us her cottage is,' Phyllis said. 'Like a museum of our childhood.'

'We were her life.' On the other side of the landing, along the passage of the East wing where their father slept, a lamp burned dimly.

'I suppose we were. How sad.'

'Why is that sad? She was ours, too, for years and years.'

At the door of the Chinese room Phyllis put her hand on the porcelain knob with its painted dragon. She did not turn it. She looked down the passage towards the faint light of the lamp. 'Have you ever told him you love him? I mean, actually told him?'

'I don't have to. He knows.'

'Does he?' Phyllis stared at the rug, her toe tracing the pattern. 'I keep thinking about something someone told me once. That it isn't a scientist's results that are the most interesting part of his experiment, it's the facts he takes for granted before he starts.'

'That sounds like something Oscar would say.'

'Does it?' She hesitated, her hand on the door knob, as though she meant to say more. Instead, she ducked her head forwards, kissing Jessica's cheek. 'I'm sorry,' she murmured. 'I should have . . . I'm sorry.'

'Sorry for what?' Jessica said but Phyllis had already closed the door.

Oscar undressed slowly. The fire had gone out in his room and it was very cold. When he got into bed he realised he had left his book in the drawing room. He reached into his knapsack and took out another. His mother's book of Gray's poems with Sir Aubrey's photographs of Ellinghurst tucked inside. He opened the cover, reading the inscription. *Thoughts that breathe and words that burn, with all my love.* He frowned at the handwriting, struck by its familiarity. Then it dawned on him. The writing was Sir Aubrey's. Not an inscription from his father to his mother at all, but from Sir Aubrey to Godmother Eleanor. His mother must have borrowed the book and forgotten to return it. He stared at the inscription. The words were different now that they no longer meant the same thing. Sliding the photographs out from between its pages, he put the book on the bedside table. He would have to leave it behind when he went back to Cambridge. The thought made him obscurely sad.

He fanned the photographs in his hand like playing cards, then laid them out, one after the other, on the counterpane. They had been printed by a machine on cheap cardboard and the images were soft, as though they were already starting to fade. They had an elegiac quality, as distant and unreal as the portraits of the Ellinghurst household that Sir Crawford had insisted on taking with a camera of his own invention, which had required an exposure time of nearly a minute so that the faces of the servants all came out blurred. As distant as the photographs on the boys' dressing tables at school, those soldiers in their smart uniforms smiling into a future that turned out not to exist at all. When his mother saw the photographs Sir Crawford had taken she said that they did not even look like people, just ideas for people that someone had got bored with in the middle, which was so exactly what they looked like that Oscar had wanted to kiss her in delight. He thought of the way she smiled to herself when he read her the Gray poem about the goldfish from the book that was not hers, the way it spread on her favourite line: *Presumptuous maid!* He missed her. Perhaps, he thought, if she were here, he might be able to bear it better, the ache that pummelled inside him like a fist trying to punch a bigger hole.

He never meant to open the letter. He only meant to look at the envelope, to draw comfort from her familiar handwriting. *To my dearest Oscar, on this happiest of days.* He thought of the way she had sat in the parlour on days when she knew he was unhappy, her stockinged feet tucked under her and her book set aside on the arm of her chair, waiting for him to be ready. One corner of the envelope's flap was not properly stuck down. Oscar picked at it, his thumbnail worrying the flap, and abruptly the gum gave way and the fold opened.

He missed her, her laugh and her frown of concentration and her silly music hall songs, the private smile over the top of her book. He wanted to believe what she believed, that one day he would marry and it would be the happiest day of his life.

The ink was blue and faintly smudged.

My dearest O, it is dawn as I write this, a grey winter's dawn. Beyond the chimney pots the dull white sun is peering from under the clouds like a child reluctant to get out of bed. I ache too much to sleep and a good deal too much to try to get up so I am writing this to you.

I know too little of marriage to give advice. I made a mess of mine. I wish I had tried harder. A love affair, however passionate, is nothing but a chemical reaction, like gunpowder or phosphorus in water, dazzling perhaps but not profound. A marriage, even an unhappy marriage, is an act of creation. Exhausting sometimes, difficult often, but always interesting. You are thoughtful by instinct, attentive, endlessly curious. You see things others do not see. You will make a fine scientist. Perhaps you are one already. You will be good at marriage.

This letter is a last kiss. A fond goodbye. It was ever so. From today your family is not the one you were given but the one you have chosen for yourself. It is not a child's majority but his marriage that topples the parent from his throne, that strips him of his power and his glory. The King is dead, long live the King. Amen to that. My father was a tyrant who terrorised my childhood but from

561

Clapham he was nothing but a querulous, peevish old man.

I wish I could tell you this instead of writing but it is too soon. This way is better, I think. When a mother dies, her child's father is his next of kin. Until he marries. When he marries, that person is his wife.

In the summer of 1899, I met Joachim. You know this part of the story. I loved him, or wanted to. Joachim was so stubbornly, unyieldingly free and I wanted to be free too. You see, for a long time I had loved a man who could not love me back and I was tired of it, angry with myself and with him. Anger made me reckless. When I told him Joachim had proposed marriage he asked for a week. One week to say goodbye. When it was over he went back to his wife and I went to Paris.

I never regretted it. How could I? There was you. And no one was hurt. Joachim never knew, never even suspected. Why would he? You were like him in so many ways. You were like them both. They say a mother has an instinct for these things. Perhaps some do. As you grew up there were times when I believed that I knew, that I knew beyond doubt, but I have noticed, as I grow old, that what we see depends mainly on what we look for. Truth alters with the light. The only certainty is that we can never be certain. We must choose what to believe. In my mind you will always have two fathers.

And you? It is for you to decide. Perhaps you will choose to choose, perhaps like me you will find you cannot. It is nobody's business but yours. Joachim is dead. As for the other, he is married with children of his own and a master at seeing what he wants to see. We have never spoken of it, not once, but I wonder if he wonders. He has been very kind. There would be worse fathers to have than Aubrey Melville.

CHAPTER 38

The knock on the door was tentative, a maid's knock. He groaned, drawing the covers over his head. His head ached and his eyes felt raw beneath his eyelids. He turned over, trying to burrow back into sleep. The motion made his stomach pitch. He thought he might be sick. He pulled the pillow over his head, willing himself back towards unconsciousness.

All night the thoughts had squirmed and coiled, swallowing their own tails. Joachim Grunewald was his father. Fatherhood was not biology. Fatherhood was shaving soap in the bathroom and German lullabies and the same unlaced pair of boots tipped on their sides at the bottom of the stairs when you came down in the mornings. It was Oscar's first conscious memory, reaching up to hold his father's hand as they crossed the road, the impossible size and slipperiness of his leather-gloved fingers. His father's hands were square with thick fingers and square nails, a potter's hands, not a pianist's. Oscar had inherited his mother's narrow palms, her long tapered fingers. The rod-shaped structures in a cell's nucleus known as chromosomes were the basis for all genetic inheritance. The association of paternal and maternal chromosomes in pairs and their subsequent separation during the reduction division constituted the physical basis of the Mendelian law of heredity.

His mother was wrong. You could not choose. Dr Mallinson, who lectured on human biology, had been very clear on that. Chromosomes were independent entities that retained their independence even in the resting nucleus. He had written it on the blackboard. The genes they contained could not be altered. A single sperm fertilised an egg to form a zygote and within that zygote were contained all the patterns and parameters of the infant's essential self, the blueprint for the person to come. A foetus did not alter because another man stroked the swelling belly and called himself Father. The cells divided and multiplied as they were determined to do, in strict accordance with the genetic code laid down inside each nucleus. A single sperm. You were your biological father's son. And sexual relations with a sister, even a half-sister, was incest and morally repugnant. The children of incestuous relationships were born deformed, idiotic, mad.

There would be no children. Phyllis did not want children and she knew how to make sure they did not come. Phyllis, whose touch convulsed him with desire, who moaned softly, her back arching, as he ran his tongue over her neck and her breasts and her belly, as he slid his fingers between her legs. Who smiled very slowly, her grey eyes on his as she pushed him backwards on to the rug and sat astride him, engulfing him in electrical currents of such intensity that he thought he would die of it. The aftershocks echoed in his pelvis, at the root of his cock, and immediately he hardened, swelling and tightening. He closed his eyes, fumbling with the cord of his pyjamas, imagining pushing his cock inside her, so deep inside her that they neither of them existed without the other and there was no knowing where he ended and she began. Cock was Phyllis's word. Fuck too. The bluntness of the words aroused him. His hand moved more frantically as he sucked his fingers, smelling her, tasting her. He was so hard he thought he might split. Tasting his sister. With a strangled cry he turned over, crushing himself painfully in his fist. There were tears in his eyes.

His sister. What kind of monster wanted to fuck his own sister?

His half-sister. Perhaps not even that. A week, his mother said. A single week, but she had gone to Paris with Joachim Grunewald. They had spent months there together. Phyllis was not his sister. If Phyllis were his sister, he would have known. It would have changed things. He could never have loved her as he loved her if he were her brother. Or Jessica, he thought, a fragment of the old dreams flickering faintly in his memory, but he stamped it out. He would not think about that. To love your sister, to desire her, it went against

566

nature, against all that was right. He was not a wicked person.

Besides, they would have looked alike, wouldn't they? He did not look like Phyllis, not in the least. Just as Phyllis did not look in the least like Jessica. Theo and Jessica had always resembled one another with their tilted eyes and their long limbs and their goldenness, but Phyllis did not look like either of them. Every human child carries two copies of the same gene, one from each parent, but in many cases only one copy produces a trait while the action of the other is masked. Mendel's ratio is three to one. Sir Aubrey's brother was a great scientist. Joachim Grunewald was a composer. Oscar had shown no aptitude for the piano but there was a strong correlation, long documented, between music and mathematics. Oscar had loved mathematics once.

In the darkest part of the night he went downstairs for whisky. A light burned outside Sir Aubrey's room but the door was closed. He took the stairs at a run but the thoughts still came with him, coiling and twisting in his head. He could not make them stop. They could still make a life together, couldn't they? Phyllis would not care. She did not want to be married. They could live in separate houses, in separate cities. They could meet as they had always met, secretly, in hotel rooms and under willow trees. No one would ever have to know. Phyllis would never have to know. When he was at school a man had been discovered living in wedlock with his sister. The other boys were almost as outraged as the halfpenny newspapers. They declared him disgusting, perverted, desperate, no better than a dog. When the man was sentenced to three years in prison they were furious. They wanted him hanged.

He drank his whisky in the dark, one hand on the drinks table to steady himself. The taste made him gag. He poured himself another. For as long as he could remember Eleanor Melville had surrounded herself with admirers. People murmured about her, when they thought the children were not listening. They said she should be more discreet. Who was to say that she, like his mother, had not had her affairs? Was that why Phyllis was not like them? Perhaps Phyllis's father was not Sir Aubrey at all but someone else entirely. Perhaps, perhaps, perhaps.

The only certainty is that we can never be certain. His mother had invited him to choose and he would choose. He would choose to forget. He would burn his mother's letter and turn back the clock to a time before, when there was no letter and his father was Joachim Grunewald. This time he would not go to London. He would not sit in Mr Pettigrew's office and ask him for the poesy rings. Mr Pettigrew would do whatever it was he did when Oscar had not come to see him and the letter would remain where it was, fastened with a paper clip to the cover of his file in its envelope with his name typed on the front.

He was Joachim Grunewald's son. That was how it was, how it had always been. Oscar Greenwood. Oskar Grunewald. Times changed. His father was dead, his mother too. It was no business but his own. *I wonder if he wonders. He has been very kind.* Sir Aubrey knew when he was born. He had mastered the principles of basic arithmetic. Was that why he had sent Oscar the letters, the photographs of Ellinghurst, why he wanted him here as he was dying? Was that why he had given Oscar his brother's books, because somewhere in his heart he believed he was his son? Well, he could believe all he liked. He could not know. No one could. You might as well toss a coin, heads or tails. Best of three. Of five. Of nine hundred and ninety-nine. Unless there was something in Oscar he recognised, some trait or distinction that revealed him, that gave him away.

What would Sir Aubrey say if he knew about him and Phyllis?

He sloshed more whisky into his glass and swallowed it down. Forget the letter, he told himself, but he already knew it was hopeless. There could be no forgetting. The possibilities wormed through the white noise of the alcohol and into the lobes of his brain, devouring, defecating, depositing their disgusting eggs. Multiplying and multiplying, a slimy white writhe of grubs burrowing into the dark folds, fattening themselves on his fears. Sir Aubrey was his father and Phyllis, Phyllis whom he loved with every cell in his body, Phyllis was his sister. It was not love. It was genetics. Every cell in his body was marked with her because contained in the nucleus of every cell was his father's chromosome. His father's and hers.

Two fools in a tub.

His bedroom door opened. He heard the faint protest of the hinges. He did not know how long he had slept. It felt like only moments but perhaps it was days. Perhaps the maid had been sent to see if he was dead. He was not dead, not yet. His brain was waking and already the thoughts were stirring, stretching their snake bodies, darting their venomous snake tongues. He pressed his face against the pillow. He heard the pad of feet.

'Oscar?'

He lifted his head. The movement hammered through his skull, sending a wave of nausea through him. Phyllis stood beside the bed in her nightdress, her hair rumpled, her face pale in the curtained gloom.

'May I get in?' she asked. He did not answer. The sickness churned in his stomach, oily waves rising in his throat. Throwing back the blankets he pushed past her and vomited violently into the basin on his washstand. He swallowed, his head throbbing, the lumps catching in his throat before it convulsed him again, vomit splashing against the porcelain. She murmured to him, her hand on the back of his neck, stroking his hair. His stomach heaved a third time. Exhausted and empty, he leaned over the basin. The pain pounded dully in his skull and clamped the back of his eyeballs, digging in its nails.

'Here,' she said, putting a tooth glass in his hand. 'Drink this.'

The water tasted of metal and dust. She took the glass from him. Then, covering the vomit-spattered basin with a towel, she carried it to the door and slid it out into the corridor. There was a key in the keyhole. She turned it and, taking his hand, led him gently back to bed.

'Shove up,' she murmured. He knew he should not let her do it, that there was a raging mob of reasons why she should not be allowed to do it, but they were too many and too loud and his head ached so that he could barely swallow, so he only closed his eyes as she climbed in beside him, pulling the blankets up over them, and when she tucked herself into the curve of him his arm moved reflexively to encircle her, holding her against him like an amulet, to ward off evil.

When he woke she was lying propped on one elbow beside him, watching him. She had drawn back the curtains and in the pale grey light of morning her eyes were almost blue. She smiled at him tentatively, her bottom lip caught between her teeth, and his heart dropped inside him, like a stone dropped in a well. He closed his eyes, pressing his hand to his forehead.

'Good morning,' she said softly. 'How are you feeling?'

'I . . . I'm not sure.'

'You deserve to feel awful. How much did you drink, anyway?'

'I don't know. Lots.'

'I thought you didn't like whisky.'

'It was . . . medicinal.'

Her laugh was rueful, like a sigh. 'I'm sorry. I avoided you yesterday, I know. I didn't mean . . . I didn't know what to do, what to say. It's my fault. I'm sorry.' She reached across the bed and took his hand, plaiting her fingers in his. He did not resist. He looked at their hands, their entwined fingers, and he thought of Jessica and Phyllis at the lunch table, Phyllis weeping silently, her shoulders hunched away from him like a shield.

'What time is it?' he asked.

Phyllis glanced at the alarm clock on the bedside table. 'Half past eight.'

'We should get up,' he said but she shook her head.

'Not yet. We have to talk.'

A sudden surge of panic swept through him. He twisted around to see his mother's letter lying where he had dropped it, among the clothes strewn on the chaise at the bottom of the bed. He wanted to leap up, to bury it, burn it, to cram it in his mouth and swallow it whole. He made himself look away.

'You're not going to be sick again, are you?' Phyllis said, making a face. He shook his head. 'Look, I want to say this, I want to say it all, and

I want you to promise you won't interrupt me until I'm finished. Do you promise?'

His head throbbed, too heavy for his neck. Even his breath was cement, weighing down his lungs. He thought of Sir Aubrey in bed, his mouth sagging open, his too-big tongue lolling in his mouth. 'All right,' he said.

Phyllis took a deep breath. She did not look at him. 'It may be too late, I mean, I understand if it's too late, but I was wrong. When I said I wouldn't marry you. You see, the thing is, well, you know I never wanted to be married, the idea of being someone's wife, it's always felt like a kind of death, a terrible slow lifetime of dying, but coming back here, seeing you, for the first time I really under-stand what it means, that I would have to live my whole life like this, without you, pretending it doesn't matter, and, you see, that's a kind of death too, or anyway a deadening, and I . . . I'm not sure I can do that.'

She faltered but before he could say anything she shook her head. 'Let me finish. When you asked me to marry you it terrified me. I know you thought it was because of you but it wasn't. It wasn't even the marriage part, or not only that. My father . . . a few months ago, my father told Jessica and me that he wanted to leave Ellinghurst to one of us. The title would go to Cousin Evelyn but the house, the house would go to whichever one of us married first. When you asked me to marry you all I could think of was Ellinghurst, of the walls rising higher and higher, incarcerating me. The thought of it . . . it was impossible. It was as though I couldn't breathe. But marriage isn't Ellinghurst. I see that now. I don't want to be married, I never have, but I want to spend the rest of my life with you. And if that means marrying you, then all right, yes, I'll marry you. I'll be your wife. There's only one condition, my father cannot know. You have to promise me that. I can't be happy here, Oscar, even with you. If we are stuck here I will suffocate, I'll make us both wretched. I have to be able to go on with my work. You know that, don't you? You've always understood that, you would never expect me to be a housewife arranging flowers and plumping cushions, I know you wouldn't, it would make you as miserable as it would make me. We can be ourselves, can't we, and still be married? Ourselves, separately and together. Marriage itself isn't anything, it's the stupid conventions that make it so, and neither of us have ever given a straw for conventions, have we? So, yes, Oscar, I'll marry you. You can't tell anyone, not a soul, but when Father is gone and all this business of the house is finished and done with I'll marry you. If you still want to, that is, if I'm not too late. Tell me I'm not too late?'

He stared at her. There was a pain in his breast-bone, as though someone had split it with a knife, but it was a good pain, a strong pain, and when he swallowed, the muscles of his throat and his oesophagus contracted, compressing the wild horrors of the night until they were nothing but a sharp black stone inside him. Joachim Grunewald was his father. He had chosen. It was nobody's business but his own.

'You're shaking,' she said, smiling awkwardly, and he realised that he was. 'I don't suppose a marriage proposal is the best cure for a hangover.'

'I don't know.'

Her smile spread, pushing up into her cheeks, creasing the corners of her eyes. 'So what do you say? Will you let me marry you after all?'

Tears prickled his eyes. He blinked them back. 'Only if you promise never to tell anyone,' he said and she laughed and he seized the silk counterpane that covered the bed and flung it back so that it fell over the chaise. Then he held out his arms.

'Come here,' he said and he wrapped his arms around her, holding her against him, and all that mattered was her mouth and her tongue and the warmth of her against him, the softness of her.

He had never loved her so much or so completely. She was his, to have and to hold, for ever and ever. He closed his eyes as she wound her fingers in his hair, mashing his face against hers, her tongue urgent, her teeth catching his lips. When she turned her head, her tongue tracing his ear, his jawbone, the side of his neck, he touched her cheek, guiding her mouth back to his, but she slid downwards out of his embrace, her fingers tugging at the buttons of his pyjama jacket, her tongue circling his nipples, tracing the raised curve of his ribcage.

'Come back here,' he murmured, but she shook her head, her nose brushing his skin as she moved down to kiss his stomach, her hand sliding into the vent of his pyjamas, and suddenly all the words were blown away in an explosion of sensation, his nerves like branches bursting into flower as she took him in her mouth and he cried out, raising himself from the pillow to gape at her as she looked up at him, his cock in her mouth, her mouth full of his cock, and he could not stop it, could not stop the rush that gathered in his stomach and roared through his pelvis, the glorious irresistible surge of it as it swept through him, the hot white blast of pure pleasure. He jerked, electrified, and was still. She smiled up at him. Her chin was smeared with his semen. She touched it, smoothing it away with her fingers, then raised them to her mouth and suddenly the nausea engulfed him, the spike pushing up into his throat, choking him, and he twisted away, his knees curling up towards his chest as he vomited yellow bile in a splattering stream onto the bedside rug.

He told her it was the whisky. Perhaps it was. She was kind. She wiped up the worst of it and brought him more water and told him to stay in bed.

'You can't just walk out of here in your night-gown,' he said. 'What if someone sees you?'

'I'm not as stupid as I look.' She gestured at a pile of clothes on the tapestry chair by the door. 'I thought ahead.'

'You knew I'd let you stay.'

'I hoped.' She smiled, then wrinkled her nose wryly. 'Of course, if I'd known about the whisky . . .'

When she was dressed she sat down next to him on the side of the bed and stroked his shoulder. 'Sleep. I'll have Doris bring you an aspirin.'

He caught her hand. 'I'm sorry. I never meant . . .'

'I know.' She kissed him lightly on the cheek. 'I'll see you later.'

'Wait.' Pushing back the blankets he got out of bed and went to the chest of drawers. He took out the silk pouch. 'We can't wear them, I know, but I wanted you to have this.' He shook out the rings and held the smaller one out to Phyllis. 'One each.'

She hesitated. Then she took it, turning it in her fingers. 'They belonged to my parents,' he said.

'What does it say inside?'

'*Du allein*. You alone.'

'You alone.' She looked at the ring and then at him. He smiled and, taking the ring from her, he slid it onto the third finger of her left hand. She looked at it and picked up the other ring.

'Here,' she said and he held out his hand so that she could put it on. The ring was too big. She smiled, entwining her fingers with his. He squeezed, then pressed her hand to his lips. Her skin smelled of him. He closed his eyes.

He had chosen. There was no going back now.

CHAPTER 39

Jessica wished Phyllis did not make Oscar so uncomfortable. Almost as soon as she had arrived he had withdrawn, retreating snail-like into his boyhood silence. At dinner Jessica had tried to bring him into the conversation, had asked lots of encouraging questions about his life at the University, but Oscar had answered in monosyllables. As for Phyllis she had been no help at all. Not for the first time Jessica had wondered if she had got it all wrong, if despite everything he was still the same infuriating weirdo he had always been, but she pushed the thought away. That kind of thinking could drive a person round the bend.

On her way to breakfast she put her head around her father's dressing-room door. When she saw Jessica the nurse smiled. Sir Aubrey, she said, had had a good night. The delirium had passed and his temperature was almost normal. Once the doctor had been, she hoped that he might be well enough to receive visitors.

Stupid with relief Jessica went to the Chinese room to tell Phyllis. There was no answer when she knocked so she nudged open the door. The curtains were still drawn but the bed was empty, the covers thrown back. Jessica went downstairs to the breakfast room.

'Is my sister up?' she asked Doris but Doris only shook her head.

'I've not seen her, miss.'

'And Mr Greenwood?'

'No, miss.'

She ate her breakfast alone. She wished the others would come down. It was not right, to have good news and no one to tell. She wondered if she should cable her mother. If Father was better there would be no need for her to come. To her surprise, that too felt like a relief.

Some time later the doctor came. Jessica waited while he went upstairs. Afterwards he kept an affronted distance, his hand clasped piously over his stomach as he reprised the nurse's diagnosis. Jessica nodded and wondered for the tenth time that morning where Phyllis was and why on earth she had bothered to come home.

'So it wasn't pneumonia after all?' she asked.

The doctor stiffened. 'But of course it was pneumonia. The excretions from the lungs were unmistakable. Your father has been very fortunate. He has recovered well. It is safe to say that the immediate danger is behind us.'

'So I can see him?'

'I don't suppose I could stop you if I tried.'

She laughed. 'No, I don't suppose you could.'

When she pushed open the door her father was

sitting up against a bank of pillows, his chin rimed with grey stubble. His good eye slid towards her. 'Jes'ca,' he whispered. Her heart lifted.

'Good morning, Father.' She smiled as she kissed his rough cheek. He smelled of laundry starch and old age. 'The doctor says you're much better.'

He made a clumsy attempt at a nod.

'Phyllis is here. She got back yesterday.' His eye swivelled sideways. Jessica shook her head. 'Not here in this room. She'll come later. We're not allowed to wear you out. Doctor's orders.'

'Osk. Wha' Osk?'

'Oscar's here too. He came just as you asked. He's been here all the time.'

His good eye blinked. He said something she could not understand. She leaned closer as he tried again. It sounded like good boy. She wished he would rest. It was painful to see the effort it cost him to speak. In his scrawny neck the tendons stretched tight and white scum formed on the corners of his mouth.

'I'm glad you asked him,' she said. 'He says you've been writing to each other, that you've been playing the game with him, the photograph game. He's much better at it than me, it's shaming. He knows so much about the house. So many stories, you wouldn't believe. He's almost as dreary about it as you.' She smiled at her father. Tremblingly he raised his good hand towards her.

'Jes'ca,' he said.

'I'm right here, Father.'

'Lisn me.' His hand fluttered. She took it. 'I wan. Osk.'

'You want to see him now? I'm not sure he's up yet.'

Her father tried to shake his head. 'Gu boy. Alls gu boy.' Always a good boy. The words were raw, clumsily shaped, each one pushed laboriously from his tongue. She had to strain to make sense of them. She took a handkerchief from the bedside table and tried to wipe his lips but he turned his head away, his good hand batting the air. 'Jus lisn.'

'I'm listening. I'm sorry.'

Her father jerked forward, his hand reaching for hers. His grip was startlingly fierce and his bad eye gaped. 'Gu husbn,' he said. 'Gu f' you. F' Melv.'

Jessica did not answer. She stared down at his hand on hers. Good husband. She felt winded, numb with shock. She did not know why. It was not as though she had not thought the same thing herself. He squeezed her hand again. She stared at him stupidly.

'Hap,' he said. She shook her head. 'Hap,' he said again.

'I don't understand.'

His mouth worked, his tongue pushing up against the roof of his mouth. 'Happy,' he pushed out. 'Osk.'

'You want Oscar to be happy?'

He frowned, frustration tugging at his forehead. 'You,' he said and perhaps it was an easier word

581

to say because he said it very clearly. He closed his eyes. His breathing was laboured.

'Father?'

At the door the nurse cleared her throat politely. 'Miss Melville? I don't mean to impose but the Patient is still very weak. If we might let him rest?'

'Father?' She patted his hand but he did not open his eyes. Reluctantly Jessica nodded at the nurse.

She went back downstairs. In the Great Hall a fire was blazing. She went into the dining room but there was no one there and on the table the breakfast china was untouched. Jessica felt a stab of resentment. Phyllis had no right to vanish so blithely when for all she knew Father had died in the night. Last night's show of conscience in the bathroom had been just that, a show. Phyllis was good at that. She managed it so that everyone always thought of her as the good one, the considerate one, but the truth was she never considered anyone but herself. She was just clever enough to do it quietly and with a concerned expression. Even her nursing had been an excuse to run away from Ellinghurst and Eleanor. She had been running ever since. As for Oscar it was the first time since his arrival he had not been up before Jessica. She thought of the window seat behind the shutters in the library where he used to hide and wondered how long Phyllis meant to stay.

There was a bowl of winter camellias on the table in the middle of the Great Hall, their white

582

heads beginning to droop. Jessica fingered a bloom and several petals dropped onto the polished wood, their waxy tongues tipped with brown. She held them in her cupped hand. *Will you, Jessica Margaret Crompton Melville, take this man to be your awfully wedded husband?*

'Good morning.'

Phyllis stood in the doorway to the servants' corridor. Jessica dropped the petals. 'Is it? Still morning, I mean?'

'I'm sorry?'

'Where have you been? I've been looking for you everywhere.'

'Actually I was talking to Dr Wilcox. He says Father is much better.'

'Better? You think paralysed for life is better?'

'According to Dr Wilcox his temperature is almost normal. That's something to be grateful for, surely?'

'He can't move and he can barely get a word out. Just how grateful do you expect him to be?' Phyllis's bewildered expression only angered Jessica more. 'You know what, Phyllis, everything's fine. I'm sorry it was a wasted journey but you're off the hook. You can go back to your tombs with a clear conscience.'

'Why are you being like this?'

'Like what, exactly?'

'Like this. So angry with me.'

'I'm not angry with you. Why would I be angry with you?'

'I don't know. Because I wasn't here. Because you think you had to do this all by yourself.'

'Because I *think* I had to? I did have to do it all by myself, Phyllis, just like I've been doing for years. You left, remember? You left and never came back.'

'Nobody made you stay.'

Jessica was silent. She crossed her arms. 'Have you seen Oscar this morning?'

'I don't think he's up. Doris said something about him having been sick in the night.'

'Sick?'

'That's what she said. She said she took him an aspirin.'

Jessica frowned. 'Do you think I should telephone Dr Wilcox? I mean, what if it's the flu or something? We can't risk exposing Father to infection, not when he's already so weak.'

'I wouldn't worry. It's probably just a hangover or something.'

'From one glass of wine?'

'Some people have no head for alcohol.'

Jessica fiddled with the camellias, pretending to arrange them. More petals fell onto the table. She did not pick them up. 'He loves this house, you know.'

'Oscar or Dr Wilcox?'

'When I told him it might have to be sold I thought he might cry.'

'Perhaps there was something in his eye.'

Jessica told her about the photograph game. 'He knew them all. Many more than I did.'

'Yes, well. He's that kind of person, isn't he? He notices things.'

'He notices the things he cares about. Otherwise he's completely oblivious.'

There was a silence. 'Have you had breakfast?' Jessica asked.

Phyllis shook her head. 'I'm not hungry.'

'You should let Doris know. Especially if Oscar's not coming down. She's left everything out.' She drew a shape around the petals on the table with her fingertip. 'He's changed, you know. Oscar. He's different.'

'Different how?'

'He used to be such a fearful drip.'

'Was he? I don't remember.'

'That's because you were a drip too.' She laughed, ducking away from Phyllis's mock swipe. 'Actually, that's not quite true. You were mostly just a swot. Oscar was a drip and a swot.'

'And now?'

'Now, I don't know, he's . . . interesting. Funny even. Funny ha-ha, not funny peculiar the way he used to be. Father thinks the world of him.'

'Is that so?'

'The thing is, Father . . .' She shook her head. She longed to confide in someone but there was no point in trying to explain it to Phyllis. She would only tell Jessica that it was ignoble and shallow and selfish to choose a husband to safe-guard a house when Jessica knew it was exactly the opposite. Phyllis claimed to be so principled but she would never understand that it was possible to love someone not exactly for themselves but for the good they could help you to do, that a large part of loving someone came from knowing that by loving them you were doing the right thing.

'He might be awake,' she said instead, picking a camellia petal and shredding it with her thumbnail. 'You should go up.'

Phyllis nodded but she did not go. She pressed her lips together, looking at Jessica as though she meant to say something.

'What?' Jessica asked.

'Nothing. I'm just glad . . . never mind. You might want to ask Mrs Johns to check on Oscar. Just in case it is the flu after all.'

Oscar came downstairs a little after midday. Phyllis was not yet back from her walk.

'I've never known anyone go for so many walks,' Jessica said. 'It's as though she's afraid of being indoors.'

Oscar smiled vaguely. Mrs Johns had said briskly that there was nothing wrong with him that fresh air and aspirin could not cure but his face was the colour of candle wax. It had a candle's waxy sheen.

'Are you sure you shouldn't be in bed?' she said but Oscar only shook his head and fiddled with something in his pocket. He seemed stupefied, only half there, but his face twitched and his leg jiggled ferociously up and down. The restlessness leaked from his skin, making the air prickle. It was as if he had snorted cocaine, Jessica thought, and pushed the thought away. The last person she wanted to think about was Gerald.

'Father wants to see you,' she said. The words seemed to startle him. 'Are you sure you're all right?'

'Yes. Sorry. Of course.'

Sir Aubrey's room was warm and stuffy. It made Oscar's head ache.

'I'm very glad to hear you're feeling better, sir,' he said and Sir Aubrey made a jerking motion with his head.

'Jes'ca,' he said and Jessica came closer. Shakily Sir Aubrey reached out and took Oscar's hand. He jerked his head again. Smiling awkwardly at Oscar Jessica put her hand on both of theirs, like the Pat-A-Cake games Oscar had played with his mother as a child.

'Look after her,' Sir Aubrey said or at least that was what Oscar thought he said. He nodded and tried to smile. The muscles beneath his ears ached. He rubbed at them surreptitiously with his spare hand. He supposed he must have clenched his jaw in his sleep. Sir Aubrey said something else but Oscar could not make it out. The only word he was sure of was Melville. He leaned forward. His head pounded.

'I'm sorry, sir?' he said but Sir Aubrey did not answer. He leaned back against the pillows and closed his eyes.

The air on the landing was cool, sweet with burning apple wood, but it was not any easier to breathe.

CHAPTER 40

He was improving. Dr Wilcox said so. Talking tired him and the tiredness made him confused, but he ate, mashed-up baby foods fed with a spoon, and his head no longer seemed too heavy for his neck. He slept a good deal of the time. Jessica cabled her mother and told her there was no longer any need for her to come home. She wrote too to Mrs Maxwell Brooke who sent a breezy letter by return saying how glad she was and how relieved dear Eleanor must be and murmuring vaguely about a visit some time in the New Year. It was nearly Christmas. Jessica spoke to Mrs Johns about bringing the boxes of decorations down from the attic. She asked Phyllis and Oscar if they thought they should have a tree but Phyllis only shrugged and said it was not for her to decide. It was too late for her to rejoin the dig in Malta but there was work she needed to do. She would leave for London the next day.

Jessica lost her temper. She shouted at Phyllis. She told her she was selfish and heartless and that it might be their father's last Christmas and what the hell was wrong with her anyway?

'What's wrong with working here?' she raged. 'If you need books have them sent. You have to stay, don't you see that? For once in your life you have to bloody stay.'

'The library won't send books.'

'Then fetch them. Fetch them and come back. Be here. Eleanor may never be coming back but you . . . you're going to bloody stay, do you hear me? This could be our last ever Christmas in this house. Doesn't that mean anything to you at all?'

'All right, all right. Fine. One night in London, then I'll come straight back.'

Later in bed Oscar held her against him. 'I could come to London with you,' he said but Phyllis shook her head, her nose rubbing his cheek.

'You should stay.' He could see the gleam of her eyes in the darkness. 'Jessica's not a fool. We can't risk her putting two and two together.'

She kissed him and he kissed her back, shutting his eyes. He did not want to see anything. It was him who insisted on turning off the lights, he said it was safer, that they would be less likely to be discovered, but the truth was that it was only in the dark that he could bear it. In the dark when he touched her, there were no thoughts, only sensations. His body led and, for a time, drowned out by the white noise of sensation, the voices in his head were quieted. They came back. In the porridgy grey dawns they came back, redoubled by their brief reverse. Outside his window, as night ended, a robin sang. Robins were aggressively territorial, quick to attack intruders. They killed their own kind.

He burned the letter but he could not burn the image of it, branded in his brain. The words returned to him randomly, shards of glass piercing his attempts at self-possession. Each time Jessica or Phyllis referred to Sir Aubrey as Father he felt the shock of it. Father. A single word like a kick in the gut.

'What is it about scientists and fire?' Jessica laughed one evening as he bent down to put a spill of paper in the flames. 'Uncle Henry was always lighting those things too,' and he dropped the paper on the rug and stared stupidly as Jessica stamped it out with her foot.

No one was hurt . . .

There would be worse fathers to have than Aubrey Melville.

He knew there was something wrong with him. A normal man would have excised those feelings the moment he read the letter, gouged out the love and the longing like a cancer, and stitched it back up with whatever it was that brothers and sisters felt for each other, affection and exasperation and a half-baked sense of belonging. Not Oscar. His tumour only metastasised, seeding itself frenziedly in his liver, his kidneys, his stomach, his bones. His whole body ached for her. It made him feel dizzy, nauseous. And yet sometimes, when she passed close to him, brushing the backs of his fingers with hers, the brutality of his repugnance stopped his throat. He wanted to kiss her, to crush his mouth against his, and at the same time to pound her with his fists, to take her white throat between his hands and squeeze.

He was sane enough to be frightened that he might be going mad.

The next day was Sunday. Phyllis left for London after breakfast. Oscar had dreaded her absence but it was easier with her gone. He thought of Kit and the other men she had nursed during the War who cried out in the ward at night, begging in their narcotic dreams to have their mangled limbs cut off all over again. The pain of an amputation was cleaner, the wound cauterised. When Phyllis was gone he and Jessica walked together down to the park. They talked about Ellinghurst and she showed him the ancient oak tree in which, as a child, she had pretended to set sail for America. Afterwards they drank tea together in the morning room and he read the newspaper while she turned the pages of a magazine. From time to time he looked up and she smiled and he smiled back, without speaking. He could love Jessica like a sister whether she was his sister or not.

After lunch, she took him to the library. She wanted to show him some of the photographs Sir Aubrey had collected for his book. The library was crowded with tables, each one stacked with books. An upended chest was spread with plans and blueprints and photographs of the tower. Jessica touched one with the tip of her finger.

'Our first kiss,' she said. 'Do you remember?'

Oscar tried to laugh. He did not want to remember.

'It was the only thing about that whole terrible day that was pure and simple and good. I told you you'd always love me, do you remember? Because I was your first.' She bit her lip, glancing up at him. 'I was pretty pleased with myself back then.'

Oscar shrugged uneasily. 'Look at that,' he said, bending over the blueprints. 'These must the original drawings. For the tower. See here, you can see the elevator your great-grandfather designed for it, where the staircase is now.'

'Oscar—'

'But, see, by the second plan it's gone and you have the spiral staircase instead. Your father said that even his grandfather was not as confident of unreinforced concrete as all that.'

'Oscar, listen to me. I know after all I've said to you you probably think . . . that is, I never imagined . . .' She screwed up her face, shaking her head. 'Oh God. I don't suppose you could kiss me and put us both out of our misery?' She smiled helplessly at Oscar who, flustered, took a step backwards and knocked the table behind him, tipping one of its folding legs underneath it in a curtsey. Papers scattered across the floor.

'I'm sorry. Here, let me . . .' He squatted, fumbling for the papers, but she was not listening because the door was open and Mrs Johns was standing there, one hand at her throat, and suddenly Jessica was running, her feet echoing along the stone flags of the corridor, and he was running behind her, taking the stairs three at a time.

The third stroke was sudden and severe. The doctor was sent for but Sir Aubrey never recovered consciousness. Jessica held his hand as his breath slowed. Afterwards she said that she thought she had seen it, the moment when the life left his body, that it shimmered above him like one of those mirages that grease the air on a hot summer's day.

'His spirit, I suppose,' she said and she put her hands over her face and Oscar put his hand on her shoulder to comfort her and she reached out for it blindly, clasping it tight.

They cabled for Phyllis to come home, and Eleanor. Jessica supposed she should send word to Mrs Maxwell Brooke too but she did not. The undertaker came to lay the body out. Dr Wilcox went away and came back. Doris brought tea. Amidst all the busyness of death Jessica sat in the drawing room, her arms wrapped around herself and her shoulders hunched as though she was afraid that the roof would fall in on top of her.

'I should telephone Cousin Evelyn,' she said to Oscar. When she began to cry he took his handkerchief from his pocket and handed it to her. She pressed it to her nose.

'Do you want me to do it?' he asked.

'It should be one of us. I'll ask Mr Rawlinson. He'll be here in the morning.' Mr Rawlinson was the Melville family lawyer.

'You don't think they should know today?'

'What difference will that make?' Jessica said bitterly. 'It's Sunday. Land agents don't work on Sundays.'

There were no late trains from London on Sundays. Phyllis caught the milk train the next morning. Pritchard collected her from the station. When Mrs Johns opened the door Phyllis hugged her quickly, tightly. Jessica was standing beside the table. Phyllis kissed Mrs Johns' cheek, and held out her hands to her sister. They looked at each other, then clasped one another close. They were both crying. Jessica had put on a black dress but Phyllis wore her scarlet coat. It was the only splash of colour in the room. Under his dark suit Oscar's chest prickled, tiny bubbles rising and bursting between his ribs. Sir Aubrey was dead and Oscar was no one's son, not any more. He was just Oscar.

He kissed Phyllis on the cheek. 'I'm so sorry,' he said. Her skin was blotched with tears. She went upstairs with Jessica. Oscar did not go with them. It was not his place. Soon afterwards Mr Rawlinson arrived. He brought a clerk with him.

'Shall I let Miss Melville and Miss Jessica know you are here?' Mrs Johns asked but Mr Rawlinson shook his head.

'We'll wait,' he said, jingling the change in his

pockets. Mrs Johns showed them into the morning room. Oscar remained in the Great Hall, unsure of where to be or what he should be doing. He stood, then sat, then walked to the bottom of the stairs and back to the fireplace. His self-consciousness was stronger than his sadness, he thought, and the realisation shamed him. His mother was right. Sir Aubrey had always been very kind.

When Phyllis and Jessica came back downstairs they were red-eyed but composed. Phyllis glanced back at Oscar as she followed Jessica to the morning room and he touched his fingertips to his lips. Jessica hesitated.

'What about Oscar?' she asked. 'Shouldn't he be there too?'

Oscar shook his head. 'I don't think so. This is a family matter.'

'Please. We want you there. Don't we, Phyll? We need someone to get us out if Mr Rawlinson goes on and on.'

Mr Rawlinson was less enthusiastic. 'I must be candid, Miss Melville,' he said. 'I had hoped to speak to you and your sister privately.'

'Oscar is one of us,' Jessica said. 'Anything you have to say you can say with him present.'

The lawyer's frown deepened. He turned to Phyllis. 'You are aware, Miss Melville, that your father made recent alterations to the terms of his will?'

'How recent?' Phyllis asked.

'Some two or so weeks ago. After his first seizure but before the second.'

'Did you know that, Jess?'

Jessica shook her head.

'He didn't speak to either of you about these . . . adjustments?' Mr Rawlinson asked.

'Not to me,' Jessica said. Phyllis shook her head.

'I see. Mr Greenwood, I wonder if I might ask you step out of the room for a few minutes while I speak privately with Sir Aubrey's daughters.'

'For God's sake,' Phyllis said. 'Whatever it is you have to tell us, having Oscar here isn't going to change it.'

The clerk looked sideways at Mr Rawlinson. The lawyer sucked in his cheeks.

'Very well,' he said. He opened his briefcase and took out a folder. 'On December 9, 1919, your father signed a new will and testament in the presence of two witnesses who deemed him to be in sound mind. In this will he stipulated the payment of an annuity to be agreed with the will's executors and commensurate with the convertible assets of the estate to both of you, his daughters, to cease upon the occasion of your marriages. A similar arrangement has been made for Lady Melville. The Ellinghurst estate, however, he bequeathed in its entirety to Mr Greenwood.'

There was a silence. Oscar could not breathe. It was as though someone had punched all the air from his lungs.

'I don't understand,' Phyllis said very quietly. 'Why would he do that?' Beside her Jessica covered her mouth with her hand.

'There are conditions,' Mr Rawlinson said. 'Mr Greenwood's inheritance is conditional upon his assumption of the Melville name and coat of arms by Royal Licence. Should he agree to do so, his heirs will henceforth become heirs to the estate. An additional clause further stipulates that both you and Jessica must be permitted to reside here at Ellinghurst for as long as you remain unmarried. It is your home. Sir Aubrey was very clear on that point.'

Jessica's leg was trembling. She pressed down on her knee to steady it.

'Are there any others?' she asked. 'Any other clauses?'

Mr Rawlinson shook his head. 'Mr Greenwood will not, of course, inherit the baronetcy. That passes by law to Evelyn Melville, Sir Aubrey's legal heir.'

'Why Oscar?' Phyllis demanded. 'Why him?'

'I understand that, as his wife's only godson and close friend of the family, Sir Aubrey considered Oscar his heir by proxy. He was adamant that Ellinghurst should pass only to someone as devoted to the house as he had been, someone who would do everything in his power to preserve it and the Melville legacy. He did not believe that his cousin would honour that obligation.'

'And what if Oscar doesn't want it?' Phyllis said. 'What then?'

'I'm not sure I—'

'Father obviously assumed that he'd agree, that he'd give up his name and everything else to keep this place limping on, but what if he won't? What if that's not what he wants?'

Mr Rawlinson folded his hands. 'If the terms of the will are not met the estate reverts to Sir Evelyn.'

'And gets sold,' Jessica added.

'That's not Oscar's problem,' Phyllis said. 'How could Father do this to him, try to saddle him with this . . . this albatross? He's not even a member of this family! Why didn't he leave it to that nurse of his? To Jim Pugh and his bloody dog?'

'The dog died.'

'Shut up, Jess, for God's sake—'

'No, you shut up,' Jessica cried. 'Father wanted Oscar in this family, don't you see? He wanted—' She broke off, biting her lip.

'What?' Phyllis challenged. 'To stifle Oscar's potential just as he stifled his own?'

Jessica glared at her. 'He wanted him to have Ellinghurst. He knew Oscar wouldn't let him down.'

'He told you that?'

'Yes. I mean, not directly, not in those words, but he tried to. Even when he could hardly speak he tried to.'

'And you never thought to mention it to me?'

'Why should I have? It didn't have anything to do with you.'

Oscar closed his eyes.

'Mr Greenwood,' Mr Rawlinson said coldly, 'are you unwell?'

Oscar did not answer. There was too much noise in his head. Sir Aubrey had known. *The only certainty is that we can never be certain.* But Sir Aubrey had been certain, certain enough to leave Ellinghurst to Oscar – Ellinghurst, which he loved as much as he loved his own daughters. More, perhaps. He had known, and he had known that Oscar knew too, that he could never betray the trust that Sir Aubrey had placed in him. Oscar Melville. Names meant nothing, Oscar knew that as well as anyone, but Oscar Melville was who he was. The name sang in his head like a struck glass. Sir Aubrey had been right, Oscar did know. He had known all along.

Someone put a hand on his elbow. He flinched, pulling his arm away.

'Steady there,' Jessica said. 'Sit down. It's the shock. It's . . . it's a surprise for everyone.' When he bent his knees his legs gave way beneath him, dropping him into the chair. His distress made her feel very tender towards him.

'Don't listen to Phyllis,' she said softly. 'It doesn't matter what she thinks. Father was right. Ellinghurst will be safe with you.'

She glared at Phyllis but Phyllis only stared into the middle distance like one of her sphinxes, surveying the bleached emptiness of the African desert. There were voices in the Great Hall. Jessica heard the brisk tap of footsteps. Then the door to the morning room flew open.

'Eleanor,' Jessica said dazedly.

'My poor darlings,' Eleanor said, holding out her arms. 'I came just as soon as I could.'

★　★　★

When Jessica came down the next morning she found an envelope with her name on it on the breakfast table. The letter was from Oscar.

> I have to go. I am humbled and daunted by your father's faith in me but I cannot pretend it has not come as a shock. I need some time alone to think. Please send my apologies to your mother.

Eleanor nodded when she heard. She said that she was glad, that it saved them the awkwardness of insisting that he leave.

'Except that we couldn't. I mean, it's his house now, isn't it?'

Eleanor stared at Jessica. 'But of course it isn't. We'll contest.'

'For what? So that the house can go to Cousin Evelyn and be sold?'

'You would rather it was stolen from under your nose? That scheming little runt preyed on your father, don't you see? He took advantage of him when he was not in his right mind.'

'That's not true. Father knew exactly—'

'Aubrey would never have left Ellinghurst to . . . to a stranger. Flesh and blood, that was what mattered to your father. The Melville line.' Suddenly her face changed. She put a hand to her mouth. There was a strange light in her eyes. 'Oh my God. So it was her. It was her all along. God, it must have gone on for months.'

600

'I haven't the first idea what you're talking about.'

'I knew it. I knew your father wouldn't be able to help himself. The way she flaunted that penniless Hun, it was so crude, so clumsy, a shrewder man would never have fallen for it, but then no one could ever have accused Aubrey of shrewdness. Oh God, how he hated it, Sylvia making googly eyes at that long-haired German good-for-nothing after all those years of trailing at his heels like a spaniel, hanging on his every word. It drove him absolutely to distraction. For once in her life she had him just where she wanted him.'

'You're not making any sense.'

'Oh, but I'm making perfect sense. I was expecting you and horribly ill, you were sucking the life out of me, and he swore, he swore that there was no one else, that all of that was over, but it wasn't true. I knew it, even then. Aubrey was a terrible liar. Sylvia Carey, on the other hand, was a master. She could have been caught flat on her back with her legs around a man's neck and still manage to convince the world she was the blessed Virgin Mary.'

Jessica thought of the letter in the bottom of the wardrobe. 'For God's sake, Eleanor,' she spat. 'That's horrible.'

'Oh, I'm sorry. I forgot you like to imagine your father as some kind of saint. Well, I hate to shatter your illusions but this is what happens when people die. The truth comes out. Sylvia Carey was a duplicitous bitch who worshipped the ground your father walked on and Aubrey? Aubrey only ever pleased himself.'

'That's not true. Father was a good man. An honourable man.'

'Honourable? And how long did he honour the memory of his dead son, tell me that? How long before he found himself another, before he set Sylvia's bastard up in his place?'

Jessica gaped at her mother, queasy with anger and revulsion. 'Have you entirely lost your mind? Oscar isn't . . . how could you even think that?'

'How could I? How could anyone think otherwise? Your father would never have dreamed of relinquishing this place to anyone but a Melville. Never in a thousand years.'

'What do you know of what Father would have done? You weren't here, Eleanor. You were never here.'

'And now you know why. What was there here for me? A faithless husband? Another woman's child flaunting himself in my boy's place?'

Jessica clenched her fists, furious tears prickling behind her eyes. 'You disgust me, do you know that? You and your vicious baseless theories. Father loved Oscar. Not just because Oscar is your godson and his mother was your best friend. He loved him because Oscar is a good, good man who is almost as devoted to Ellinghurst as Father was. He trusted him. He trusted him to fight.'

'Oh, Jessica, you can't honestly believe that your father would leave Ellinghurst to Oscar Greenwood because he loves the place? Why not Pritchard? Why not Jim Pugh? This house was the only thing your father ever loved. He would have burned it to the ground before he let it pass out of the Melville line.'

Jessica dug her nails into her palms. She had never meant to confide in her mother but she could not help herself. She could not endure to listen to any more of her vicious lies. 'And that's why he did what he did. Don't you see? Father wanted me to marry Oscar. That's why he left him the house. For us both.'

'He told you that?'

'Yes. He had had two strokes. He knew he was dying. He wanted to know Ellinghurst would be safe.'

'So he arranged your marriage? How very thoughtful. And did he give you any choice in this matter?'

'It wasn't like that. Ellinghurst is my home.'

Eleanor stared at her. She shook her head, exhaling a disbelieving laugh. 'So Aubrey was hedging his bets? How very unsavoury.'

'For God's sake, that's enough!' Jessica cried, flinging her arms out in fury. 'Oscar is not Father's son!'

Coolly Eleanor picked up her teacup, eyeing her daughter over the rim. 'And you can be quite sure of that, can you? You'd marry him anyway, to please your dead father, this boy who may or may not be your half-brother?'

'Don't!'

'My advice exactly. It's perfectly clear you don't love him. Besides, your children might have three heads.'

Jessica crossed her arms. She was shaking with anger. 'Why did you come back, Eleanor?'

'What else would I do? Aubrey was my husband.'

'Ah, the grieving widow, back to spread her poison and seize her share of the spoils. And your Frenchman? I suppose you brought him with you?' It was only a guess but she knew from the flicker that crossed Eleanor's face that she was right. 'Jesus, Eleanor.' It might be amusing, she thought bitterly, if it were not so utterly pathetic. Turning, she walked towards the door and suddenly she found herself thinking with a pang of tenderness of Gerald, devastated by the death of his wife Christabel. She hoped he was all right, wherever he was.

'I shan't let you do this,' Eleanor said quietly. 'Rawlinson will be here at eleven. Phyllis and I shall see him, with or without you.'

Jessica shook her head. 'No. You won't.'

'I'm doing this for you, Jessica. Do you really imagine I can stand back after what you've told me? How could your father have even . . .? I shan't allow it. I shall tell Rawlinson we mean to fight it, if it takes every last penny we've got. That scheming little bastard of Sylvia's will never take my son's place.'

Jessica stopped in the doorway. She turned

wearily, her shoulders slack. 'Oh, Eleanor, don't you understand? What you want doesn't matter, not any more. You can howl and rage all you like. Theo is dead. He's dead. What matters now is keeping hold of what we have left.'

'And what is that, without Theo?'

'If you don't know how can I begin to tell you?' Eleanor hesitated.

'Go back to France, Eleanor,' Jessica said. Her voice was flat. 'We don't want you here.'

'And if I don't?'

'If you don't then I shall speak to Rawlinson about contesting your part of Father's legacy. He had begun divorce proceedings against you, after all, and your adultery is hardly in question. Perhaps it was not the wisest decision, in the circumstances, to bring your lover to your husband's funeral. I just hope he is patient. Do you know how long these things take to grind through the courts?'

'Don't you dare threaten me.'

'Oh, I wouldn't call it a threat. More of an insurance policy.'

'You wouldn't.'

'You don't think so? Go home, Eleanor. There's nothing left for you here. Take your Frenchman and go back to your graveyard before either of us do something we'll regret.'

'Jessica—'

'Goodbye, Eleanor,' she said. Turning, she closed the door behind her. She could feel her knees shaking, her heart thumping in her chest. More than anything she wanted to be somewhere else, somewhere her mother was not. Halfway across the Great Hall she broke into a run. She took the stairs in bounds, two at a time.

At the gallery she stopped, breathless, looking over the balustrade to the Great Hall below. She could feel them still, the coils of her mother's lies, clinging to her like seaweed. Oscar was not her brother. Of course he was not. Eleanor's assertions were nothing but fantasies and lies, the foul effluence of her rotting grief.

And yet. Her father had chosen Oscar. According to Rawlinson he had changed his will after his first strokes. He had not waited for Jessica. Whatever her father had hoped for, he had never spoken to her directly, never attempted to elicit any promises. He had said only that he wanted her to be happy, that he wanted them both to be happy. He had never meant her to do something she did not want to do. That was why he had done what he had done. He had left Ellinghurst to Oscar and made it safe. With or without Jessica, Oscar would be a Melville. The law would see to that. It was no longer up to her. Whatever she did, Ellinghurst was his.

The realisation lifted her like wings. Ellinghurst was Oscar's, and the debts and the mortgages and the inexorable creeping decay were Oscar's too. From now on the burden was his. He would bear it. He was kind and clever and good and he loved Ellinghurst. He would not let anything bad happen.

He would keep it safe for all of them. And for as long as Ellinghurst was his it would be hers too, no matter what else she chose to do. Her mother's lies were ludicrous, the poisonous fantasies of a lunatic, but what did that matter? What did it matter if Oscar were her brother or her uncle, if he were the son of the Kaiser or the devil or the second Son of God? Her father had made him a Melville. He was one of them. She did not have to marry him. She did not have to marry anyone. She could take lovers and travel the world. She could even go back to work. Joan would help her if she asked. She could leave all this behind, the leaking roof and the impossibility of finding servants and the ceaseless nagging anxieties about money, safe in the certainty that it would always be here to come back to, an anchor and a sanctuary. Hers but not hers, like family, to love and to depend on. To take for granted.

Gripping the balustrade tightly, she pushed herself forward, balancing on her stomach. The rail was wide, she would not fall, but she still felt the old exhilaration, as though she were flying. She stretched out her neck, feeling the tendons pulling at her breastbone, and closed her eyes.

Ellinghurst was Oscar's. She was free.

CHAPTER 41

The day was almost over, the light a last smear of silver where the sky met the sea. In the gloom the graceful concrete pillars that supported the window arches were pale as skin. Oscar touched one, running his hand down its cold flank. Beneath him the darkness congealed in the trees. It was a long way down.

Ellinghurst was not his, not yet. Mr Rawlinson had explained to him that the Melville name and arms could be transferred only by means of a Royal Licence, which would require the submission of a petition first to the Ministry of Justice and then to Buckingham Palace. He foresaw no difficulties but the process was slow. It would take several weeks.

By then Phyllis would be gone. She had deferred her archaeology studies for a year and was travelling to Egypt to rejoin Mr Carter's dig in the Valley of the Kings. There was still no trace of the boy-king, Tut-ankh-Amen, but Mr Carter's faith remained unshaken.

'He has the courage of his convictions,' she said to Oscar and he said nothing, because there was nothing left to say. Sir Aubrey had been dead less than two weeks. One day, he thought, he would be able to look at her and it would hardly hurt at all.

That afternoon, after Eleanor had arrived, she told him she was going for a walk. He watched her cross the lawn towards the woods, her hands deep in the pockets of her scarlet coat. He knew she was going to the tower. Some time later, while Mr Rawlinson argued with Eleanor in the morning room, he followed her. His legs were stiff, like whalebone. He stumbled through the woods, brambles tearing at his trousers. When he pushed open the door she was sitting on one of the broken benches in the Tiled Room, staring out of the window. The glass was clouded, lacy with cobwebs. In the watery grey light her face was very pale. She did not have her arms around her knees but she looked just as she had when she was eighteen, shivering in her jersey. She turned to smile at him. Her eyes were the same grey as the cobwebbed window. His heart turned over.

'I wasn't sure you knew where I was going,' she said.

'I knew.'

She held out her hand. He took it numbly, waiting for the pain.

'You're bleeding,' Phyllis said softly. She kissed the scratch and, like an anemone, Oscar's fingers closed into a fist. He pulled his hand away.

'Mr Rawlinson,' she said. 'Is he still there?'

Oscar nodded.

'We need to tell him. The longer you leave it the more complicated it gets. We need to go back there and tell him you won't do it. My father's will specifically said that in order to inherit you had to take the Melville name and arms. If you refuse there's nothing they can do.'

Oscar was silent. He stared at the floor, at the eight-pointed stars like crossed ribbons, the lattice-work of the repeating patterns that enclosed them.

'I'm sorry, Oscar. My father had no right to do that. To make it your responsibility like that, out of the blue. To . . . force it on you. It was cowardly. Cowardly and wrong.'

'I'm going to do it.'

Phyllis stared up at him. She shook her head.

'There's no point in trying to talk me out of it.' The words were ground glass in his throat. 'I've made up my mind.'

'I don't understand. You can't. We . . . we agreed.'

'I'm sorry.'

'Are you saying you'd rather have Ellinghurst than me?' she said, trying to laugh, and her voice cracked on the last syllable. Oscar felt something inside him crack too. He clenched his fists more tightly, digging his nails into his palms.

'I've made up my mind,' he said. 'I'm sorry.'

'So – what? I thought . . . I thought you loved me.'

'I'm sorry.' It was the only true thing he could think of to say.

'Why?' She looked up at him. She was crying. 'Why?'

The pain was starting. It spread out from the centre of him, waves and particles, stabs of it jumping like electrons from one orbit to another, radiating pain and more pain, scintillating light. He made himself breathe. He would never tell her. He had promised himself that. It was the only gift he had left to give her, that she never had to know. It was better that she hated him than appalled herself.

'I owe it to your father,' he said.

Oscar leaned out of the window of the tower, closing his eyes, willing the icy wind to scour his mind, but in the darkness the image was clearer, sharp as a film. Her eyes between her parted fingers, her open mouth in the space between her palms, the tear that ran slowly over the knuckle of the index finger and down her left hand. Her ring hand. He put his hand in his pocket, fumbling for the poesy ring, slipping it over his thumb and pressing down until the metal bit against the bone. It had become a kind of ritual, like his mother's ritual with the magpies.

Good morning, Mr Melville, where's your brother?

'You owe it to my father?' she echoed and, when he nodded, she cried silently into the palms of her hands. She had not looked at him. When she was finished she wiped her face with her fingers.

'So that's it,' she said and she stood up and shook the leaves from the skirt of her scarlet coat.

Her eyes were red-rimmed, the grey touched with pink like the inside of seashells. He did not think he had ever loved her so fiercely.

'I'm sorry,' he said and she gave a high choked gasp as though there was something stuck in her throat.

'So you keep saying,' she said and she pushed past him and out of the tower, a blaze of scarlet against the harsh grey-brown of the winter wood.

He did not follow her. He sat on the broken bench, his head in his hands, and he thought of something Kit had said to him once, that it was not Einstein's rearrangement of time and space that had proved the greatest jolt to man's preconceived idea of the universe but Rutherford's dissolution of all that seemed solid into tiny specks floating in the void. The immense void of interstellar space was awe-inspiring, mind-boggling even, but it was the void within the atom that meant it was no longer possible to believe that things were more or less as they seemed. Perhaps she would go back to Kit. They were alike, Phyllis and Kit. Apart from his mother they were the only two people in the world he had ever properly loved.

He had not spoken to her again. The next morning he had gone to London and waited for time to pass. Christmas came and went. There were parties to see in the New Year. He saw the lights in the windows, heard the music and the voices and the drunks staggering out of public houses to urinate against alley walls. Then he returned to Ellinghurst for the funeral. She was polite. She kissed his cheek, her face folded like a blank envelope. Jessica hugged him.

'Dear Oscar,' she said affectionately, as though she were starting a letter. Neither of them mentioned Eleanor. Oscar thought of her in France and wondered if there were some kinds of anguish a heart never recovered from, that extinguished forever the possibility of feeling anything ever again.

He put his hand in his pocket. His fingers found the photograph. He drew it out, turning it over to read the message he had written on the back. *One fool in a tub.* There was a box of matches in his pocket too. He took it out and struck one, touching the flame to the corner of the photograph. It went out. He struck another and this time it caught, the chemicals in the paper flaring green. He let it go. It fell and the wind caught it, tumbling the flame in the darkness. Jessica was right, it was beautiful. Then it was gone.

Slowly he made his way down the unlit staircase, one hand on the wall to steady him. It was a matter of putting one foot in front of the other. Tomorrow he would return to Cambridge. This term a fellow at Emmanuel would teach the University's first course in quantum theory. The Prof was ambivalent. Quantum physics was still equivocal, makeshift, messy. There were members of the faculty who believed that a logical theory of the atom was simply beyond the capacity of the human mind.

The lamps were on in the library as he walked back across the lawn, spilling light out onto the terrace. In the far window he could just make out the profile of eyeless Mr Albus, the curls of his marble hair. Albert Einstein had once told the Prof that the idea that an electron exposed to radiation chose of its own free will not only when but in which direction to jump orbits was intolerable to him. He said that if that was the case he would rather be a cobbler than be a physicist. The way the Prof told it, it sounded like a threat. Oscar thought it sounded like a surrender. Einstein was famous these days, the closest thing science had to royalty, but electrons cared nothing for fame. The greatest physicist since Newton could mend boots to his heart's content and electrons would still continue as they always had, jumping or not jumping, choosing or not choosing, driven by an imperative that defied human understanding. There was no point in believing, like Captain Ahab, that one man's rage and resolve could prevail against the inexorable might of the white whale. Ahab had thought his madness sane because he could explain it. He banged his whalebone leg against the deck and the thump was like a tom-tom, summoning him to war. But Ahab was wrong about the whale. A whale was neither malicious nor vengeful. A whale, like an electron, followed its own impenetrable laws. The dark realms of the sea were like the black wastes of the universe, beyond human reach. Moby-Dick rose and blew, as whales had done since the start of time, and, even as he sounded and Ahab was swallowed by the sea, he sang, impervious, unaware that such a thing as men existed.

When Oscar was a boy he had thought that knowledge was everything. He thought that if you knew everything then you could understand everything. He did not think that any more. Perhaps he would make a good cobbler. They could go into business together, Einstein & Greenwood. Einstein & Melville. And Sons. Einstein had two boys. He was also divorced. The newspapers had made much of that. He had divorced and married again. His new wife was also his first cousin. They would have a good deal to talk about, Oscar thought, as they stitched uppers and banged nails into worn heels.

He walked around the terrace, peering in through the library windows at the chaos of papers and books on every surface. One table was entirely covered in boxes of photographs, all printed with the name H. GRAHAM PHOTOGRAPHY in large capitals on the side. Perhaps if the cobbling went well, Oscar thought, Einstein & Melville could diversify. Out of habit he tried the double doors at the end of the library and to his surprise they opened.

Sir Aubrey's desk was just as he had left it. His fountain pen lay discarded on a pile of handwritten notes. On the desk and on the floor beside the chair were stacks of matching notebooks, all bound in the same dark morocco like the volumes of a huge encyclopaedia. Oscar opened one. It was a diary from 1837, the year that Jeremiah Melville had embarked on the building of the castle. He turned the pages.

> Nicholson proposes a moat, less for authenticity than for the romance of the reflection, and over it a drawbridge but, unless it lifts, I should just as well have a ponderous and mysterious-looking entrance. One should feel very much that, crossing it, one is entering a separate and better world.

Somewhere in the house a gong sounded. Oscar glanced at his watch. It was almost time for dinner. Eleanor would be there and Jessica and Marjorie Maxwell Brooke and her mother. As the only man he would be placed between the two older women. He would not have to talk to Phyllis.

The name caught in his heart like a thorn. He closed his eyes, waiting for the pain to ease. He knew he should go up and change. Instead, he pulled out Sir Aubrey's chair. Sitting down, he began to read.